The Aftermath

'The science fiction author who will have the greatest effect on the world.'   Ray Bradbury

Ben Bova is the author of many novels including:

Mars
'A splendid book . . . of his many books, *Mars* must be the most important.'   Arthur C. Clarke

'Extraordinary . . . this kind of story is the reason science fiction exists in the first place.'
                                        Orson Scott Card

Venus
'Fun, thought-provoking, pacy and stylish . . . Gives a good read while turning your eyes to what might be in the not so distant future, just like Clarke and Asimov used to do so well.'   *SFX*

Jupiter
'Vivid, poetic and wonder-provoking.'   *Foundation*

The Rock Rats
'Bova is a masterful storyteller and the narrative is co_____ *Vector*

About the author

The author of more than one hundred futuristic novels and non-fiction books, Ben Bova is also an award-winning editor, President Emeritus of the National Space Society and a Fellow of the British Interplanetary Society.

Ben Bova holds degrees from the State University of New York and Temple University, Philadelphia, and a Doctor of Education degree from California Coast University. In 2005, he received the Arthur C. Clarke Foundation's Lifetime Achievement award.

His most recent novel, *Titan*, won the John W. Campbell award, given annually to the best science fiction novel of the year.

BEN BOVA

THE AFTERMATH

HODDER

First published in Great Britain in 2007 by Hodder & Stoughton
An Hachette Livre UK company

First published in paperback in 2008

1

Copyright © 2007 by Ben Bova

A CIP catalogue record for this title is available from the British Library

ISBN 978 0 340 82399 6

Type in Plantin Light by Hewer Text Ltd, Edinburgh
Printed a TD

Hodder & wable
and recy able
forests. to
conform gin.

To Laurie and Fred Towers:
new friend, old friend, dear friends both.

And to Lloyd McDaniel, for suggesting one
of the themes of this novel; thanks, buddy.

I do not believe in a fate that falls on men however they act; but I do believe in a fate that falls on men unless they act.

— G. K. Chesterton

BOOK I

Attack and Survival

I wage not any feud with Death
For changes wrought on form and face;
No lower life that earth's embrace
May breed with him, can fright my faith.

Ore Ship *Syracuse*: Main Power Bay

'Don't touch that switch!'

'Ow!'

His father's shouted warning made Theo Zacharias jerk upright. He banged his head painfully on the steel shelf that jutted out over the power bus recess set into the floor plates of the cramped compartment.

'You could trip all the breakers on the power bus,' Victor Zacharias admonished his son. 'The whole damned ship would go dark.'

Fifteen-year-old Theo sat there surrounded by relays and circuit breakers, his knees poking up from the recess like a pair of folded ladders. He rubbed his throbbing head with one hand and glowered sullenly at his father.

'How many times do I have to tell you to be careful?' Victor demanded. 'Do you have any idea of how many megavolts are in those circuits?'

'Twenty-two point six,' Theo muttered. 'You've told me often enough.'

Victor offered a hand to his son and helped to pull him out of the recess. 'I'll handle it,' he said, climbing down to where the teenager had been.

'Yeah. Right,' said Theo, thinking he knew what his father had left unsaid: Never send a boy to do a man's job.

Nearly an hour later Victor clambered out of the recess and hunched beneath the low overhead alongside Theo.

'That ought to hold until we get back to Ceres,' he said. 'Come on, Thee, help me put the deck plates back in place.'

Theo skinned his knuckles wrestling with the heavy deck plates, but he avoided mashing his fingers, as he'd done once before. The fingernail on his left ring finger was still black from that one. They finished and crabbed out into the passageway, where they could at last stand erect. Theo stretched to his full height, several centimeters taller than his father. While Victor was thickset and bullnecked, his once-trim midsection had spread, stretching the fabric of his coveralls. Theo was tall and slender, but youthfully awkward, all gangling arms and legs. Victor's hair was jet black and thickly curled; Theo's was a light sandy brown, like his mother's.

'How's your head?' Victor asked gruffly as they started back toward the living quarters.

Theo rubbed the spot he had whacked. 'No lump,' he said. He flexed the fingers where he'd skinned his knuckles; the hand stung, but not badly.

'This old vessel needs a lot of tender loving care,' Victor said, more to himself than to his son. 'We've got to nurse her along until we put in at Ceres for a major overhaul.'

Theo started to reply, but his mouth went dry. He knew what he wanted to say, but found that it wasn't easy to speak the words. At last, working up his courage, he tried, 'Dad, when we get to Ceres . . .' But the words dried up in his throat.

His father's expression turned hard. 'What about when we get back to Ceres?'

Theo blurted, 'I don't want to spend the rest of my life taking care of this rust bucket.'

'Neither do I, son. I thought we'd spend a year or two out here in the Belt and then cash in. But it hasn't worked out that way. The years just seem to slip past.'

Theo had heard the sad story many times before. 'I don't want to be a rock rat all my life,' he said.

'You don't want to be like me, is that it?' Victor asked, his voice suddenly sharp.

Feeling miserable, Theo replied, 'It's not that, Dad. It's . . . jeeze, there's got to be more to life than running around the Belt picking up ores and delivering them to Ceres, for cripes sake.'

'Don't let your mother hear that kind of language. She expects you to be a gentleman.'

'Yeah, I know,' Theo sighed.

More softly Victor said, 'Theo, this ship is our home. It's our whole life—'

'Your life,' Theo muttered. 'I want something more.'

'Like what?'

'I don't know. I'm not sure. I'm getting good grades in my science classes.'

'High school classes over the ednet are a far cry from real science, Thee.'

'The guidance program says my test scores are good enough for a scholarship.'

'Scholarships pay tuition. Who's going to pay all the other expenses?'

'I can work, support myself. Selene University scholarships include transportation, at least.'

'Selene?' Victor stopped in the middle of the passageway, forcing Theo to stop and turn to face him. 'You want to go to the Moon?'

'Just long enough to get a degree in biology.'

'And then what?'

'Maybe I could go to the research station at Jupiter. They need biologists to study the life forms there.'

'Jupiter,' Victor murmured, shaking his head. He clutched at his son's arm hard enough almost to hurt. 'A biologist. At the Jupiter station.'

'If I'm good enough to make it.'

'You'll have to be pretty damned good,' Victor told his son. Then he chuckled and added, 'If you don't kill yourself first trying to keep this ship going.'

Theo did not laugh.

Ore Ship *Syracuse*: Galley

'Let's face it, Mom,' Theo mumbled into his bowl of yogurt and honey, 'Dad doesn't trust me. He thinks I'm still a kid.'

His mother, Pauline, stood at the one microwave oven that was still functioning and smiled understandingly at her son.

'I don't think that's true, Theo,' she said gently.

'I'm fifteen!' Theo burst. 'Almost sixteen! And he still doesn't trust me with anything.'

'Your father has an awful lot of responsibility on his shoulders,' Pauline replied. 'This ship, our lives . . . there's a war going on out there, you know.'

'And he doesn't trust me.'

Pauline sighed, wondering if the microwave was functioning properly. *Syracuse* was an old, creaking bucket of an ore carrier. The family spent most of their time on maintenance and repairs, just trying to keep the vessel going on its lonely circuit through the Asteroid Belt. The galley was a tight little compartment, its bulkheads and deck scuffed and dulled from long years of use.

Theo sat hunched over his bowl, muttering unhappily into his unfinished breakfast. His sister Angela, sitting across the galley's narrow table from Theo, was slightly more than two years older; she was still carrying more weight than she should, still wearing an extra layer of teenage fat. Theo taunted her about it. She responded by calling her lanky, gawky brother 'the giraffe.'

When Pauline looked at her daughter she could see a dark-haired, dark-eyed beauty waiting to blossom. We'll have to be careful about her once we put in at Ceres, she reminded herself. There'll be plenty of young men chasing after her.

'Dad's got enough to worry about, Thee,' Angie said, in the authoritative voice of an older sister.

'I could help him if he'd let me,' Theo grumbled.

'Like you fixed the leak in the fuel tank? Dad had to come down and—'

'Hydrogen's tricky stuff!' he protested. 'It seeps right through ordinary seals.'

'Never send a giraffe to do a man's job.' Angela smirked.

'Like you'd do better, hippo?'

'Mom! He's calling me names again!'

'You started it!'

'Both of you, stop this at once,' Pauline said firmly. 'I won't have you calling each other ugly names.'

The microwave dinged at last. As Pauline opened it and pulled out her own breakfast of steaming oatmeal, she said, 'Let me talk to your father about this, Thee. Perhaps there's something that we can do.'

Theo brightened a bit and sat up a little straighter. 'I could pilot the ship into Ceres!'

8

'I don't know . . . .'

'Dad lets Angie pilot the ship sometimes.'

'I'm more mature than you,' Angela said loftily. 'You have to be reliable, you know.'

But their mother smiled. 'We'll see.'

Ore Ship *Syracuse*:
Master Bedroom

Pauline Zacharias looked into the mirror as she sat at her dresser. I'm getting old, she realized, studying the fine lines that were beginning to spiderweb across her face.

She had never been a beauty, not in her own critical estimation. Her jaw was too long, she thought, her lips too thin. Her gray eyes were large and Victor often called them luminous, the dear. But her hair. It was sorrowful. Dirty blonde. Victor called it sandy. It never behaved. Pauline had cropped it short, close to the skull, and still it stuck out all around in a sea of cowlicks. She tried to consider her good points: she was tall and her figure still slimly elegant. She had always strived to carry herself proudly, chin up, shoulders back, head erect. Now she was beginning to wonder if it was worth the effort.

Victor stepped into the bedroom and slid the door shut. The lock didn't catch at first; he had to jiggle it a few times.

'This whole tub is breaking down around our ears,' Victor Zacharias muttered.

He was right, Pauline knew. Glancing around their bedroom she saw that the dresser and cabinets were badly in need of upgrading. Even the wall screens had developed an annoying little flicker. But the bed, she would never replace their bed. Victor had ripped out the compartment's built-in bunk when they'd first leased *Syracuse*, and he'd built a handsome oversized bed with his own hands. Painted the plastic paneling to resemble real wood. Made a mattress out of discarded elastic water bags. Their one luxury, their bed.

'We'll do an overhaul when we get to Ceres, won't we?' she asked.

'I was just talking to Ceres,' he said, walking across the little compartment and kissing her absently on the crown of her head. 'Three more ore ships have been hit, so prices are up.'

'Three ships?' she asked, alarmed.

'Corporation ships, Pauline. Nobody's attacking the few independents, like us. Not even the mercenaries.'

'Still . . .'

Ignoring her unspoken fears, Victor mused, 'If we can get this cargo of ore to the market before prices dip again, we'll make a nice profit. Then we can overhaul the ship good and proper.'

'Will we be able to afford a rejuve therapy, too?' Pauline blurted.

'Rejuvenation?' Victor looked genuinely shocked. 'You? Why?'

She loved him, not least because her husband always seemed to see her through adoring eyes. He was short, barrel-chested, starting to get potbellied. That hardly mattered to her. His real strength, Pauline knew, was in his character. Victor Zacharias had pride, yes, but more than that he had intelligence. When she'd first met him, Victor had been strong enough to bend steel rods with his bare hands. What really impressed her, though, was that he was sharp enough to talk his way out of confrontations, clever enough to win fights without violence.

And he had that beautiful, thick, curly, midnight black hair. Pauline envied her husband's luxuriant dark ringlets. This many months out in the Belt, he had allowed his hair to grow down to his collar.

'I think it's time for a treatment,' Pauline said. 'I'm not getting any younger.'

'Pah!' He dismissed the idea with a wave of his hand. 'People back at Ceres think you and Angie are sisters.'

'That's not true, Vic, and you know it.'

'It *is* true,' he insisted. 'You just don't notice it.'

'Nonsense.' But she smiled.

He sat beside her, just one hip on the corner of the dresser's little padded bench, and put an arm around her slender waist.

'You're gorgeous, Pauline,' he said into the mirror.

'Not as gorgeous as I used to be.'

He raised his dark brows, then took a breath. 'I think it's gilding the lily, but if you want a rejuve treatment when we get back to Ceres, go ahead and do it.'

'We'll be able to afford it?'

He nodded. She leaned her head on his shoulder and he curled around and kissed her.

And slid off the bench, plopping onto the threadbare carpet. They laughed together.

Later, as they lay in their handsome waterbed together, Pauline said into the shadows, 'Victor, Theo thinks you don't trust him.'

'What?'

She turned toward him, sending a gentle wave through the bed. In the darkened room she could make out the curve of his bulky shoulder, the outline of those raven ringlets.

'He wants more responsibility, darling. He's almost sixteen now—'

'And he's a terrible klutz,' Victor said, chuckling. 'All arms and legs, no coordination.'

Pauline smiled, too. She remembered Theo's disastrous attempt to repair one of the galley's faulty microwave ovens. It was functioning poorly when Theo started tinkering with it. It was a complete loss by the time he gave up.

But she coaxed, 'You could let him relieve you in the command pod now and then, couldn't you? Like you let Angie sit in. After all, the ship's cruising on automatic, isn't it?'

'We're on course for Ceres, yes.'

'Couldn't Thee watch the panels for an hour or two? It would free you up to work on repairs. And it would mean so much to him.'

'As long as he doesn't touch anything,' Victor muttered.

'Maybe he could even work with you on more of the maintenance chores,' Pauline suggested.

'I'm not sure I have the patience for that,' he said.

'But you'll give him a chance?'

She sensed him smiling.

'He wants to go to Selene University and study biology,' he said.

'Leave us?' She felt startled by the thought.

'Sooner or later,' said Victor. 'I can't keep him on this ship against his will. Not for long.'

'But he's not even sixteen.'

'He will be.' Victor fell silent for a moment. Then, 'I wonder what kind of a man he'll turn out to be. I've tried to teach him. . . .'

'Give him a chance,' Pauline urged. 'Show him that you trust him.'

'I suppose you're right,' he said softly. 'I'll have to give him a try.'

Ore Ship *Syracuse*:
Approaching Ceres

Syracuse was shaped like a giant wheel, with two long intersecting spokes bracing the rim: a pair of three-kilometer-long buckyball tubes running perpendicular to each other. The ship's control center was nothing more than a pod attached to the rim at the end of one of the spokes: The ship spun slowly through space, producing a sense of almost a full Earth gravity along the rim of the wheel.

'Now remember,' Victor said to his son, 'watch everything, touch nothing.'

Sitting in the control pod's command chair with his father standing at his shoulder, Theo nodded unhappily.

'This is a big responsibility, son. I'm going to leave you in charge for a couple of hours.'

To Theo, his father's heavy-browed, dark-haired face looked somehow menacing. Victor looked like a solid, sawed-off stump of a tree, his torso thick and powerful. He wore faded gray shorts and a sweat-shirt, the sleeves cut off to show his hairy, muscular arms. Theo kept his own skinny arms hidden inside long sleeves.

The command chair in which Theo sat was wedged into a curving bank of screens that displayed every aspect of *Syracuse's* systems: propulsion, navigation, life support, logistics supplies, communications, emergency equipment, and the fourteen thousand tons of asteroidal ores held in magnetic grips at the center of the slowly turning buckyball tubes.

'We're on the approach course for Ceres. The controls are locked in, so you don't have to worry about navigation. Are you sure you can handle the responsibility of being in command?' Victor asked anxiously.

That's a laugh and a half, Theo said to himself. The ship's on automatic and I'm in command of nobody. Plus I'm not supposed to touch anything. Some responsibility.

Misunderstanding his son's silence, Victor said, 'It's a dangerous world out there, Thee. There's a war going on.'

'I know,' Theo muttered.

'Ships have been attacked, destroyed. People killed.'

'Dad, the war's between the big corporations. Nobody's bothered independent ships, like us.'

'True enough,' Victor admitted, 'but there are mercenaries roaming around out there and out-and-out pirates like Lars Fuchs—'

'You told me Fuchs only attacks corporate ships,' Theo said. 'You said he's never bothered an independent.'

Victor nodded gravely. 'I know. But I want you to keep your wits about you. If anything unusual happens – anything at all – you call me at once. Understand?'

'Sure.'

'At once,' Victor emphasized.

Theo looked up at his father. 'Okay, okay.'

With a million doubts showing clearly on his face, Victor reluctantly went to the command pod's hatch. He hesitated, as if he wanted to say something more to his son, then shrugged and left the pod.

Theo resisted the impulse to throw a sarcastic two-fingered salute at the old man.

At least, he thought, it's a beginning. I'll just sit here and let him take over once we've entered Ceres-controlled space. It's a beginning. At least Mom got him to let me babysit the instruments.

Slightly more than an hour later, Theo sat in the command chair, his brows knitted in puzzlement at the fuzzy image displayed on the ship's main communications screen.

Syracuse was still more than an hour away from orbital insertion at Ceres. But something strange was happening. Theo stared at the crackling, flickering image of a darkly bearded man who seemed to be making threats to the communications technician aboard the habitat *Chrysalis*, in orbit around Ceres, where the rock rats made their home. The image on the display screen was grainy, the voices broken up by interference. The stranger was aiming his message at *Chrysalis*: Theo had picked up the fringe of his comm signal as the ore ship coasted toward the asteroid.

'Please identify yourself,' said a calm, flat woman's voice: the comm tech at *Chrysalis*, Theo figured. 'We're not getting any telemetry data from you.'

The dark-bearded man replied, 'You don't need it. We're looking for Lars Fuchs. Surrender him to us and we'll leave you in peace.'

Lars Fuchs? Theo thought. The pirate. The guy who attacks ships out here in the Belt.

'Fuchs?' The woman's voice sounded genuinely puzzled. 'He's not here. He's in exile. We wouldn't—'

'No lies,' the man snapped. 'We know Fuchs is heading for your habitat. We want him.'

Theo realized that something ugly was shaping up. Much as he hated to relinquish command of *Syracuse* – even though his 'command' was nothing more than monitoring the ship's automated systems – he reluctantly tapped the intercom keyboard.

'Dad, you'd better get up here,' he said, slowly and clearly. 'Something really weird is going on.'

It took a moment, then Victor Zacharias replied testily, 'What now? Can't you handle anything for yourself?' There was no video: voice only.

'You gotta see this, Dad.'

'See what?' He sounded really annoyed.

'I think we're sailing right into the middle of the war.'

'Ceres is neutral territory. Everybody knows that and respects it.'

'Maybe,' Theo said. 'But maybe not.'

Grumbling, Victor said, 'All right. I'm on my way.'

Only then did Theo notice that the blank display screen's indicator showed his father was in the master bedroom. He felt his cheeks redden. He and Mom . . . No wonder he's cheesed off.

Ore Ship *Syracuse*: Control Pod

Theo sat in the command chair, watching and listening to the chatter between *Chrysalis* and the strangely menacing stranger.

His father stepped into the control pod, dark face scowling.

Theo swiveled the command chair and got to his feet, crouching slightly in the confined head space of the pod. Gangling, awkward Theo had his father's deep brown eyes, but the sandy hair and tall, slender build of his mother. There was the merest trace of a light stubble on his long, narrow jaw. His denims were decorated with decals and colorful patches. 'What's got you spooked?' Victor asked in a heavy grumbling voice as he lowered himself gingerly into the command chair. He had injured his thigh months earlier while loading *Syracuse*'s cargo of ores from one of the rock rat miners deeper in the Asteroid Belt. The leg still twinged; Victor had scheduled stem cell therapy when they arrived at the *Chrysalis* habitat.

Gesturing to the main display screen that covered half the curving bulkhead in front of them, Theo replied, 'Take a look.'

But the menacing stranger had apparently cut his communications with *Chrysalis*. To Theo's dismay, the main screen showed nothing more than a standard view of the approaching asteroid and its environs. At this distance Ceres was a discernable gray spheroid against the star-spattered blackness of space. Circling in orbit about the asteroid, the habitat *Chrysalis* glittered light reflected from the distant Sun: a Tinkertoy assemblage of old spacecraft linked together into a ring to make a livable home for the rock rats. They had built the makeshift habitat to escape the dust-choked tunnels that honeycombed Ceres itself.

Radar displays superimposed on the screen showed the images of nearly a dozen ships, mostly ore carriers like *Syracuse* or massive factory smelters, in orbit around the asteroid; their names and registrations were printed out on the screen. Two other ships were visible, as well. One was labeled *Elsinore*, a passenger-carrying fusion torch ship from the lunar nation of Selene. The other had no name tag: no information about it at all was displayed on the screen. From the radar image it looked like a sleek, deadly dagger.

Victor Zacharias scratched absently at his stubbled chin as he muttered, 'By god, that looks like a military vessel – an attack ship.'

'She's not emitting any telemetry or tracking beacons,' Theo pointed out.

'I can see that, son.'

'They were talking to *Chrysalis* before you came in,' Theo explained. 'Sounded threatening.'

Victor's blunt-fingered hands played over the comm console. The main screen flickered, then the image of the bearded man came up.

'Attention *Chrysalis*,' he said in a heavy, guttural voice. 'This is the attack vessel *Samarkand*. You are harboring the fugitive Lars Fuchs. You will turn him over to me in ten minutes or suffer the consequences of defiance.'

Theo said to his father, 'Lars Fuchs the pirate!'

'The rock rats exiled him years ago,' Victor muttered, nodding.

The voice of *Chrysalis*'s communications center said annoyedly, 'Fuchs? God knows where he is.'

'I know where he is,' *Samarkand* replied coldly. 'And if you don't surrender him to me I will destroy you.'

His image winked out, replaced by the telescope view of Ceres and the spacecraft hovering near the asteroid.

Victor began to peck intently on the propulsion keyboard set into the curving panel before him, muttering, 'We've got to get ourselves the hell out of here.'

'Huh? Why?'

'Before the shooting starts.'

'*Chrysalis* is unarmed,' Theo said. 'They don't have any weapons. Everybody knows that.'

'We don't have any weapons either,' said his father.

'But they wouldn't shoot at an unarmed ship. That doesn't make sense.'

'You hope.' Victor's fingers were flicking across the controls.

Turning a massively laden ore ship is neither a simple nor a quick maneuver. It takes time and lots of space. Theo glanced at the control screens and saw that *Syracuse* was slowly, painfully slowly, coming about.

Something flashed on the main screen.

'He's fired on her!' Victor shouted.

Theo saw a red-hot slash cut through the thin metal hull of one of *Chrysalis*'s modules. A glittering cloud puffed out and immediately dissipated. Air, Theo realized. The module seemed to explode, shards of metal spinning out dizzily. And other shapes came tumbling, flailing into the airless emptiness of space. Bodies, Theo saw, his heart suddenly thundering, his guts clenching. Those are people! He's killing them!

'Stop!' screamed a voice from the habitat's comm center. 'Stop or you'll kill—'

The voice cut off. Theo watched with bulging eyes as invisible laser beams from the attack ship methodically sliced one module of the habitat after another, slashing, destroying, killing. A cloud of spinning debris and twisted bodies spread outward like ripples of death.

'You've got to do something!' Theo shouted.

'I am,' his father replied. 'I'm getting us the hell away from here.'

'Something to help them!'

'What can we do? You want to join them?'

As *Syracuse* slowly, ponderously turned away from its approach to Ceres, its telescopic cameras maintained their focus on the slaughter of the *Chrysalis* habitat. Module after module exploded soundlessly, corpses and wreckage flung into space.

22

Tears in his eyes. Theo leaned over his father's broad shoulder and shouted into his face, 'You can't just leave them there!'

His eyes fastened on the carnage displayed on the main screen, Victor told his son, 'The hell I can't! I've got to protect you and your sister and mother.'

'You're running away!'

Victor nodded bleakly. 'Just as fast as I can get this ore bucket to fly.'

Theo glanced up at the main screen once more, then down again to his father's grimly determined face. He saw beads of perspiration on his father's brow; his knuckles were white as he gripped the chair's armrests.

'But there must be *something* we can do!'

The bearded man's image appeared again on the main screen, sharp and steady. 'Ore ship *Syracuse*,' he said, 'just where do you think you're going?'

Theo's blood froze in his veins.

Battle Frenzy

'Are you harboring the fugitive Lars Fuchs?' asked the stranger, his voice dagger-cold.

Victor replied evenly, 'We're inbound from the deeper Belt, carrying fourteen thousand tons of ore.' Then he added, 'No passengers.'

'How do I know that's the truth?'

'You're welcome to come aboard and see for yourself.'

The dark stranger lapsed into silence, apparently deep in thought. Theo thought his eyes looked strange, their pupils dilated wider than he had ever seen before.

'Damn!' Victor growled. 'The intercom's down again.'

'We just fixed it yesterday,' Theo said.

'Not well enough.' Victor leaned on the comm console's mute button and whispered urgently to his son, 'Get down to the habitation module and get your mother and sister into suits. You suit up too.'

'What about you?'

'*Do it!*'

Theo scrambled out of the control pod, nearly banging his head on the rim of the hatch, and clambered up the rungs set into the tubular passageway that ran the length of the three-kilometer-long buckyball tube. With each rung the feeling of weight lessened, until he let his soft-booted feet rise off the rungs and started scampering along the ladderway like a racing greyhound, his fingers barely flicking on the rungs. The closer he got to the ship's center of rotation the less g force he felt: soon he was literally flying through the narrow tube.

Meanwhile Victor sat alone in the control pod, his mind working in overdrive. *He's a killer. He's wiped out the habitat, must have killed more than a thousand people, for god's sake. The nearest help is days away, weeks. Hell, it takes more than half an hour just to get a message to Earth. We're alone out here. Alone.*

The stranger aboard the attack vessel seemed to stir to life. 'Well? Where is Fuchs?' he demanded.

'Who am I speaking to?' Victor asked, stalling for time. 'You know who I am but I don't know who you are.'

The man almost smiled. 'I am your death unless you surrender Fuchs to me.'

His fingers racing across the control keyboard like a pianist attempting a mad cadenza, Victor Zacharias answered, 'Lars Fuchs isn't aboard this ship. Send an inspection party if you want to. I assure you—'

Syracuse shuddered. *We've been hit!* Victor realized. *The bastard's shooting at us!*

A bank of red lights flared angrily on the control panel. *The main antennas. He's silenced us. And the fuel tanks below the antennas; he's ripped them open!* With a swift check of his other diagnostics, Victor hesitated a heartbeat, then punched the key that released the ship's cargo. *Syracuse* lurched heavily as fourteen thousand tons of asteroidal rock were suddenly freed from their magnetic grips and went spinning into space between the ore carrier and the attack vessel.

That's the best shielding I can provide, Victor said to himself as he punched up *Syracuse*'s propulsion controls and goosed the main fusion engine to maximum acceleration. In the main display screen above his curved control panel he saw glints of laser light splashing off the rocks that now floated between him and the attack ship. Come on, he silently urged the fusion engine. Get us out of here!

'You can't run away,' came the voice from the attack ship, sounding more amused than angry.

I can try, Victor replied silently.

Theo banged painfully against the rungs protruding from the central passageway's curving bulkhead. Dad's accelerating the ship, he thought. Trying to get away. He grabbed a ladder rung and pulled himself along the tube. Within seconds he was no longer weightless but falling toward the habitation module, where his mother and sister were. Careful now, he told himself, remembering how he'd broken his arm a few years earlier in a stupid fall down the tube. He jackknifed in midair, banging his knee painfully against the rungs, and turned around so that he was falling feet first.

He heard a hatch creak open down at the end of the tube and, glancing down, saw his sister Angie starting to climb upward toward him.

'Go back!' he yelled at her. 'Get into a suit! Mom too!'

'What's happening?' Angie shouted back, her voice echoing off the tube's curving bulkhead. 'The intercom isn't working.' She sounded more annoyed than frightened.

'We're being attacked!' Theo hollered, scrambling toward her as fast as he dared. 'Get into suits, you and Mom!'

'Attacked? By who? What for?'

The lights flickered and went out. The dim emergency lights came on.

'Get into the goddamned suits!' Theo roared.

Angie began backing toward the hatch. 'No need to swear, Theo.'

'The hell there isn't,' he muttered to himself.

He clambered down the rungs and dropped the final couple of meters through the open hatch and onto the bare metal deck of the auxiliary airlock. Long habit – backed by his father's stern discipline – made him reach overhead to close the hatch and make certain it was properly sealed. Then he pushed through the inner hatch and entered the family's living quarters.

The accommodations were spare, almost spartan, but they were all the home that Theo remembered. A small communications center, crammed with electronics equipment; its deck was polished plastic tiles, its overhead decorated with a fanciful ancient star map that showed the constellations as the beasts and legendary heroes of old. When he was a little kid Theo loved to sneak in here at night and gaze at the glow of the fluorescent figures.

No time for stargazing now. The next hatch led into the main living area, with its wide glassteel port that looked out into the depths of space. Well-worn comfortable sofas and cushioned chairs. Through the port Theo saw a jumble of rocks spinning off into the distance, flashes of light glinting off them.

Dad's jettisoned our cargo, he realized. And that bastard's shooting at us, whoever he is.

The lighting was normal here. Theo hurried through the living area and into the equipment bay that fronted the main airlock. His mother was helping Angie into her space suit, sliding the hard-shell torso over his sister's head and upraised arms. Angie's head popped out of the collar ring; she looked as if she'd been swallowed by a robotic monster.

Angie glared at Theo, more nettled than scared, he thought. She thinks this is all my fault, as usual, he said to himself.

It was hard to tell if his mother was worried or frightened. Pauline Zacharias seemed calm, unruffled. Theo couldn't imagine anything that would rattle his mother. She knows Dad wouldn't tell us to get into the suits unless we were in deep spit, but she seems totally in control of herself.

Angela was tucking her thick dark hair inside her suit's collar, looking thoroughly annoyed. Funny, Theo thought, how Angie got Dad's height and coloring and I got Mom's light hair and long legs. Genes can be peculiar.

His mother reached for the gloves resting on the locker shelf beside Angie's helmet.

'You can put these on yourself,' she said in a low, cool voice. 'Quickly now. I've got to help Theo.'

Angie took the gloves, her eyes still on Theo. 'You sure that Dad wants us in the suits, Thee, or is this just one of your little stunts?'

'Didn't you feel the ship lurch?' he answered hotly. 'We're being attacked, for god's sake!'

'That's stupid,' Angie said as she tugged on her gloves. 'This old boat is always shaking and groaning. Besides, who'd want to attack us?' But she sealed her gloves to the cuffs of her suit's arms and reached for her helmet.

'Who's attacking us?' his mother asked. 'And why?'

Pauline was a handsome woman with the steady gray eyes and firm jaw of someone who had weathered her share of troubles. She was slightly taller than Theo; he had always measured his height against her, not his stubby father. She wore her sandy blonde hair cropped short, not the stylish shoulder length that she allowed her daughter to flaunt.

'I don't know who's attacking us,' Theo said, 'but he's smashed up *Chrysalis* pretty awful.'

'But Ceres is neutral territory!'

'Not anymore.'

Pauline opened her son's suit locker.

'Mom,' Theo said, stretching the truth only slightly, 'Dad said I should help you with your suit before I get into mine.'

'What about me?' Angie snapped.

Theo smirked at her. 'He knew Mom would have his precious little chubbo all suited up by the time I got here.'

'Mom!' she yowled.

Pauline sat down on the bench that ran in front of the lockers. 'Don't you two start,' she warned. 'This is no time for bickering.'

'Yes, ma'am,' said Theo. But he saw Angie stick her tongue out at him behind their mother's back. As he pulled his mother's suit torso from its rack he thought that his sister might be two years older than he, but she was still nothing more than a bratty girl.

Dad had spoken more than once about buying new nanofabric space suits for them, the kind you could pull on like plastic coveralls and be suited up in a minute or less. But they cost too much. All they had aboard *Syracuse* were these old-fashioned cumbersome hard-shell suits, with their big ungainly boots and heavy backpacks and glassteel bubble helmets. At least the suits ran on oxygen at normal air pressure; you didn't have to spend an hour prebreathing low-pressure oxy like the earliest astronauts did.

They said little as they donned their suits. The ship shuddered and jolted a few times, whether from being hit by the attacker's laser beams or from Dad jinking to get away, Theo had no way of knowing. Dull booming noises echoed distantly. Angie's eyes widened with every thud and shake; their mother looked grim.

Leaving the visors of their helmets up, the three of them inspected each other's suits, making certain all the connections were in place and the seals tight. Theo noticed that his hands were trembling slightly.

'What do we do now?' Angie asked. Theo thought her voice sounded shaky. She's scared now, he realized. I am too, but I can't let them see it. I've got to be the man here.

Pauline said, 'Now we wait. If the ship is badly punctured we can live inside the suits until we repair the damage.'

Theo pressed the stud on his left cuff. 'Dad, we're suited up. Waiting for your orders.'

No answer.

'I told you the intercom wasn't working, chimp-brain,' Angie said.

'The suit radios are on a different frequency, dumb-butt,' Theo told her. 'Dad, we're in our suits. What's your situation?'

Nothing but silence. Not even the crackle of the radio's carrier wave.

'Dad!' Theo shouted.

Angie's face went ashen. 'Do you think . . .'

Theo turned from his sister to his mother. For the first time in his life she looked fearful.

Victor Suleiman Zacharias

He was born in one of the tent cities strung along the craggy ridges of eastern Kentucky; his parents were refugees from the greenhouse flooding that had inundated most of Chicago. Victor's father had once owned a restaurant in the part of that city called Greek Town. His mother was a Palestinian exile who had barely managed to escape the nuclear devastation of Israel and Lebanon. Victor was their only child; his father refused to bring another baby into a world ravaged by the savagery of nature and the cruelty of men.

At sixteen his mother died and Victor ran away from the tattered city of tents to join the army. He was short, underweight and underage but the recruiters asked few questions. After four years of guarding food warehouses and putting down riots, he won a scholarship to study – of all things – architecture at Syracuse University in the middle of New York state. He graduated just as the earthquakes in the Midwest brought on a new wave of flooding, and the Gulf of Mexico washed halfway up the Mississippi valley. Returning home, he found that his father had drowned while doing forced labor on a press gang building levees.

There was plenty of work for builders, but little for young architects who wanted to create something more than barracks for flood victims or cookie-cutter new cities for refugees. Victor was attracted to the lunar nation of Selene, far from the miseries and despair of Earth: he heard there were plans afoot to build an astronomy complex on the Moon's farside.

He won a job over several other aspiring young architects and went to the Moon, spending the next four years of his life shuttling between the underground city of Selene and the complex of astronomical observatories and housing units being built on the farside. There he met Pauline Osgood, a Selenite by birth who had never been to Earth. They returned once, to get married, and stayed for the funerals of Pauline's parents, victims of a food riot in Denver.

Back on the Moon, Victor settled in to work on the slow but steady expansion of Selene's underground accommodations. For more than a year he helped to design the resort complex at Hell Crater, then signed up with Astro Manufacturing when they began their new manufacturing base at the Malapert Mountains, near the lunar south pole. He'd become the father of a baby girl by then, and while still working on the Malapert designs Pauline became pregnant once more, this time with the son that he so badly wanted.

Victor was dragged into the Asteroid Wars almost by accident. Pancho Lane herself, CEO of Astro Manufacturing, asked him to head a small design team working on a space habitat that could serve as Astro's military headquarters. Flattered, Victor completed the design within three months. He was aboard the unfinished habitat in its L-2 libration point site when it was attacked by ships of Humphries Space Systems. Victor was not injured, but seeing his construction project slagged into twisted structural beams and shattered living compartments angered him beyond words.

The Asteroid Wars had started as a personal feud between Martin Humphries and Lars Fuchs. An uneven battle: Humphries was the wealthiest man in the solar system, founder and master of Humphries Space Systems. Lars Fuchs was a lone individual, too proudly stubborn to bow down to Humphries. He had taken to piracy out in the dark depths of the Asteroid Belt as his only means of survival. The First Asteroid War ended in the only way it could, with Humphries triumphant and Fuchs exiled from the rock rats' habitat at Ceres.

With peace came unemployment. Astro Corporation was not building any new facilities and Selene's expansion had been halted for no one knew how long. Victor cashed in his modest savings, borrowed a lot more, and leased an aged ore vessel from Astro, which he dubbed *Syracuse*. With his young family he headed out to the Belt.

He became a rock rat, content to ply the Belt buying ores from the miners who worked the asteroids and transporting them to ships waiting at Ceres to carry the raw materials to the Earth/Moon system. While billions of international dollars changed hands, very little profit remained for Victor Zacharias's pockets. Yet he was contented. His children were growing, his wife was happy. Life was serene.

Until the Second Asteroid War broke out. This time there was no pretense: the war was a struggle for control of the Belt and its enormous resources, a struggle between Humphries Space Systems and Astro Corporation. Lars Fuchs was nothing more than an excuse for the two giant corporations to go to war.

Now Victor Zacharias sat hunched in *Syracuse*'s control pod, sweating hard as he desperately tried to maneuver the lumbering ore ship out of range of the attacker's fire.

The attacking ship, much more agile, was swinging clear of the jumble of rocks that Victor had released. In another few minutes, he saw, the attacker would have a clean shot at *Syracuse*; then it would be merely a matter of time before the ship was utterly destroyed and everyone aboard killed. Pauline, he thought. Angela. Theo.

He couldn't even call his attacker and surrender, Victor realized. The bastard's knocked out my antennas. We're mute. And deaf. He could be singing Christmas carols to me and I'd never hear him.

The intercom link with the ship's living quarters was down, too. He saw the sullen red lights glaring at him from the control panel.

How can I . . . ?

A desperate idea popped into his head. Looking up at the display screen again he saw that the attacking ship was at the edge of the swirling, tumbling cluster of rocks he'd released. It was only a matter of seconds now.

His pulse hammering in his ears, Victor lifted the safety covers over the escape system's dual butter yellow buttons.

'Goodbye, Pauline,' he murmured. Then he pressed his stubby fingers against the twin buttons.

Explosive bolts blew away the connectors holding the command pod to *Syracuse*'s main body. The pod's internal rocket engine lit automatically; Victor felt himself pressed deep into the command chair's padding. The control panel's lights flickered madly, then winked out.

He stared fixedly at the main screen. The camera view jerked violently, then swung its focus back on the attack vessel. Just as Victor had hoped, just as he'd prayed, the attacker swerved to follow him.

They both left *Syracuse* far behind, dwindling into an invisible speck against the starry black of space.

He thinks I'm carrying Fuchs with me, Victor thought gratefully. He thinks I'm trying to help Fuchs escape. He's following me and leaving Pauline and the kids alone. I've saved them. I've saved them.

Abandoned

Dad's going to be boiled at me if he ever finds out, Theo thought as he hesitated at the lip of the auxiliary air lock hatch. He was fully suited up, with his helmet visor down and sealed. Standing on the ladder leading up to the hatch set in the ceiling, his head and shoulders above the hatch's edge, Theo saw the long tube leading from the family's living quarters to the control pod stretching above him, a narrow dimly lit tunnel of buckyball filament, stronger than steel, lighter than plastic.

So he boils, Theo said to himself. This is an emergency. And he started climbing up the rungs set into the tube's circular interior. It was laborious work in the cumbersome space suit. The emergency hatches were closed tight, he saw. Every hundred meters the tunnel was divided by double hatches that served as mini-airlocks. Usually they were kept open, but if a part of the tunnel was punctured, the hatches automatically sealed shut to prevent all the air from escaping into space. Now they were closed.

Not a good sign, Theo told himself. The tunnel's been punctured somewhere.

Gravity melted away as he climbed; soon he was taking the rungs three, four, five at a time. As he approached the tunnel's midpoint, where the g force was effectively zero, his booted feet weren't touching the rungs at all.

Once past the ship's center, he allowed himself to fall, slowly at first, then with increasing speed as he neared the end of the tunnel. But the closed hatches of the airlocks stopped him from dropping all the way. He had to stop and manually open each hatch, then proceed to the next one. No tunnel diving, the way he used to when he was just a kid, eight or nine years old. Just drop from the midpoint to the end of the tunnel, let yourself fall like a stone. When his father had found out, the old man had exploded with fearful anger.

'You could kill yourself falling against the rungs!' Victor had roared. 'Tear your arms out of their sockets when you try to stop! Break every bone in your empty head!'

But tunnel diving was too much fun to ignore. Theo had even gotten Angie to dive with him. Of course she banged herself up, broke an arm, and loudly wailed Theo's guilt. Dad had confined Theo to his sleeping compartment for a week, with nothing to do but watch old vids.

Now, encased in the hard-shell suit, he worked his way down the tunnel from one sealed hatch to the next. Finally he planted his boots against the last hatch, the one that opened into the command pod. Theo let out a gust of breath. The journey had been hard work instead of fun.

No time for complaints, though. At his feet was the airtight hatch that opened into the command pod.

Dad's in there, Theo said to himself. Maybe his comm system's been shot away. Maybe he's hurt, wounded.

He had to carefully, painfully turn himself around so he could see the hatch's control panel. Its status light glared bright red. Vacuum on the other side of the hatch! Cripes, did Dad have enough time to get into his suit? The pod must be punctured!

Theo was literally standing on his head, clinging to the ladder's rung with one gloved hand. He reached for the hatch's control panel, but stopped his shaking hand just in time. If I open the hatch to vacuum it'll suck all the air out of the tunnel. But the tunnel's already been punctured and the emergency hatches are shut. Whatever air we're gonna lose we've already lost. Still he hesitated. Be better to conserve the air we've still got, he thought. We might be out here for who knows how long. *Chrysalis* is all torn up; there's no help back at Ceres for us.

Standing on a ladder rung, he punched at the suit radio's keyboard on the wrist of his suit.

'Mom?' he called.

She answered immediately, 'Yes, Theo.'

'I need you to pump the air out of the tunnel.'

He heard her sharp intake of breath. 'There's vacuum on the other side of the hatch?'

Sharp, Mom, he thought. 'That's what the hatch pad says. And the tunnel's been punctured someplace; all the emergency airlocks are closed. Pump out the air and store it in the standby tanks.'

Pauline said, 'All right. Can you talk with your father?'

Theo hadn't even tried that. 'I'll see.' He called over the suit radio. No answer. He pounded a gloved fist against the hatch. No response.

'He . . . he doesn't answer,' he said at last.

Again his mother hesitated before replying, 'The tunnel's evacuated.'

'Right.'

It took Theo two tries to peck out the combination that opened the hatch, his hand was shaking so much. When it finally did slide noiselessly open, his heart clutched in his chest.

There was nothing there! The entire control pod was gone! Gasping, wide-eyed, Theo slowly climbed three more rungs until his head and shoulders were through the open hatchway.

He was in empty space. Hard pinpoints of stars stared down at him from the black depths of infinity. The ship that had attacked them was nowhere in sight. Their cargo of ore was a distant cloud of rocks, spinning farther away every heartbeat. The wheel-shaped structure of the ore ship curved away on either side of him but there was no trace of the control pod. Theo saw the severed stumps of the struts that had held the pod in place, blackened by the blast of their explosive bolts.

Gone. Dad's gone. He's left us.

'Theo?' his mother's voice called in his helmet earphones. 'Is your father hurt? Or . . .'

'He's gone,' Theo said, feeling a deadly cold numbness creeping over him. 'He's abandoned us, Mom.'

Adrift

'Your father did *not* abandon us,' Pauline Zacharias said firmly.

Theo thought she looked angry. At me. She's boiled at me because Dad took off and left us. She's not mad at Dad, she's spitting mad at me.

He was sitting tensely on the sofa in the family living room, feeling tired and angry and scared. Angie sat on the armchair at one end of the sofa, rigid and staring hard-eyed at him, as if he'd done something wrong. Mother was pacing slowly across the room, past the family portrait they'd taken years ago, when Theo was barely ten.

'He didn't abandon us,' Pauline repeated.

'He blew the explosive bolts and took off in the control pod,' Theo said, his voice low, stubborn. 'He left us here drifting.'

His mother stopped pacing and looked directly at him. 'What your father did,' she said in a hard, cold voice, 'was to draw that attack ship away from us.'

'Yeah,' Theo retorted. 'And he left us without controls, without the navigation computer, without communications. The main tunnel's been punctured, spit knows what other damage the ship's taken.'

41

Pauline stared at her son for a long moment, then sank into the nearest chair, her face frozen in a mask of doubt and worry.

Angie broke the silence. 'But we'll be okay. Won't we? I mean, we can get back to Ceres and—'

'There's nothing left at Ceres!' Theo snapped. 'He killed them all! And we're heading outward, deeper into the Belt, toward Jupiter!'

For an instant Angie looked as if she would burst into tears. But Pauline reached across the space between them and grasped her arm.

'It's not that bad,' she said calmly. 'We have plenty of food and water. We have the main engine—'

'Which we can't control.'

'Can't control?' Angie's eyes went wide.

'The command pod's gone. All the controls're gone.'

Pauline fixed her son with a stern look. 'There's the backup command pod.'

'If it works,' Theo said sourly. 'Nobody's even been in there for more'n a year.'

'It will work,' Pauline said flatly. 'That's your responsibility, Theo. Yours and Angela's. Get to the backup command pod and get it up and running. We can't let ourselves continue to drift outward; we've got to get control of this vessel back in our hands.'

'Yeah, sure,' he groused.

'Yes, certainly,' Pauline said, with iron in her voice. 'We're not going to sit on our hands and do nothing. If we're going to be saved, we've got to save ourselves.'

'Can we . . . ?' Angie murmured.

'Of course we can,' said Pauline. 'And as soon as you get into the backup pod you set up a tracking beacon so your father can home in on it and get back to us.'

Theo started to answer that his father had run away from them and wouldn't be likely to come back, but he held his tongue. Some things you just don't say to your mother, even if they're true, he thought.

Turning to Angie, Pauline said, 'I want the two of you to work together. No bickering. Do you understand?'

Angela nodded. 'I will if he will.'

'I'll be all right,' Theo said to his sister. Then he added, 'As long as you don't try to lord it over me.'

'Lord it over you? When did I ever—'

'You're always pulling that older sister stuff, like you know it all.'

'That's not true!'

'Yes it is, dammit!'

'Stop it!' Pauline shouted. 'Stop it this instant! Theo, I won't have you using such language. And Angela, you will treat your brother with respect. Is that clear? Both of you?'

Angela nodded, her lips pressed into a thin bloodless line.

'Theo?' his mother demanded.

'Yes, ma'am. Sorry about the language.'

'You should be. If your vocabulary is so limited you should study your dictionary.'

'Yes, ma'am,' he mumbled again. It was Mom's old line, about the dictionary. He looked over at Angie; she glared back at him.

'You two have to work together,' their mother insisted. 'We don't have time for your little spats and name-calling. You both have to start behaving like adults.'

Angie behave like an adult? Theo grumbled silently. When the universe stops expanding, maybe.

Pauline stood up. 'Now then, if we all work together we can get through this. It'll be quite an adventure to tell your children about!'

'Your grandchildren,' Angie said, with a faint smile.

Theo shook his head. Busywork, he said to himself. Mom just wants to keep us busy so we won't have time to think about the fix Dad's left us in. But she's right; nobody's going to help us, so we'll have to help ourselves. Or die.

'Theo, we need the backup command center up and functioning. The sooner the better.'

'Right,' he said, thinking, Maybe she's right. Maybe, if I can get the backup command pod on line, maybe we *can* patch up this bucket and steer it back to civilization. There's nothing left at Ceres; we'll have to get back to the Earth/Moon vicinity. Or maybe the exploration base at Mars. Where is Mars now? On our side of its orbit or all the way over on the other side of the Sun? I'll have to check that once I get the nav system running.

Or maybe, he thought, we could make contact with the research station around Jupiter. We're heading in that direction anyway.

His mother clapped her hands lightly, interrupting his thoughts. 'Very well, then. On your feet, both of you! We all have work to do.'

Theo started toward the auxiliary airlock, but his mother stopped him. 'Thee, you'll have to get into your suit.'

'I know.'

'And before you do, I want you to take a shower and put on clean clothes. You don't smell very good, you know.'

'Aw, jeezus—'

Pauline leveled a stern finger at him. 'Language, young man!' Then, despite herself, the beginnings of a smile curled the corners of her lips. 'You're not so big that I can't wash out your mouth with detergent.'

'Why should I take a shower now?' Theo protested. 'I'm just gonna get sweated up again inside the suit.'

'Then you can take another shower when you get back.'

Angie smirked at him. But Pauline went on, 'Angela, you'll have to suit up and check the damage to the tunnels.'

'All right.'

'I'll try to save some hot water for you, Angel face,' Theo said, grinning maliciously at his sister.

'He's going to use up all the hot water on purpose, Mom,' Angela accused.

Pauline shook her head. Some things never change, no matter what, she thought. Then she added, Thank god.

I've got to be strong, she told herself. For both of them. They're only children and they're frightened. I've got to get them working, get them to repair the damage to the ship and put us on a trajectory that will

45

take us back to civilization. It's up to me. There's no one else until Victor returns to us. I've got to make them feel that they're contributing to our salvation, make them understand that they can save themselves – and me.

After a lightning-quick shower, Theo went alone to the main airlock and started pulling on his suit leggings. Mom's being a pain in the butt, he said to himself. Shower first. Shower afterward. You'd think I smell like a garbage dump, the way she talks. And Angie just sits there and sneers at me, the dumb hippopotamus. As he wormed his feet into the insulated boots he thought, What if the backup pod's been hit? Maybe that bastard took it out on purpose.

Theo looked up at the blank, scuffed metal bulkhead. Jeezus, if the backup pod's out we're not just up the creek without a surfboard. We're dead.

Ore Ship *Syracuse*:
Backup Command Pod

Theo wormed into the leggings of his space suit, then pulled on the thick-soled boots. As he hefted the suit's torso over his head and slid his arms into its sleeves he thought about turtles back on Earth with their shells. Born on the Moon, Theo had never been to Earth, had never faced a full Earthly g, although his parents had always insisted that he and Angie spend hour after pointless hour in the cramped little centrifuge in *Syracuse*'s gym.

'Your body's genetically equipped to handle a full g,' Dad repeated endlessly, 'but you've got to make sure that your muscles are trained up to their full potential.'

Yeah, right, Dad, Theo thought as he worked his arms into the straps of the suit's cumbersome backpack. Make sure we're ready for any emergency. And when it happens, you split out of here as fast as you jackrabbit can.

Theo felt angry. And betrayed. And guilty that he should feel this way about his own father.

He was locking the helmet into the suit's collar ring when his mother came into the equipment bay, her face tight, tense.

'I'll check you out,' Pauline said.

'Where's Angie?'

'She'll be here in a few minutes.'

'Maybe I should check the tunnels,' he said.

'No. Let your sister do it. There's more than enough to keep you both busy.'

And separated, Theo realized. Mom's pretty sharp.

'You be careful, Thee,' said Pauline. 'Make certain the pod's safe before you do anything else.'

He nodded inside the helmet. 'I'll be okay, Mom.'

'I know you will. I just fret.'

'Yeah.'

'Theo . . . your father did not abandon us. I don't want you thinking that he did. He'll come back, you'll see.'

Theo couldn't answer. He knew that if he spoke he'd say something that would hurt his mother.

But she could see the anger in his face. 'He did *not* abandon us,' she repeated.

'Yeah.' He slid the visor down, hoping it would keep his mother from seeing his expression, and clumped in the heavy boots toward the equipment bay hatch.

Up the central tunnel he climbed, the g load getting lighter with every step, and through the mini-airlocks that had automatically shut. When he came to the cross tunnel he floated weightlessly through the hatch and started downhill, toward the backup control pod. He was always surprised at how much effort it took to move himself in zero-g. You'd think it'd be like floating on a cloud, he thought as he clambered along the tunnel's protruding rungs. Instead, you had to consciously exert your muscles all the time. If you relaxed

48

you curled up into an apelike crouch with your arms dangling chest-high.

The cross tunnel was filled with air at normal pressure, according to the sensors on the right wrist of his suit. Theo stayed buttoned up inside the suit anyway, just to be on the safe side. When he finally arrived at the end of the tunnel, the telltales on the hatch's control panel were all in the green. He puffed out a sigh of relief. The backup pod hasn't been punctured, he said to himself. Then he added, If I can believe the sensors.

He tapped out the code on the hatch's panel and the hatch slid open with a slight grating sound. Hasn't been used in a while, Theo realized. Dust gets into everything sooner or later.

Cautiously he pushed himself through the hatch and climbed to his feet inside the pod. It was a near-duplicate of the main control center: curving panel of instruments and sensors; electronic keyboards right, left and center; display screens arrayed above the panel; command chair fastened to the deck by its short rails. But the screens were all blank, the instruments and sensors dark.

Theo took a deep double lungful of canned air, noticing for the first time how flat and metallic it tasted. His suit's sensors told him the air in the pod was perfectly fine. Cautiously, he cracked his helmet visor a millimeter or two and sucked in an experimental breath.

'Nothing wrong with that,' he said aloud.

He raised the visor all the way, made a full turn, and decided to take off the helmet altogether.

First, though, he called his mother. 'I'm in the pod. It's undamaged.'

'Good.' He heard a world of relief in his mother's solitary syllable. She must be using one of the suit radios, he realized. The intercom's still out.

'Now to get all the systems up and working,' he said.

'Don't take off your suit,' she cautioned. 'Even if you're breathing ship's air.'

'Right.' But as soon as he clicked off the suit radio he unlatched his helmet and lifted it off his head. Easier to see and work without the helmet in my way, he reasoned.

Victor Zacharias sat in his sweatshirt and shorts, staring into the emptiness displayed on the pod's central screen.

'He's gone,' Victor muttered to himself. He made the cameras do a full global scan of space around the pod, but there was no sign of the vessel that had attacked him. Nothing out there but dark emptiness and the cold, distant stars watching him like the eyes of ancient gods.

'He's gone,' Victor repeated. He wiped out *Chrysalis*, smashed our ship, and now he's gone off somewhere. Looking for Lars Fuchs, he said. The man must be insane, a total barbarian. Unable to believe that the attacker would just peel away, Victor scanned the area again. Nothing to be seen but dark emptiness and the distant unblinking stars.

Has he gone back to find *Syracuse*? The thought frightened Victor. No, he told himself. *Syracuse* is accelerating toward the outer edge of the Belt. He won't follow them that far. I hope. If I were religious I'd pray. Then he realized, Even if he is going after them there's nothing I can do about it now. Not a goddamned thing.

No time for remorse, Victor said to himself. I've got to figure out where I am, where I'm heading.

They call it the Asteroid Belt, but the region is actually just as empty as a vacuum can be, almost. The asteroids sprinkled through the area are rare and small, most of them the size of dust grains. Ceres, the largest of them, is barely a thousand kilometers across. Put all the millions of asteroids together and they wouldn't amount to a body as large as Earth's Moon, Victor knew. Some 'belt,' he thought. More like an enormous football stadium with only a few dozen people scattered among the seats.

'No time for philosophy,' Victor told himself sternly. 'See where you are and how quick you can get back to the ship.'

He began running through the navigational computer's data. The pod's thruster had fired him off roughly in the direction of Ceres, while *Syracuse* – with Pauline and the kids in it – had been accelerating in the opposite direction, toward the Belt's outer fringes. Not good, he thought. Not good at all.

The pod had no real propulsion system, only the rocket thruster that had hurled it clear of the ship once he'd fired the explosive bolts to separate from *Syracuse*. He had small cold-gas jets for fine maneuvering, but no engine that could turn him around and head him back to the ore carrier.

'Okay,' he said to himself. 'Then where am I heading?'

Again, the news was not good. The pod was on a trajectory that would miss Ceres by several thousand kilometers. Not that there was anything or anybody left at Ceres who could help him. *Chrysalis* was destroyed, and its rock rat inhabitants slaughtered. The few ore carriers and smelter ships that had been in orbit around Ceres must have lit off and fled out of there as fast as they could.

'Besides,' he said aloud, 'I don't have any communications that could reach them. I'm deaf and mute.'

No sense moaning, he told himself. Find out where in hell you are and where you're heading.

He ran through the navigation program twice, then a third time. The numbers did not change. The control pod was coasting through space sunward. It would miss Ceres by exactly seventeen point nine thousand kilometers and continue sailing inward, past the orbit of Mars – which was all the way over on the other side of the Sun now – then past the orbits of Earth, Venus and Mercury. It looked as if he would miss running into the Sun and instead would swing around it and start heading outward again. If he didn't broil first as he approached the Sun's searing brilliance.

His outbound course would bring him back almost to the exact spot where he'd separated the pod from *Syracuse* – in roughly four and a half years.

Victor didn't bother to calculate the perturbations on his course that the gravitational fields of the inner planets would cause. Why bother? Long before he reached even Mars's orbit he'd be dead of starvation. Of course, if the pod's cranky air recycler crapped out, he could die of asphyxiation long before that.

In *Syracuse*'s backup command pod, Theo felt like screaming or pounding his gloved fists against the control board. He had carefully switched on the pod's electrical power, then booted up the control instruments and sensors one at a time, to make certain he didn't overload the system and trip any circuits.

Now he stared at the red lights glaring at him from one end of the panel to the other. Propulsion fuel tanks. Air reserve tanks. Structural integrity. All in the red. The fusion reactor and main engine were undamaged, apparently, but the level of hydrogen fuel left in the battered tanks was dangerously, critically low. The fusion reactor generated the ship's electrical energy and powered the main engine. At the rate the engine was roaring along now, the tanks would be totally dry in hours.

Theo shut down the main engine. We're going to need that aitch-two for electrical power, he thought. We can coast for the time being: Dad had us going like a bat out of Hades to get away from that murdering son of a female dog.

He began to use the cameras on the ship's tiny maintenance robots to assess the damage to the ship's structure.

'God, she's falling apart,' he whispered to himself. When the attacker slagged the antennas his laser beams sliced through the hull of that section of the wheel, gutting their main propulsion fuel tanks. Penetrated to the tunnels, too, Theo saw. That's how we lost the air in there.

Sitting in the command chair, Theo realized that *Syracuse* was badly damaged and heading deeper into the Belt, away from Ceres, away from any chance of help. The antennas are gone, our fuel is down to a couple of days' worth, we're going to lose electrical power and die.

For the first time since he'd been a baby Theo wanted to cry. He wanted to curl up into a fetal ball and let his fate overtake him. But that would mean Mom and Angie would die too.

He lifted his chin a notch. It's up to me, he told himself. I've got to repair this damage. Angie can't do it, not by herself anyways. I've got to get this ship back in operating condition and heading toward civilization. I've got to keep Mom and Angie alive.

He thought that his father would know what to do and how to do it. But Dad's gone. There's nobody here but me.

'It's up to me now,' he said aloud.

Ore Ship *Syracuse*: Lavatory

Angela stepped out of the shower stall vigorously rubbing a towel over her body. As she tucked it around her and wrapped a second towel over her wet hair she muttered something.

Pauline was at the sink brushing her teeth. The mirror was fogging from the steam of her daughter's shower. She rubbed a clear spot with a hand towel as Angela finished drying herself.

'It's not fair,' Angela muttered again.

Pauline rinsed her mouth, then asked, 'What's not fair?'

'Theo's got a lav all to himself while we're bumping into each other in here.'

'Theo shared the other lav with your father when he was here,' Pauline said.

'Still, it's not fair. He ought to—'

Pauline silenced her daughter with a stern glance. 'Angela, you've got to stop fighting with your brother.'

'Me?' She seemed genuinely shocked. '*He*'s the one who's always calling me names, yelling that I boss him around. I'm the older one, he ought to be taking orders from me.'

'Young lady,' Pauline said, the way she always did when she was about to tell her daughter something

Angela didn't want to hear, 'I will say this only once more. I want you to stop arguing with Theo. He's had an enormous burden of responsibility dumped on his shoulders.'

'Me too!'

'Yes, I know, but Theo's a male and he automatically assumes he's got to take charge.'

'That's dumb.'

'Maybe it is, but you and I will have to deal with it. Thee would welcome help from you if only you'd be pleasant about it and stop calling him names.'

'I don't—'

'Angela, you're the older sibling. It's up to you to set the tone between you and your brother. I will *not* have you two bickering over every little thing that comes up. We're in enough danger here, we all need to work together if we're going to survive.'

Angela sagged back onto the edge of the sink. 'Are we really in that much trouble?'

'Yes, we are.'

She stared down at her bare toes for several moments. Then, in a low voice, 'Do you think Dad really ran away?'

'Not for a picosecond,' Pauline said firmly. 'He lured that attacker away from us. He saved our lives.'

'Do you think he's . . . he got killed?'

Pauline had to pull in a breath before she could reply, 'No.'

'Really, Ma? Really and truly?'

'Really and truly, my little angel. He's not dead.

56

I know it in my bones. He's out there somewhere trying to find us, trying to save us.'

Angela threw her arms around her mother's neck. 'I'll be good, Ma, I promise,' she said tearfully. 'I'll treat Theo better, you'll see.'

'I know,' Pauline said, holding her daughter in her arms. 'I know.'

That night, as she slipped into her oversized bed alone, Pauline thought that she should have a talk with Theo, as well. It takes two to make a fight; Angela's not the only one who needs to improve her behavior.

She turned out the lights and lay back on her pillow. The bed seemed empty, lonely without Victor beside her. He's not dead, Pauline told herself. He left us to decoy that attacker away from us, to save us from being destroyed. He got away, I know he did. I'd know if he were dead. I'd feel it, somehow.

Pauline Osgood Zacharias was made of strong fiber. Born in Selene while her astronomer parents were teaching at the university there, she had grown up in the sunless corridors and confined living quarters of that underground city. To Pauline, the 'outdoors' meant strolling along the winding pathways of Selene's Grand Plaza, beneath its arching concrete dome, admiring the miniature trees and shrubbery that the lunar citizens so lovingly tended.

She was fifteen before her parents allowed her to go without them out onto the surface of the giant crater Alphonsus. Selene was dug into the crater's ringwall mountains, and the area out on the flat was dotted with solar-cell farms, factories that took advantage of the

Moon's airlessness, and the Armstrong Spaceport, where ships took off for Earth or other worlds deeper in the solar system.

She studied astronomy, just as her parents had. But by the time she was ready to graduate, a family crisis arose. Her parents were preparing to return to Earth. Despite the greenhouse floods and the devastation of so many cities – or perhaps because of that – her parents felt they had to go back to the homeworld, back to their roots in Colorado. Pauline desperately wanted to stay on the Moon. She was working as a teaching assistant at the new astronomy complex being built at Farside. She had met Victor Zacharias and fallen in love with him.

Her parents left for Earth, with Pauline's promise that she and Victor would come to visit them as soon as they could. But by the time Pauline and her newly married husband reached Denver it was too late: both her parents had been killed in a food riot.

She clung to Victor then, returned to the Moon, bore him two children, and went with him when he decided to become a rock rat, to live aboard a rattletrap ship he had managed to lease, to ply through the Asteroid Belt collecting ores from the miners and selling them to the big corporations at Ceres. She raised her daughter and her son, content to make the tiny world of the ore carrier *Syracuse* her island of home, her whole universe.

When the occasional violence in the Belt flared into the Second Asteroid War, Victor told her, 'Not to worry. We don't belong to either corporation. Nobody's going to attack the independents; that would stop the flow of resources from the Belt and neither Humphries nor Astro wants that.'

She believed her husband. Until that moment when their ship was nearly destroyed by an anonymous attacker.

Now she tried to sleep, alone in her bed, desperately afraid that she would never see Victor again, almost frantic with the fear that she kept stifled all day, each day, every waking moment. She couldn't let her children see her fear. But alone in the dark, it threatened to overwhelm her.

Ore Ship *Syracuse*: Galley

Theo eyed the steaming roast on his plate.

'Eat up,' his mother urged. 'This is the last feast we're going to have for a long time. Tomorrow we start rationing our provisions. We've got to make them last.'

Theo was too tired to eat. For the past six days he had spent virtually every waking moment trying to repair the ship, directing the tiny-brained maintenance robots to weld patches where the wheel and the tunnels had been punctured, worming his way into the narrow access tubes to reconnect wiring, digging through the logistics storage bays to find the spare parts that he needed for the repairs. Most of his evenings he spent in the backup command pod, bringing systems back on line. He saw through eyes bleary with fatigue that one by one the red lights on the display panels were turning to green or at least amber. Mostly amber, but that was the best he could accomplish.

The fuel supply for the fusion reactor worried him most. Without the reactor the ship's electrical power systems would go down. When that happened, the lights, the air and water recyclers, the food refrigerators and microwave cookers would go down too.

The navigation program told him that they were coasting deeper into the Belt, away from help, away from the rest of the human race. He knew the ship didn't have enough fuel to change their course significantly. For a while he hoped that they might drift outward far enough to reach the research station orbiting Jupiter, but the navigation program showed that would be impossible unless they added a major jolt of thrust to their velocity vector, and there wasn't enough hydrogen left in the tanks for anything like that.

They were going to die aboard *Syracuse*, Theo realized: probably of asphyxiation, certainly of starvation. All his brave thoughts and hard work could not change that.

'Theo,' his mother said gently. 'I know you're tired. But you've got to eat to keep up your strength.'

He focused on her face smiling encouragingly from across the narrow galley table.

'Right, Mom,' he mumbled, digging a fork into his dinner.

Angie's appetite seemed normal, even better than normal, he thought. His sister was chewing on a slab of roast pseudomeat: artificial protein created by cellular biologists and marketed to the rock rats and other spacefarers as Faux Beef (or pork, or veal, or even pheasant).

'So our food stores are okay,' he muttered, pushing the meat around his plate listlessly.

'Enough for years, if we're careful,' his mother said guardedly as she got up and went to the galley's stainless steel sink.

Theo glanced at Angie, munching away. Dieting will do her good, he thought. But he didn't say it. Instead, he told his mother, 'We're going to need enough for years.'

Angie looked up at him, startled. 'For years?'

'Looks that way.'

'But you said the fusion engine was okay, didn't you?'

He gave his sister a bleak look. 'The engine's fine, Angie. But when that freaking illegitimate slagged our antennas he ripped up the fuel tanks as well. They're just about dry. Only two cells out of twenty have any hydrogen left in them.'

He saw his mother's hands clench on the sink's edge; her knuckles went white.

'I've shut down the engine until I can figure out some way to get us turned around and headed back to civilization. We're coasting now.'

Pauline made a brittle little smile. 'Then I suppose we'll just have to coast for a while.'

'For how long?' Angie asked, looking suspicious, as if this was some kind of trick Theo was playing on her.

He pursed his lips, then replied, 'Right now we're on a trajectory that takes us halfway to Jupiter before we curve back and start toward the inner Belt again.'

'How long?' Angie repeated.

He had memorized the numbers. 'Three thousand, one hundred and thirty-seven days,' Theo said.

'Three thousand—'

'That's eight years, seven months and four days.'

'Eight *years*? I'll be twenty-six years old!'

'That's to get us back to Ceres,' Theo explained, 'where we were when we were attacked, more or less.'

Pauline went to her daughter and laid a calming hand on Angie's shoulder. 'We have enough food to last that long,' she said. 'If we're careful. And we recycle our water and air, so life support shouldn't be an issue.'

If all the equipment keeps on working, Theo countered silently.

'Can't you do something, Thee?' Angie asked, her face agonized. 'I mean, eight years!'

'I'm working on it,' he said. 'Maybe we can use what little fuel we have left to cut the time down. But I've got to be real careful. I don't want to make things worse than they are now.'

'How could they get worse?' Angie grumbled.

'Is there any chance of repairing the antennas?' Pauline asked. 'Then we could call for help.'

Theo nodded. 'That's my next priority. There must be some ships in this region of the Belt. Miners, other rock rats.'

'Sure!' said Angie, brightening a little.

'Trouble is,' Theo went on, 'we've been busting along at a pretty high delta vee. Dad goosed the main engines before he split.'

'So we're accelerating too much for another ore ship or a miner to reach us?' Pauline asked.

'I've shut down the main engine,' Theo repeated. 'We're not accelerating anymore, just coasting. But still, we're spitting along damn fast. I don't know if one of the rock rats could catch up to us, even if they wanted to.'

His mother didn't flinch at his minor vulgarity. She's just as scared as Angie, Theo thought, but she hides it better.

'Eight years,' Angie repeated, in a whisper.

Theo nodded. He knew their hydrogen fuel wouldn't last anywhere near that long. The reactor would shut down and the ship would lose all its electrical power well before then. They'd freeze and choke to death when the heaters and air recyclers shut down.

'Well then,' their mother said, as brightly as she could manage, 'once the antennas are working again we can call for assistance. With *Chrysalis* gone, there must be a lot of rock rats stranded out here in the Belt calling back toward Earth for help.'

'Guess so,' Theo said.

'So fixing the antennas is our first priority,' Pauline continued. 'Thee, what can we do to help you?'

He glanced at Angie and thought, Keep out of my way. But to his mother he said, 'I don't know yet. I've got some studying to do.'

For the next two days Theo stayed mostly in his own compartment studying the tutorials and maintenance videos about the antennas. He saw that he would have to go outside to assess the damage that the attacker's laser beams did. The maintenance robots could be helpful, but only if he could program them with exact instructions.

He was stretched out on his bunk, so intent on the maintenance video that he didn't hear the scratching on his privacy partition.

'Thee? You in there?' Angie's voice.

He yanked the plug out of his ear and looked up. His sister inched the accordion-fold partition back a sliver. 'Can I come in?'

'*May* I come in,' he corrected.

Angie pushed the partition wide open. 'May I. All right. Satisfied?'

'Come on in,' he said, swinging his stockinged feet to the tiled deck. He clicked the remote and the instruction vid disappeared from the screen built into the bulkhead at the foot of his bunk.

Angie sat in the spindly little desk chair, her fists clenched on her knees.

'How's it going?' she asked.

'Okay. I'm learning a lot about how the antennas work. I'll have to go outside and check the damage. Prob'ly tomorrow.'

'You want me to go with you? You know, like backup?'

He started to say that she'd be more trouble than help, but bit back the reply and answered instead, 'You could be a big help by monitoring me from the control pod.'

Angie's eyes widened eagerly. 'I could do that,' she said.

'Okay. Good. I'll tell Mom.'

'Thee?'

'What?'

'She cries.'

'Who? Mom?' A blast of something close to panic jolted through him.

Nodding, fighting back tears herself, Angie said, 'At night. After we go to bed. I can hear her in her compartment. She tries to muffle it but I can hear her crying.'

Theo couldn't believe his mother was afraid of anything. 'It's about Dad, I bet. She's crying about Dad.'

'You don't really think he ran away from us, do you?'

'What else? We're here and he's not.'

'But Mom says he did it to protect us. To draw the attack ship away from us.'

A thousand thoughts raced through Theo's mind, all jumbled up, blurring together.

'Thee, you don't really think he abandoned us, do you?'

He shook his head. 'It doesn't matter what I think. Dad's prob'ly dead.'

'No!'

'Most likely. But we're alive, and I intend to keep us that way.'

Victor Zacharias was alive, but starving.

The pod in which he was coasting sunward carried only a minifridge's worth of packaged food: mostly sandwiches and preserved fruits. He had been living on one sandwich and one piece of fruit per twenty-four hours. His stomach rumbled hollowly.

As the pod sailed silently through the dark emptiness he had plenty of time to think. And plan.

The pod had an emergency transponder that could beam out a distress signal. But it was a notoriously weak signal, Victor knew, and bound to be swamped by the comm chatter that would be sweeping over the area where *Chrysalis* once orbited Ceres. It was bitterly ironic, he thought: There must be whole fleets of rescue and salvage ships heading for Ceres, a regular armada of vessels and people. But they wouldn't be looking for a small, weak-voiced pod hurtling inward from the Belt, thousands of kilometers from the asteroid.

How can I get them to notice me? Victor asked himself. He pondered that question through the long, lonely hours he spent in the command chair, staring at his useless instruments and sensors. He dreamed about it when he cranked the reclining chair back and willed himself to sleep. He worried that the nanobatteries powering the pod's systems would run dry, but then he realized he'd starve to death long before that happened.

At first he thought his hunger would be a sharp prod that would make him think. After a week he realized that starvation dulled the mind. No brilliant ideas surfaced; all he could think of was food.

He wished he had the mental discipline of a Buddhist monk, capable of submerging himself into deep meditation. Victor's mind was not so trained. He wanted an idea, a plan, a scheme. He wanted action, not the oblivion of Nirvana.

He wanted, above all, to get back to Pauline and the children. With a shake of his head he reminded himself, They're not children anymore. Angela's ready for marriage. Theo is a man in every way except experience.

And still the pod drifted, like a leaf caught in a tide, like a man-made asteroid sweeping along in its mindless orbit.

Feeling weaker each day, Victor forced himself to check and recheck every item of equipment in the pod. Every piece of hardware, every computer program, every system. There's got to be something here that I can use as a tool, something that I can use to get noticed, to get rescued.

Again and again he checked his inventory. There was a communications laser built into the pod's outer hull, but lasers were strictly for line-of-sight communications. Radio waves spread out like ripples on a pond, but the tight beam of a laser was good for communications only if it was pointed directly at the ship you wanted to communicate with.

I could make the laser swing around in a circle, Victor thought. That might catch some ship someplace. But he knew that was a tactic of desperation. The chances of his pencil-thin laser beam reaching another ship's receiving sensor were little better than the chances of being struck by lightning out here in the middle of empty space.

Yet that night he dreamed of a star shining in the soft night sky of Earth. The star pulsated. Shepherds gathered in the desert and marveled at it.

When he woke he thought he must be getting irrational. 'Next thing you know you'll be dreaming about Santa Claus," he growled at himself.

He fought off sleep but eventually it overpowered him. And he dreamed again of the star blinking in the cloudless sky of a desert on Earth. Blinking. Blinking.

Victor awoke with a new sense of purpose. The first thing I've got to do is modify the laser, he told himself. Get its pulses down into the petasecond range. The shorter the pulses, the more power in each pulse. Each pulse will carry megawatts worth of power, plenty bright enough to see on Earth. There must be thousands of astronomers looking at the stars each night. They'll have to notice me!

But first I've got to modify the laser.

Theo was soaking in a hot shower after long hours in his space suit, working outside on the slagged antennas. Whoever their attacker was, he had done a thorough job of destroying the antennas: long ugly gashes sliced through the metallic monolayer that had been sprayed along *Syracuse*'s curving outer hull and gutted the fusion engine's propellant tanks beneath them.

He let the steaming water relax his cramped and aching muscles. Neither Mom nor Angie tried to hurry him out of the shower. What the hell, he rationalized, the water's recycled. We're not losing any of it: it just goes into the purifiers and back to the holding tank. He remembered when he was a kid, maybe seven years old, and he'd taken a pair of welder's goggles into the shower with him and pretended he was swimming underwater on Earth, like the vids he'd seen. After three-quarters of an hour Dad got sore, he recalled, but Mom laughed when Dad told her about it.

I can repair the antennas, Theo told himself. I know what to do and how to go about it. The maintenance robots can do most of the outside work, all I've got to do is program them and feed them the right materials. Tomorrow I'll go through the logistics files and find what I need.

But the next morning he found that the monomolecular spray that made up the antennas was not listed in the logistics files. Theo spent the next two days searching through the stores in the ship's storage bays. No antenna spray.

Spit in my hat, he groused to himself, I'm gonna have to make it up from scratch.

By dinner time of the second day he was thoroughly angry.

'How could Dad let us sail out here without the proper materials to repair the antennas?' he grumbled into his bowl of soup.

'Are you sure – ' Angie began.

'I'm sure!' Theo snapped. 'The stuff isn't there. Never was. He let us cruise through the Belt without the material we need to repair the antennas. Our main antennas, for crying out loud!'

Pauline kept her face from showing any emotion. 'You'll have to produce the antenna spray from the materials we have on board, then, Theo. That's what your father would do, I suppose.'

He glared at her. 'No. Dad would just wave a magic wand and the antennas would fix themselves.'

'Theo.'

'Or more likely the antennas wouldn't dare get damaged long's Dad's in charge.'

His mother drew in a long breath. Then she said, 'Theo, the antennas did get damaged while your father was on board. Now it's up to you to repair them.'

He stared down into his unfinished soup. 'Yeah. It's up to me.'

Columbus, Ohio:
COSETI Headquarters

Even after more than three quarters of a century, the headquarters of the Columbus Optical Search for Extra Terrestrial Intelligence was hardly imposing. It consisted of a lovingly preserved but unpretentious wooden frame house, a much newer brick two-story building for offices and workshops, and the Kingsley Observatory, which housed beneath its metal dome a sturdy two-meter Schmidt reflector telescope.

The homes adjacent to COSETI headquarters had long been demolished after being inundated time and again by the Scioto River, which had overflowed much of Columbus in the greenhouse floods. Now the headquarters grounds were surrounded by a low earthern levee, almost like the long mysterious mounds that the original Native Americans had built in the region a thousand years earlier.

Jillian Hatcher was bubbling with excitement. She bent over the desk of the observatory's director, a small, slim blonde woman filled with the energy and exhilaration of discovery.

'It's real!' she shouted, tapping the computer screen on her boss's desk. 'I found it! I found it!'

She practically danced around the small, cluttered office.

Dwight Franklin smiled at her. Although he contained his excitement as best as he could, he too felt a thrill shuddering along his spine. 'After all these years,' he murmured.

Franklin had a square, chunky build. His thinning hair was combed straight back from his high forehead. Sitting behind his desk in his shirtsleeves and suspenders, he looked more like a clerk or an accountant than a world-renowned astronomer.

'The pulses are regular!' Jillian said, dancing back to his desk. 'It's a message! A message from an extra-terrestrial civilization!'

'Looks intriguing, I've got to admit,' said Franklin. 'Where in the sky—'

'The region of Sagittarius!' she crowed. 'The heart of the Milky Way!'

'And it's fixed in its position? It's not a satellite or a spacecraft?'

Jillian's beaming face faded a little. 'I haven't tracked it yet.'

Franklin got up from his creaking desk chair. 'Let's see if we can get a firm fix on it.'

She sank into silence and followed him out into the chill November night. Clouds were building up along the western horizon but most of the sky was clear as crystal. Orion and the Bull sparkled above them. Jillian picked out the Pleiades cluster and bright Aldebaran.

The observatory was freezing cold with the dome open but they walked past the silent framework of the

Schmidt telescope and into the tiny control room. It was heated, and Jillian was grateful for that.

Half an hour later her excitement had evaporated like a shallow pan of water over a hot fire.

Franklin looked up from the computer screen, a fatherly look of sympathy on his face.

'It's a spacecraft, I'm afraid.'

'Are you sure?' Jillian asked, desperate. 'Positive?'

He gestured toward the display. 'See for yourself. It's out in the Asteroid Belt, and it's definitely moving.'

'It's not a star.'

'I'm afraid not.'

'Not a message from an extraterrestrial intelligence.'

'No.'

Jillian felt like crying. But then a new thought popped into her head. 'So why is a spacecraft out in the Belt sending pulsed laser messages toward Earth? What's he trying to say?'

Ore Ship *Syracuse*: The Workshop

The workshop smelled of machine oil and dust. The overhead lamps bathed the big chamber in glareless, shadowless light. Theo sat at a long workbench in one corner where shelves of chemical compounds were stacked high on both sides of him. He was bent over an ordinary optical microscope, feeling frustrated and cranky, when his sister came through the open hatch that led back to the family's living quarters.

He didn't hear her enter, nor the soft footfalls of her slippered feet as she approached his workbench. He was studying the jiggling Brownian motion of the metallic chips that he had mixed into a sample of liquid plastic. Although the instructions in the maintenance videos had been quite specific, Theo found that the supplies his father had stored were far short of what he needed to repair the ship's antennas. He was trying to make do with what was available in the storage bays. And it wasn't going well.

'Thee?' Angie called timidly.

Her voice startled him. He jerked up straight on the stool he was sitting on.

'I didn't mean to scare you,' Angie said.

'I'm not scared,' he snapped. 'You just surprised me, that's all.'

'You didn't come in for lunch,' his sister said. 'And now it's almost dinner time.'

'Okay. Okay. Tell Mom I'll be there.' But he turned back to the microscope.

'How's it going?' Angie asked.

'Lousy.'

'Really?'

He looked up at her. 'Really. Lousy. I don't have the electrolyte I need. And the polymer filler is so old and goddamn gooey I don't think it'll be workable.'

'Theo, I really—'

'Go tell Mom about the language.'

'It's not that.' Angie took a breath, then went on, 'Is it really going to take eight years for us to get back to Ceres?'

He heard the stress in her voice. 'Unless I can figure out a way to shorten it.'

'Eight years?' she whimpered.

Trying to fight down the anger rising inside him, Theo said, 'Yes. Eight years, seven months and four days.'

'You don't have to be so happy about it!'

'I'm not happy, Angie.'

'You're gloating! You don't care how long it takes. You don't care about me at all!'

'I told you I'm trying to figure out a way to shorten it,' Theo protested. 'What more can I do, for Christopher Columbus's sake?'

She plopped herself down on the bench beside him. 'Eight years! I'll be an old woman by the time we get back.'

'If we get back,' he said. He knew he shouldn't have said it but there it was.

'If?'

'There's a good chance we'll die on this bucket. The recyclers might wear out, the fusion reactor could fail, our hydrogen fuel is going to run out—'

Angie clapped her hands to her ears. 'I don't want to hear it! You're just being spiteful!'

'It's the truth, Angie.'

'No,' she said. 'We'll live. We're not going to die here. If something breaks down we'll fix it.'

'If we can.'

'And you'll find a way to get us back to Ceres quicker, too, won't you? You're just teasing me, trying to make me cry.'

'Angie, I'm just telling you the facts.'

'I can't sit here for eight years, Theo! I'll be twenty-six years old by then! Twenty-six! All the guys my age will already be married.'

Suddenly Theo understood what was really bothering her.

'Angie,' he asked, 'that bozo you dated when we were docked at *Chrysalis* last year—'

'He's not a bozo! His name is Leif Haldeman.'

'How serious are you about him?'

She blinked several times before murmuring, 'I love him, Theo.'

'Have you been to bed with him?'

Her cheeks flamed. 'That's none of your business!'

'Does Mom know? Or Dad?'

'There's nothing for them to know. I love Leif and he loves me. We were going to tell Mom and Dad about it when we got back to Ceres.'

'He was living on *Chrysalis*?'

'He was looking for a job with one of the rock rats. He's a mining engineer.'

Feeling totally miserable, Theo said softly, 'Angie, if he was still on *Chrysalis* when we were approaching Ceres . . .'

Angie's eyes went wide as she realized what her brother was trying to tell her. 'You think he was killed?'

'I don't think anybody aboard *Chrysalis* survived, Angie.'

'No,' she said, shaking her head. 'He probably found a berth on one of the mining ships. He was probably out in the Belt somewhere when *Chrysalis* was attacked.'

'I hope so,' said Theo.

'He had to be!'

'I hope so,' he repeated.

Victor was roused from a troubled sleep by a beeping noise. Any sound at all aboard the cramped little pod was alarming. The muted hum of the air fans and the constant buzz of the electronics had long since faded into an unnoticed background. But a new sound – a ping, a beep, a creak – meant danger.

Instantly awake, Victor swiftly scanned the control board. No red lights, all systems functioning nominally.

The beeping sounded again, and Victor saw a yellow light flashing in a corner of the control panel.

The comm laser, he realized. What's wrong – His breath caught in his throat. *That's the message light!* Wiping sleep from his eyes with the heel of one hand, he punched up the communications system on his main screen.

TORCH SHIP *ELSINORE*. The yellow letters blazed on the otherwise dark screen. His mind raced. *Elsinore* was one of the vessels in orbit around Ceres when the attack started.

Victor pounded on the comm key. '*Elsinore*, this is *Syracuse*. What's left of it, anyway.'

A woman's voice replied, 'We have you in sight. Will rendezvous with you in twenty minutes. Be prepared to come aboard.'

Victor wanted to kiss her, whoever she was. But then he remembered, 'I don't have a suit. I can't go EVA.'

Several heartbeats' silence. Then a man's voice answered, 'Very well, we will send a shuttlecraft and mate to your airlock.'

'Thank you,' Victor said fervently. He had never felt so grateful in his life. 'Thank you. Thank you.'

After dinner Theo was so tired that all he wanted was to crawl into his bunk and sleep. But as he got up from the galley's narrow table, Angie said, 'Thee, isn't there anything I can do to help you?'

He looked down at his sister. Was she asking out of a sense of duty, or because their mother had told her to? She looked sincere.

'I mean,' Angie went on, 'I just sit around here all day with nothing to do but keep the kitchen appliances in working order.'

'You're helping me work out our diets,' Pauline said, from the sink where she was scraping dishes and putting them into the microwave dishwasher. Instead of using precious water, the dishwasher blasted everything clean with pulses of high-power microwaves. Theo wondered if it wouldn't be better to wash the dishes with recycled water than use the fusion reactor's dwindling fuel supply to power the microwave cleaner.

'Mom, that's nothing more than busywork,' Angie said. 'I want to do something *useful*.'

Theo was impressed. Angie had never shown a desire to be useful before. Their parents had always raised Angie to be a little queen, he thought, lording it over him while Mom pampered her. Maybe her telling me about her boyfriend is bringing us closer together, he thought. But then a different voice in his head sneered, Or maybe she just wants to stay close to you to make sure you don't tell Mom about her love life.

'Don't look so surprised, Thee!' Angie demanded. 'What can I do to help you?'

He blinked, then grinned. 'Well . . .' he started, drawing out the word, 'most of what I'm doing in the workshop is dogwork chemistry: mixing things and seeing if the mixtures have the conductivity I need for repainting the antennas. . . .'

'I could help you do that, couldn't I?' Angie asked. 'I mean, you could tell me what to do and I could do it.'

Slowly he nodded. 'Yeah. I guess so.'

'Good!' Angela seemed genuinely pleased. 'Tomorrow morning I'll go to the workshop with you.'

Theo glanced at his mother, still by the sink. She was smiling. Did Mom get Angie to do this? he wondered. With a mental shrug, he said to himself, Doesn't matter. Maybe Mom talked Angie into it, or maybe Angie's growing up and trying to take some responsibilities. Or maybe she just wants to keep an eye on me now that I know about her boyfriend. Whichever, it's okay.

If my spoiled brat sister actually lets me tell her what to do in the workshop, he added.

Torch Ship *Elsinore*

It's a freaking floating palace, Victor thought as the two
uniformed crew members – one man and one woman –
led him through the carpeted corridors and spacious
lounges of the *Elsinore*.

The lounges were empty and quiet, the corridors
nearly so. The crew seemed to far outnumber the
passengers.

The same two crew members had flown a shuttlecraft and plucked Victor from the command pod that
had been his home for nearly two weeks. They had
delivered him to *Elsinore*'s small but well-stocked infirmary, where a pair of medics – again, one woman
and one man – checked him thoroughly and pronounced him physically fit, except for slight dehydra-
tion.

Now they walked him through the ship.

'Where are we going?' Victor asked at last, as they
climbed a carpeted staircase.

'To meet the man who diverted our ship to pick you
up,' said the crewman walking on Victor's right side.

'The captain? I'd certainly like to thank him.'

'Not the captain,' replied the woman on his left.

'Who then?'

They reached the top of the stairs. Another lounge, with fabric-covered walls and muted music purring softly from overhead speakers. Two people were sitting at one of the little round tables; the lounge was otherwise empty except for the human bartender standing behind the bar. The man at the table rose to his feet like the Sun climbing above the horizon: a huge mountain of a man with wild red shaggy hair and beard and a mug of what had to be beer in one ham-sized hand.

Victor recognized him immediately: George Ambrose, chairman of the ruling council at Ceres. Big George, the rock rats' leader. A brightly attractive woman was sitting at the table with George. She too looked familiar to Victor but he couldn't quite place her. She appeared to be young, with bountiful blonde hair framing her pretty, smiling, cheerleader's face.

'You're Victor Zacharias?' Big George asked in a surprisingly sweet tenor voice. He was not smiling, however. If anything, he looked grimly angry.

Victor extended his hand and Big George engulfed it in his massive paw.

'We've met before,' Victor said, 'but it was in a crowd at a party aboard *Chrysalis*; I don't suppose you remember me.'

'*Chrysalis*,' George muttered, plunking himself down on his chair; it groaned beneath his weight.

Victor turned to the woman.

'I'm Edith Elgin,' she said, still smiling as she raised her hand toward him.

'Edie Elgin. The news anchor,' Victor said, recognizing her at last. 'But I thought you lived in Selene.'

'I came out here to do a story on the war in the Belt,' she said, her smile fading.

'And walked into a fookin' massacre,' Big George growled.

A moment of awkward silence. Then George hollered over to the bartender, 'We've got a thirsty man here!' Turning to Victor he added, 'I guess maybe you want a drink, too, eh?'

Despite himself, Victor grinned. He asked the barman for a glass of red wine. Edith Elgin shook her head when the barman offered to refill her glass of soda.

'I want to thank you for picking me up,' Victor said. 'I didn't think anybody—'

'Got a message from some astronomers Earthside,' George interrupted. 'They saw your laser signal. Thought they'd found fookin' little green men, at first. Big disappointment to them.'

'I'm not disappointed,' Victor said. He picked up his stemmed wine glass and took a long, slow, delicious sip. 'You weren't aboard *Chrysalis*,' he asked Big George, 'when . . . when it happened?'

George swung his red-maned head. 'I was here on *Elsinore*, chattin' up our visitor.'

'What happened to you?' Edith Elgin asked Victor. 'How did you get into this mess?'

Victor began to speak, but the words caught in his throat. 'My family . . . they're still out there. . . .'

'Where?'

'I don't know!' Victor groaned. 'The ship was heading outward. . . .'

'*Syracuse?*' she asked.

For the first time in his adult life Victor had to struggle to hold back tears. He nodded at the two of them and managed to choke out, 'He attacked us. For no reason! I separated the pod, drew him away. My wife . . . two children . . . they're out there, drifting outward.'

Edith Elgin looked up at George Ambrose. 'We've got to find them.'

Big George sat unmoving, like an implacable mountain. At last he said, 'How can we find 'em when we don't know where they are?'

'They're drifting outward,' Victor said.

'Yes, but what's their track? We can't go traipsin' all over the Belt to search for them. There's too much to do here and too little to do it with.'

'Can't you scan the area with radar?' Edith Elgin asked. 'They have those huge radar arrays back Earthside. They can pick out a thumbtack a million kilometers away.'

George slowly shook his shaggy head. 'They can pick up a beacon from a spacecraft, that's what they do.'

Edith turned back to Victor. 'Your ship's sending out a beacon, isn't it? A tracking beacon?'

Victor felt totally hollowed out. 'He destroyed our antennas. *Syracuse* can't send out any kind of signal.'

George took another huge gulp of beer, then placed his mug firmly on the tiny table.

'Face it, mate,' he said to Victor. 'Your family's gone and there's nothin' we can do for 'em.'

Ore Ship *Syracuse*:
Theo's Compartment

Theo was stretched out on the bunk of his tight little compartment, VR goggles over his eyes and sensor gloves on his hands, deeply immersed in the virtual reality program. He knew he should be studying the navigation program, but he'd spent all day staring at graphs and lists and numbers. Now he was trying to relax with an entertainment VR he had smuggled past his parents' watchful eyes.

I'm old enough to have adult VRs, he said to himself. Old enough to really experience what these women are doing. Full sensory input: sight, sound, touch . . .

He heard a faint tapping and then the squeak of his accordion-pleated door starting to slide open. With a sudden twitch of guilty fear he yanked the goggles off his head and pulled off the gloves.

'May I come in, Theo?' his mother asked.

Shoving the goggles and gloves under his pillow, Theo sat up, swinging his long legs off the bunk.

'I knocked at your door, Thee,' said Pauline as she entered the compartment, 'but I guess you didn't hear me.'

Not over the panting and moaning of the scene you interrupted, Mom, he replied silently.

'Are you all right?' his mother asked, sitting in the compartment's only chair, the spindly little plastic one that fit under the desk.

'Yeah. I'm fine, Mom.'

'You've been working terribly hard, I know.'

'I just can't get the right mixture for repairing the antennas. Nothing I've tried has the right electrical conductivity. I just can't find the proper materials.'

'You'll find the right mixture sooner or later.'

'I've been working on the nav program, too. Trying to find some way to cut our trajectory so we can get back to Ceres sooner.'

'Angela's very anxious to get back to Ceres as soon as we can.'

'I . . . I know.'

His mother took a deep breath, then said, 'The thing is, Theo . . . I want to know, in all honesty, what is your feeling about our chances of getting through this? Our chances of survival.'

He looked into her pearl gray eyes and saw that she expected the worst.

'I don't know, Mom. If I can get the antennas working – even just one antenna – if we could send out a distress call, then we might have a chance of being picked up.'

'And if not?'

'Then we just keep on sailing out toward Jupiter until the reactor runs out of hydrogen. Or the recyclers start breaking down.'

'You could repair the recyclers, couldn't you?'

'Maybe. I think so. Unless we run out of spares.'

87

Pauline seemed to put it all together in her mind. 'Then it comes down to a question of how long our food will last.'

Theo nodded glumly, thinking, It's really a question of how long the hydrogen lasts.

'All right then.' She got to her feet and Theo stood up to face her, almost eye to eye. 'We'll just all go on stricter diets and make the food last as long as we possibly can. It will do Angie good to slim down. Me too.'

'Mom, even if I can fix the antennas, even if we can send out a distress call . . .'

'I know. No one may answer. We may be too far away to be rescued. We may all die.'

He grasped both her wrists. 'I won't let that happen, Mom. I'll take care of you. Angie too. We'll get through this. I'll get us back to safety.'

His mother smiled, but there was sadness in it. 'I know you will, Theo. I have no doubts about that at all.'

He was glad she said it, even though he knew she didn't really believe it.

'I won't let you die, Mom.'

'Of course not. Besides, your father will come back for us, sooner or later. He's probably searching for us right now.'

Theo didn't reply to his mother. But to himself he said bitterly, Like hell he is.

Ceres Sector: Six Months Later

It was simple economics, brutally simple economics and nothing more. Victor needed a ship to search for his family, drifting somewhere in the outer region of the Belt aboard *Syracuse*. A ship cost money. He had none.

On the other hand, Big George Ambrose was in a frenzy to recover the bodies of *Chrysalis*'s slaughtered men, women and children.

'You can work with one of the recovery teams,' George had told Victor. It wasn't a suggestion. It was a command.

So for six months Victor Zacharias worked as a crewman aboard *Pleiades*, once a cargo vessel that ferried supplies to the research station orbiting Jupiter, now pressed into duty recovering the dead. The cargo bays that once held food and scientific equipment now held corpses as *Pleiades* wandered through the space around Ceres in an ever-widening spiral, seeking bodies wafting, tumbling, drifting through the silent dark mausoleum of space.

It was soul-killing work, following a blip on the ship's radar screen, hoping that it actually was the remains of a human being, catching up to it only to find – in most cases – it was a fragment of one of *Chrysalis*'s exploded modules, or a chunk of rock, another uncharted minor asteroid. Or – worst of all – a bloody piece of a body that had been ripped apart.

Grisly work. The hell of it, though, was that Victor knew the pay he was receiving would never be enough to lease a spacecraft to search for his family. I'll have to steal this ship, he told himself, just as soon as the opportunity comes up.

So, for day after gruesome day, week after hideous week, month after sickening month, Victor pulled on a nanofabric space suit and went out to investigate the dark blob that the radar had found. The bodies were mangled and caked with dried blood: the sudden decompression when they'd been hurled into the vacuum of space had literally exploded their lungs and blood vessels. Their skins had been burned black by the Sun's harsh unfiltered ultraviolet radiation.

One day he found the bloody remains of a young woman clutching a baby to her chest with both arms; their eyeballs were gone, nothing but empty dark accusing sockets. Victor bullied the ship's medic into giving him enough alcohol to get thoroughly drunk that night.

The ship's captain was a steel-eyed woman with the unlikely name of Cheena Madagascar. She obviously didn't like this corpse-seeking mission any more than he did. But Big George Ambrose had the ear of Selene's governing board, which in turn had the International Astronautical Authority in the palm of its hand, so the IAA was paying for the rescue operation – at minimum rates. Selene agreed with George's insistence that all the bodies had to be found and accounted for. All eleven hundred and seventeen of them.

Selene and the IAA faced the harsh necessities of simple economics, too. Selene and the research outposts scattered across the solar system needed the resources of the asteroids: the metals and minerals, the oxygen and water baked out of asteroidal rock or melted from icy 'roids. Big George made it abundantly clear that there would be no mining or smelting done until the rock rats could rebuild their habitat at Ceres – and the bloody war between Humphries Space Systems and Astro Corporation was brought to an end.

Douglas Stavenger, the power behind Selene's governing council, hammered out a peace agreement between Martin Humphries and Astro's CEO, Pancho Lane. Meanwhile, Victor Zacharias and the other crewmen of *Pleiades* hunted for the dead bodies drifting through the Belt.

The morning after his drunken oblivion Victor stayed in his bunk instead of reporting for duty. That earned him a visit from the ship's medic. The young woman looked decidedly nervous as she entered Victor's privacy cubicle unannounced.

His head still buzzing, Victor lay on his back and blinked blearily at her, tugging at the bedsheet that half covered him.

'I need a day to recover,' he told her before she could say anything.

Her lips were pressed into a thin line. She was slim, with long legs like a colt; her shoulder-length hair was dark, her cheekbones high, her deep brown eyes were flecked with gold.

'We're both in trouble,' she said, in a near-whisper. Victor's brows rose.

'The captain wants to see us both. Immediately.'

He puffed out a breath. 'I'll have to get dressed, then.'

'Please hurry.' And she stepped outside his cubicle.

Sitting up was an exercise in teeth-gritting will-power. The tiny cubicle swam giddily for long moments. But at last Victor got to his feet – shakily – and pulled on his coveralls and softboots.

As he pushed his doorscreen open and stepped into the crew's common area, he asked, 'Do I have time to wash my face and do my teeth?'

The medic gave him a distressed look.

'Comb my hair, at least?'

'Be quick.'

Nine minutes later, Victor and the medic were standing before the sliding partition of the captain's quarters. The medic rapped lightly on the bulkhead.

'Enter,' came the captain's voice.

Her quarters were a surprise to Victor: very feminine, pale pink covers on the bunk, an ornate vase on the desk filled with colorful flowers. Artificial, of course, he thought.

Cheena Madagascar herself was a collection of contradictions. She wore a set of jet black coveralls with a bright pink scarf around her throat, its ends tucked into her unbuttoned collar. Soft doeskin boots and a wide black belt studded with asteroidal silver, midnight dark hair cropped military style close to her skull, but silver rings glittering with gems on seven of her fingers and silver earrings dangling from her lobes. She was no taller than Victor, almost as slim as the medic, but her tight coveralls showed ample bosom and hips. Cosmetic nanotherapy, he guessed.

Without preamble, she demanded of the medic, 'You gave this man alcohol to drink?'

'Yes, ma'am, I did,' the medic whispered.

She turned to Victor and he saw that her eyes were the same gold-flecked brown as the medic's. 'You got yourself so plastered that you couldn't report for duty?'

'That's right,' Victor answered.

'Or maybe it was an excuse to take a day off?'

'No. Not that.'

The captain glared at him. 'Not that, huh?'

'Not that,' he repeated.

She turned to the medic. 'You may go.' Before the younger woman had a chance to turn around, the captain added, 'And no more dispensing alcohol. To anyone. Understand me?'

'Yes, ma'am.' Barely audible.

'Get out of here.'

The medic fled, leaving Victor alone with the captain.

'Do you have any excuse for your behavior?'

Victor thought of the mother and baby he had recovered. But he said, 'Not really.'

'Not really, huh? I heard you picked up something really stomach-turning. Is that right?'

'A woman. With a baby in her arms.'

'Upsetting.'

Before he realized he was saying it, Victor revealed, 'I have a wife and children somewhere out in the Belt. . . .' He stopped himself.

The captain stared at him for a long moment. Then she said, more softly, 'I have a family too. I keep them with me.'

He recognized the sculptured cheekbones, the gold-flecked eyes. 'The medic?'

'One of my daughters. The other one's an engineer with the flight crew.'

'Is your husband aboard too?' he asked.

'Never had one. Never wanted one. Cloning works fine.'

Victor's insides felt hollow, his legs weak. 'I don't know where my family is now.'

She seemed to stiffen, and drew herself up to her full height, eye to eye with Victor. 'Well, you're aboard my ship now and you'll do the work you've signed on to do. No more booze and no more days spent in your bunk. Understand me?'

'Yes, captain.'

'Report to the infirmary at once. I want you to take a full physical and psych exam. I want you detoxed; get that alcohol out of your bloodstream.'

'Yes, captain.' Victor turned to leave.

'At twenty hundred hours, report back here.'

He blinked with surprise. 'Here?'

'To my quarters. Twenty hundred hours. Understand me?'

'Yes, captain.'

Ore Ship *Syracuse*: The Galley

Pauline Zacharias wondered why they had these meetings in the galley. The family's living quarters included a perfectly comfortable sitting room, but somehow whenever they had something to discuss the three of them always huddled together over the narrow table of the galley.

Like old-time families on Earth, she thought, coming together in the kitchen. Maybe it's instinct. Gather where the food and warmth are centered, where the air smells of cooking and everybody feels at ease. But *Syracuse*'s galley didn't smell of cooking, except for the brief moments when the cranky old microwave was opened and she was taking a sizzling hot prepackaged meal to the table. The galley wasn't homey and warm; it had no fireplace, no cookpots simmering; its metal bulkheads and plastic deck tiles were cold and worn.

Still, Pauline thought, it's the closest thing to a safe cave that the children know.

Children, she thought. They're not children anymore. Angela's old enough to start a family of her own. And Theo, he's aged five years in the past six months, working night and day to keep this ship's systems going, to keep us alive.

95

Theo was sitting at the head of the little table, Angela on his left. Pauline herself sat with her back to the row of freezers and microwave ovens. She had placed a meager bowl of thawed fruit on the table and a glass of reconstituted juice at each of their three places.

Theo was saying, 'I've been working with the navigation program at night, trying to figure out some way to cut our trip time down and get us back to the Ceres area in less than eight years.'

'And seven months,' Angela muttered.

'And four days,' Theo added, grinning at her. Pauline realized that six months ago he would have lost his temper with his sister. Now he simply let her grumbles roll off his back. Theo's growing up, she thought. All this responsibility is making a man of him.

Angela is maturing too, she realized. She's become a real help to Theo; she can run the command pod's systems just as well as he can. Pauline smiled to herself: The idea of Theo and Angela working together on repairing the ship's antennas would have been preposterous six months ago; yet they've slaved away at it together without fighting, without calling each other names. Even when it became painfully clear that they wouldn't be able to get the antennas functioning again, they didn't blame each other.

Theo blames his father, though. He says Victor didn't store the proper supplies for repairing the antennas. Maybe he's right. None of us expected to be attacked. None of us expected the antennas to be so badly damaged.

That was her greatest worry. Not that they were drifting halfway to Jupiter, alone and unable to call for help. Not that they might run out of food or have the recyclers break down past the point where they could be repaired. Pauline's greatest worry was that Theo blamed his father for this, blamed Victor for not supplying the ship adequately, blamed him for running away and abandoning them.

'We might be able to cut the trip time in half,' Theo was saying, 'but it's an awfully risky maneuver.'

With an effort of will, Pauline focused her attention on what her son was telling her.

'We put it all on a graph,' Theo said, fingering the palm-sized remote in his hand.

'We?' Pauline asked.

'Angie and me.' He hesitated, then admitted, 'Angie's a lot better at math than I am.'

A multicolored map appeared on the smart screen on the galley's far bulkhead. Thin yellow lines looped across its gridwork background. Pauline realized that they were the orbits of major asteroids. A pulsing red dot was at its center.

'The red dot is us,' Theo explained. 'And here's our current trajectory. . . .'

A blue curve arced outward. The view enlarged to show *Syracuse*'s trajectory soaring out the far side of the Asteroid Belt halfway to Jupiter before it finally swung back toward Ceres again.

'I've gone through all the numbers a dozen times—'

'We both did,' Angela said, without a hint of rancor.

He dipped his chin in acknowledgement of his sister. 'And here's what we might be able to do.'

A dotted blue curve appeared, much shorter than the solid one.

Theo explained, 'The nav program shows that we can get back to Ceres in a little more than four years if we fire the main engine and decelerate the ship.'

'Four years, two months and sixteen days,' said Angela, looking almost happy about it. 'Right, Thee?'

'Right. Give or take an uncertainty of five percent.'

'Couldn't we make it less than that?' Pauline asked.

Theo grimaced, then answered, 'We don't have the fuel for a longer burn, Mom. This maneuver's gonna use up our last drop of hydrogen.'

Pauline thought about that for a moment. 'You don't mean *all* our hydrogen?'

'All of it, Mom. Down to the last molecule.'

'But how will we generate electricity if we use all the fuel? The reactor needs hydrogen.'

'That's the risky part.'

'We can't run for four years without electricity! We couldn't last four days.'

'I know. But we have water.'

'Drinking water,' Pauline said. 'Which we need.'

'We recycle it,' said Angela.

'But what's our drinking water got to do with hydrogen for the fusion reactor?' Pauline asked. She was fairly certain she knew the answer but she wanted to hear what Theo had come up with.

Theo gnawed on his lip for several heartbeats. With

a glance at his sister, he explained, 'Here's what Angie and I have figured out. Water contains hydrogen. We electrolyze some of our water and feed the hydrogen to the reactor to keep it going.'

'We use the electricity that the reactor generates to split the water into hydrogen and oxygen,' Angela added.

Pauline felt confused. 'Now wait a second. You use electricity from the reactor to produce hydrogen fuel for the reactor?'

They both nodded.

'It sounds . . .'

'It's a bootstrap operation, I know,' said Theo. 'But the numbers show that it could work.'

Angela said, 'The hydrogen fusion produces a *gajillion* times more energy than it takes to split the water molecules.'

'Something about this doesn't sound right to me,' Pauline insisted.

'Angela's right, Mom,' Theo replied. 'The fusion process produces a lot more energy than it takes to electrolyze the water. We'll be on the happy side of the curve.'

'You're certain of this?' Pauline asked.

Again Theo hesitated. Then he said, 'That's what the numbers show.'

'Then why can't we produce enough hydrogen to feed the main engine and get us back to Ceres sooner?'

'Propulsion needs reaction mass, Mom. Our hydrogen doesn't just generate electrical power; we use most of it to push through the engine's jets and provide thrust.'

'That's what most of the hydrogen in our tanks was

for,' Angela chimed in. 'Reaction mass. Only a fraction of it goes to generating electricity.'

To make sure she understood what they were telling her, Pauline said, 'So you think you can generate electrical power for the ship even after you've used up all the hydrogen in the fuel tanks.'

'Yes.'

'And cut our trip time in half.'

'Just about.'

'And the risk is . . . ?'

Angela said, 'The risk is that we might use up too much of our drinking water to keep the reactor generating electricity.'

'The reactor doesn't need all that much fuel to generate electricity,' Theo explained. 'A glassful of water can produce enough electricity to keep the ship running for a month, just about.'

'Fusion's a powerful thing, Mom,' said Angela. 'It's what powers the stars, y'know.'

Pauline looked from her daughter's eager face to her son's more somber expression. Theo looks so much like his father now, she thought.

'We can do it, Mom!' Angela urged. 'We can get back to Ceres in four years!'

She's so anxious to get back to civilization, Pauline thought. But what if we use up all our water before we get back?

'Theo,' she asked, 'do you really think this will work?'

'That's what the numbers show,' he repeated.

'But what do *you* think?'

'I think we can do it, but it's not just up to me. We all have a vote in this.'

'Let's do it!' Angela said.

Realizing she would be outnumbered if she decided to vote against the scheme, Pauline made herself smile at her children.

'All right,' she said slowly. 'Let's try it.'

Cargo Ship *Pleiades*: Infirmary

It was weird, knowing that the medic was the captain's cloned daughter. Victor allowed her to put him through the scanners for a thorough physical, then sat in a soundproofed cubicle for more than an hour with the psych computer, answering questions while hooked up to blood pressure, voice analysis and other stress sensors. Finally he went through the thoroughly unpleasant experience of having his blood pumped out of his arm, through a detoxifying dialysis machine, and back into his arm again.

The medic said barely a word to him through the whole long procedure. At last she pulled the tubes from his arm and sealed his wounds with medicinal spray-on patches.

'You're free to go now,' she said in her near-whisper.

Victor swung his legs off the gurney, got to his feet and took a deep, testing breath. He felt good, no shakes, no weakness.

'I'm sorry I got you into trouble,' he said to the medic.

'It was my own fault,' she replied, hardly looking at him. Then a tentative smile emerged on her face. 'She doesn't stay angry very long.'

'Your mother?'

The medic nodded. 'The captain.'

'Well,' he said, 'thanks for everything.'

Her eyes evaded his. 'Good luck.'

It wasn't until Victor had left the infirmary and was halfway along the passageway that led to the ship's galley that it struck him that 'Good luck' was a strange thing to say. What did she mean by that? he wondered.

The galley was jammed with crew members eating dinner. Victor had to squeeze in at a table already occupied by six of his mates.

'Took the day off, didja?' one of the men said, elbowing him in the ribs hard enough almost to make Victor slosh the coffee out of his mug as he edged his tray between the others already on the table.

'The easy life,' joked the woman sitting across the table from him, grinning widely at him.

'I wasn't up to it today,' Victor said, turning his attention to the dinner tray before him.

One of the other women said, 'We heard about what you picked up yesterday, Vic.'

The table fell silent.

Victor put his fork down and looked up and down the table. They were all staring at him.

With a shrug he said, 'Let's forget about it.'

'Yeah. Shit happens.'

'Not much you can do about it.'

They all started eating again.

Victor half-finished his meal, then hurried back to his own cubicle. A message was blinking on the wall screen above his bunk: REPORT TO CAPTAIN'S QUARTERS AT 2000 HOURS.

'Aye-aye, captain,' he muttered.

At precisely 2000 hours, dressed in fresh coveralls, Victor rapped smartly on the frame of the captain's sliding doorscreen.

'Enter,' she called.

He slid the door back and stepped in. Captain Madagascar was still in her black uniform, sitting at her desk. She blanked the computer screen and got to her feet.

'Exactly on time. Good.'

'I went through the medical—'

'I know,' said Cheena Madagascar, jerking a thumb toward the dead display screen. 'I reviewed your medical records. You're in good condition, physically and psychologically.'

Victor nodded.

She slid a partition back and Victor saw a kitchenette laid out along the bulkhead: steel sink, minifridge and freezer, microwave, cabinets overhead.

'Had your dinner?' the captain asked.

'Yes, ma'am.'

'I haven't.' She pulled a prepackaged meal from the freezer. 'Sit down, relax.'

The little round table in the middle of the room was already set for two, he saw. He pulled out one of the delicate little chairs and sat on it carefully.

'Want some wine?' the captain asked as she slid the dinner package into the microwave.

'You said I shouldn't drink anything alcoholic.'

She broke into a wry grin. 'I told my daughter I didn't want her to give you any alcohol. That doesn't mean you can't have a glass of wine with me.'

Thinking of the detox dialysis, Victor said, 'I'd better stay away from—'

Cheena Madagascar interrupted, 'When the captain invites you to have a glass of wine, you say, "Thank you, captain. I'd be delighted."'

Victor saw where this was heading. With a shrug he said, 'Thank you, captain. I'd be delighted.'

He sipped at the chilled white wine slowly as she ate her dinner. The wine tasted like biting the cold steel blade of a knife.

'We're almost finished with this body hunt, you know,' the captain told him as she chewed away. 'There's only a few dozen more to account for.'

'George Ambrose won't be satisfied until every single one is found,' Victor said.

Madagascar nodded. 'He's got the clout to make 'em do what he wants.'

'Them?'

'The IAA. Selene. The university consortium that runs the research stations orbiting Jupiter and Venus. The big-ass corporations.'

'The powers that be,' Victor muttered.

'If they don't do what Big George wants, the rock rats won't supply resources.'

'What's left of the rock rats.'

'There's plenty of 'em left. The people on *Chrysalis* were mainly storekeepers and clerks. The miners and smeltery workers were on their own ships, scattered all across the Belt.'

'My family's out there somewhere,' Victor said.

Madagascar took a healthy slug of wine. Putting the stemmed glass down on the tabletop, she said, 'Face it, Zacharias: Your family's most likely dead.'

'No,' he said.

'You know better than that,' she insisted. 'If they're not dead already they're as good as dead, drifting out there in the Belt somewhere. Nobody's going to find them.'

'I will.'

'You will? How?'

'I'll need a ship.'

'Damned right you will.'

And then it hit him. 'And I'll need Big George's clout.'

Captain Madagascar smiled like a lynx. 'I could help you with Big George. And with this ship.'

Victor nodded. He knew what she wanted in return.

Ore Ship *Syracuse*:
Backup Command Pod

The command pod was crowded with all three of them in there. Theo felt the body heat of his mother and sister, the tension of their anxieties, their expectations, their fears.

'Three minutes to go,' he said, trying to keep his voice firm and clear.

He was sitting in the command chair. Theo had configured the electronic keyboard to control the propulsion system program. Now his eyes were fixed on the main display screen. Almost everything in the green, so far. Angie was standing behind him on one side, his mother on the other.

Pauline placed her hand on his shoulder. He glanced up at her.

'Theo, I want you to remember that this was a family decision. We all agreed to do it.'

'I know, Mom.'

'If it doesn't go right, I don't want you to blame yourself. We're all in this together.'

Angie said, 'It'll go right, Mom. Don't worry.'

Theo thought that his sister's voice sounded high and brittle. Angie's worried too, he thought, but she doesn't want to show it.

Theo focused his attention on the control board. He and Angie had checked the pumps that fed the main engine a dozen times. With their mother helping them, they had inspected every centimeter of the propulsion system's piping and electrical wiring. The board showed no red lights, only a pair of ambers and they were minor backup circuits, not crucially important; everything else was in the green.

'Two minutes and counting,' the computer's synthesized voice said. Theo realized the computer sounded almost exactly like his father's voice. Naturally, he thought. Dad programmed it himself.

They heard a thump and a groaning rattle from deep in the bowels of the ship. Before Angie or his mother could say anything, Theo told them, 'Main pump powering up.'

Angie was leaning over his shoulder now, squinting at the countdown checklist displayed on the screen to his right. 'Open the hydrogen feed lines at T minus ninety seconds.'

He nodded and placed his finger on the proper key. It's programmed to open automatically, but I'll punch the manual command anyway, he said to himself.

'T minus ninety,' came the synthesized voice. 'Hydrogen feed line open.'

A new green light winked on.

'Confirm feed line open,' Theo said, his own voice sounding slightly shaky in his ears.

'T minus sixty seconds. Automatic sequencer on.'

'Confirm automatic sequencer.'

New lights were springing up across the panel. All

green, Theo saw. He could hear his mother's rapid breathing. Something deep in the ship shuddered. Hydrogen's flowing, Theo realized. Liquid hydrogen, at more than two hundred fifty degrees below zero. If anything's going to go wrong, he thought, it'll be now.

'T minus thirty seconds. Electric power activated. Magnetic field on.'

'Confirm mag field,' Theo said crisply. The liquid hydrogen seemed to be flowing smoothly: leakage rate minor, no damage to the insulated piping.

'Ten . . . nine . . . eight . . .'

Hydrogen was flowing from the propellant tank to the main engine's thruster. The engine's superconducting magnets were on at full strength. The ship's fusion reactor was putting out its maximum power level.

'. . . three . . . two . . . one . . . engine thrusting.'

Theo pointed a finger at the central display screen. It showed a green line rising steadily. Thrust. The thrust they needed to slow the ship and get it looping back toward civilization eventually.

'It's working!' Pauline exclaimed, clapping her hands together.

'I don't feel anything,' said Angie, sounding disappointed.

'You won't,' Theo said, feeling enormously relieved. 'I told you, remember? You can't blast this old bucket like some rocket ship in an adventure vid. We nudge her gently.'

Angie replied, 'I know the thrust level's real low, Thee, but I thought we'd feel *something*.'

He grinned up at her. 'Watch yourself pouring liquids tonight. They'll be skewed a little.'

'You did it, Theo,' his mother said, gripping his shoulder tighter. 'You did it.'

'We did it,' he corrected. 'Angie and me.'

His sister beamed at him.

It wasn't until Theo tried to get up from the command chair that he realized he was soaked through with perspiration.

'You better take a shower, Thee,' Angie said, wrinkling her nose. 'You smell pretty disgusting.'

Theo laughed. Back to normal, he said to himself.

That evening, while they were relaxing in the sitting room after a celebratory dinner of real frozen chicken, Theo mused, 'If there was only some way to get the antennas working.'

'If there *were* only,' Angie corrected, sitting across the coffee table from him. 'Subjunctive. Right, Ma?'

Pauline nodded. 'After the conditional *if*.' She was on the sofa, to Theo's right.

With a shrug, Theo said, 'If we could get the antennas working we could call for help.'

'But you said we don't have the materials you need to repair the antennas,' Angie pointed out.

'Yeah, that's right. But I'm wondering if there isn't some other way.'

'Like what?'

'Like . . . I don't know.'

Before Angie could say anything, their mother

asked, 'Is there anything else on board that could be put to use as a beacon?'

'Or a comm system, so we could call for help.'

Theo shook his head. 'We've got all the communications gear we need. It's just that the godda . . . er, godforsaken antennas are gone. No antennas, no signals out. Or in.'

'Is there something else we can use for an antenna?' Angie asked.

'Not that I can figure out,' Theo answered. 'I've looked all through every piece of equipment on the ship. Nothing usable.'

Pauline asked, 'Don't we have a radar system?'

'Collision avoidance radar,' said Theo. 'That antenna's a mess of melted goo, just like the rest.'

'You mean we're flying blind?' Angie yipped. 'We could run into an asteroid?'

'Yes, we're flying blind. No, we won't hit an asteroid big enough to do much damage. It's *empty* out there, Angie.'

'For real?'

'For real. The chances of us getting hit by anything bigger than a dust flake are about the same as . . . well, it's pretty blinking remote.'

Angela did not look relieved.

Pauline asked, 'We are getting hit by micrometeoroids, though?'

'Yes'm. Every day. Nothing big enough to penetrate the hull, but sooner or later I'll have to go out and replace some of the meteor bumpers.'

'Isn't there *anything* we could use for an antenna,

Thee?' Angie persisted. 'I mean, we've got a whole ship's worth of supplies. Can't we jury-rig some wires or something?'

Theo didn't answer for a long moment, his mind churning, his self-control tottering.

'I've tried,' he said at last. 'I've really tried.'

'We know,' his mother said.

'I mean, I've gone through everything I can think of. I really have. I just don't know enough. I've checked all the maintenance vids, all the logistics lists, everything. I can't make it work. I just don't know how to do it!'

They were both staring at him.

'I've failed,' Theo admitted, close to tears. 'I can't fix the antennas. I've tried and tried and tried and I can't do it.'

'It's all right, Thee,' Angie whispered.

His mother reached out and touched his shoulder. 'You've done your best, Theo. No one can ask more than that.'

'I feel so damned *stupid*!' he blurted, banging the arm of his chair with his fist.

'You are not stupid,' said Pauline firmly. 'No child of mine is stupid. You simply don't have the materials you need to repair the antennas. That's not your fault.'

'It's not your fault, Thee,' Angie consoled. 'It was the stupid designers. Why'd they have to put all the antennas on the same section of the hull? That was just plain stupid.'

'They weren't designing a man-of-war,' Pauline said. 'They never expected an ore carrier to be attacked.'

Fighting to hold back tears of frustration, Theo looked across the coffee table to his sister. 'Maybe we could figure out some way to rig up an antenna, Angie.'

'You think so?' she asked.

'I don't know. I can look through the maintenance vids again, I suppose.'

'Do you think there's something in them?' Pauline asked softly.

'I'll look. It's better than doing nothing, I guess.'

'Good. That's all we can ask of you.'

'I'll go through the vids with you, Thee,' said Angie. 'Two heads are better than one.'

Theo started to glare at her, but it melted into a grin. 'Unless they're on the same person,' he said tamely.

They all laughed together.

Ore Ship *Syracuse*: Outside

Theo's nose twitched at the sharp tang of his own perspiration that pervaded his space suit. He was floating at the end of a buckyball tether, watching the squat little maintenance robots place a new section of meteor bumper atop the ship's outer skin.

'Your suit temperature has risen five degrees in the past ten minutes, Thee,' Angie's voice sounded in his helmet earphones. She didn't seem worried about it; just doing her job of monitoring his EVA from the command pod.

'Turning up the suit fans,' Theo obediently replied, jabbing a gloved finger on the proper key in the control pad on his left wrist. He heard the pitch of the suit's cooling fans rise slightly. His father had often said the fans sounded like the whine of mosquitoes on a summer night; Theo had never heard mosquitoes, never experienced a summer night on Earth.

'Ten more minutes on the timeline,' Angie called.

He nodded inside his bubble helmet. 'We're gonna run a little long. They haven't got the bumper fastened in place yet.'

'We have an extra thirty minutes built into the timeline.'

'Right.' Theo knew his suit held enough air for another hour and more. No sweat, he told himself, then grimaced at the phrase. He was sweating plenty inside the heavily insulated suit. Funny, he thought, this far from the Sun you'd think it'd be freezing out here. But even the wan distant Sun was powerful enough to drench him with perspiration. The suit didn't let heat out, he knew. Maybe I ought to build a radiator into the backpack for long excursions like this.

He had ventured out the main airlock four hours ago to direct the robots in their task of removing this section of pitted old meteorid bumper and replacing it with a new section, straight from the storage bay. The robots, about the size of a snare drum with four many-jointed dexterous arms, were programmed for simple, repetitive maintenance tasks. Something as compli-cated as removing the old bumper and replacing it with the new one required constant commands from a human being.

Theo imagined himself to be some kind of wizard out of an old fantasy vid, commanding a squad of trolls or gnomes. He wondered if he could build voice synthesizers into the robots and have them say, 'Yes, master,' to him.

At last the job was done. The shiny new bumper was in place and the robots had used their cutting lasers to slice up the pitted old one into sections small enough to feed into the ship's miniature smelter, to be melted down into new raw material.

Theo pictured himself leading an army of laser-armed robots against the type of murdering bastard who had attacked their ship. Slice 'em to bloody ribbons, he told himself.

'What did you say?' Angie asked.

'Huh? Nothing.'

'You mumbled something.'

'Nothing important. I'm coming in now.'

Victor lay in bed, wide awake, beside Cheena Madagascar, who was snoring softly. I ought to feel guilty, he thought, sleeping with this woman instead of my wife. But life takes strange twists. If I want to use this ship to search for Pauline and the kids I've got to keep the captain happy.

Despite himself, he grinned into the shadows of the darkened bedroom. You've got to admit, he said to himself, that if this is what it takes to keep her happy, well . . . it's better than being poked in the eye with a sharp stick.

Cheena was an accomplished lover, he'd found. At first he'd been surprised at her demand, thinking that a woman who'd prefer to have her children through cloning and avoid being tied to a man in marriage would probably not be all that interested in sex games. But he'd been wrong. Captain Madagascar was passionate in bed, demanding. He'd done his best to satisfy her, and apparently his best was good enough to please her.

According to her calculations, they were nearly finished with the grisly task of picking up the dead bodies from the *Chrysalis* massacre. Soon – perhaps as soon as the next few days – Captain Madagascar could report to Big George Ambrose that the job was completed.

Then what? Victor wanted this ship so he could go deeper into the Belt and find his family, drifting aboard what was left of *Syracuse*. For that, he'd need not only Cheena's agreement, but Big George's as well. They'll tell me my family is dead by now, Victor thought. They'll say searching for them would be a waste of time and effort.

He clenched his jaw in the darkness. And I'll tell George that my family are victims of the *Chrysalis* massacre, too. We've got to find them even if they're dead, like all the others.

But they won't be dead, he told himself. They're alive. Pauline is keeping them alive. *Syracuse* is keeping them alive. I'll find them. If I have to steal this ship from Cheena, I'll find them.

Then a new thought struck him. What if they agree? What if Cheena takes me out searching for *Syracuse*? And we find them? What happens when Pauline and Cheena meet?

'Theo?'

He opened his eyes, surprised to realize that he'd fallen asleep on the sofa. His mother was bending over him.

'I guess I nodded off,' he said, feeling slightly sheepish.

'You've been working very hard,' said Pauline. 'We all have.'

She sat on the sofa beside him.

'Angie's gone to bed?' he asked.

'Yes. She was tired too.'

He nodded and pulled himself up to a sitting position. 'She was really good today, monitoring my EVA. She sat there all suited up for nearly five hours, ready to go outside if I got into trouble.'

Pauline smiled faintly. 'Angela's growing up.'

'I guess she is.'

'You are too.'

'Think so?'

'I know so. You've taken charge of the ship, Theo. Six months ago you were complaining that your father didn't trust you—'

'He always did everything himself. He never gave me a chance to learn, to show him what I can do.'

'Yes, I know,' Pauline said gently. 'I understand. But I trust you, Theo. I know that you've put us on the right course to get back to Ceres and you'll keep this ship running until we get there.'

Theo felt a warm glow inside. But he didn't know what to say, how he should respond to his mother's praise.

'Now don't you think you'd better get some sleep?' Pauline suggested. 'Tomorrow's another day.'

'You're right.' He swung his long legs off the sofa and got to his feet.

'Good-night, Theo,' said Pauline.

'Good-night, Mom.'

She's right, he thought as he padded to his own cubicle. Tomorrow's another day. With fifteen hundred and thirty-four more to go.

BOOK II

Three Years Later

Eternal process moving on,
From state to state the spirit walks;
And these are but the shatter'd stalks,
Or ruin'd chrysalis of one.

Smelter Ship *Hunter*: Bridge

They made an unlikely pair.

Although Elverda Apacheta was near the end of her long life, she was still a regally tall, slim woman with the carriage of an empress. Yet her once haughty eyes of sparkling jet now looked out at the world with a weariness that grew heavier each passing day. Her high flaring cheekbones and imperious nose spoke of her Andean background, but her long colorfully woven robe hung loosely on her emaciated body and her dead-white hair was disheveled, chopped unevenly, as if she no longer cared who saw her.

Her only companion on *Hunter* had already died once, or tried to. When he had been a mercenary soldier he had pressed a mini-grenade to his chest and set it off. Now he was as much machine as man, a cyborg whose face was half metal etched with swirling hair-thin lines. He wore the threadbare remains of a military uniform, all insignias and signs of rank rudely ripped off its fabric. He called himself Dorn and said he was a priest. He and Elverda Apacheta had been on this lonely, interminable, thankless mission for more than two years.

She had once been a worlds-renowned sculptress, the woman who carved *The Rememberer* out of a two-kilometer-long asteroid. The magnificent sculpture rode in a high orbit around Earth, a work of art that attracted tourists from the Earth, the Moon, and the man-made habitats in space between the two.

Now she and Dorn searched for the dead, out in the silent darkness of the Asteroid Belt. And fled from the mercenaries who had been hired to kill them.

Hunter was a massive ship, much too large for just the two of them. It had originally been built to smelt asteroidal ores on the way from the Belt inward to the Earth/Moon vicinity. But the advent of nanotechnology made such bulk smelters obsolete. Virus-sized nano-machines separated pure elements out of the asteroidal rocks. *Hunter* went on the market at a bargain price. Dorn had use for the smelter, so Elverda Apacheta had emptied her retirement accounts to buy the vessel.

For all its size and mass, *Hunter* was capable of bursts of high acceleration when they needed to flee an intruding vessel. They had not seen another ship, though, in several months.

'We're approaching the coordinates you plugged into the navigation computer,' said Elverda into the ship's intercom microphone. She was sitting in the command chair on the ship's compact bridge; Dorn was some-where in the bowels of *Hunter*'s equipment bay.

'I will come to the bridge,' his deep, heavy voice replied. She always wondered what his voice had been like before his shattered body had been turned into a cybernetic organism.

'No hurry,' she said. 'It will be an hour before we reach the exact spot.'

Dossier: Dorn

He was born Dorik Harbin in a Balkan village that was swept up in one of the bloody frenzies of ethnic cleansing that swept that region of Earth every few generations.

Shortly before his twelfth birthday, the militia from the next valley descended on his village, raping, killing, burning everything in their fervent zeal. Dorik Harbin saw his mother nailed to a cross, naked, bleeding, dying. The young boy ran away, lived like an animal in the hills until he was caught pilfering an apple from the kitchen tent of a different militia band. Brought before the group's commander, he was given the choice of joining the militia or being shot.

He learned to kill. Remembering what had been done to his mother, his sisters and brothers and father, he marched into other villages and killed everything living in them, down to the livestock and household pets. Carrying an assault rifle that was almost as big as he was, he became an adept killer.

But his sleep was haunted by terrible dreams. He saw those he killed, heard the pleas for mercy that he never listened to in waking life. Sometimes, in his dreams, he killed his own mother. That was when he began taking the drugs that were freely available among the roving militia bands. The narcotics helped him to sleep, helped him to keep on killing despite his nightmares.

Peacekeepers from the newly reorganized United Nations finally suppressed the militias and established an uneasy peace in the region. The dead were buried, the fires extinguished, the acrid smoke that hung over the region finally cleared away.

Dorik Harbin was sixteen by then. The Peacekeepers recruited him into their forces and tried to train him to enforce the peace with a minimum of killing. It was nonsense, and young Dorik knew it, but he allowed his superior officers to believe that he had been rehabilitated. They smiled at his progress as a model Peacekeeper and turned a blind eye to his growing dependency on what they termed 'pharmaceuticals.'

He was among the Peacekeeper troops who were sent to the Moon in the UN's ill-fated attempt to wrest control of Moonbase from its rebellious citizens. After that fiasco, once Moonbase became recognized as the independent nation of Selene, Dorik Harbin quit the Peacekeepers and joined the private security forces of Humphries Space Systems, Inc.

In a short time he was killing again, this time as commander of spacecraft that attacked other spacecraft in the dark emptiness of the Asteroid Belt. His prowess came to the attention of Martin Humphries himself, who personally assigned Harbin to the task of tracking down and killing his archenemy, Lars Fuchs.

Humphries also saw to it that Harbin had an adequate supply of specialized drugs, pharmaceuticals that enhanced his battle prowess, that made him sharper, faster, drugs that fed his inner rage.

It was in such a drug-enhanced fury that he methodically destroyed the rock rats' habitat, *Chrysalis*, killing all of the one thousand seventeen men, women and children aboard. Attacking the ore ship *Syracuse* was merely a minor skirmish in the immediate aftermath of that slaughter.

Once his mind cleared and he realized what he had done, Dorik Harbin held a minigrenade to his chest and detonated it. He knew of no other way to end the horror that obsessed his sleep.

But the corporation that literally owned his body would not let him die. Their medical specialists tested their own skills and theories and turned him into a cyborg, half machine, half human. And sent him back to his duties as a mercenary soldier in the employ of Humphries Space Systems, Inc.

The Asteroid Wars were over by then, forced to an end by the shock of the *Chrysalis* massacre. Dorik Harbin took no credit for the unexpected result of his atrocity. Humphries Space Systems saw to it that no one learned that the cyborg was the mass murderer. Dorik Harbin went about his unexciting duties as mechanically as if he were entirely a machine. But still he dreamed.

Then he was assigned to head the security detail for a small asteroid that the corporation had quietly bought from a rock rat family, deep in the Belt. Martin

Humphries himself was coming from his home on the Moon to inspect the asteroid. There was something inside the rock, something artificial, something staggeringly unusual, something that was perhaps not made by human hands.

As part of his duties Dorik Harbin inspected the artifact buried deep inside the asteroid. The experience shattered him. He saw his life, all the pain and horror, all the grief and remorse that filled his dreams.

Every day he stood before the artifact. Every day the deeds of his life were peeled away, moment by moment, murder by murder. It was if he were being flayed alive, one layer of skin after another stripped from his bleeding, quaking flesh.

At last there was nothing left. The personality that he had built for himself since he'd been twelve had been stripped bare and a new persona, one that had been hidden deep inside his old one, at last came forth.

He tore all the insignias of rank from his uniform, turning it into the tattered gray costume of a penitent. Dorik Harbin ceased to exist. Out of the warrior came a priest named Dorn, as single-minded in his quest for atonement as he had once been in his missions of murder.

He still dreamed when he slept, but now his dreams were of mercy and justice.

Smelter Ship *Hunter*: Bridge

Elverda saw a glint reflected in the bridge's main display screen. It was Dorn stepping through the hatch, silent as a wraith, the metal half of his face catching the light from the overhead lamps.

Touching a keypad with a long, slim finger, Elverda superimposed a navigation grid on the scene their forward camera showed.

'There,' she said, tapping the screen with her fingernail. 'That's the spot.'

She sensed Dorn nodding as he leaned over her shoulder.

'It's empty,' she said, turning her head slightly. The human half of his face was so close she could feel its warmth, hear his slow, steady breathing.

'It wasn't empty five years ago,' said Dorn. 'We destroyed a dozen Astro warships here. Led them into a trap and ran a swarm of pebbles into them.'

'A dozen ships? How many . . .' She caught herself and choked off her question.

But Dorn understood. 'There must have been at least ten mercenaries in each ship. Probably more. I've tried to get the exact number from Astro Corporation but they refuse to release such information.'

'A hundred and twenty men and women.'

'At least.'

Elverda knew what came next. They would fly a search spiral expanding outward from this site, probing with radar and telescopes for the bodies of the dead that had been drifting in space since the battle that had killed them. It would take weeks, perhaps months, to find them all.

If they lived that long.

With his prosthetic hand Dorn tapped out a command on the keyboard. The image on the screen changed subtly.

'Ultraviolet?' she asked, slightly puzzled.

'Lyman alpha,' he replied. 'Ionized hydrogen.'

'Why are you looking for ionized hydrogen?'

'Exhaust trail.' With the cool metal fingers of his left hand Dorn worked the keyboard.

Even after knowing him for more than two years Elverda shuddered at the sight of the mechanical hand. She looked up at the main screen and saw that he was panning the cameras three hundred and sixty degrees, then up and down doing a complete global sweep around their ship.

'Nothing,' she said.

Dorn did not reply. The screen's view climbed up, then swung downward.

'We're alone.'

'Are we?' he countered. 'Humphries's people know that a battle was fought here. They know that we will come here to seek the dead and give them proper rites.'

She gestured toward the screen, empty except for the unblinking stars, so distant and aloof. 'There are no ships out there.'

'Perhaps,' he said. 'But there is a small asteroid that does not appear on the nav charts.'

Almost feeling annoyed at his wariness, Elverda said, 'Asteroid orbits change constantly. The charts are never up to date.'

'True enough,' he said. 'But let's check out that rock before we proceed further.'

'It's barely twenty meters across,' Elverda objected. 'It can't be a camouflaged vessel.'

'I know.'

Elverda stared at him for a long, disquieting moment. Dorn looked back at her, his electro-optical eye unblinking, the overhead lights glinting on the etched metal of his skullcap. With a sigh that was half exasperation she punched in the commands that would bring *Hunter* to within fifty meters of the tiny asteroid.

They shared a modest lunch in the galley while *Hunter* cruised at minimum thrust and established itself in co-orbit near the asteroid. When they returned to the bridge, they saw that the object outside was a jagged chunk of debris, a shard torn from what had once been a spacecraft, probably an attack vessel. They trooped down to the main airlock, where she helped Dorn into a nanofabric space suit. When she had first met Dorn she'd been surprised at how agile he was: the metal half of his body was lithe and supple, not at all like a cumbersome clanking machine. Now, though, more than two years later, he seemed slower, more careful, as if his mechanical half were developing the robotic analog of arthritis.

At last she returned to the bridge to monitor his EVA. Within half an hour he was back from the airlock, a small black object in the palm of his prosthetic hand.

Elverda peered at it.

'A sensor,' said Dorn. 'It was attached to the piece of debris out there. It must be programmed to detect the arrival of a ship in this area and send a message back to whoever planted it here.'

'They've been waiting for us?'

He nodded minimally. 'I imagine they have planted such sensors at every site where there was a battle.'

'Humphries wants to find us.'

'He wants to kill us.'

Elverda knew it was true, yet she still found it hard to accept the idea in her heart, emotionally. The concept that someone wanted to kill her was so bizarre, so alien to her outlook, to her entire life, it was like being told that the world was flat.

Martin Humphries wants to kill us, she told herself. He wants to kill me. She had only known Humphries for the few weeks it had taken to fly to the asteroid where the alien artifact had been found. Where Dorn had transformed himself from a cyborg mercenary soldier to a cyborg priest. Where Humphries had gone insane with fear and guilt once he'd seen the artifact.

And now that he's recovered, now that he knows we saw him in his terror and his shame, he wants to erase all memory of his collapse. He wants to eliminate the witnesses. He wants to kill us.

Under the pretense of preserving the artifact for scientific study, Humphries's corporate minions had thrown a protective guard of ships and mercenary troops around the asteroid and sealed off the artifact itself – burrowed deep inside the rock – from all visitors. Not even scientists from the International Consortium of Universities were allowed to visit the asteroid. The news media had been totally stonewalled, to the point where it was widely believed that the reports of an alien artifact were nothing more than a legend concocted by some of the UFO crackpots among the rock rats.

Elverda Apacheta knew how powerful the artifact was. It had changed Dorn from a murderous mercenary soldier into a priest intent on atoning for his former life. It had shaken her own soul more profoundly than any experience in her long life. Before she had seen the artifact she had been ready for death, weary of the trials and disappointments of living, convinced that her talent had shriveled within her disenchanted soul. But once she looked upon that mystical, amorphous, shifting work of wonder she was overwhelmed with new purpose. Before the artifact she had regarded Dorn with a distaste that was almost loathing; after the artifact she realized that Dorn was the child she had never borne, the tortured soul who needed her solace, the man whom she would help and guide and protect even at the cost of her own existence.

The artifact had changed Martin Humphries, of course. His swaggering, self-confident ego had been shredded into a whimpering, pathetic figure huddled into a fetal ball, pleading for escape. But the effect had been only temporary; Humphries recovered. Now the wealthiest man in the solar system was determined to erase the two witnesses of his moment of weakness.

Staring at the sensor in his metallic hand, Elverda asked Dorn, 'What do you want to do?'

Slowly, Dorn crushed the miniaturized sensor. It crunched like a crisp wafer. Then he answered, 'Find the dead. Treat them with respect, if not honor.'

Attack Ship *Viking*:
Communications Center

Thoroughly bored, Kao Yuan curled his lip at the image on his comm screen. Not that the woman who was speaking to him would see his expression. This was a one-way transmission: the latest orders from Humphries Space Systems headquarters on the Moon to Yuan and his three-ship formation. Besides, he was certain that the image he was watching was a computer-generated persona; Martin Humphries might not deign to speak to him personally, but he didn't want any additional people to know about this mission he'd sent Yuan on, either.

'Mr. Humphries is pleased with your idea of seeding the battle sites with sensors,' the image was saying, 'but he wonders if all the battle sites are recorded. Dorik Harbin did a lot more than attack the *Chrysalis* habitat, of course.'

'Of course,' Yuan murmured, feeling slightly bemused to be talking to a pile of computer chips. At least the woman's image was voluptuously beautiful. Humphries has an eye for buxom young women, he thought.

'Mr. Humphries stressed once again that this matter must be handled very discreetly. The fugitive Dorik

Harbin is not alone in his ship. There is at least one accomplice with him. Both of them – and anyone else with them – must be eliminated. They must disappear and never be found. There must be no way for anyone to discover that Mr. Humphries has ordered their executions. That must be clearly understood.'

Yuan's bored smile grew slightly less tolerant. 'I understand,' he said to the unhearing image on his screen. 'My crew understands. The crews of the other two vessels also understand. Clearly.'

He had received these same instructions, or closely similar ones, from this computer persona at least twice a month for the past eight months. Humphries wants Harbin or Dorn or whatever he's calling himself killed. And his accomplices with him. But he doesn't want anyone to know about it. They must simply disappear out here deep in the Asteroid Belt. All of them. No sweat, Yuan thought. All I have to do is find them.

A strange mission, Yuan thought. Track down a mass murderer and his accomplices, but do it in secrecy. Why doesn't Humphries want the credit for executing the man responsible for the *Chrysalis* massacre? And what's Harbin doing out in the Belt, anyway? They claim he's trying to recover the bodies of the mercenaries killed in battles. That sounds flaky. Maybe it's just a hallucination that HSS intelligence dreamed up. Maybe the intel flunkies are popping the wrong pills.

Yuan had been hunting for the renegade for nearly eight months now, without success. He had planted sensors at most of the old battle sites where HSS intelligence had told him that Harbin/Dorn was likely to visit. Now he simply waited for the fugitive to show himself.

'It's only a matter of time,' he said to the screen as the image prattled on. 'If your brain trust is right about him traveling to the old battle sites.'

Growing impatient, Yuan got to his feet, left the soundproofed booth that served as *Viking*'s communications center and stepped back onto the bridge. He was an imposing figure, even in his unadorned coveralls, nearly two meters tall in his softboots, broad of shoulder and narrow of waist. His inky black hair was brushed straight back from his forehead; it was long enough almost to touch his collar. No military buzz cut for him: Yuan preferred to look casually dashing. A dark little tuft of a Vandyke decorated his chin. He had deep brown eyes and a crooked little grin that he thought – no, he *knew* – that women found enticing.

Yuan had never intended to be a mercenary warrior. His father had been a chef in his native Jiangsu province; his restaurant was recognized as the finest in the region. And the gambling room in back was always filled with fools who thought they might beat the forbidden computer games the old man had smuggled past the government's censors. 'All this will be yours one day,' his father had told him so often that Yuan actually began to believe it. By the time he was ten, Yuan was not only a decent cook, he was the best computer gamer in the province. People signed in from as far away as Shanghai to play against the child prodigy. He let them win only often enough to assure that they'd return and spend more of their money.

But when the greenhouse warming shifted the rains and the province's rice paddies turned to dust, his father's restaurant was closed by the government and Yuan was drafted into the 'volunteer' army that took possession of Vietnam and its invaluable rice bowl in the well-watered Mekong delta. Then the greenhouse floods swept over the delta and he was lucky to escape alive.

The strangest turn in his life, Yuan thought, was when the government sent him to the Chinese base on the Moon to help build the hydroponics farms there. He hated living underground. Trying to feed several thousand workers from the meager crops grown in the long hydroponics trays was a challenge, but not an enjoyable one. Better was the fact that he could jigger the base's computers to run gambling games; better still, most of the women at Base Mao found him more attractive than the stolid soldiers and technicians who made up the base's male population.

Yuan dreamed of returning to Earth once his tour of duty in the army was finished. But once he realized that the government back home would press an unemployed former cook into service wherever they wanted him to work, he signed up with Humphries Space Systems and became a mercenary soldier. Mercenaries had to eat, and Yuan was ready to feed them. HSS pay was far better than the army's, the uniforms were smarter, and the selection of women was more diverse.

What he hadn't expected was that he'd be forced to fight. And kill. Aboard the stripped-down attack vessels that battled for control of the Belt, even a cook had to take his turn at the weapons console. During the bitter years of the Second Asteroid War, Kao Yuan found that he was good at the cat-and-mouse chases in the dark emptiness of space. He had always been a winner at computer games; now he maneuvered a real ship and fired real lasers. The enemy vessels were little more than blips on a screen or distant dots in an observation port. They twisted and dodged but he always – almost – caught up with them and won the game. His youthful skills earned him rapid promotion from cook to captain.

This mission to find the renegade and whatever accomplices riding with him was strange, though. For some reason Martin Humphries himself wanted them erased. The war was over; this mission was a personal quest, an exercise in vengeance. God knows what they did to make Humphries so determined to kill them, Yuan thought. He had not the slightest interest in finding out what it was. I don't want that powerful egomaniac after *me*, he told himself.

As he looked over the three crew members sitting at their posts on the bridge, Yuan thought, Find the renegades, destroy them, and earn the bonus Humphries has promised. Then you can go back to what's left of Shanghai and open the best restaurant they've ever seen.

His goal was to own the best of restaurants. With a gaming room in back, a gaming room from which he could challenge the best gamers in the world. Maybe even play against the slickwillies of Selene, them and their smug airs of superiority to any flatlander on Earth. That was his goal. The means to reach it was murder in the depths of space.

Kao Yuan was quite content to have things this way.

His communications officer glanced up at him as he closed the soundproof door of the comm both and went to his command chair.

'Sir,' she said, brushing a long lock of hair from her almond eyes, 'the message from headquarters is still running.'

Yuan favored her with a grin. 'Keep recording it. I'll listen to the rest of it when I've got nothing better to do.'

The comm officer smiled back at him. 'I mean, sir, that other messages are piling up in storage.'

'Other messages?' Yuan asked, surprised. 'Who's calling us out here?'

She glanced at her screen, pushing that stubborn tress from her face again. 'A call for assistance from a miner whose propulsion system has malfunctioned.'

'Not our problem,' Yuan murmured. *Viking* was running silent, not emitting either a tracking bacon or telemetry. The vessel was built to return as small a radar profile as possible. *Viking* was virtually invisible and Yuan intended to remain that way.

'A medical emergency on another rock rat ship.'

Yuan shook his head. 'I'm not interested in general chatter. Is there anything specifically for us?'

'One of the snoops reported a vessel in its area. Then it went dead.'

'What?' Suddenly alert, Yuan stepped to her comm console and bent over her to peer at the screen. 'Where?'

The comm officer displayed the coordinates on her screen. Yuan couldn't help noticing the subtle intoxication of her perfume. With the touch of a keypad, she had the computer pull up data on the sensor's location.

'That's where he wiped out Gormley's fleet!' Yuan said, excited. He called to the man at the navigation console, 'Set a course for these coordinates, top acceleration.'

Yuan didn't believe that the renegade was visiting the sites of his old battles to recover dead bodies, despite what Headquarters claimed. But he didn't press for more information, either. My job is not to know why, he told himself. My job is merely to find him and kill him. And whoever is with him.

Smelter Ship *Hunter*: Bridge

Out of the corner of her eye Elverda watched Dorn as he sat next to her in the ship's bridge. He had been staring at the crushed remains of the round black sensor, still in the palm of his artificial hand.

She glanced at the screens and instrument readouts displayed on the panels curving around them and saw that the ship was functioning normally.

'What do you want to do?' she asked.

Dorn turned slowly toward her, his human eye looking sad, the other emotionless.

'Find the dead,' he answered.

'But they'll be coming to find *us*.'

The human eye closed briefly. Then, 'They are probably already on their way here.'

'Shouldn't we get away, then? There are other sites, other locations where battles took place.'

'They'll have planted sensors there, too.' Dorn's voice sounded heavy with resignation.

'Then what should we do?' she repeated.

'I should speed you back to Earth at maximum acceleration. You would be safe there. Not even Martin Humphries would dare to harm you where you are surrounded by friends and admirers.'

'And you?'

'I will return to the Belt and try to complete my mission. As much of it as I can.'

'I could tell the news media about this. That might protect you.'

Dorn's lips ticked, as close to a smile as he could come. 'You would tell them that you are trying to protect the monster who is responsible for the *Chrysalis* massacre? If the general public knew that Humphries was hunting me down they would give him an award.'

'I can't let him murder you.'

'There is no way that you can stop it.'

Elverda felt as if she were locked in a closet with the walls closing in on her. 'There must be *something*—'

Dorn shook his head slightly, a ponderous swiveling of that half-metal, half-flesh construction. 'Besides, I will die anyway, soon enough.'

'Die? What are you talking about?'

'My systems are failing.' He raised his right arm slowly. 'The power pack needs replacement. Joints need lubrication. I have the mechanical analog of old age.'

'We can go to Selene and get you overhauled, rejuvenated.'

'The monster responsible for *Chrysalis*? Who would even think of helping me?'

'They wouldn't know. No one knows that—'

'Humphries knows. Returning to Selene would be a death warrant for both of us.'

Elverda stared at him for a long, silent moment. What can we do? she kept asking herself. What can we do?

Dorn broke the silence. 'The bodies from this battle have spiraled outward from this site for hundreds of thousands of kilometers. We should find as many of them as we can and give them proper rites before Humphries's assassins find us.'

'And then what?'

'And then we die, I suppose.'

She stared into his impassive face. When I met him, Elverda thought, I was ready for death. I thought my life was over, that I'd outlived my purpose. Now I don't want to die! This man – this half-machine – has given me a reason for living.

He reached out with his human hand and touched her arm. 'It's all right. I'll escort you back to Ceres. The rock rats are almost finished building their new habitat—'

'*Chrysalis II*,' Elverda murmured.

'Yes,' said Dorn. 'You'll be safe there, and you can find passage back to Earth or Selene. Without me.'

'You'll return here,' she said.

He gave no answer. None was required; she knew his need.

Abruptly, Elverda turned in the command chair and began to peck at the communications console.

'What are you doing?' Dorn asked.

'I'm calling the news media. There's a woman in Selene, Douglas Stavenger's wife, she's a famous news anchor.'

'No,' said Dorn.

'Why not? Once the world knows what we're trying to accomplish, not even Martin Humphries would dare to harm us.'

'You'd tell them you're with Dorik Harbin, the monster?'

'I'll tell them I'm with Dorn, the priest, the man who had dedicated his life to recovering the bodies of those killed in the wars.'

'Humphries knows who I am,' said Dorn. 'He has whole battalions of public relations experts. Your story will be swamped by his. Vigilantes will come out here to find me. The hunt will become a news event. Our deaths will be called executions.'

She took her hand away from the keyboard. 'You want to die, don't you?'

'I deserve to die,' he said.

'I need a ship,' said Victor Zacharias.

Big George Ambrose leaned back in his swivel chair and nodded resignedly. 'You've been tellin' me that for nearly three fookin' years now.'

The two men were sitting in Big George's office in the half-finished *Chrysalis II* habitat. It was hardly an imposing room, no larger than most of the office spaces aboard the habitat. George's massive desk and intimidating figure made it seem even smaller. The walls were blank at the moment: smart screens that could display anything in the habitat's computer files or show views of the outside, where teams of engineers and robots were working to complete the structure.

Victor's jet black ringlets were neatly trimmed, but in the three years of his enforced stay at Ceres he had grown a thickly curled beard. He wore the maroon coveralls that identified him as a member of the habitat's technical staff. Big George still looked like a shaggy mountain man with his untamed mane of brick red hair and wild beard. His coveralls were light blue, rumpled, frayed at the cuffs from long wear.

With the icy calmness of a man who was trying hard to control his anger, Victor said, 'My family is out there somewhere and I've got to find them.'

George shook his busy head. 'Look, Vic, you've gotta face facts. They're dead by now.'

'No,' Victor insisted. 'The ship had plenty of provisions and—'

'Why haven't we heard from them, then? In all this time? It's been more'n three years, hasn't it?'

Victor glared at his boss. With that dark beard, he would have looked fiercely intimidating to anyone else. But George Ambrose knew better. By the time the task of finding all the bodies from the massacre of the original *Chrysalis* was finished, Big George had learned that Victor Zacharias had been an architect, a builder. As head of the rock rats' governing council, George had persuaded the International Astronautical Authority to fund the building of a new habitat in orbit around Ceres. The IAA got support for the project from Selene and the major corporations involved in space industries.

The new habitat – *Chrysalis II* – would not be a ramshackle Tinkertoy assemblage of old and disused spacecraft. George Ambrose wanted a structure that was designed and constructed specifically to be a home for the rock rats. And he wanted Victor Zacharias to head the team that built it.

Victor reluctantly agreed to do the job, but only if Big George would provide him with a ship afterward.

'Face it, Vic,' George said from behind his desk. 'They're gone.'

'You promised me a ship,' Victor said again, relentless.

'When the job's done. It's only half finished.'

'The design is complete,' Victor insisted. 'The major structural work is finished. You don't need me for the rest of it. A couple of trained chimpanzees could finish the job.'

'Nearest trained chimps are Earthside, Vic. But you're here and you're gonna stay here until the fookin' job's finished. And that's it.' George slapped his heavy hands on the desktop and rose to his feet, an imposing red-bearded giant of a man who would brook no further discussion.

Victor got out of his chair, his eyes smoldering. But he said nothing further. He knew that this conversation was finished. Silently he walked to the door.

'By th' way,' Big George called to him, '*Pleiades* is due in later t'day. Cheena Madagascar'll be lookin' you up.'

Over his shoulder, Victor grumbled, 'Thanks for the good news.'

Attack Ship *Viking*:
Captain's Quarters

It's good to be the captain, Kao Yuan thought as he lay stretched out in his double-sized bunk. His communications officer, the lissome young brunette with sloe eyes and surprising athletic abilities, was in his shower stall, singing to herself. Off-key, Yuan realized. But what the hell. She's got other talents.

Tamara, he pronounced silently, rolling her name around in his mind. Tamara Vishinsky. In bed, she had told Yuan that she'd studied for ballet as a child. The training serves her well, he thought.

HSS headquarters had added her to his crew at the last moment, flying her all the way out from the Moon to reach *Viking* before Yuan started his hunt for the renegade. She came with high qualifications in communications systems. And in sexual gymnastics, Yuan thought, grinning inwardly.

He badly wanted to turn over and sleep for another hour. I deserve the rest, he told himself. But *Viking* and its accompanying two ships were fast approaching the area where the sensor had reported Dorik Harbin's vessel to be. We could be in battle today, he knew.

Reluctantly, Yuan rolled out of bed and padded to the steamy shower stall. Opening the door, he said sternly, 'This is your captain speaking. Now hear this.'

The comm officer reached out with both arms and pulled him into the hot, sudsy stall. He slid his arms around her and pressed close. We've got plenty of time, he thought. Plenty of time.

Elverda paced the short passageway between *Hunter*'s bridge and the hatch that led into the main airlock. Despite all the rejuvenation therapies, you are still an old, old woman, she reminded herself. You must exercise your legs. After a lifetime in low-gravity environments the ship's acceleration was punishing her, even though Dorn kept it well below one g.

He was up in the bridge, sitting in the command chair as impassively as a sculpture of steel. Is he fleeing from the assassins coming after us, Elverda wondered, or rushing to find the bodies of the slain? Some of both, she concluded. We seldom do anything for merely one reason.

And you, she asked herself, what are you fleeing from? What are you rushing to?

Death, she answered. The answer to both questions is the same.

Her creative career had been finished many long years ago. Decades ago. She was going through the motions of teaching at Selene University when Martin Humphries swept her out to the Asteroid Belt, agog to see the artifact that a rock rat family had accidentally discovered.

It has to be the work of alien intelligence, Elverda told herself. No human could have made it. Yet it related to humans in a way that stirred the soul, viscerally, beyond the five senses. The artwork – for Elverda was convinced it was a work of superhuman artistry – bored directly into one's mind, into the depths of the unconscious intellect that lay hidden and disguised beneath the conscious personality.

When Elverda had seen the artifact she had been ready for death, eager to end the pain and loneliness of her life. Then she had looked into its glowing depths and saw herself, saw the mother who had loved her so completely, saw the baby she had never borne, the path of her life from its beginning and through all the twists of fate and pride and remorse.

She was ready to face life again after seeing the artifact. She had the strength to stand next to Dorn, the self-mutilated ex-mercenary who had tried to atone for the thousands he had slaughtered, and failed.

Martin Humphries had seen the artifact and it nearly killed him. She saw in her mind's eye once again how Humphries staggered out of the crypt that housed the artifact: his handsome face twisted and sweating, his eyes wild with fear; how he curled into a fetal ball, crying, spittle dribbling from his lips, babbling frantically, helplessly.

It must have shown him his own life, Elverda thought, shown him how despicable he's been, shown him all the people he's destroyed. Now Humphries has sent assassins to kill us, because we saw him in his moment of pain and weakness. He has learned nothing from the artifact. Nothing.

She wondered what had happened to the artifact. There had never been a report about it in the news media: Humphries had prevented that. But the rumor floated through the cold emptiness of the Belt; not even Martin Humphries could keep the news of an alien artifact completely suppressed. The tale spread to the Moon and to Earth, she was certain, where most people took it as gossip from the rock rats, a fable from the frontier, a legend without basis in fact.

Strange that the scientists of the IAA and the universities haven't spoken out, Elverda thought. Has Humphries silenced them? Money can buy almost anything, she knew, but would all the scientists in the solar system remain silent?

Then a new thought struck her. Perhaps he's destroyed the artifact! Blown up the little asteroid in which it was found, wiped it out of existence. That would be just like Humphries: destroy what he feels is threatening him. Just as he is determined to destroy us.

'Radar contact.' Dorn's voice issued from the intercom speaker set into the passage's overhead, as flatly unemotional as a computer's synthesized announcement.

He's human, Elverda reminded herself. Despite the machinery that keeps him alive, he's a human being. He has feelings, emotions, just as I do. We wouldn't be out here trying to recover the dead if he didn't.

Yet that machinery is failing. One day he'll be as dead as the corpses we're trying to retrieve.

She hurried along the passageway to see what he'd found.

Freshly showered and dressed in a set of coveralls that bore his captain's stripes on its cuffs, Kao Yuan slid into the command chair and nodded to the man sitting at the communications console.

'Give me a channel for all three ships,' he commanded.

A green light in his chair's armrest winked on.

'This is the captain speaking,' Yuan said, trying to make his voice firm, authoritative.

'We are about to enter battle against an experienced and ruthless opponent. I have every confidence that if each of us performs his assigned task properly we will destroy our adversary.

'The Asteroid Wars have been over for some years now,' Yuan went on, 'but the mission we're on is a piece of unfinished business. The enemy we seek is the man who wiped out the *Chrysalis* habitat. He slaughtered more than a thousand defenseless men, women and children. Our mission is to bring justice to him and anyone aboard his ship assisting him. Our goal is to avenge those thousand people he murdered.'

The others on the bridge were staring at him. Keeping his face solemn, Yuan added, 'We have been sent on this mission by Mr. Martin Humphries himself. He has a personal interest in seeing that the last remnant of the old wars is erased once and for all. Once we've fulfilled our mission and returned to Earth, each of us will receive a very generous bonus – but our real reward will be the knowledge that we have paid a rightful and fitting retribution to the mass murderer, Dorik Harbin.'

Yuan looked around the bridge. All his officers' eyes were on him. He half expected applause but they simply gazed at him, waiting for his next words.

So he said, 'All ships, battle stations.'

Habitat *Chrysalis II*:
Observation Blister

Victor Zacharias stood alone in the observation blister and looked out at the distant, uncaring pinpoints of light. The stars gazed back at him, cold and silent. Jupiter glowed in the darkness; Victor thought he could make out two sparks of moons near its ruddy, flattened disk. Off to his left a blue light gleamed: Earth.

Curving away on either side of the glassteel blister was the massive wheel shape of the unfinished habitat. Victor knew every girder, every panel, every weld. To one side of him the wheel was nothing more than unfinished ribs of metal, like the fossil bones of a giant dinosaur. He saw flashes of welders' lasers flickering in the darkness out there. Construction crews worked twenty-four/seven under the booming roar of Big George's demands.

But the construction of *Chrysalis II* was not urgent to Victor. His family was, and he chafed under the inflexible restraints that Ambrose had bound upon him. It's not Big George, Victor told himself. It's the war, it's that murdering sonofabitch who wiped out the original *Chrysalis*, it's the laws of physics, it's fate. Victor felt the weight of the universe trying to bow him down, bend his knees.

He squared his shoulders and stood straighter. 'I'll find you,' he muttered. 'Through hell and time and space I'll find you out there.'

Ceres was a pitted ball of rock, close enough, it seemed, to reach out and touch. None of the other asteroids were bright enough to be seen but Victor knew they were swinging in their ever-shifting orbits out there in the cold darkness. And among them was a ship, his ship, *Syracuse*, and the family he wanted to save.

Are they already dead? he asked himself for the thousandth time. And he found the same answer as always: *No*. They're alive. The ship may be crippled but they're alive. They have provisions enough to last for years. Pauline will keep them going. She's strong, brave, resourceful.

It all depends on Theo, he realized. He's the one with the technical smarts and know-how. But he's only fifteen! Then Victor realized, no, he must be nearly nineteen by now. A young man, with the responsibility of keeping the ship's systems functioning. Pauline can help him, but Theo's the one I was training to run the ship.

And Angela, my little angel. What of her? She should be here at Ceres finding a husband, starting her own family, starting her own life. Instead she's marooned on a crippled ship drifting through the Belt.

I've got to find them, Victor told himself again. I've got to get a ship, one way or the other, and find them.

He heard the soft hiss of the hatch sliding open, a tinkle of bracelets clinking together.

'I thought you'd be here.'

Pulled out of his thoughts, Victor turned to see the darkly clad figure of Cheena Madagascar step through the hatch into the dimly lit glassteel blister.

'It's like standing in empty space, isn't it,' she half-whispered once the hatch slid shut behind her and the lights dimmed again. 'Like a god walking among the stars.'

He snorted disdainfully. 'Take a good look at Ceres, pitted and cracked and ugly as sin.'

Cheena chuckled in the shadows. 'Very romantic, Victor.'

'I hate this place.'

She came up and stood beside him. He could see her gold-flecked eyes shining in the shadows of the diffused lighting.

'I like the beard,' she said. 'Makes you look . . . dangerous.'

He didn't know what to say, so he merely shrugged his shoulders.

'You've been avoiding me,' she said softly.

Despite himself, he smiled at her. 'It's best to avoid temptation.'

'Really? You didn't avoid me when you were on *Pleiades*.'

'You were the ship's captain. I had to follow orders.'

'You seemed to enjoy the duty.'

He shrugged. 'I'm only flesh and blood.'

'What a compliment.'

'Cheena, please, what happened aboard *Pleiades* was very good, but—'

'No buts,' she whispered, sliding her arms around his neck.

'This isn't right, Cheena. I have a wife. She's alive, I know she is.'

'Even if she is, my reluctant lover, she's far, far away and I'm right here, in your arms.'

He hadn't realized that he'd wrapped his arms around her waist. She was pressing close to him. He could smell the clean tang of her shampoo, feel her breathing, the beating of her heart.

'Life belongs to the living, Victor,' Cheena murmured.

'She's not dead,' he insisted, in a whisper.

'I'll make you a deal,' she said, with a teasing smile in her voice. 'I'll let you use my ship for six months. If we haven't found them in six months you'll give it up and stay with me.'

'Six months . . .'

'You'll be mine until we find them. If we don't, it wouldn't be so terrible to stay with me, would it?'

Before he could decide rationally he was clasping her to him in a fiercely passionate kiss. Six months, said a voice in his mind. Six months. You can search for them. You can find them.

Then the voice added, If you can get away from Big George.

Smelter Ship *Hunter*: Main Airlock

'It's definitely a body,' Dorn said. He tugged on his nanofabric space suit and began sealing its front.

Elverda nodded as he pulled up the hood and inflated it into a bubble of a helmet. She had never gone outside the ship, never taken a space walk. What did the technical people call it? she asked herself. EVA. Extravehicular activity. How pretentious! How bloodless! Spacewalk is much more descriptive.

They had flown more than eighty thousand kilometers from the coordinates where the old battle had been fought, radars probing in every direction. Twice they had found chunks of debris. This was the first corpse they had located.

Elverda remembered the other bodies they had found from other battles. Desiccated, like ancient mummies. Hollow-eyed, shriveled, skin blackened by the hard ultraviolet radiation of space. Many of the dead were in space suits: they had gone into battle as fully protected as possible. Still it did them no good. They died when their ships were destroyed. Elverda shuddered at the thought of drifting through space alive, knowing that there would be no rescue, knowing that within hours or days or perhaps weeks the air in the suit would give out or you would starve or die groaning of thirst.

Worse were the poor devils who had been blown out of their ships without a space suit. Their lungs exploded in showers of blood. Their eyes burst out of their sockets. Elverda vomited the first time Dorn had brought such a corpse aboard.

'Where there is one body,' Dorn said as he clumped to the airlock's hatch, 'there must be others. They've scattered, but they're out there waiting to be found.'

'Be careful,' she said as she always did.

With the swipe of his human fingers, Dorn sealed the helmet to the collar of his suit. She saw him nod. 'Of course,' he said.

Then he stepped over the hatch's sill and touched the control button that slid it shut. He raised his other gloved hand in what might have been a hesitant wave.

Elverda watched the lights on the airlock panel cycle from green through amber to red as the lock pumped down to vacuum and the outer hatch opened. Nodding to herself, she hurried along the passageway to the bridge to monitor Dorn's EVA.

He had been a soldier all his life, from childhood. This she knew from what little he had told her about himself. Most of his revelations were confessions. As calmly as if he were talking about someone else, he told her that while in a drug-heightened rage of jealousy he had murdered a woman who claimed she loved him. Later, his mind again boiling in drugs that his employer distributed freely to enhance the mercenaries' battle prowess, he methodically wiped out the habitat *Chry-*

salis. And attacked another ship, *Syracuse,* immediately afterward.

Now he lived a life of atonement, searching for the dead who'd been left to drift through the Asteroid Belt after the war's battles. But Elverda knew that it was more than atonement that Dorn sought: he was waiting for death. He had tried to kill himself and been prevented from succeeding at that. Now he waited for death's hand to reach him.

And it was coming, Elverda knew. Martin Humphries's assassins were tracking through the Belt searching for them. His own cyborg body was beginning to break down, as was her human one.

How can I save him? she wondered. How can I protect him? How can I heal him?

'It's gone, sir.'

Kao Yuan planted his fists on his hips as he loomed before the two crewmen who'd gone out to find the tiny chunk of debris on which they had planted the sensor many months earlier.

'Gone?'

They stood in the compartment just outside the ship's main airlock, where the suit lockers stood in a silent row. The two crewmen were peeling off their nanofabric space suits as they reported to their captain.

'Gone, sir. He must have found the sensor on it.'

Yuan nodded. 'That explains why it stopped transmitting its signal.'

He turned abruptly and strode back toward the bridge. The renegade found my sensor. He knows he's being tracked. What will he do now? Which way will the mouse jump?

By the time he reached the bridge and slid into his command chair he'd made up his mind. 'Navigator, program a search spiral course. He can't be far from here.'

The navigator said, 'Search spiral. Aye, sir.'

Yuan grinned inwardly. It still gave him a special pleasure to realize that he was actually captain of this ship. This isn't a computer game, he told himself. It's real! I'm captain of an actual attack ship. I've got two other ships under my command.

And once I've destroyed the renegade, I'll have enough money to go back to Shanghai and open the best restaurant the city's ever seen.

Life is good, thought Kao Yuan. Life is good.

The body was in an old-fashioned hard-shell space suit. Thank god, Elverda thought gratefully. Until Dorn slid its helmet visor open and she saw the agonized expression on its shriveled, wrinkled face. Lips pulled back over its teeth in terror, eyes wide and staring as if to ask, 'Why me? Why is this happening to me?'

Dorn stared into those blank, dead eyes. 'I wonder what I will look like when death reaches me.'

Elverda had no answer for him.

Working together, they laboriously removed the space suit from the stiffened corpse. Dorn put the suit together again and tossed it back into the airlock, then popped it out into space again.

'Maybe our pursuers will follow it,' he said, 'and give us a little more time to continue our work.'

Elverda smiled weakly.

Then Dorn tenderly lifted the corpse in his strong arms and carried it to the cremation chamber. He had personally built this oven, modified from the ship's standard smelting furnace, the kind that the rock rats had once used to refine the ores they pried out of metallic asteroids. Elverda always felt uneasy in this part of the ship, as if she were trespassing in a haunted house. The spirits of the dead hover around us here, she thought. This is a chamber of desolation.

Yet Dorn seemed to smile as he carefully placed the desiccated body in the exact center of the oven. He had to stoop inside the low-ceilinged chamber; when he stepped back outside it and stood beside her his face looked satisfied, at ease, almost happy.

'Your atoms will rejoin the cosmic dust,' he intoned as he swung the metal door shut and primed the heaters. 'The substance of your body will someday help to build a new star, new worlds.'

Elverda knew it was Dorn's desperate attempt at salvation, his belief that the universe recycles constantly, that nothing is ever wasted, not even the tiniest atom.

The smelter furnace roared to life. Elverda felt its heat, welcomed its warmth on her aged bones. Inside the star-hot oven the corpse was quickly vaporized, flesh boiled into gases. Finally Dorn shut down the smelter and pressed the buttons that exhausted its gases out of the ship, into the interplanetary void.

'It is finished,' he said.

As if in counterpoint, the ship's synthesized computer voice announced, 'Radar contact.'

They both hurried to the bridge.

Attack Ship *Viking*: Bridge

'Sir, there's nobody inside this suit.'

Kao Yuan's brows knitted as he stared at the main display screen. The three other officers on the bridge were also focusing their attention on the view of two crewmen outside the ship in nanofabric space suits grasping an empty hard-shell suit. They had unfastened the suit's helmet as they floated in the vacuum: one of the crewmen had tucked it under his arm, like a severed head.

We've been tracking an empty suit, Yuan said to himself. He's damned clever, this Dorik Harbin or whatever he calls himself now. Send out the suit as a decoy to lead us on a wild goose chase.

'Bring it inside,' he commanded. To his navigation officer he asked, 'Can you backtrack the suit's trajectory? I want to know where his ship is.'

The woman looked uncertain. 'I can try, sir.'

'Do so.' Turning to his propulsion officer, Yuan said, 'Minimum power. Communications, I want a full sweep at all frequencies. That ship of his can't be too far away from here.'

But a nagging voice in his head countered, Yes it can. He could have released that suit days ago. He got you to chase after it while he's heading off in a different direction altogether.

Where would he be heading? According to the intelligence from HSS headquarters he's on some fanatical mission to recover the bodies of all those killed in the war's battles. That's most likely dope smoke, but he was at this site, I've got to admit. We've got the other battle sites pinpointed, but the bodies hurled out of exploding ships could fly fifty, a hundred thousand kilometers over the years since the battles were fought. Farther, even. And they won't all be near the ecliptic, either; some of those bodies might have gotten flung out at high inclinations.

Lips pressed together in a troubled, almost angry line, Yuan realized, Crap! I might have to spend years chasing after this nutcase.

Then he realized that the other officers on the bridge were all watching him, waiting for his next orders. He straightened up in his command chair and put on a careless grin.

'We'll find him,' he said. 'We'll find him.' Suddenly a new realization popped into his mind. Cheerfully he told them, 'And I know how to do it!'

The radar contact turned out to be a shard of metal, a fragment of a ship destroyed long ago.

Dorn leaned over Elverda's shoulder as she sat in *Hunter*'s command chair and traced a finger along the navigation screen. She wished he were on her other side, with the human half of his face toward her. Even though she admired its workmanship, his metal half felt cold, heartless to her.

'A body here,' his flesh-and-bone finger tapped the screen, 'and a fragment of a ship here. We must be approaching a cloud of debris.'

'And bodies?' she asked.

'And bodies,' he confirmed. 'Yes, there will be bodies.'

Elverda pursed her lips, then heard herself ask, 'Would it be possible to retrieve some of the debris?'

She could see no expression on the metal side of his face, but she heard the puzzlement in his voice. 'You want to pick up pieces of debris?'

'Nothing too large,' she said.

For several heartbeats Dorn said nothing. Then, 'You wish to create a sculpture.'

'I didn't realize it until just now. Yes, a sculpture. Nothing grand. Just a small monument that we can leave drifting through the Belt.'

He made a sound that might have been a chuckle. 'I should have expected it.'

'Me too,' she said.

Dorn turned like a machine pivoting and went to the hatch. 'I'll suit up.'

'You don't have to take this piece. Later, when you're going out anyway for the bodies. There'll be scraps of metal there, won't there?'

'Very likely,' he said, his prosthetic leg already through the hatch. 'But we might as well take this one. It will give you something to start with.'

★　　★　　★

Yuan said to his navigation officer, 'Plot a course for the next nearest battle site.'

'Sir?' she asked, uncertainty in her voice, her face.

Smiling patiently, Yuan said, 'Break off the pursuit course we've been on and get us to the next nearest battle site.'

His first mate, a chunky dour Hawaiian sitting at the propulsion console, said, 'Captain, he's not at that site. He's—'

'I know he's not there yet,' Yuan said, still smiling but with an edge of steel in his voice. 'But he will be. And when he gets there we'll be waiting for him.'

All three officers were clearly unhappy with their captain's order.

Yuan asked, 'How many hard-shell space suits are we carrying?'

'We haven't used the cermet suits since we were issued the nano—'

'I didn't ask that,' Yuan snapped. 'How many of the old suits are still in storage?'

His first mate tapped into the logistics program. 'Six, sir,' he said grudgingly.

'Check with the other two ships and see how many they're carrying.'

Plainly perplexed, the first mate asked, 'Sir, why do you want—'

His smile turning smug, Yuan said, 'Our quarry used an empty suit to lure us away from him. Well, two can play at that game. Only, we'll use empty suits to lure him *toward* us. Like bait for our trap.'

Habitat *Chrysalis II*:
George Ambrose's Office

'No,' said Big George. 'Not until the fookin' construction job's finished.'

Sitting in front of George's desk, Victor tried to hold on to his temper. 'All the design work is done. There's nothing more for me to do but supervise the work crews. You don't need me for that.'

It was difficult to tell George's expression beneath all that flaming red hair, but Victor heard the inflexible tone of his voice. 'Look, Vic, gettin' the habitat finished isn't the most important thing. It's the *only* thing! You're not leavin' Ceres until the last weld's welded and the last pisser's plumbing is workin'."

'That's my reward for helping you for more than three years?'

'Listen, mate: You're alive because we picked you up and saved your bloody butt. You'd be floatin' into the Sun, already dead, if it weren't for me. You owe your life to me and the people of this habitat, what's left of 'em.'

Victor clenched his jaw so hard that pain shot through his head.

'The people of this habitat?' he snapped. 'The original people of this habitat were slaughtered by the same madman who attacked my ship.'

'There are plenty of newbies streamin' in. We need *Chrysalis II* to house 'em. Prob'ly have to enlarge the fookin' habitat before we even finish it.'

'My family's out in the Belt,' Victor insisted. 'I've got to find them!'

'Your family's dead, Vic. Admit it. It'll simplify your life.'

Every impulse in his body was urging Victor to leap over the desk between them and squeeze George's windpipe until his eyes popped out. But his rational mind told him that the giant redhead would pull him loose like a gorilla flicking off a flea. And then where would I be? he asked himself.

George leaned forward, resting his beefy arms on the desktop. 'Look, Vic, I'm not bein' unreasonable. Another six months, a year at the most, and you'll be free to go wherever you want.'

'The habitat will be finished in six months,' Victor muttered. 'Seven, at most.'

'There y'are,' said George. 'Then you're free as a bird.'

'Unless you decide to start enlarging the place.'

George shrugged massively.

His innards trembling with rage, Victor slowly rose to his feet. 'As soon as the habitat's finished I'm leaving.'

'You'll need a ship, of course.'

'I'll get a ship.' Mentally he added, One way or the other.

George got to his feet, too, like a ruddy jagged mountain rising out of a geological fault. He stuck out his hand. 'Till the habitat's finished.'

Victor kept his hands at his sides, balled into fists. 'Until my sentence is served out.'

He turned his back to George and went to the door.

'Don't go gettin' any ideas about skippin' outta here,' George warned. 'I'm puttin' security on notice. Nobody's gonna allow you anywhere near a dockin' port.'

His back still to George, Victor nodded. 'So be it,' he muttered.

Elverda pushed up her goggles with one hand and clicked off the handheld laser welder with the other. The work was not going very well, she thought.

For three weeks Dorn had been recovering bodies left drifting in space, and bringing back scraps of metal and plastic, the twisted remains of spacecraft that had been shattered in battle.

The trouble is, she said to herself, that you have no clear vision of what you want this monument to be. She glared critically at the coiling column that was growing from the deck plates of her makeshift workshop. The compartment had once been the ship's loading bay, where asteroidal ores were brought aboard before being fed into the smelter. Now it was a grimy, empty, low-vaulted echoing chamber of gray metal, darkly shadowed except for the brilliant pool of light that Dorn had rigged for her. Broken chunks of metal lay scattered on the deck around her and her unfinished construct, looking hopelessly useless.

The column itself seemed just as utterly pointless to Elverda. It's going nowhere, she told herself. It says nothing. Your talent has left you, long years ago. There's nothing remaining: no imagination, no inspiration, no soul.

'Do you need more material?'

Dorn's voice startled her. She hadn't heard him enter the capacious bay.

Turning, she saw that he was eying the misbegotten sculpture intently.

'I need more ideas,' Elverda said unhappily. 'I need more talent.'

Dorn shook his head slowly, a ponderous shift from side to side. 'No,' he said. 'You need more time.'

She placed the hand laser carefully down on the deck. 'I've put enough time into it today.'

'Are you ready for dinner, then?'

'I'm not hungry.'

He seemed to smile. It was sometimes difficult for her to tell. 'Will you join me, though? It's depressing to eat alone.'

She grinned at him, widely. 'You're trying to psych me into eating, aren't you?'

'A little broth,' he coaxed. 'It will do you good.'

Once in the galley she sipped at the broth, then forked down the slivers of pseudomeat that he put on the table in front of her.

'Do you feel better now?' Dorn asked as he took their dishes to the sink.

'I feel full,' she admitted. 'How about you?'

'I feel puzzled.'

'Puzzled? About what?'

He returned to the table and sat down heavily. 'The ship that is tracking us . . .'

'We haven't seen a ship.'

'No, but there is one following us. Perhaps more than one.'

Elverda nodded. Yes, she thought, Humphries must have sent someone to track us down.

'It hasn't approached us.'

'They haven't found us yet,' she said.

'Why not? They must know the locations of the old battles just as well as we do. They know what we are doing. Why haven't they reached us?'

Elverda said, 'We've been retrieving bodies. That takes us on an erratic course. It makes us harder to find.'

He seemed to think about that for several moments. At last he muttered, 'Perhaps.'

'Or perhaps,' she suggested, 'we've been wrong all along and Humphries isn't trying to find us.'

Again Dorn fell silent. Then he asked, 'Do you really believe that?'

'No,' she admitted. 'He wants to silence us. I'm certain of that.'

'Yet his ships are not pursuing us.'

'Are you sure?'

'I've spent much of the day scanning the region as deeply as our equipment allows. No radar blips, no ion trails, nothing.'

'Have they given up?'

'More likely they've returned to Ceres or Vesta to refuel and resupply.'

Nodding, Elverda said, 'That could be it.'

'No matter,' said Dorn. 'Our work here is finished. We've recovered all the bodies in the area. Now we move on to the next site.'

'How far is it?'

'A week, at one-half g.'

Elverda knew that he kept the acceleration gentle to accommodate her; she had spent most of her life in low-g environments.

'And how many sites after that?' she asked.

He puffed out a sigh. 'At least two, that I know of. There must be more, but we'll need more information from Humphries or Astro to confirm that.'

At least two more sites, she thought. And what will be waiting for us when we get to them?

Habitat *Chrysalis II*:
Control Center

It took almost a month for Victor Zacharias to prepare for his escape. He thought of it as an escape. He was going to flee not only George Ambrose and the construction task he had imposed; he was going to get away from Cheena Madagascar and her demands as well.

Not demands, he told himself. It's not fair to call it that. You're willing enough. Cheena's a temptation, a siren that I'm not strong enough to resist. The only thing I can do is run away.

It wasn't easy. Big George knew that Victor was thoroughly unhappy with his forced labor on the rock rats' new habitat. Security personnel watched Victor: not obviously, not as if he were under guard. But Victor knew his every move was scrutinized by security cameras, night and day. Even when he spent the night with Cheena, he saw the unavoidable red eye of a surveillance camera in the passageway leading to her door, and it was still watching when he left the following morning.

Slowly and surely he drew his plans. Now, as he walked through the habitat's control center, he was ready to set them in motion.

The control center was *Chrysalis II*'s brain. It hummed with constant activity, alive with the buzz of electrical circuitry and the muted talk of the men and women who observed every aspect of the habitat. Along one sweeping wall of the low-ceilinged chamber was a row of display screens, each set of six monitored by a human observer equipped with a communications set clipped to one ear. Walking slowly down the line behind them, Victor could watch every section of the habitat, oversee the construction teams working on the unfinished areas, check on the status of the life support systems, the electrical power supply, the water recyclers, everything.

On one set of screens he saw the docking ports where *Pleiades* and other ships were moored. A few screens down the row he could see an outside view of the maintenance robots installing new meteor bumpers on another ship's hull.

Victor glanced up at the master clock on the wall above the screens. Its digits read 15:44. A little more than eight hours to go, he told himself.

At exactly 16:00 hours he left the control center, as usual, and walked down the passageway to the main cafeteria, where he loaded a tray with his last meal aboard *Chrysalis II*. Or so he hoped. As he ate, an island of solitude at a small table in the midst of the bustling, noisy cafeteria, he thought that if his scheme didn't work this might be the last meal of his life. Big George would probably be angry enough to kill him.

He ate for sustenance, chewing without tasting the food. In his mind he went over every facet of his plan. It should work, he thought. He could find nothing wrong with it. If they're watching you night and day, you have to blind them. It's that simple. And that dangerous.

As he left the cafeteria Victor wondered if he should visit Cheena Madagascar one last time. No, he told himself sternly. But her quarters are closer to the docking port than mine, he argued with himself. What of it? the other part of his mind answered. You've timed it all out. You'll be able to get to the ship from your own quarters with minutes to spare.

He knew he should avoid the temptation. Still, it was a struggle. He went to his quarters, glanced up at the unblinking red light of the security camera at the end of the passageway, opened his door and stepped inside. Now you stay here until 12:01, he told himself.

The working shift in the control center changed at midnight. Usually the incoming crew began filtering in, in ones and twos, a few minutes before the hour.

As the relief crew started showing up at the control center, one of the observers at the security console frowned at a set of red lights that appeared suddenly on his board.

'Damn,' he said to the woman sitting next to him. 'Cameras are down in sections fourteen and fifteen.'

'You've had trouble with them before, haven't you?' she said.

'Last friggin' week,' he replied, tapping at his keyboard. 'Guess I'll have to roust maintenance.'

'And security,' the woman reminded him. 'There's a special security watch in those sections.'

'Yeah, right.' He frowned. 'They're gonna love getting goosed at midnight.'

The woman shrugged. 'You've gotta do it. Regulations. Can't leave the surveillance cameras down.'

He gave her a sour look. 'Like somebody's gonna steal something while the cameras are down? Most people are sleepin', this time of night.'

'It's regulations,' she repeated.

He reached for the communications link to the maintenance department, grumbling, 'If I don't report it I'll catch hell.'

The woman pushed her chair back and got to her feet. 'Let the next shift call it in. Let them listen to the bitchin'.'

At that moment, his relief sauntered over to the console, grinning casually. 'You going to stay for my shift? I'll go back to bed, then.'

The man hopped to his feet. 'Not bloody likely. I'm leaving. The cameras are down in fourteen and fifteen again.'

'Again?' said the relief observer, sliding into the warm chair. 'We had trouble with them last week. You call maintenance?'

'Not yet. It's all yours, pal.'

'Thanks a lot!'

'You gotta call security, too, y'know. Have fun.'

'Shit!'

It was a mistake, Victor thought, to try to keep the man in charge of building this habitat from getting away. I know all the systems and how to finagle around them.

The only question was timing. How long would it take the maintenance crew to bring the cameras back up? How quickly would security send a team to check on him? Victor hurried past the dead camera up on the ceiling of the passageway and made his way to the docking ports.

The security guard at the entrance to the ports was frowning at the blank screen on his desk.

'What's the trouble?' Victor asked him.

'Dunno. Goddamn screen just went blank on me. I can't get anything on it.'

'The system's gone down before,' said Victor. 'It usually comes up again in a few minutes.'

'Yeah,' the guard said, his voice thin with uncertainty.

Victor stepped around the desk to the seated guard's side.

'Uh, Mr. Zacharias,' the guard said uncertainly, 'You're not supposed to be in this area, y'know.'

'I know. I just thought I could help you with your screen.'

'Why'd it hafta go blooey just when I start my shift?' the guard grumbled. 'I can't get any calls in or out.'

'Let me have a look at it. . . .'

Victor took in a deep breath, then chopped at the back of the guard's neck as hard as he could. The man slid out of his chair, banged his chin on the desk top, and slumped to the floor.

'Sorry,' Victor muttered. He dashed up the passageway that led to the docking ports. Undogging the hatch that led into *Pleiades*'s main airlock, he rushed straight to the ship's bridge, slipped into the command chair, and began powering up the ship's systems.

No alarms yet. Good, he thought. Even if maintenance gets the cameras back on, there's nothing for them to see in the passageways. I'm okay until the guard comes to. So far so good.

Now comes the tricky part.

Victor had filed a departure plan for *Pleiades* with the habitat's flight control computer several days earlier. The flight controllers normally were not in the same loop as the surveillance cameras or security guards. Normally they seldom talked to one another. Victor hoped this was a normal night.

He had made certain that all the maintenance and repair work on the ship had been completed. Cheena Madagascar had no intention of leaving *Chrysalis II* for another week, he knew. She had offered to take Victor with her, to search for his family. For six months. Victor knew it would take longer than that, and he didn't want Cheena or any other distractions on the ship when he started out on his search.

So he had updated Cheena's own departure plan, hoping that the human flight controllers wouldn't ask the ship's captain why she had changed her departure date.

Sitting in the command chair, Victor took a deep breath, swiftly reconfigured the electronic keyboard to handle the communications system, then pecked at the keys once they lit up.

'*Chrysalis* flight control, this is *Pleiades*,' he said. 'Ready for departure.'

A wait that seemed endless, then, '*Pleiades*, you're twelve seconds behind your schedule.'

'So sue me,' he growled.

The flight controller chuckled. 'Okay. Lemme check you out. Right. Okay. You are cleared for undocking.'

'Undocking,' he said, tapping the controls. He felt the ship shudder as it was released from the grapples that held it to the habitat's dock.

'Initiate separation maneuver,' said the flight controller.

'Initiating separation,' Victor confirmed. Jets of cold gas nudged *Pleiades* away from the dock.

'We need the captain to request final departure clearance,' the flight controller said.

Voiceprint identification, Victor knew. He tugged out the palmsized digital recorder he had been carrying in his coverall pocket. It had taken him weeks of talking with Cheena and editing her words to get the message straight.

'*Pleiades* standing by for departure clearance,' said Cheena Madagascar's voice. It sounded stilted to Victor, herky-jerky.

But the voiceprint identification computer was not programmed to analyze the cadence of speech, merely the frequency pattern of the voice that was speaking.

A wait that seemed endless. Then, '*Pleiades*, you are clear for departure,' said the flight controller.

'*Pleiades* on burn,' Victor said. He clicked off the communications link, lit the ship's main fusion engine, then howled an utterly triumphant, 'YAZOO!' as *Pleiades* headed out into the Belt.

Attack Ship *Viking*: Weapons Bay

Yuan studied his first mate's beefy face as they checked the laser's double row of capacitor banks. The man was clearly unhappy, troubled.

'What's the matter, Koop?' The first mate's name was Kahalu'u Kaupakulu'a. Everyone on the ship called him Koop. 'Nothing,' he answered. He was almost as tall as Yuan, but much broader in girth, built like a fleshy brick. Before meeting Koop, Yuan had thought of Hawaiians as smiling, gracious souls, always relaxed and contented. Koop was just the opposite: moody, dark, always looking worried.

The weapons bay was narrow, its overhead so low that Yuan hunched over as he squeezed through the equipment that crammed the compartment. With the blocky Hawaiian in it, the bay seemed on the verge of bursting.

'Don't try to con me,' Yuan said, keeping his tone light. 'We're alone in here, nobody's going to hear you. What's eating you?'

Koop wouldn't meet his eyes. 'I don't want you to think I'm trying to second-guess you,' he said. His voice was a soft, gentle tenor.

'You're not after my job?' Yuan joked.

The Hawaiian's eyes flashed wide. 'No! Honest! I just . . .' His voice trailed off.

'You just what?' Yuan asked, trying to hide the irritation growing inside him. Do I have to drag it out of you? he wondered silently.

'This business of running away,' Koop said.

'Running away?'

'Well, maybe not running away, but . . . I mean, how's it going to look back at headquarters? We were on his track and then we backed off.'

Yuan edged past the laser's copper mirror mounting as he replied, 'Why should we go chasing all over the Belt when we can make him come to us?'

'We were on his track.'

'And he spoofed us with an empty suit. So now we're heading for a spot he'll come to and we're baiting a trap for him.'

'With empty suits.'

'That's right. According to the crystal ball readers from headquarters, he's out there picking up bodies from all the battles he fought in during the war. Must be crazy with guilt or something.'

'Or something,' Koop muttered.

'So we'll give him some bodies to find.'

'Decoys,' said Koop.

'Bait.'

Koop shook his blocky head slowly. 'I don't know. Most of the crew thinks it's a mistake.'

'You've been talking with the crew about this?'

'Some of them. You know how it is. They'll tell me stuff they wouldn't say to the captain.'

'And they think I'm making a mistake, do they?'

'Sort of. Tamara says—'

'Tamara?'

'Yeah. You know, Cap, if you're worried about somebody being after your job, worry about her, not me.'

Yuan felt his brows rise. But he forced a smile. 'Really?'

Koop nodded unhappily.

'Thanks for the input,' Yuan said. 'I'll keep it in mind.'

'You know, as comm officer she hasta make daily reports back to headquarters.'

'Strictly routine,' Yuan said, thinking of the microsecond bursts of laser messaging that she sent every day, his only contact with HSS headquarters back on the Moon.

'Maybe,' said Koop.

There was a world of meaning in those two syllables, Yuan realized. Koop's telling me that I can't trust Tamara, that she's been sleeping with me just to keep me from suspecting . . . suspecting what? That she wants to take the captain's post away from me? That she's a spy from headquarters?

Looking into the Hawaiian's dark, cheerless eyes, Yuan thought, Does Koop want Tamara for himself? Is that what's going on here?

'Thanks for letting me know,' he said. 'I appreciate it.'

'I'm loyal,' said Koop.

Meaning, Yuan decided, that Tamara isn't.

★   ★   ★

Elverda felt tired. Even sitting in the padded command chair her body ached sullenly. It's the acceleration, she told herself. Half a normal Earth gravity has become more than my old bones can accept.

Should I ask him to slow down? No, she decided, I shouldn't. He wants to get to the next site, find the bodies left coasting through space after the battle, give them a decent death rite.

And what happens after we've found them? she asked herself. He'll want to search for others. Already he's talking about other battles, other sites to search. He'll never stop. Not until someone stops him.

She looked up at the main display screen. It showed emptiness, cold dark vacuum lit only by the pitiless stars strewn through the endless black. So many stars! Elverda marveled. Why are there so many of them?

'Could you come down here to the workshop?' Dorn's deep voice came through the intercom speaker. 'I . . . I need your help, please.'

'Of course.' Elverda got out of the command chair, winced at the twinge of pain from her hip, and headed down the passageway that led to the workshop and, beyond it, to the fusion reactor and propulsion system, deep in the bowels of the ship.

The hatch to the workshop was open. She gasped as she stepped in and saw Dorn bent over his own left arm resting on the table. His left shoulder socket was empty; tiny telltale lights winked inside the open socket.

He heard her and turned slowly on the swivel stool he sat upon. The human side of his face twitched with what might have been an apologetic grin.

'I can't get it back on again without help,' he said.

'What happened? How did—'

'The arm was malfunctioning. I couldn't apply full power to my hand. It felt . . . weak, almost paralyzed.'

Standing beside him, she couldn't take her eyes off the disembodied arm. 'We should get you back to Selene,' Elverda said.

'Not necessary,' he replied. 'I found the faulty circuit and repaired it. But I can't reattach the arm without your help.'

'Tell me what to do.'

He nodded gravely. 'One final test, first.'

Dorn picked up an oblong metal box, about the size of a hand-held remote control wand, and thumbed the keys on its face. The arm on the table top flexed slightly at the elbow. The fingers of the hand clutched and opened, clutched and opened. Elverda shuddered.

'The power readout is fine,' Dorn said, his voice flat and emotionless. Turning to Elverda, he put down the remote and said, 'Now let's see if we can get the arm back where it belongs.'

It was heavy, far heavier than she had expected it to be. Elverda could barely lift it. Dorn gripped it in his human right hand and held it steady for her.

'Put it flush against the shoulder socket,' he told her, 'then rotate it until it clicks into place. Please.'

With hands sweaty from the exertion Elverda guided the arm into its socket and heard the clear mechanical snap as the connectors locked.

Handing her a pencil-shaped probe, he said, 'Kindly

check each of the connectors. They're marked by blinking lights.'

Elverda worked the probe all the way around his shoulder. One by one the telltale lights winked out.

'Now for the acid test,' he said. Standing, he raised the arm over his head, then swung it in a full arc, flexing his fingers as he did so.

'It's fine,' said Dorn. She thought she heard a note of relief in his voice. 'Thank you very much.'

'De nada,' she murmured.

As they headed back toward the bridge Elverda asked, 'When it isn't working properly, do you feel . . . pain?'

'Something akin to pain,' he said. 'The circuits send electrical signals to the biocomputer that's linked to my brain. My conscious mind interprets those signals as . . .' he searched for a word, '. . . as a sort of dull ache. A discomfort, not the same as a pain in the organic side of my body.'

Elverda nodded as they stepped into the bridge. 'And the mechanical side is powered by a nuclear source?'

'It's well shielded,' he said. 'You don't have to worry about radiation.'

'I was wondering how long it will last,' she said as she sank gratefully into the command chair.

'It's only a small thermionic system,' said Dorn. 'It will need to be replaced in a hundred years or so.'

Elverda laughed. Humor from Dorn was rare.

The radar pinged. Suddenly alert, Elverda called up its display on the main screen. A tiny pinpoint of a gleam, artificially colored bright red by the computer. Near it, a slightly larger blip, which the computer painted in blue. It appeared slightly oblong to Elverda, even at this distance.

'We have a radar contact,' she said.

'I see,' Dorn answered.

Working the keyboard, Elverda overlaid a gridwork of navigational lines atop the radar image. Numbers came up automatically. They were twelve hours away from the contact, fourteen hours from the second blip, the location of the battle that was their destination. While most of the old battle sites were empty spaces, this location was centered on a five-kilometer-long asteroid; the callout on the screen labeled it as 66–059.

The asteroid was registered in the IAA files, Elverda saw. She called up its file photo: an ungainly oblong of rock, its lumpy surface strewn with boulders and smaller stones, dented here and there with craterlets. Ugly, she decided, like a face marred by hideous scars and pimples. It had been claimed by Astro Corporation years earlier. A battle had been fought over it; men and women had died for it. Now it rode silently through the vacuum of the Belt, alone, forgotten, as it had coasted through space for all the billions of years since the solar system had been created.

Not forgotten, Elverda told herself. One of the warriors who fought here has remembered you. One of the mercenary soldiers who fought other mercenaries here has returned as a priest to pay final tribute to those he killed.

Dorn leaned in over her shoulder. Elverda saw his reflection in the main screen, his prosthetic eye gleaming red as he studied the chart and the radar image beneath it.

'Sixty-six oh five nine,' Dorn read the asteroid's designation from the screen. 'I remember this battle. We were outnumbered, but we won.'

'What do you make of the other image?' she asked.

'Too far away to tell,' Dorn replied, 'although it must be fairly large to give a return at this distance.'

'Not a body, then?'

'Perhaps a cloud of debris.' He straightened up, then rubbed his chin of etched metal with his human fingers. 'But I would expect that a debris cloud would have expanded much farther than that in the time that's elapsed since the battle.'

'Could it be in orbit around the asteroid?' Elverda mused aloud. 'Held there by the rock's gravity?'

Dorn refused to speculate. 'We'll find out in twelve hours' time. While we wait, let's take a meal.'

Elverda smiled up at him. He's like a little boy sometimes: when there's nothing better to do, eat.

Cargo Ship *Pleiades*: Bridge

Like most of the deep-space vessels plying the Asteroid Belt, *Pleiades* was built on the circular plan of a wheel, so that its rotation could impart a feeling of gravity to its crew and passengers.

But on this flight, the vessel had no passengers and only one crew member. Victor Zacharias was flat on his back on the deck underneath the main control panel, cursing fluently, an electro-optical magnifier over one eye as he traced the microthin circuitry of the ship's control systems through the labyrinthine innards of the command consoles. Access panels and electronic modules were strewn across the plastic tiles of the deck around him. He had banged his head at least a half-dozen times, his knuckles were skinned, and his temper was fraying badly.

It wasn't enough to steal the ship; now he had to control it. By himself. So he was working, fuming, struggling to reconfigure the ship's control systems, to automate as much of them as possible and bring the rest of them together so that one man could operate all the controls from one console on the bridge.

It wasn't easy. Unlike his rickety old *Syracuse*, *Pleiades* had been designed to be operated by a crew of six. Cheena Madagascar could sit in her command chair like a queen and have her lackeys run the vessel while she did nothing more than utter commands. Victor didn't have lackeys: only himself.

He found himself wishing that he had Theo here to help him; even the teenager's clumsy efforts would have been some relief. That started him thinking about Pauline and Angela and the three of them alone on *Syracuse* drifting out to god knows where and . . . He squeezed his eyes shut. Stop it, he commanded himself. Stop it or you'll drive yourself crazy.

Hunger finally made him crawl out from under the consoles and climb stiffly to his feet, scratching at his sweaty beard. *Pleiades* was racing outward from Ceres under a full g acceleration. The ship's main wheel had ceased its rotation and all the compartments inside it had pivoted on their bearings to orient themselves properly to the acceleration. If Victor closed his eyes it felt as if he were standing on Earth.

'I'll cut the acceleration in an hour or so,' Victor said aloud as he headed for the galley. He was certain that no one was chasing after him. Cheena Madagascar was probably sputtering with anger, Big George was undoubtedly volcanic, but there was really nothing much that they could do. Send a ship after him? They'd have to be willing to spend the money for a ship and crew, and even then Victor had such a good lead on any potential pursuer that a chase would be fruitless.

Besides, he was running silent, emitting neither a tracking beacon nor telemetry reports on his condition. He didn't want to be found. Not yet.

*   *   *

It had been a tricky maneuver, hunkering down so close to the pitted, boulder-strewn surface of asteroid 66–059. *Viking* was almost as wide as the oblong, elongated rock's breadth. The bridge was absolutely silent as Yuan piloted the wheel-shaped vessel to within a few meters of the asteroid's grainy, dusty surface. It's like a computer game, he told himself as he worked the fingertip controls on the armrests of his command chair with practiced delicacy. Easy does it. Easy.

'Close enough,' Yuan breathed as he cut the ship's maneuvering jets. He saw that his officers had their eyes locked on him, then realized his face was beaded with perspiration.

'We'll rotate with the rock,' he said. 'If they probe with radar they won't be able to distinguish us against the normal backscatter.'

'Their resolution will get better as they come closer,' Tamara countered, from her comm console.

'By then it'll be too late for them,' Yuan snapped.

Koop nodded slowly, but the expression on his face said, *I hope you're right.*

Yuan's other two ships had dispersed to a distance of an hour's flight, at one g acceleration, and gone silent. No communications now, Yuan told himself. Now we sit and wait, quiet as a tiger crouching in the reeds by a waterhole.

'Computer shows we're drifting slightly,' the navigation officer said, almost in a whisper.

'Maybe we should grapple the rock,' Koop suggested.

Yuan shook his head. 'No. I want to be able to jump out at an instant's notice.' To the nav officer he asked, 'How bad's the drift?'

'One point four meters per minute. We can correct for it, captain.'

'Cold jets only. I don't want to give them any signature that they can pick up.'

'Yes, sir.'

'Better get yourselves a meal while we're waiting,' Yuan said. Then he added, 'One at a time. Fix a tray in the galley and bring it back here.'

Tamara got up from her comm console. 'I'll make a tray for you, captain.'

Yuan suppressed a pleased grin. 'Do that,' he said.

The human half of Dorn's face was frowning as he studied the image on *Hunter*'s main screen.

Sitting beside him on the bridge's padded rolling chair, Elverda said, 'It looks like bodies. Five . . . no, six bodies.'

'How could they still be so close to the asteroid?' Dorn asked. 'The battle was more than four years ago. They should have dispersed far into space, like the others we've recovered.'

Elverda shrugged her frail shoulders. 'Does it matter? The bodies are there.'

'Yes,' he murmured. Tapping on the keyboard before him, he called up the velocity vectors of the images on the screen.

'They all have the same velocity,' Elverda saw.

'Within a hair's breadth.'

'Is that normal?'

'If they were all blasted into space at the same time, by the same explosion.'

Elverda felt a chill creeping along her spine. There is something eerie about this, she thought. We've never seen a group of bodies clustered together this way.

'If you multiply their velocities by the length of time since the battle was fought,' Dorn said, 'they should be thousands of kilometers from the asteroid. Tens of thousands of kilometers.'

'But they're not. They're here.'

'Which means that they were placed here recently. Perhaps only a few days ago.'

'Could there have been another battle here?'

Dorn sank back in the command chair, his eyes never leaving the radar image on the screen with its superimposed vector numbers. Elverda looked at him, waiting for him to make a decision.

'I've sworn to recover all the bodies that have been left drifting through the Belt,' he said, as much to himself as to her.

'Humphries knows that,' she whispered.

'This could be a trap, then.'

'Do you think . . . ?'

'There's one way to find out,' Dorn said, tapping the keyboard to call up the propulsion program.

Into The Trap

'He's accelerating!' the nav officer shouted.

'I can see that,' Yuan said testily as he leaned forward in his command chair so hard that the meal tray slid off his lap and clattered to the deck.

'He's turning away,' Koop said.

'Power up,' Yuan commanded. *'Now!'*

'He didn't fall into your trap,' said Tamara. 'He's too smart for that.'

Feeling the surge of acceleration as *Viking* climbed away from the asteroid, Yuan said, 'It doesn't matter. He's close enough for us to get him.'

Fingers flicking on the keyboards set into his armrests, Yuan called up the weapons display on the bridge's main screen. 'Comm, tell the other ships to power up and converge on the target's vector.'

'Yessir,' Tamara said.

Yuan smiled as he peered at the main screen. The renegade's ship was nothing but an electronic blip, accelerating away from him. But he knew how to play this game. His other two ships would close the trap while he moved in for the kill.

To his first mate he commanded, 'Koop, activate the laser.'

The big Hawaiian pecked at his console's keys. 'Activating weapon system, sir.'

'I'll handle the weapons officer duty,' Yuan said. 'You're my backup, Koop.'

'Backup. Right.'

Yuan couldn't see Koop's face, but he heard the resignation in his voice. Maybe it was resentment, he thought. The first mate was ordinarily the weapons officer in battle. But Yuan wanted that task for himself. That's where the fun is. The chase and then the kill.

Dorn had swung *Hunter* into a wide turn away from the asteroid. Sitting beside him, Elverda watched the image of the asteroid as their ship's cameras swiveled to keep it in view. Off in the distance behind the rock she could see the faint gleam of the cluster of bodies floating in the emptiness.

And then a ship rose up from behind the rock, a big vessel that radiated power, purpose, menace.

'I'll have to increase our acceleration,' Dorn said, a tendril of concern in his voice. 'You'd better get to your compartment and into your bunk.'

'I'll stay here,' Elverda replied, 'with you.'

He turned his head to look at her, but said nothing. His prosthetic hand pushed the throttle forward. Elverda sensed nothing at first, but then inexorably the thrust built up and she felt herself sinking into the chair's liquid-filled cushions.

'We have a chance,' Dorn said, 'if we can accelerate quickly enough. He's starting from a standstill.'

'He was hiding behind the asteroid,' she said, puffing out the words.

'Clever. But we can outrun him.'

'If he's alone.'

He turned toward her again. 'Yes. If he's alone.'

Yuan's two other ships were designated *Viking 2* and *Viking 3*. They were smaller than *Viking* itself, each crewed by only three people.

Yuan bared his teeth in a feral grin as his main screen showed their quarry's vector racing away from the asteroid – and toward his other two ships, which were now accelerating to an intercept point on the renegade's extended track.

The screen was showing a holographic view now, allowing Yuan to see the game in three dimensions. It's not a game, he told himself. This is real. This is what Humphries is going to pay that bonus for. But he couldn't help smiling grimly as he watched the three-dimensional view. It's so simple. I played more complex games when I was a kid. This one's easy.

'He's increasing his distance from us,' the navigation officer said. Then she added, 'Sir.'

'For the moment,' Yuan murmured. 'We'll catch up with him.'

Tamara said, 'Two and three report they're on course to intercept.'

'I can see that,' said Yuan, without taking his eyes from the main screen.

'Do you have any further orders for them?'

Despite his focus on the screen, Yuan noted that Tamara did not address him properly.

'Officer Vishinsky,' he said. 'You will use correct military respect when speaking to your captain. Is that understood?'

'Understood, captain,' she replied instantly.

'Good.' *The whole crew knows we're sleeping together,* he said to himself. *Can't have them thinking that our sex life gives her any special privileges. Can't allow discipline to get sloppy.*

Glancing at her, he saw that Tamara was sitting rigidly at the comm console, looking neither right nor left. *You don't have to call me captain in bed,* he said to her silently. Then he turned his attention back to the game that was unfolding on the main screen.

'We're outrunning him,' Elverda said. It came out as a gasp, almost. The acceleration was weighing her down, making her bones ache, her chest almost too heavy to speak.

'Get into a suit,' Dorn said.

'Why? We're pulling away—'

Dorn raised his arm and pointed. Two new radar images were gleaming on the main screen.

'He isn't alone,' said Dorn.

'We're trapped!'

'It looks that way.' But his fingers were playing on the console keys. 'I'm cutting our acceleration. Get into a suit, please.'

'What about you?'

'You first.'

194

Elverda struggled to her feet. The acceleration made her feel heavy, as if her legs were made of lead. But lead wouldn't hurt so much, she said to herself. She took three steps toward the hatch, then felt a red-hot searing pain flash through her chest. She turned back, groped for the chair and sank into it again.

'I can't . . .' she panted.

'If I cut the acceleration much lower they'll catch up to us in less than an hour.'

'Do what . . . you need . . . to do,' Elverda said through teeth gritted by pain.

'Strap in, then.'

She fumbled for the restraint straps from the seat's back and buckled them across her chest and lap. The pain was getting worse, flaring down her arm now, even along her jaw. Her thoughts swimming, she wondered if the chair's wheels were locked into their grooves on the deck. I should check that they're locked. But she could barely move her head.

'They'll be firing at us soon,' Dorn said. His voice was flat, as unemotional as ice.

Elverda could feel her heart clenching beneath her ribs. How many g's are we pulling? she asked silently.

The ship rocked. Red warning lights sprang up on the console.

'Good shooting,' Dorn muttered.

Elverda's vision was blurring. The radar images on the main screen looked like streaks to her, arrows hurtling toward her. It was all going gray and hazy.

Through the fog of agony she saw Dorn turn toward

her, the human side of his face twisted with sudden alarm.

As if from a great distance she heard Dorn's voice: 'Cease firing. We have a sick woman on board. She needs immediate medical assistance. We surrender.'

Attack Ship *Viking*: Bridge

'A sick woman?' Yuan echoed, startled by Dorn's plea, and shaken even more by the sight of the cyborg's half-machine face on his main screen.

'It's a ruse,' said Tamara.

Dorn's voice, taut with stress, came through the speaker again. 'I have Elverda Apacheta with me. I think she's having a heart attack.'

'He's slowing down,' the nav officer reported. 'Two and three have him boxed in.'

'They're requesting permission to fire,' Tamara reported.

'Permission denied,' Yuan snapped. 'Who the hell is Elverda whatever-her-name? Sounds familiar, but—'

'The sculptress,' Koop said. 'She's famous.'

Radiating suspicion, Tamara protested, 'What would a famous artist be doing on that killer's ship? It's a trick. It has to be a trick.'

Yuan's mind was racing.

'Please!' Dorn urged. 'She's dying!'

'Let me see her,' Yuan said to the screen.

The view enlarged to show a half-unconscious woman sitting beside the cyborg. She looked very old. Her face was gray and sheened with perspiration, her eyes half closed, her mouth hanging open slackly.

'I've seen pictures of her,' Koop said, his voice rising eagerly. 'That looks like Elverda Apacheta.'

'But what's she doing—'

'You can't just let her die,' Koop urged. 'She's famous! It'd start a shitstorm if anybody found out we let her die.'

If anybody found out, Yuan thought. Humphries's orders are to kill the renegade quietly. No fuss. No news reports. He's just to be erased, eliminated. And his accomplices with him.

But a worlds-famous artist? If we let her die how can it be kept a secret? *Somebody* must know she's out here in the Belt.

Tamara said, 'I can message headquarters for orders on how to proceed.'

'It'd take an hour or more to get a reply,' Yuan muttered, as much to himself as to his crew. 'She'd be dead by then.'

With a slight lift of her shoulders, Tamara replied, 'Then the problem would be solved, wouldn't it?'

He glared at her.

'Sir,' she added belatedly.

Grimacing with a responsibility he never wanted, Yuan decided, 'Take her on board.'

'Sir?' Tamara asked.

'Now,' he snapped. 'Do it now.'

Koop smiled brightly, and jabbed a finger into the nav officer's shoulder. She began pecking out a rendezvous course.

To the screen, Yuan said, 'We're going to rendez-vous and give your companion immediate medical care. How many others are on your vessel?'

'Only the two of us,' said Dorn.

'Very well. Consider yourself my prisoner, then. No tricks or we'll execute you both.'

'No tricks,' Dorn repeated. Then he added, 'Thank you, captain.'

Yuan sat alone in his compartment peering at the flow of information about Elverda Apacheta that was scrolling down his screen. The half-dead woman they had taken aboard was indeed the famous sculptress: her face matched the computer file's image and her DNA matched her medical record.

He called up images of *The Rememberer*, the asteroid that this woman had carved into a memorial to the history of her Andean people. He saw the ionospheric paintings she had produced, making artificial aurorae high in Earth's atmosphere with electron guns to paint ephemeral pictures that glowed with delicate shimmering colors briefly at twilight, then faded as the Sun went below the horizon: the *Virgin of the Andes*, the serenely beautiful *Heavenly Pastures*, the *Star Children*.

What is she doing in a ship deep in the Belt with a mass murderer? Dorik Harbin had come aboard *Viking* peacefully and admitted that he was the man who had wiped out the *Chrysalis* habitat. Yuan's crew stood in awe of the cyborg, their hands on their sidearms as they marched the half-machine to one of the ship's empty storage bays and locked him in.

Yuan had sent a message to HSS headquarters on the Moon, informing them that he had captured Dorik Harbin and that the killer had been accompanied by Elverda Apacheta. Now, as he waited for their reply, he wondered all over again why Humphries wanted Harbin executed in the deep darkness of the Belt, rather than bringing him back to civilization and taking the credit for tracking down the criminal.

A gentle knock on his door startled Yuan out of his thoughts. He touched a key and his screen showed it was Tamara out in the passageway.

'Come in,' he said sharply, without getting up from his desk chair.

She slid the door back and stepped in to his compartment, a sheet of plastic flimsy in her hand, a self-satisfied little smile on her delicately boned face.

'Headquarters' answer,' she said, handing the sheet to him. 'It's encrypted. For your eyes only.'

Yuan took the sheet and slid it into his scanner. Tamara turned to leave.

'Hold on a minute,' he said.

She turned and stood framed by the open doorway.

'Shut the door.'

She slid it closed and turned back to him, her smile a little more tentative now.

Without asking her to sit down, Yuan said, 'You've been too informal with me on the bridge.'

'You told me so, in front of the others.'

'Discipline in small things is important. I can't have the crew think I'm showing favoritism toward you.'

Her brows arched.

'What we do in the privacy of this compartment is one thing. On the bridge is another.'

'I see.'

'I hope you do.'

The scanner had finished its decrypting task; its yellow READY light was blinking. Yuan swiveled his chair to face the display screen. Tamara made no move to leave.

He looked up at her over his shoulder. 'You already know what this says, don't you?'

She didn't reply, but she didn't look surprised by his question, either.

'Headquarters assigned you to watch me?'

'Mr. Humphries assigned me to watch you. He considers this mission extremely important.'

'Humphries himself?'

'Yes. The message is from him, personally.'

Yuan was surprised that the news didn't startle him. He realized that he'd half expected something like this. Wheels within wheels. A labyrinth for the lab rats to run through.

He told the screen, 'Display message, please.'

The letters glowed bright red against a yellow background: ELIMINATE THEM BOTH IMMEDIATELY.

Attack Ship *Viking*: Infirmary

Elverda's eyes fluttered open. A blank and featureless ceiling hung low over her, a pale cream color. She smelled the faint tang of disinfectant, heard a soft beeping sound. For long moments she lay still, trying to work up the courage to see if she could move her head. Slowly she realized that the pain was gone. Her entire body felt relaxed, languid.

Then she stiffened with the memory of her last waking moments. The agony flaming through her. And Dorn's words, tense and urgent: '*Cease firing. We have a sick woman on board. She needs immediate medical assistance. We surrender.*'

He surrendered. He slowed the ship and surrendered to our pursuers because he wanted to save me. Have they already killed him? Are they going to kill me?

She turned her head and saw that she was in a hospital of some kind. More likely the infirmary aboard the ship that was chasing us. Her bed was surrounded on three sides by blank off-white partitions. The fourth side was a metal bulkhead, with a bank of sensors stacked against it; they were making the beeping sounds she heard.

Tentatively, Elverda tried to lift her head off the pillow. No pain. No dizziness. The beeping changed its tone slightly. She let her head sink back again into the softness of the pillows, too weak to even think about sitting up.

One of the partitions slid back and a bulky, blocky man stepped in. Suddenly the area was overcrowded. He was dressed in light gray coveralls, with marks of rank on his cuffs. His face was square, heavy-set, his skin a light brown, almost golden. Polynesian? Elverda wondered.

'You're awake,' he said, in a surprisingly light tenor.

'Yes.' Elverda realized that her throat was very dry, rasping.

'I'm Kahalu'u Kaupakulu'a,' he said, smiling gently. 'Don't bother to try to pronounce it. Just call me Koop. Everybody calls me Koop.'

'You must be the ship's medical officer.'

'First mate,' he corrected. 'We don't carry a medic.'

'I see. Where's Dorn?'

'Dorn?'

'The man who was with me. What—'

'He's Dorik Harbin, isn't he? We have his files. Even with half his body replaced by machinery he has the same DNA.'

'He was Dorik Harbin. Now he is Dorn.'

Koop shook his head. 'Whatever he calls himself, he's locked up, waiting for the captain to make up his mind about him.'

'Don't hurt him! He's been hurt enough already.'

'Not my call, Ms. Apacheta.'

'You know my name.'

'I've seen *The Rememberer*. When I was a teenager. It knocked me out.'

She decided it was a compliment. 'Thank you.'

'We injected stem cell activation factor into your heart. It's repairing the damage.'

'How did you know . . . ?'

'Med program. We have an up-to-date diagnostic program in the computer, and a good stock of medical supplies.'

'I see.'

'It's not a total fix, y'know. You oughtta see a specialist when you get back to Earth. Or Selene, whatever.'

Elverda nodded, knowing that it would be many months before she returned to the Moon, if ever, and she could never face the heavy gravity of Earth.

Glancing up at the sensors lining one side of her bed, Koop said, 'Seems to be workin'. You should be able to get outta bed by tomorrow.'

'But Dorn? Dorik Harbin? What's going to happen to him?'

Koop shrugged his heavy shoulders. 'That's for the captain to decide.'

Captain Kao Yuan stared at his prisoner. The crew had locked Dorik Harbin in an emptied storage locker. The man had come aboard *Viking* peacefully. Yuan had ordered a thorough search of his ship, *Hunter*. No one else was aboard. No weapons of any kind. Just ordinary stocks of food and replacement parts. Nobody but him and the old woman.

Now Yuan stood in the open doorway of the storage locker. Two of his biggest crewmen stood out in the passageway, sidearms strapped to their hips. Dorik Harbin stood in one corner, looking back at him.

Yuan felt distinctly uneasy. This isn't a man, his mind told him: he's more machine than human. Half his face is metal, etched metal covers the top of his head like a skullcap, one arm is prosthetic, and one leg. Does he have balls? What are his insides like?

'You can come in,' said the half-machine. 'I won't attack you.' His voice was deep, calm. It made Yuan think of the huge lake he used to swim in when he was a child, before the greenhouse warming dried it out.

Yuan stepped fully inside the storage locker. It was small, meant to house medical supplies. The crew had emptied its shelves and moved the supplies to an unused bed space in the infirmary, where the old woman was being kept.

'You admit you are Dorik Harbin?' Yuan asked.

The lips on the half-face bent slightly. 'I was Dorik Harbin. Now I am Dorn.'

'You are the man who destroyed the *Chrysalis* habitat?'

'I am the beast responsible for the *Chrysalis* slaughter, yes.'

Yuan licked his lips nervously. What more is there to ask? He admits it. My orders are to kill him.

'The woman who was with me,' the cyborg said slowly, as if he had to ponder each word. 'She had nothing to do with Dorik Harbin's crime. I did not meet her until years after that.'

'Why is she with you?'

'I wonder.'

'Is she really a famous artist?'

'She is Elverda Apacheta, yes.'

'What made her come out to the Belt with you? For that matter, what in the name of hell are you doing out here?'

'You don't want to know.'

'Don't get smart with me! I'm the captain of this vessel. I can have you executed like that!' Yuan snapped his fingers.

'And I can kill you, too, if I choose.' Dorn's prosthetic hand flashed through the air and grabbed one of the empty storage shelves, ripped it out of the bulkhead and crushed it in his metal fingers.

Yuan jumped back. The crewmen pulled their pistols from their holsters.

'Relax, gentlemen,' said Dorik Harbin, scorn dripping from his tone. 'That was merely a demonstration. I can make threats too.'

Yuan wished he'd carried a gun with him.

'I have no intention of resisting whatever sentence you pass on me,' Dorik Harbin went on. 'But I would like your assurance that Elverda Apacheta will not be harmed. She has not done anything to be punished for.'

'Then why's she with you?' Yuan insisted.

The cyborg fell silent for several endless moments. Yuan felt its eyes boring into him: one human eye, dark, pained; the other an unblinking red, like a laser.

'I chose my words poorly a few seconds ago,' Dorik Harbin said. 'It would be in your best interests not to know why she decided to accompany me.'

'My best interests?'

'Yes.'

'You'll have to explain that.'

Again the cyborg hesitated before answering. 'My mission is to retrieve the bodies of those who were killed in the war and left to drift alone, unwanted, uncared for.'

'Retrieve the dead bodies?'

'And give each of them a proper death rite.'

Yuan stared at him. 'That's what you've been doing?'

'Yes.'

It was impossible to read his half-metal face. Yuan started to ask, 'But why—'

Dorik Harbin held up his human hand, stopping his question in mid-sentence. 'Again, it would not be in your best interests to probe too deeply.'

And Yuan believed him.

Attack Ship *Viking*:
Captain's Quarters

'You believed him?' Tamara asked. 'You swallowed his ludicrous story? You let him get away with this mysterious tripe?'

Sitting on the edge of his double-sized bunk, Yuan nodded unhappily. 'I didn't want to believe him, but I really think he's telling the truth.'

Tamara Vishinsky stood by the compartment's closed door. She was in her off duty coveralls, with the front unzipped enough to show considerable cleavage. Ordinarily Yuan would have found this enticing, suggestive. Not now.

Planting her hands on her slim hips, Tamara scorned, 'You actually believe that he's wandering through the Belt looking for bodies of dead mercenaries? It's a lie, and a pitiful one at that.'

Scratching his head, Yuan shot back, 'What else could he be doing out here? Going from one battle site to the other?'

Tamara said, 'What else indeed? Why don't we find that out before we get rid of him? He might know things that would be valuable to us.'

'Us?' Yuan asked. 'Us, meaning you and me? Us,

meaning the crew of this task force? Or us, meaning you and Humphries?'

She started to answer, caught herself, then replied, 'He's searching for something out here in the Belt. I'd like to know what it is. Wouldn't you?'

'What in the name of all the dragons in hell could be out here?'

'That's what I want to find out.'

'My orders are to kill him. Immediately. You know that.'

'But we can interrogate him first.'

Yuan shook his head. 'He won't be easy to pry information out of.'

'Maybe the woman will be easier.'

'No!' Yuan snapped. 'It's bad enough we have to kill her.'

Tamara walked to the bed and sat down beside him, close enough for their shoulders to touch.

'They're out here in the Belt searching for something,' she whispered in his ear. 'It must be something valuable, or else why would they be doing it? It might be something that could make us rich.'

'Buried treasure?' Yuan sneered.

'Information is the basis of wealth,' Tamara purred. 'Information that we can sell or trade or use to make us rich.'

Yuan smelled the faint perfume she wore. He knew the places on her body where she daubed her skin with the scent.

'He says he's searching for bodies,' he muttered, 'to give them proper last rites.'

'But what is he *really* doing?'

'Do you actually think he's up to something else?'

'He's got to be,' she said.

'I . . . I don't know.'

'Let me interrogate him. We're going to eliminate them both anyway. Let's find out what they've been doing, first.'

'I don't like it,' Yuan said.

'I'll take care of it. You can question the woman and be as gentle as you like.'

'Let me talk to her first. Maybe I can get what we want out of her.'

Tamara got to her feet and headed for the door. 'All right,' she said. 'You do that.'

And she left Yuan sitting on his bunk, alone.

'Whatever did you do to Martin Humphries to make him want you dead?' Yuan asked.

He had invited Elverda to his quarters for dinner. And some questioning. She had come hesitantly, wondering how well her heart had been repaired. But aside from a slight breathlessness when she first got out of bed, she felt all right. She thought she'd felt her heart skip a beat or two when she'd first stood up, but she put that down to her imagination.

Elverda looked up from the salad taken from the hydroponic tank that Yuan had built for the crew.

'It might be better if you didn't know,' she said softly.

Yuan studied the aged sculptress. Her face was seamed with years, her hair white and cut short: poorly, he thought. Yet there was strength in that imperious face, natural dignity in the firm set of her frail shoulders beneath the woven robe she wore.

'Mr. Humphries is a bad enemy,' Yuan said, trying to keep his tone casual. 'He has a long reach.'

'And a longer memory,' said Elverda. Then she took a forkful of the salad. 'Delicious. I missed fresh vegetables. We had nothing but prepackaged meals and supplement pills aboard *Hunter*.'

Yuan saw that she was trying to change the subject and decided to go along with her, for the moment.

'What were you doing on your ship?'

She looked at him from across the little table with onyx eyes of endless depths. 'Didn't Dorn tell you?'

'He said you were searching for dead bodies.'

She nodded. 'Mercenaries killed in the war and left to drift through space.'

'This . . . person you call Dorn, his real name is Dorik Harbin.'

'His name once was Dorik Harbin,' Elverda conceded. 'But he has changed his life, his entire personality. So he's changed his name, as well.'

Yuan leaned back in his chair. 'Do you expect me to believe that you were searching for bodies? Like a pair of ghouls?'

'That's what we were doing,' Elverda replied. A small smile bent her thin lips slightly. 'Not like ghouls, though. More like priests. Missionaries, perhaps.'

Feeling his brows knit in a frown that he didn't want to display, Yuan said, 'Mr. Humphries's orders are to execute you both.'

'I'm not surprised.'

'Which brings us back to my first question: What did you do to make him so angry with you?'

'He's not angry. He's afraid.'

'Of what?'

Elverda seemed to think about that question for a moment. Then she replied, 'He's afraid of himself, I believe.'

Yuan picked up his napkin, started to daub his lips, but instead threw it onto the table in frustration.

'This is getting us nowhere!'

Elverda said nothing.

'I want to know why Humphries is out to get you,' Yuan said, his voice rising. 'If you won't tell me, I'll have to pry it out of Harbin.'

'Dorn.'

'Don't play games with me, woman.'

She put down her fork. 'Captain Yuan, have you considered the possibility that if you knew why Humphries wants to kill us, then he might want to kill you, too?'

Yuan blinked.

'In fact,' Elverda went on, 'I would imagine that the chances are very good that once you do kill us, Humphries will have you murdered as well.'

Yuan's jaw dropped open.

Attack Ship *Viking*: Communications Center

Tamara Vishinsky decided that the soundproofed comm center was the best place to interrogate Dorik Harbin. The booth was small, but it was adjacent to the bridge, and once its door was shut no one could see or hear what was going on inside it. So she had Koop and the burliest of the crewmen strap Harbin firmly into the chair while she searched through the ship's medical stores for the necessary drugs.

Now Harbin sat in the narrow booth facing her, his arms pinned tightly, his booted feet clamped to the deck. He had not struggled against being bound; he had not resisted in any way.

Standing in front of him, with a shelf full of hypodermic sprayguns at her side, Tamara eyed the cyborg. Harbin seemed impassive, the human half of his face as expressionless as the etched metal half.

'Now then,' she began coolly, 'do you expect me to believe that you have been wandering through the Belt looking for the bodies of mercenaries killed in the wars?'

'That's the truth,' said Harbin. His voice was a deep, flat and calm baritone.

'You call yourself Dorn. Why?'

'I am a different person from Dorik Harbin. Suicide and death are life-changing experiences.' His lips did not curve in the slightest; he gave no indication that he appreciated the irony in his statement.

'You tried to kill yourself.'

'And failed.'

'When did you decide to search for the dead?'

For the first time, he hesitated. 'After another life-altering experience.'

'What was that?'

Harbin stared at her steadily. Tamara felt uneasy under the gaze of those eyes, one human, one artificial, both burning intently.

'It would be better if I didn't tell you.'

'That's what you said to Captain Yuan.'

'Yes, it is.'

She picked up one of the hyposprays. 'I'm not satisfied with that answer.'

His shoulders surged slightly against the restraining straps. Tamara reflexively flinched back, banged her hip against the booth's bulkhead. He can't break those straps, she told herself. Besides, there's an armed crewman outside and all three of the bridge officers on duty.

But Harbin seemed to relax. 'I'm thinking of your welfare, not my own. What you want to know could put you in danger.'

'Danger? How?'

'Martin Humphries.'

'I work for Martin Humphries,' Tamara said. 'I report to him personally.'

'I've met him. I've seen into his soul.'

Tamara slapped the flesh side of his face. 'This mystic mumbo jumbo is getting us nowhere. What was the life-altering experience you mentioned? What do you know about Martin Humphries?'

'I know that he's capable of murdering you and the entire crew of this ship if it suits his purposes.'

'Why would he do that?'

Harbin shook his head slightly, the barest movement from side to side.

'Very well,' Tamara said, holding the spraygun before his eyes. 'If you won't tell me voluntarily . . .'

'Psychotropic drugs may have unforeseen reactions with my body chemistry,' Harbin said calmly.

'You mean pain?'

'I mean . . . unforeseen. I warn you—'

'*You* warn *me*?' She began to push up the sleeve on his human arm.

Harbin grimaced as she held the spraygun against his bare biceps and pressed its activator button. There was a slight hiss.

'Now then,' she said, removing the emptied cylinder from the syringe, 'we'll wait a few moments for it to take effect. And if that dosage doesn't work, we'll go higher. Or try something stronger.'

Harbin's metal chin sank to his chest. He muttered something almost too low for Tamara to understand: 'Stay dead.'

He could close his human eye but with his arms bound behind him he couldn't reach the prosthetic eye to dial it shut. Still, the scene before him began to swirl and shift. He saw the artifact again, glowing too brightly to look at directly. An alien construct, blazing brighter than a star, burning straight into his soul.

Tamara thought he'd passed out. She lifted his chin. The metal felt cold in her fingers. Harbin opened his eye and stared at her ferociously.

'Still defiant?' She turned for the shelf of medications.

'Don't,' he warned.

She took his word as a plea for mercy.

'What was your second life-altering experience?' she demanded, picking up another hypospray.

If I tell her and Humphries learns of it . . .

'What made you come out here to search for dead bodies?' she demanded.

Dorn heard her voice, but it was distorted, echoing weirdly in his mind. He tried to say, 'I don't want to hurt you,' but his tongue was too swollen and dry to get the words out.

Tamara jammed the spraygun against his bare flesh and pressed it home. Harbin's head snapped back; his whole body seemed to spasm, arching against the straps that held him pinned to the chair.

'Harbin,' she said sharply. 'What happened that made you decide to search through the Belt? What are you really doing out here? You can't expect me to believe—'

He saw the artifact, looked into its molten glowing heart and saw the faces of the dead. A woman screaming as she clutched her baby to her. A harmless old man, his face distorted with the sudden realization that he was about to die. Children. Men. Women. All the people of *Chrysalis*, staring at him in terror. Some of them pointed at him. Some of them pleaded with him. All of them died.

I killed them, Harbin knew. And before them, years and years before. The people of the village where he'd grown up. Burn their homes. Shoot them as they come running out, in flames. Kill them all. All.

Tamara saw that he was drifting into unconsciousness. She slapped him again, harder.

'What made you change your name?'

'The artifact.' His voice seemed to come from a million kilometers away.

'Artifact? What artifact?'

'Alien. Humphries saw it. Went insane.'

'Martin Humphries? Alien artifact?' She was suddenly breathless. 'Where? When?'

He smiled: a strange, twisted, brutal smile. 'Now I've killed you, too.'

'Talk sense, damn you!'

I am Dorik Harbin, he said to himself. I have killed thousands. I am death.

He growled like a feral beast, looking up at her, both eyes glaring. His mechanical arm yanked free of the restraints, popping the straps like ribbons of straw. Tamara backed away, hit the bulkhead, turned in blind panic and fumbled with the locked door.

Harbin rose to his feet, pulled his boots from the floor clamps and grabbed her by the hair with his human hand. She screamed uselessly in the sound-proof chamber.

His face mere centimeters from hers, its human half twisted into a mask of fury, he snarled, 'You've unleashed the monster.'

He threw her against the chair. With his prosthetic arm he smashed the door of the booth open, knocking the startled guard on the other side halfway across the bridge. Harbin stepped through the suddenly open doorway. The three officers on the bridge jumped to their feet. He grabbed the nearest one by the jaw and lifted him off his feet; bones snapped audibly and the man screeched in agony. Throwing him to the floor, Harbin saw the half-stunned guard on the deck groping for the pistol in his holster.

Harbin turned toward the guard, who pulled the laser pistol free and fired squarely at his chest. The laser pulse burned through Harbin's shirt and splashed off the metal of his torso. The fabric of the shirt smoldered as Harbin leaped on the guard like a pouncing lion, ripped the gun from his hand and flung it across the bridge. He took a handful of the guard's hair and bashed his head against the deck plates.

On his feet again, he pounded the control console. Metal bent, glass shattered. He reached for the woman standing frozen in shock, tossed her across the bridge, grabbed the next man by the shoulder and smashed his face into the control console. Blood spurted. He ripped the command chair out of its deck clasps and threw it against the main display screen. All in a blur of raging power.

Tamara staggered to the ruptured door of the comm booth, her eyes wide, her jaw slack.

'You!' Harbin shouted, pointing at her with his human arm. 'You!'

She froze, hands gripping the doorway's sides. For an instant no one moved, no one made a sound. Then Harbin turned and punched the wall panel that controlled the hatch that led off the bridge. The hatch slid smoothly open and he ducked through and lurched down the passageway, leaving the bridge in a shambles, its officers stunned and bleeding.

Kao Yuan had holed up in his quarters. He wanted no part of Tamara's interrogation of their prisoner. My prisoner, he reminded himself. But she's got the upper hand. She reports straight to Humphries himself. I'm just the captain of this ship, the commander of this little task force. She probably sleeps with Humphries when she's back at headquarters.

He heard a muffled roar, then thumps and heavy banging and screams of agony. Yuan jumped out of his bunk and slid his door open just as Harbin came boiling up the passageway from the bridge.

He managed to say, 'Hey!' before Harbin whacked him on the forehead with the heel of his human hand, knocking Yuan backwards to crash painfully into his bunk and slide to the deck.

His head spinning, Yuan pulled himself to his feet and stumbled to the bridge. It was a disaster area: consoles smashed, officers on their knees groaning and bleeding. He ripped my command chair out of the fucking deck! Yuan screamed silently.

'He's gone amok!' Tamara gasped, staggering to him and collapsing into his arms.

Yuan couldn't suppress a grim smile of satisfaction.

He helped her to one of the still functional chairs, then leaned on the intercom button. 'General alert! General alert! Our prisoner is loose and extremely dangerous. Arm yourselves and hunt him down. Use whatever force necessary to subdue him. I repeat, he is extremely dangerous! Use whatever level of force necessary to subdue him, including lethal force.'

Attack Ship *Viking*: Infirmary

They had not bothered to assign Elverda quarters of her own; she was still housed in the infirmary. From her bed she heard the captain's frantic warning over the ship's intercom.

Their prisoner? she thought. He means Dorn!

'Lethal force is authorized,' the captain was repeating.

'He's a maniac! Don't take any chances with him!'

Elverda got up from the bed. She had been drowsing but now she was entirely awake, alert, alarmed. They'll kill him, she realized. God knows what's happened.

Pulling her robe from the closet by the bed, Elverda rushed out into the passageway. It was empty and silent.

What's happened? she wondered. What did they do to him?

The captain ought to know, she reasoned. He'd be up on the bridge, most likely. She headed toward the bridge, using the maps displayed on the wall screens along the passageways. Crewmen ran past her, strapping holsters to their hips, their faces strained with apprehension. They ignored her as they raced down the passageway.

When she got to the bridge, she found Captain Yuan standing in the midst of chaos. Equipment was smashed, crew members were writhing on the floor with others bending over them, spraying bandages on them. Koop was tenderly lifting one of the women officers to a sitting position, she saw.

'Captain,' Elverda called, stepping across shattered shards of glass and plastic toward him.

'Get back in the infirmary,' Yuan snapped. 'We've got a madman on our hands.'

'Don't hurt him,' Elverda pleaded.

'Don't hurt *him*?' Yuan spread his arms in a broad, sweeping gesture. 'Look what's he's done here!'

'What did you do to him?'

The captain glanced at a dark-haired woman sitting huddled on one of the serviceable chairs. She looked pale with shock.

'He's hiding somewhere on my ship. We've got to catch him before he does more damage. Before he kills somebody.'

'Let me go to him,' Elverda said. 'I can talk to him, calm him down.'

'He's insane,' said the dark-haired woman. 'A homicidal maniac.'

Elverda hated her instantaneously. 'Did he kill anyone?'

'Not because he didn't try.'

'He could have snapped your neck like a twig,' Elverda said. 'You must have done something to set him off.'

'Those damned drugs,' Yuan muttered.

'Drugs? *Madre de dios*, you didn't give him drugs, did you?'

Again Yuan looked toward the dark-haired woman. She would not meet his eyes.

'I've got to find him before one of your crew kills him,' she said, heading back toward the hatch.

'Or before he kills one of my crew, more likely,' Yuan shouted after her.

Dorn sat hunched on the deck plates next to the thrumming power generator, his head sunk in his hands.

How close to the surface lurks the beast, he was saying to himself, over and over. How close. How close.

Just beneath the surface lies the monster. You thought you'd buried him deep, but the drugs brought him back. One little dose and all your discipline cracked like an eggshell.

He looked up bleakly, seeing nothing but his own misery.

Was it really the drugs? Maybe that was just an excuse, a justification to allow the monster out of his cage.

It felt good to be free! He shuddered at the realization of it. It felt good to smash and rage and let the fury boil out. To scatter them. To break their bones. To see the terror on their faces.

He pounded both his fists on the metal deck plates. I'll never be free of him! I'll never be rid of the beast. He wanted to cry but he had no tears.

He knew what he should do. Get to your feet, go out and meet them. Let them shoot you. Finish it, once and for all.

But something within him held him fast. A mocking voice in his head laughed bitterly. For all your talk of death, you cling to your miserable life. You know you deserve to die, but you're not willing to face it. Not again. Once was enough for you. Beneath all the fury and violence is the ultimate cowardice.

I killed myself once, he said to the voice. I tried to atone. They wouldn't let me die. They wouldn't let me pay for my crimes. They want men like me. They need killers in their employ.

Unbidden, a quatrain of Khayyám came to his mind:

Up from Earth's Centre through the Seventh Gate
I rose, and on the Throne of Saturn sate,
And many Knots unravel'd by the Road;
But not the Knot of Human Death and Fate.

Human death and fate, he repeated silently. I could have killed them. That woman who questioned me. The stupid oafs on the bridge. I could have killed them all. Maybe I did kill one or two of them. But I tried not to. Despite it all, despite the rage of the monster inside, I kept myself from deliberately killing them.

That's something, he told himself. Not enough to save your own pitiful life, but at least I tried to stay my hand from murder.

Slowly he clambered to his feet and, for the first time, took a good look at his surroundings. Power generator, he saw. It feeds off the hot plasma ejected from the fusion reactor. He smiled to himself. Even in a blood-red rage your rational mind led you here, where the crew will be afraid of firing lasers at you for fear of damaging their power equipment.

He saw that he was in a narrow aisle between man-tall bulkheads that housed machinery. They'd have to come at you one at a time, he said to himself. I could slaughter them like Samson against the Philistines. I wouldn't even need the jawbone of an ass.

Turning, he saw that this narrow aisle widened into a small chamber fitted with a diagnostics console. They could come at me from both sides, front and back. Unless they have to come through this aisle to get to the console station.

He heard footsteps approaching. They were trying to be stealthy, tiptoeing, but the scuff of boots on the deck plates was easy enough to hear, even over the steady hum of the generator.

He retreated with soft, lithe steps to the diagnostics chamber. There was a hatch at its far end. They'll be able to come at me from both directions. It's too roomy in here, he decided. Better to fight in the narrow aisle.

Why fight at all? he asked himself. Why not just surrender to them? Would they accept that? Or will they be so frightened of me that they'll try to kill me straight off? It would be easier for them in the diagnostics chamber. But why should I make it easy for them? Or for myself?

'Dorn!'

Elverda's voice. High, quavering with tension.

225

'Dorn, come out. Show yourself. They won't harm you. I have the captain's word.'

He grunted. The captain's word. He's under orders to kill us both, Harbin replied silently to the old woman.

'Dorn, come out. It will be all right, I promise you.'

She treats me as if I'm a child. Her little boy. Harbin thought back to his own mother, raped and crucified by the soldiers sent to cleanse his village.

They'll kill us both, he thought. They'll kill you, Elverda. They've got to.

Unless I can prevent it, he told himself.

That was a new thought. Can I prevent them from killing her? Can I save her life? Could saving her one life possibly balance the scales for all the lives I've snuffed out?

Could she be the path to my atonement, my final peace?

'Dorn!' she called again.

'I'm here,' he called back. 'I'm coming out.'

Confrontations

Koop was leading a squad of four crew members, two of them women, down the passageway that led to the power generator bay. The ship's surveillance cameras showed Harbin huddled behind the generator itself, sitting on the deck plates with his knees pulled up in front of his face. He was unarmed, but Koop had seen what the freak could do with his bare hands.

Elverda Apacheta had insisted on coming with them. Now she stood beside Koop, calling out to Harbin. She called him Dorn.

He stopped his little team at the hatch that led into the generator bay. It was open. 'Okay,' he told them, 'we wait here until the captain signals.'

Yuan was leading the rest of the crew members who were able to walk, a total of five men and women, around the long way through the ship's wheel to come up behind the generator bay. His plan was to trap Harbin between the two squads.

'I'll go in and talk to him,' Elverda said.

Koop shook his beefy head. 'Orders are to wait here. I don't want you in the line of fire when the shooting starts.'

'I can make him come out without shooting,' she insisted.

'No,' said Koop. 'You stay here with us.'

She tried to stare him down, but Koop grasped her bony wrist in his massive paw and said gently, 'I don't want you to get hurt. Stay here. Please.'

Elverda almost smiled. Instead she turned and shouted through the open hatch, 'Dorn, come out. Show yourself. They won't harm you. I have the captain's word.'

No response. I can't blame him, Elverda said to herself. He knows they want to kill him. Kill us both.

Koop checked the charge on his laser pistol. He had seen the carnage Harbin had unleashed on the bridge, watched the security camera's playback of the mayhem. Gonzolez hit him square in the chest with a laser shot and all it did was burn a hole in his shirt.

'If we have to shoot,' he muttered to his crew, 'go for his face, or his human arm. The metal half of him splashes laser beams like a stream of water.'

'You'll kill him!' Elverda hissed.

'If I have to,' said Koop, as the others checked their pistols. He wished he had a more powerful weapon: a high-velocity rifle, maybe, or an armor-piercing missile.

Elverda cupped her hands to her mouth and called again, 'Dorn!'

From somewhere in the generator bay he called back, 'I'm here. I'm coming out.'

Koop's team stiffened and gripped their guns tighter.

Yuan had led his team halfway around *Viking*'s wheel-shaped main body and then down the connecting tunnel that opened on the far side of the generator bay. He wished he had more crew members and heavier weapons, but these five officers and crew were all that were left unhurt. They all looked nervous, frightened, as they hefted their pistols in trembling hands.

Tamara Vishinsky had stayed on the bridge, at Yuan's orders. Ostensibly, she had the ship's con. In reality, Yuan didn't want her anywhere near the renegade.

'I don't want him to see you,' Yuan had told her. 'It might set him off again.'

She hadn't argued the point. In fact, she looked relieved. The three other members of the crew were in the infirmary, two with broken noses, the third heavily sedated, his jaw shattered.

Now Yuan raised his free hand to bring his little team to a halt. The hatch that opened onto the generator bay stood before them. It was shut. Holstering his pistol, Yuan pulled out his palmcomp. Its tiny screen showed the surveillance camera's view of the bay from up in the overhead. He could see Harbin crouched behind the generator, his back to the hatch that was no more then five meters from Yuan and his squad. He was pulling a cover plate off the generator, using one finger of his prosthetic hand as a screwdriver.

Thumbing the palmcomp's keyboard, Yuan called in a low voice, 'Koop?'

A moment's delay, then the first mate's face filled the screen. 'Sir?'

'We're in position, ready to go in.'

'He says he's willing to come out, captain.'

'He'll surrender?'

'He wants us to guarantee we won't hurt Ms. Apacheta.'

Yuan grunted like a man who's just received news that could be both good and bad.

'I'll have to talk to him,' he said.

Dorik Harbin – Dorn – realized that there must be surveillance cameras throughout the ship. Peering up into the shadows of the overhead support beams, he spotted the unwinking red eye of a camera. They can see me, he said to himself.

He got slowly to his feet and raised his hands above his head.

'I'll come out,' he said to the open hatch in front of him. He could see Elverda standing there in her threadbare robe, and several members of the crew, all of them armed with pistols.

'I'll come out,' he repeated, 'under one condition. You must promise that you won't hurt my companion.'

The big, burly Hawaiian stepped in front of Elverda. 'That's a decision that only the captain can make,' he said.

'Then I'll stay here until the captain decides.'

It took several minutes and a flurry of chatter into handheld communicators. At last Koop told him, 'The captain's in the passageway behind you. He's going to open the hatch so he can talk to you.'

'I understand,' said Dorn.

'Nobody's going to come any closer than these hatches,' Koop assured him.

'I understand,' Dorn repeated, knowing that with laser pistols they could shoot him quite easily from the open hatches. The laser beams weren't powerful enough to do more than singe his metal skin, but they would of course aim for his flesh.

The hatch behind him started to creak open, slowly. Dorn turned to face it.

'I'm willing to surrender to you, captain, if you'll guarantee that no harm will come to Ms. Apacheta.'

Yuan frowned at Harbin. 'You're in no position to make demands.'

'True enough, but that's what I want. Otherwise you'll have to come in here and get me.'

'We're prepared to do that,' Yuan said.

Harbin lifted the plate he had removed from the generator and held it before him like a shield. 'Are you prepared for the casualties you'll take?'

'Dorn!' Elverda shouted. 'Stop this nonsense! Now!'

He turned and looked at her with the human side of his face. She pulled loose from Koop's restraining hand and stepped through the hatch, toward him.

Harbin dropped his shield. It clattered to the deck.

'No more fighting,' Elverda said, her tone softer.

'No more fighting,' he agreed.

They marched the two of them to the galley, where Yuan offered them a meal. Elverda made herself a cup of tea. Harbin sat in brooding silence at the end of the table that ran the length of the narrow compartment.

'You know I'm under orders to execute you both,' Yuan said, almost casually, as he poured a mug of tea for himself.

'I understand,' said Harbin, 'that Humphries wants us dead.'

'I don't have any choice in the matter.' Yuan sat himself at the head of the table.

'None of us really do,' Harbin said.

Elverda clutched her mug in both hands, soaking up its warmth. 'Could you at least wait until our mission is finished?' she asked.

Yuan turned toward her. 'You mean picking up dead bodies? That could take years.'

'Yes, but—'

Tamara Vishinsky stepped into the galley. Harbin tensed at the sight of her and she froze where she stood.

'There won't be any more interrogations,' Yuan said hastily. 'You can relax, both of you.'

Tamara went to the urn and took a mug. 'For what it's worth,' she said without looking at Harbin, 'I'm sorry I pumped you. I didn't know what your reaction would be.'

'I'm sorry also,' Harbin said. 'The man with the fractured jaw . . . ?'

'Koop injected him with stem cells. The medical computer predicts he'll be recovered in six days.'

'I regret injuring him.'

Yuan said, 'The two of you are under a sentence of death. I don't like it, but those are my orders.'

'And if you don't carry them out, Humphries will send assassins after you,' Elverda said.

Nodding, the captain said, 'He sure as hell will.'

A gloomy silence filled the galley. Yuan looked from Harbin to Apacheta to Tamara. He felt uneasy, almost sick to his stomach. It's one thing to ping a ship, he thought. Like a computer game. Bang, he's dead. But these are real, living people. Even Harbin: he's half machine, but he's a human being nonetheless. What am I supposed to do with them? Shoot them between the eyes? Give them lethal injections? Pop them out an airlock without suits?

Tamara broke the silence. 'Tell me more about this alien artifact, Harbin.'

'His name is Dorn,' Elverda said.

'I want to know more about the artifact.'

'Artifact?' Yuan asked.

Dorn fixed Tamara with a gaze. 'Humphries wants us killed because we saw the effect the artifact had on him.'

'You mean it's real?' Yuan asked. 'I've heard rumors, everybody has. Tales . . . but I thought—'

'It's real,' said Elverda.

'It made Humphries crazy?' Tamara's voice was brimming with anticipation.

'Temporarily,' Elverda said, placing a hand on Dorn's human arm to keep him silent.

But Dorn added, 'The artifact merely brought his underlying insanity into the open.'

'And you saw him crumble?'

'He won't like finding out that you know what happened to him,' Elverda warned.

Undeterred, Tamara asked, 'You both saw the artifact, too, didn't you? And it affected you, too, didn't it?'

'It did,' said Dorn.

'It changed your lives,' Tamara said, her eyes glittering.

'Yes,' Elverda admitted.

Leaning across the table toward Dorn, Tamara asked, 'Where is this artifact?' ·

'It's buried inside an asteroid.'

'Which asteroid?'

'IAA designation 67-046,' said Dorn mechanically.

'What are its coordinates? Could you pilot us back to the asteroid where the artifact is?'

Cargo Ship *Pleiades*: Outside

Victor Zacharias paused in his work and looked up at the stars. He had pulled on one of the ship's nanofabric space suits to go outside and repair a malfunctioning maintenance robot, thinking to himself, *Quis custodiet ipsos custodes?* Who will watch the watchmen? Or, in this case, who will maintain the maintenance robots?

'I will,' he muttered from inside the inflated bubble that covered his head. 'There's nobody here to do it except me.'

It was a lot easier to work in the nanofabric suit than in the old hard shells. The nanofabric gloves were thin and flexible, not like the stiff cumbersome gloves of the older suits. Even with miniature servomotors on their backs, it was hard to move your fingers in the old gloves; it was like wearing boxing mitts, almost. Victor lifted a hand to eye level and flexed his fingers easily.

The stars drew his attention. Stars everywhere, spangled against the infinite blackness of space. Stars strewn so thickly that he could barely make out the constellations that he'd known as a child in the muted skies of Earth.

Earth itself was out there, he saw: a warm point of blue. He couldn't find Mars but Jupiter was so big and bright he thought he could see the flatness of its disk.

And Pauline is out there, he told himself. Pauline and Angela and Theo. Somewhere out there.

He had only the roughest idea of where they might be. When he'd separated from *Syracuse*, in the midst of that madman's attack, he hadn't had time for a careful navigational fix. They were rocketing outward, he knew, on a trajectory that would swing completely out of the Belt and then loop back again toward Ceres.

So Victor piloted *Pleiades* across the sector that he guessed his family would return to, crisscrossing the region like a man groping blindly in a dark alley for a coin he had lost.

I'll find them, he told himself, again and again. I'll find them.

He had worked hard to upgrade *Pleiades*'s search radar so it could send a powerful probing pulse out into space. *Syracuse* was deaf and dumb, he knew. The attack had ruined the ship's antennas. He could expect no call from his family, no signal to guide him to them.

Unless . . .

No, he said to himself. You can't expect Theo to know enough to help you. He's only a teenager. He can't repair the antennas, they were too badly ripped up for repair. But is Theo smart enough to use the suit radios? Will he think of that?

The radios built into the ship's space suits were low powered, barely strong enough for crew members to chatter back and forth. Their signals faded away into

236

the background hiss of the stars at only a few kilometers' distance.

But on Earth there are powerful radio telescopes, antennas that can pick out the microwatt signals from robot spacecraft way out in the Kuiper Belt and beyond. Antennas that had been listening for signals from extraterrestrial civilizations, until the religious fanatics that controlled most of Earth's governments had shut down almost all of them.

But the antennas are still there, Victor thought, listening to the signals from the outposts orbiting around Venus and Jupiter and Saturn. Communicating with the power satellite project at Mercury. And some of those scientists were sneaking time to listen for ET signals, too, Victor was certain.

If Theo was smart enough to use the suit radios to call for help, or just to identify *Syracuse*'s position . . . If, Victor thought. If.

The timer on his wrist comm pinged, making him flinch with surprise. I've been out here two hours!

He lifted the diagnostic tool from its magnetic grip on the ship's hull and ran it over the squat little robot he'd been repairing. Its lights blinked green. Nodding, satisfied, Victor activated the robot itself. It trundled off along its track, spindly arms unfolding, ready to repair any damage to the meteor bumper from impacts. Just as if it had never malfunctioned, Victor said to himself. No memory at all. Almost, he envied the simple little machine.

He clambered through the airlock hatch, unsealed the space suit and hung it up neatly in its rack, then went to the galley for a sandwich and a beer. Cheena set a good table, he thought. The galley's well stocked.

Ducking into the bridge, Victor was startled to see that the ship's sensor log showed that *Pleiades* had been pinged by a powerful radar pulse seventeen minutes earlier. And the yellow message light was blinking on the communications console.

'That can only be bad news,' he growled. He'd been running silent: no tracking beacon, no telemetry to identify himself. He hadn't yet turned on the search radar he'd worked so hard to upgrade. He didn't think Cheena Madagascar would be chasing him, but he was taking no chances.

'No harm in listening to it,' he mumbled. He sat down in the command chair, the mug of beer still in his left hand, and touched the REPLAY key.

A handsome cheerful face smiled brightly from the display screen.

'Hailing unidentified vessel,' he said, in a crisply confident tone. 'This is the salvage ship *Vogeltod*. If you are in need of help, we will assist you. If we receive no reply, we will assume you are a derelict. In that case we will board you and claim you as salvage.'

The image on the screen froze. Victor scowled at the man's face. He had a thick mop of sandy blond hair, a strong jaw, big teeth. Broad shoulders beneath a non-descript tan shirt. His smile had a hint of the predator about it. Victor thought of a shark.

Salvage? Victor asked himself. Are there enough abandoned or wrecked ships out here to make a salvage operation profitable? There must be, he decided.

If I don't answer him, he'll board me. I'm just one man; he's probably got a crew of least four or five people. Maybe more.

But if I do answer him he'll figure out pretty quickly that I've stolen this ship. Then he can board me, take over and bring me back to Ceres. Back to Cheena. And Big George.

Victor glowered at the frozen image in his comm screen. Damned if I do and damned if I don't.

Kao Yuan leveled a finger at Tamara. 'Do you realize what you're proposing to do?'

'Yes,' she said, delighted, enthusiastic. 'We're going to find that alien artifact.'

'If Humphries hasn't destroyed it,' Dorn said.

'Destroyed it? He wouldn't do that! He couldn't! Why would he destroy it?'

'Because he hates it,' said Elverda, from across the galley table.

'Worse,' Dorn amended. 'He fears it.'

Undeterred, Tamara said, 'He hasn't destroyed it, I'm certain of that.'

Yuan shook his head, more in wonder than contradiction.

Leaning slightly toward Dorn, Tamara said, 'You know the asteroid's coordinates, Harbin. You're going to lead us to it.'

'And if I refuse?'

She gestured toward Elverda. 'We'll kill your friend.'

'Now wait!' Kuan said, brows knitting. 'I'm the captain here, not you.'

Tamara smiled at him, coldly. 'I report directly to Mr. Humphries. I outrank you, Kao.'

'Not on this ship.'

'Why do you want to see the artifact?' Elverda asked.

Her smile thinned. 'Martin Humphries is the most powerful man in the solar system, right? Well, this artifact, whatever it is, can give me a lever on him. If I can control the artifact I can control Humphries! It's that simple.'

'It may be a lot of things,' Yuan said, 'but it's not simple. All you're going to accomplish is getting yourself killed. And me along with you.'

'Don't be a chick, Yuan. We're talking about real power here!'

'You're crazy.'

Her smile winked out. 'Listen, *captain*,' she mocked, 'I'd prefer to do this with you, but I can do it without if I have to. Koop can replace you easily enough.'

'You're talking mutiny,' Yuan growled.

'Yes, I am,' said Tamara.

Attack Ship *Viking*: Infirmary

Yuan escorted Elverda and Dorn back to the infirmary, looking decidedly unhappy.

'You'll be comfortable enough here,' he said, motioning them through the open hatch. 'This ship isn't built to accommodate passengers.'

Elverda thanked him and stepped through; Dorn followed her. Yuan closed the hatch and left them alone.

'She's mad. Insane,' Elverda said as she went to her bed and sat on it. Three sides of the bed were partitioned off.

'Is she?' Dorn wondered, standing next to her. 'She seems to understand how powerful the artifact can be.'

'But how can she hope to control Humphries through it? If he hasn't already destroyed it he must have it heavily guarded, sealed off from the rest of the world.'

'Perhaps. But she's a gambler, and she's willing to play for the very highest stakes.'

'Our lives.'

'And her own. If she's wrong about controlling Humphries, he'll snuff her out like a candle flame.'

Elverda felt tired, bone weary. Yet . . . 'Perhaps there's some way we can use the artifact to bargain for our lives.'

'Your life,' he said. 'I'm ready to die.'

'No!'

He looked away from her. In a voice so low she could barely hear it, he said, 'Today I realized how brittle this façade is. I could have killed her – all of them.'

'That was the drugs.'

'In my body,' he retorted. 'My brain. My mind. I could have killed them all. I *wanted* to.'

'But you didn't.'

He shook his head slowly. 'I don't want to go through that again. I want to be released from all this . . . this . . . living.'

Elverda searched for something she could say to help him, to ease his pain, to bring him back from his despair. But she found nothing.

With the enormous reluctance of a man who knew he would regret his decision, Victor keyed his comm console.

'This is the cargo ship *Pleiades*,' he said, trying to keep his voice firm, unruffled. 'We are not in trouble. I repeat, not in trouble. We do not require assistance. Thank you.'

Hardly a moment later the smiling young man's face appeared on Victor's comm screen.

'You're not emitting a tracking beacon, *Pleiades*,' he said. 'We thought you were abandoned.'

Victor could see a glint of sunlight off a ship's hull on his main display screen. *Vogeltod* was still too far away for the cameras to show its shape.

'No, we're not abandoned.'

'But you're running silent, eh?'

'For the moment, yes.'

The man's toothy grin widened. 'My name is Valker. What's yours?'

Thinking swiftly, Victor said, 'Kaneaz.'

'Kaneaz?' Valker echoed. 'What's that, German?'

'Greek.'

'Ah! That's why I didn't understand it. It's Greek to me!' Valker burst into a hearty laugh.

Making himself smile back at the man, Victor said, 'Well, thanks for your offer of assistance. I'll be powering up soon and heading deeper into the Belt.'

Valker's handsome face turned crafty. 'Wait a minute. According to the IAA register on my screen, *Pleiades* is captained by Cheena Madagascar. Can I talk to her?'

'The captain gave orders she's not to be disturbed.'

'Did she?'

'Yes.'

'Well, you'd better wake her up, Greekie. We're coming aboard.'

Victor's main screen showed a flash of rocket exhaust against the starry background. He hesitated a bare fraction of a second, then punched his main propulsion controls. *Pleiades* lurched into acceleration.

Sinking back in the padded command chair, Victor said to himself, Now it's a question of who's faster. And better armed.

Kao Yuan went from the infirmary straight to the bridge. Koop was in the command chair, Tamara leaning over him in whispered conversation.

'Koop,' Yuan called. 'Come with me.'

The big Hawaiian looked like a guilty little boy as he pulled himself to his feet.

'You too, Tamara,' he said.

It was crowded in the captain's quarters with the three of them there, but Yuan slid his door shut and leaned against it for a moment, eying them. Tamara went directly to the double-sized bunk and sat on its edge. Koop looked at the flimsy desk chair, decided against it, and remained standing.

'Take the recliner,' Yuan said, pointing to the cushioned chair.

'It's okay, captain,' Koop said. 'I'll stay on my feet.'

'We've got a command crisis here,' Yuan said, without moving from the door. 'Tamara thinks she can give the orders aboard my ship.'

'I report directly—'

'To Humphries, I know,' said Yuan. 'But I'm the captain of this ship. Like Ahab said, there's one god in heaven and one captain of the *Pequod*.'

Koop's chunky face screwed up in bewilderment. '*Pequod*?'

'You hold the balance of power here,' Yuan said to his first mate. 'Whose orders are you going to follow, hers or mine?'

'Yours,' the Hawaiian answered without hesitation.

'You're certain?'

'Sure, captain. You're the captain and that's it.'

'Even if she goes to bed with you?'

Koop's face flamed red. Tamara actually smiled.

'We've already been in bed together,' she said, her

244

smile turning into a self-satisfied smirk. 'It was very enjoyable.'

'I see,' Yuan said tightly.

'That's got nothin' to do with who's captain,' Koop said.

Yuan looked into his steady brown eyes. 'This is important, Koop. I can't have her going over my head.'

'You've made your point, *captain*,' Tamara said. 'I'll follow your orders without question.'

'No calling back to headquarters behind my back,' Yuan said.

Smiling again, she replied, 'I won't go over your head, or behind your back, or under your toes.'

'All right, then.'

'But we are going to find the artifact, aren't we?' she added.

Yuan hesitated. He knew that she wouldn't want to tell headquarters that she knew anything about the artifact. Humphries wants the renegade and the sculptress killed because they know about it. He'll kill all of us if he knows that we know.

Impatient with his silence, Tamara went on, 'We have Harbin and the artist. Our mission is completed once we eliminate them. But if we can get the artifact—'

'We could get ourselves killed,' Yuan snapped.

'Or be in control of the most powerful force in the solar system,' she purred.

Cargo Ship *Pleiades*: Bridge

Victor kept the fusion drive accelerating at one full g and watched *Vogeltod* dwindling in his wake. Nodding to himself, he thought, Scavengers like Valker aren't looking for a long and difficult chase. They want easy pickings, and there must be lots of them scattered around the Belt: ships that were blasted in battle during the war, ships that are abandoned, or their crews killed.

It wasn't until *Vogeltod* had disappeared altogether from his screen that the frightening thought hit him. What if a scavenger finds *Syracuse* before I do?

What if that bastard Valker follows me and finds *Syracuse* because I lead him to her?

No. He shook his head to clear the idea from his mind. It'll take months, maybe years before I find Pauline and the kids. Valker won't have that kind of patience. He's looking for prey, he wants to feed himself and his crew, he can't wait that long. His own crew would slit his throat first.

Still, Victor shut down the main engine and used the cold-gas maneuvering jets to shift *Pleiades* away from the outbound vector it had been following. He kicked *Pleiades* into a trajectory that climbed well above his original course. Most ships travel close to the ecliptic:

that's where the asteroids are. He might not think of looking up. Go silent again, don't leave a trail for him to follow, he told himself. Don't take any chances.

Once he had convinced himself that he had lost *Vogeltod*, he called up the navigation program and restudied his options.

I've got to stay farther away from the Ceres sector, he realized. Parasites like Valker must be combing the region, looking for derelicts to scavenge. But that means I'll have to cover a wider arc to have any hope of intercepting Pauline and the kids.

He decided to cruise silently for at least three days before turning on the search radar. Then he decided to make it a week. He didn't want to take any chances of giving Valker or anyone else a signal they could home in on.

Vogeltod's bridge was a strange assortment of equipment, most of it taken from vessels that Valker and his crew had seized and retrofitted into the old bucket. Valker himself sat in a command chair that had once belonged to Admiral Gormley, the victim of a bloody ambush during the war.

Valker was a big man, almost two meters tall, broad in the shoulders, deep in the chest. He was almost always smiling, a bright devil-may-care smile that showed lots of teeth. Where another man might show tension, even fear, in a dangerous situation, Valker smiled and fought his way through. During the war he'd been a mercenary, first with Astro Corporation, then with Humphries Space Systems.

When the shooting stopped, most mercenaries were at a loss. For years there had been plenty of work for them, and good pay. Not that they fought all the time. Much of their work involved building bases or scouting through the cold emptiness of the Belt, looking for prey. They seldom engaged in battle against other mercenaries. No percentage in that. Instead, they swooped down on hapless cargo ships and smelters, like hawks going after pigeons.

The official end of the war finished that. For the most part. Some mercenaries became outlaws, pirates, still attacking peaceful vessels. But they soon learned that no one would buy the cargoes they captured. Big George Ambrose and the other rock rats busily building their new habitat at Ceres had no time or money to hire a police force to go after the pirates. They simply saw to it that no one in the Belt bought stolen cargoes. The pirates soon realized there was little profit in their piracies. And there was always the risk that Big George's people would execute you without delay.

Valker was smarter than that. When the Second Asteroid War broke out he had just graduated from the University of Pisa with a double degree in economics and marketing. He had been a star on the international soccer team he himself had helped to organize. His plan was to spend three years – perhaps as much as five – in the Belt, working as a prospector, locating asteroids rich in metals and minerals, claiming them as an independent corporation and then selling them to the highest bidder.

The Asteroid War made such ventures far too hazardous. Valker saw that either he joined one of the major corporations or he went back to Earth empty-handed. Or got himself killed. So he became a mercenary – until the war abruptly ended.

While most of the mercenaries found themselves out of work, and flooded back to the Earth/Moon region to look for jobs, Valker realized that there was an economic niche available in the Belt: salvage. There were plenty of vessels abandoned by their crews, drifting through the Belt, there for the taking. He could claim the vessels as salvage, then sell them back to the rock rats for a handsome profit.

He was a born salesman. With his rugged good looks and winning smile, he talked a banker into leasing him a small ship, *Vogeltod*. It wasn't difficult to round up a crew: he picked nine men, all former mercenaries, all quite prepared to stretch the laws of salvage once they were out in the Belt and away from the prying eyes of Big George and the IAA.

They searched for abandoned vessels. Some were battered hulks, little more than junk. Most had equipment in them that could be scavenged. But the real money was in ships that were intact. Valker and his crewmates pounced on lonely vessels deep in the Belt, killed the crews and brought the ships back to Ceres for sale. There were always questions, raised eyebrows, lurking suspicions. Valker smiled his way through and sold the 'abandoned' vessels to the highest bidder. There were always newcomers from Earth or the Moon with money in their accounts to invest in a new career in prospecting and mining.

Now Valker sat in Admiral Gormley's old command chair and studied the data splashed on *Vogeltod*'s main screen. *Pleiades* was listed back at Ceres as stolen. Its captain and owner, Cheena Madagascar, had even posted a hefty reward for the ship's return. Big George Ambrose had declared the thief, somebody named Victor Zacharias, to be an outlaw and placed a modest price on his head.

'*Gesuto*,' Valker said aloud, 'we could take this ship and bring it back to Ceres and we'll be heroes, no less.'

The other men on the bridge grinned at him.

'The rewards don't add up to all that much,' he continued, 'but the goodwill could be helpful.'

'He's no fool, though,' said the man at the nav console. 'He sprinted away and now he's shut down his main engine.'

'Trying to be invisible,' Valker muttered.

'And doing a good job of it. Radar ain't picking up anything.'

Valker nodded absently. 'You're right: he's no fool.' He pecked out a command to the ship's computer on the keyboard set into the armrest of his chair. Let's see what Ceres has on file about this thief. Know your customer, he said to himself. That's the first rule of marketing.

Attack Ship *Viking*: Bridge

Everything stopped as Koop brought the cyborg and the old woman onto the bridge. The two crewmen who were still working at repairs of the equipment Dorn had smashed glanced at him warily, as did the officers at their consoles, two of them with spraytape covering their broken noses. Elverda's face was drawn tight with tension. It was impossible to read any expression on the cyborg's half-metal face.

Tamara, at the comm console, half turned in her chair as Koop led them in. Yuan glared at her, a warning to keep her mouth shut. I'm the captain, he said silently to her, I'm in charge.

'Harbin,' he began, 'I want—'

'My name is no longer Dorik Harbin. Please call me Dorn.'

Yuan grimaced. 'All right. Dorn. I want you to give my navigation officer the coordinates for the asteroid where the artifact is located.'

Elverda saw that all of them were staring openly at Dorn now: the three bridge officers, the captain, the pair of technicians, even the strapping Hawaiian. For a long moment Dorn said nothing; the bridge was absolutely silent except for the hum of electrical power and the whisper of air from the ventilation ducts.

'It will be very dangerous to go there,' Dorn said at last.

Yuan waved a hand impatiently. 'That's for me to worry about, not you. Give my nav officer the co-ordinates.'

'He may have moved the asteroid to a different orbit, or even destroyed it completely.'

'Just give the coordinates to my nav officer,' Yuan insisted.

Again Dorn hesitated. Then, 'I want your promise that Ms. Apacheta will not be harmed.'

'The coordinates, dammit!' Yuan shouted. 'Now!'

'I don't care what happens to me, but I want her to be safe.'

Tamara said, 'Do you want us to start pulling her fingernails out?'

Clenching his metal fist, Dorn said, 'The rest of this bridge will be destroyed if you try that. Some of you will die.' His voice was flat, unemotional, but the others on the bridge shot uneasy glances at one another.

Before anyone could reply, Yuan broke into a forced chuckle. 'All right. All right. I won't touch a hair of her head. Does that satisfy you?'

'No,' Dorn said calmly. 'I want your guarantee that no harm will come to her, neither by you nor any other member of this ship's crew.'

Elverda complained, 'Stop talking about me as if I'm not here.'

Ignoring her, Dorn said to the captain, 'You are

under orders to kill us both. You can kill me, but let her go free.'

'And what happens when Mr. Humphries finds out I've let her go?'

Dorn smiled with the human side of his face. 'Once I give you the coordinates you will go to the asteroid and try to gain control of Humphries through the alien artifact.'

Yuan glanced at Tamara, who nodded minutely.

'If you succeed in getting the upper hand with Humphries, then allowing Ms. Apacheta to go free will be of no consequence. If you fail we will all be killed.'

'Including you,' said Yuan.

'I will die one way or the other. That doesn't matter. The life of this woman does matter. Very much. To me.'

Moving beside him, Elverda said softly, 'Dorn, I can't let you throw your life away—'

'If you finish the work we've started, if you find the other bodies and give them decent death rites, then my life doesn't matter. It never did, except to cause agony and death. You can complete my atonement.'

'Atonement?' Tamara blurted. 'Is that what you're after?'

'Atonement,' Dorn repeated.

Yuan said, 'All right. Ms. Apacheta won't be harmed in any way. Now give the coordinates to my nav officer.'

Without another word, Dorn turned and stepped to the navigation officer's console, then leaned over his shoulder and began pecking on his keyboard with both his hands.

Turning to Tamara, Yuan commanded, 'Notify *Viking Two* and *Three* to proceed to Ceres immediately.'

She arched an eyebrow. 'You don't want them to go with us?'

'No,' he said. 'Do you?'

She thought it over for all of two seconds. 'No, you're right. We do this by ourselves.'

Elverda, still standing next to the captain's chair, asked, 'What about our ship, the *Hunter*?'

'We don't need it now. Let it drift.'

Valker whistled softly as he read Victor Zacharias's dossier from the computer screen built into the bulkhead at the foot of his bunk.

He was sitting up with the pillows bunched behind his back. His quarters were small but as sumptuous as he could make them, crammed with furniture and fixtures scavenged from salvaged vessels: a massive desk of actual teak filled one corner of the compartment, elephants and monkeys carved into its flanks and front; colorful draperies hung from the overhead; the entire lavatory had been ripped out of a luxurious corporate torch ship and shoehorned into place, gold faucets and all; the rich dark faux leather recliner that had been rammed into the other corner of the compartment had been taken from a prospector's ship, the one luxury its late owner had possessed.

Valker took all that for granted, including the fact

254

that he had to maneuver carefully around his pilfered treasures to get across the jam-packed compartment. His attention was fully focused on Zacharias's dossier. The man had a family – wife and two teenagers – but they'd been lost after being attacked by the same monster who'd wiped out the original *Chrysalis* habitat.

So what's he doing in a stolen ship this deep in the Belt? Valker asked himself. Searching for his family? Valker shook his head. Can't be. It's three years and more since his family disappeared. They're dead by now. Have to be. Only a fool or a madman would still be searching for them. Only an idiot would steal a ship, make himself an outlaw with the rock rats, to go searching through this wilderness for his wife and kids.

'Only a fool or a madman,' Valker repeated aloud, softly.

Why track after a madman? Even if you find him you'll have to kill him; he won't give up that ship without a fight. And even if we do take the ship, once we bring it back to Ceres its rightful owner will claim it. We'll get the reward, but that's peanuts compared to the price the ship would bring.

Why bother? Let him go searching for his family. Let him die out there. Sooner or later we'll run across his ship and take it.

The message light beneath the display screen began to blink.

'Answer,' Valker called out.

His first mate's bearded face filled the screen. 'Contact, captain. Looks like a derelict. Seems intact, but there's no beacon, no answer to our calls.'

'Identification?'

'Computer says its radar profile matches one of the ships in its files: *Hunter*. Some woman's listed as the owner, Elverda Apacheta. Sounds like some Latina to me.'

Valker nodded and swung his legs off the bunk, careful not to bang his shins against the big recliner.

'I'm coming to the bridge,' he said.

A derelict, Valker thought as he tugged on his softboots. If she's really intact she'll bring top dollar back at Ceres.

He hurried to the bridge.

Attack Ship *Viking*:
One Month Later

'By god, there it is,' said Kao Yuan in a hushed, almost awed voice.

From the navigation console, Koop wondered aloud, 'Are you sure?'

Yuan pointed to the main screen. 'How many rocks out here have five – no, six ships patrolling around them?'

'APPROACHING VESSEL, IDENTIFY YOURSELF.' The voice coming through the comm speaker sounded like a computerized synthesizer.

It had taken a month for Yuan to track down asteroid 67–046. It hadn't been at the coordinates Dorn had given. Sure enough, Humphries had moved the rock to a different orbit that swooped far below and then high above the ecliptic, out of the plane of the usual traffic through the Belt. For an entire month *Viking* followed trajectories that the navigation computer worked out, guesses based on the asteroid's original orbit and the amount of energy it would take to move a rock of its mass.

During those frustrating weeks of searching the dark emptiness, Yuan asked Tamara again and again, 'But what do we do when we find the 'roid? It's bound to be protected. Humphries won't let it just sit there without guarding it.'

Again and again Tamara would smile knowingly and say, 'Leave that to me. I'll get us past the guards.'

'You'll get us killed,' Yuan groused.

He did not sleep with her anymore. He wanted to, but the realization that she'd been using him angered him too deeply. Instead he crooked his finger at one of the other crew members, a weapons specialist, young and slightly plump, but with silky dark hair and a willing smile. It's good to be the captain, Yuan told himself. But he was certain that Tamara was sleeping with Koop now.

'APPROACHING VESSEL, IDENTIFY YOURSELF. THIS AREA IS PROPRIETARY TO HUMPHRIES SPACE SYSTEMS, INCORPORATED. NO UNAUTHORIZED VESSELS ARE PERMITTED HERE.'

Yuan looked at Tamara, who pressed the TRANSMIT key on her console and said crisply, 'This is HSS vessel *Viking*. Authorization code delta four six nine.'

'ONE MOMENT. VERIFYING AUTHORIZATION CODE.'

Tamara glanced over her shoulder at Yuan, a self-satisfied smile curving her lips.

The main screen abruptly showed a square-jawed man with iron gray hair cropped close to his skull. He wore a pale blue tunic with a high choker collar.

'I am Commander Hugh Bolestos,' he said in a gravelly voice. 'Your authorization code is out of date.'

'We've been on special duty in the Belt,' Tamara answered smoothly. 'We haven't updated our comm codes for several months.'

Commander Bolestos's stern expression did not change by a millimeter. 'I've had no word from headquarters to expect you.'

'As I told you, we're on special duty. My name is Tamara Vishinsky. Check your personnel files.'

Bolestos's eyes shifted away for a moment, widened noticeably, then returned to his main screen.

'Says here you report personally to Mr. Humphries himself.'

'Yes, I do,' said Tamara. 'May I come aboard your vessel, please, commander?'

'Certainly, Ms. Vishinsky! Of course!'

Valker approached *Hunter* cautiously. The vessel certainly looked abandoned. No tracking beacon, no telemetry signals, no reply to his repeated calls.

Elverda Apacheta, he had discovered from a computer search, was a famous sculptress. But very old. She had bought *Hunter* on a whim, apparently, and disappeared into the depths of the Asteroid Belt several years earlier.

A dotty old lady, Valker concluded. Maybe she came out here to carve more statues out of asteroids.

'Vectors matched,' his navigation officer announced. 'Close enough to board her.'

Valker nodded. 'I'll go aboard.'

'Alone?'

'Yes.' He pointed to two of the crewmen who had crowded into the bridge. 'Nicco and Kirk, stand by to come aboard when I give the signal.'

The two crewmen went to the airlock with Valker, where they all pulled on nanofabric space suits that had been taken from the same luxury yacht that the captain's oversized desk had come from.

'Wait here. If there's trouble, I'll holler.'

'Right,' they said in unison.

And if there isn't trouble, Valker thought as he stepped into the airlock chamber, I want to look through that ship and see if there's anything worth taking for myself.

Yuan was shocked at the ease with which Tamara disposed of the guards protecting the artifact's asteroid.

She, Koop, and four crew members transferred to Commander Bolestos's vessel. Less than an hour later her image appeared on *Viking*'s main screen, smiling smugly. 'You can come aboard now. No need for weapons.'

Feeling puzzled, uneasy, Yuan went to the airlock and floated through the spongy plastic tunnel that connected *Viking*'s airlock with that of the security guards' orbiting vessel.

On the bridge he found Koop sitting in the command chair with Tamara bending over him, spraying a bandage on his upper arm. A laser beam had burned through Koop's sleeve and seared his flesh. Then Yuan saw Commander Bolestos and his guts heaved: the older man lay crumpled like a rag doll in a corner, his chest soaked with blood, his wide-eyed face looking very surprised.

'You killed him?' Yuan gasped.

'Change of command,' said Tamara. She pointed to the control panel that spanned one side of the bridge.

'Now I've got all his authorization codes. I'm in charge of security for the artifact now. The grunts on the other ships are taking my orders, like good little corporate robots.'

Yuan understood her tone clearly. *I'm under her command now, too.*

'Bring the woman and the freak here,' Tamara said. 'I want them to lead us down to the artifact.'

Yuan couldn't take his eyes off the corpse. He'd never seen a dead body before. All his kills had been at a distance, clean, impersonal.

'You didn't have a gun with you. How did you . . .?'

Tamara flicked her right wrist and a wire-thin blade slid into her hand. 'With this,' she said. 'Close up and personal.'

Then she added, 'There are four other crew members down in the galley. And one of our people. The crew tried to make a fight of it.'

'They're all dead?' Yuan asked, his voice squeaking, his insides quaking.

With a quick nod Tamara replied, 'Can't make an omelet without breaking eggs.'

Yuan wanted to throw up.

'Now get the woman and her cyborg friend over here. We're going down to the asteroid.'

The Artifact

'You're making a mistake,' Dorn warned.

The four of them – Tamara, Yuan, Elverda and Dorn – were walking down the sloping tunnel inside the asteroid that led to the chamber where the artifact was housed. Tamara had placed Koop and a crewman at the tunnel's opening, up on the surface, inside the glassteel dome that protected the hatch.

'Don't be stupid,' Tamara shot back, walking beside Dorn. 'You can't change my mind.'

'The artifact won't give you control over Humphries,' Dorn insisted. 'You have no idea—'

'Shut up!' she snapped.

He walked in silence for several paces, then turned to Elverda and asked in a lower voice, 'Do you want to see it again?'

'Yes,' she said, with only a little trepidation. 'And you?'

'I see it every night in my dreams.'

Bringing up the rear of the little group, Yuan felt a mix of anticipation and dread. This asteroid was weird: it was one of the rocky type, but it seemed to be honeycombed with burrows that were apparently natural. Less than a kilometer in length, still the gravity here inside this tunnel was at least half an Earthly g: definitely *not* natural. And it was warm down in this tunnel, too; something, someplace was heating the area. Overheating, Yuan thought, feeling slightly uncomfortable.

What if this alien contraption actually does give us power over Humphries? Yuan wondered. The cyborg says it won't but what if it does? We'll be in control of the richest, most powerful man in the solar system! But then he thought, Humphries isn't a man to be fooled with. If he finds out what we're doing he'll have us all killed. If we can't control him, what we're doing here is writing our own death warrants.

I've played plenty of computer games, he said to himself, but nothing like this. Tamara's a real gambler. She's willing to risk all of our lives for this. His throat felt dry, his insides fluttery.

Still, he followed Tamara along the downward sloping tunnel. The rock walls narrowed; the ceiling got so low that Yuan began to stoop slightly. The old woman had slowed down so that she now walked beside him, her eyes bright and eager in her aged, withered face. Up ahead, the cyborg matched Tamara stride for stride.

Tamara. She killed Bolestos, he reminded himself. She stood right next to the man and stabbed him in the heart. She's a murderer, a cold-blooded killer. Yuan realized that she'd been in charge of this mission all along. I only thought I was the captain; she pulled my strings and reported my every move back to Humphries himself. Now she's rebelling, gambling for the

263

chance to seize all of Humphries's power. And I'm being towed along; she hasn't even asked me what I want to do. She's in charge and there's nothing I can do about it.

The tunnel ended abruptly at a blank stainless steel wall.

'Open it,' Tamara said to Dorn.

'It slides open by itself,' Dorn told them.

'When?'

'On its own schedule. When the artifact was first discovered I was in command of the security detail Humphries sent here. I knew the gate's timing down to the second. But I've been away so long that its schedule may have changed.'

'We'll have to wait, then,' said Elverda.

'It might take days,' Dorn said.

'We could blast the door down,' Tamara said.

'No,' said Dorn. 'You can't.'

'Why not?'

'The gate is protected by some sort of energy field,' he replied. 'Besides, an explosion might damage the artifact, if it was powerful enough to blast the gate open.'

'All right,' Tamara decided. 'We'll wait.'

Elverda took the colorful shawl from her shoulders, folded it into a makeshift pad, and sat on the stone floor. Dorn stood beside her like a protective guard.

Tamara turned to Yuan, her face shining with anticipation.

'We could still turn back,' he said. 'It's not too late to forget this whole scheme.'

'Never!' she snapped. 'This is the biggest opportunity of them all and I'm playing it out, all the way.'

Yuan nodded. He knew she'd say something like that. Still, he wished he were a trillion kilometers away from here.

'Whatever happened,' Elverda asked no one in particular, 'to the scientists who were studying the artifact?'

'Humphries never allowed the universities to send scientists here,' Tamara replied. 'The IAA was furious, but Humphries had a legal claim to utilization of the asteroid's resources, and that gave him the right to restrict visitors. He moved the 'roid out of its original orbit just to make it more difficult for anyone to reach it.'

Dorn said, 'I would have thought he would destroy it.'

'He wanted to,' Tamara said. 'He still might, if we give him the chance.'

'That's too much power for one man to have,' Elverda said.

Tamara smirked at her. Yuan could read the expression on her face: soon one woman will have all that power.

At the other end of the tunnel, inside the glassteel dome built on the asteroid's surface, Koop's communicator buzzed. He flicked it open and saw the face of a security guard in one of the ships orbiting the asteroid. The woman looked upset, apprehensive.

'We just received a message from headquarters. They want to know what your ship, *Viking*, is doing at this location.'

Koop frowned back at the guard. 'How's headquarters know *Viking*'s out here? Who told 'em?'

'There's an automated identification system planted on the 'roid's surface. It reports any vessel that comes within our perimeter back to headquarters.'

Koop grunted. Headquarters was on the Moon, he knew, which meant that messages took half an hour or more to go one way.

'I'll relay the message to Commander Vishinsky,' he said. 'She's inside the rock right now, out of range of my handheld.'

'Headquarters sounded pretty antsy,' the comm officer said. 'And they also want to know who put Vishinsky in command.'

'Whatcha tell them?'

'Same thing she told me: Commander Bolestos died and she took over for him.'

Koop thought it over for a second or two. 'Good enough,' he said. 'For now.'

'It's opening!' Tamara breathed.

Noiselessly, the metal gate was sliding upward.

Elverda began to clamber to her feet. Dorn lent her a supporting hand.

Yuan felt perspiration beading his lip. *Once Tamara takes a step past the gateway we're all in this for keeps, one way or another.*

'You first,' he said to Tamara.

She hesitated. 'No.' Turning to Elverda, 'You go first.'

'Me?'

266

'You've seen it before. I want you to see if it's the same as it was then.'

Yuan thought, Or if it causes the old woman harm.

Elverda nodded, looking slightly anxious. 'Very well,' she said.

She handed her folded shawl to Dorn, then stepped firmly past the thin groove in the dusty floor that marked where the gate had rested.

Yuan saw a diffuse light coming from beyond the gateway. Elverda walked toward it, her frail figure erect, unbent. Then she turned a corner and disappeared from his view.

Dorn stood like a stolid figure carved from ironwood. Tamara was on tiptoes, her arms extended as if she were about to take flight. Yuan heard his pulse thumping in his ears.

No one spoke a word. The tunnel was absolutely silent.

Elverda stepped toward the light, her own pulse racing. The only other time she had seen the artifact it showed her a vision of her own life, of the mother who bore her and loved her, of the baby she had never had. It transformed her from a bitter old woman ready for death into a companion for the man-machine Dorn, willing to ply the cold emptiness of the Asteroid Belt to help him find his atonement.

Now she ducked into the grotto where the light glowed coolly. She stopped and stared into the radiance. Its brightness softened, and she saw vague shapes forming and dissolving over and over again, like waves lapping up on a beach, like clouds wafting through the summer sky. She wanted to see her mother again, wanted to hold her and tell her what she'd never been able to say in real life, that she'd always loved her.

But when the shapes coalesced it was not her mother who faced her: it was Dorn, half human, half machine, reaching toward her with both his arms. Like a helpless baby. Like a boy reaching toward his mother. Like a man who felt lost and despairing, desperate for a helping hand. And she knew that she had to sculpt this semi-human, make his heroic statue for all the world to see, make it out of metal and stone, etch every fine tracery on his metal side, make the stone glow like the living flesh of his other half. That was her task, her duty, her goal, to immortalize this man and make his final atonement a memorial to human conscience.

The figure faded, the light dimmed down to a soft pastel radiance. Elverda knew she was finished here. The artifact had opened her mind again and made her understand the path she must take.

With a heavy sigh that was part thanksgiving, part regret, she turned and walked back to the three who were waiting for her.

'Well?' Tamara asked, even before Elverda stepped over the line that the gate had made. 'Is it the same?'

Elverda smiled at the woman. 'Yes, the same. And different.'

'What does that mean?'

Gesturing toward the grotto, Elverda said, 'See for yourself.'

Tamara licked her lips. Dorn remained unmoving. Yuan wondered what he would see – if he worked up the nerve to face the artifact. Better to let Tamara go in, see how it affects her first.

'All right,' Tamara said. 'I will.'

She took a deep breath, like a fighter facing an unknown opponent, and strode past the open gateway.

And the gate began to slide shut behind her.

'Wait!' Yuan yelled, lurching toward the metal gate. He tried to hold it, but the impassive steel slipped past the palms of his hands and settled firmly on the stone floor.

'It's never done that before,' Dorn said, his deep voice sounding puzzled.

'How long will it stay closed?' Yuan asked.

'I don't know,' replied Dorn.

'She's trapped inside there,' Elverda said, 'with the artifact.'

Tamara heard the soft whisper of the gate sliding shut, heard Yuan's startled, 'Wait!'

Whirling about, she saw the gate coming down slowly, inexorably. It settled on the stone flooring, cutting her off from the others. For the flash of an instant she balled her fists to pound on the impassive metal, but she realized it would be futile.

Looking around, she saw that she was in a womblike grotto, a natural hollow in the rocky body of the asteroid. Or was it deliberately carved out by whoever created the artifact? she asked herself.

The artifact. Tamara saw a soft glow coming from around a bend in the grotto. It must be in there. She glanced back at the gate again, felt a pang of alarm that it had closed her in. But there's air to breathe, she realized. It's warm and snug in here. It'll open again. The cyborg says it operates on its own schedule. I just happened to be on the inside when it automatically shut. It'll open again. It hasn't deliberately trapped me in here.

Summoning up her courage, she stepped softly, hesitantly, toward the light. It seemed to glare brighter as she approached it, pulsing like a living heart, blazing so intensely that she closed her eyes to mere slits and yet they still watered painfully. Tamara threw an arm over her brow. It was like staring into the Sun.

But there were shapes in the brilliance. Shifting, undulating shadows that seemed to beckon her closer, closer.

She saw a ten-year-old girl in leotards practicing at a barre before a ceiling-high mirror. Herself, at school in Novosibirsk. The day . . . *that* day. Tamara felt the strength ebb out of her legs. She wanted to sink to the floor. She wanted to cry. But she could do neither; she was frozen where she stood. Yes, there was the sour-faced school nurse coming to tell her. Your mother, Tamara Vishinsky. Your mother is dead. Car accident on the icy road.

Ten-year-old Tamara did not cry. She walked stiffly to her locker to change into her school uniform. But Tamara saw the expression on her own young face: the world had come to an end for her. She never danced again.

Her father. Drunk, almost always. Petting her when he wasn't beating her. Tamara learned that it was better to be petted. She learned how to soothe her father's drunken rages, how to warm his bed and take her mother's role in his life. Daddy. She saw him in his coffin with the snow sifting down like frozen tears.

And he stirred to life and became Martin Humphries. Humphries, who bedded her the first day he saw her. Humphries, who commanded her. Humphries, whose half-insane anger reached across the solar system to bring death to those he feared.

And she understood how to soothe him, how to control him, how to turn his own wrath into a weapon to use against him.

Of course! It's so simple! Tamara laughed despite the pain. She had known it all along: how to control a man, how to keep him from hurting you. But now she understood far more. How to use her innate power not merely to protect herself, but to control a man, to make him do what she wanted, to be in command of him. So simple. So primitive. So powerful.

Two deaths, perhaps three, and Martin Humphries would welcome her back to his bed. From there she could control the most powerful man in the solar system. From there she would wield the power. Humphries would do her bidding. Gladly.

But the pain. The searing, merciless pain that cut through her like a red-hot knife. The pain persisted. It would never go away.

Asteroid 67-046

Koop stood uneasily at the lip of the hatch that led down to the artifact. He and the armed crewman with him were both in nanofabric space suits, despite being inside the pressurized and heated glassteel dome that Humphries Space Systems engineers had built on the surface of the asteroid.

Outside the dome's airlock sat the squat, spindly shuttlecraft they had used to fly from *Viking* to the asteroid's surface. A segmented access passageway connected the shuttle's airlock to that of the dome. To Koop it looked like a giant earthworm.

'How long've they been down there?' the crewman asked, echoing Koop's own nervousness.

Without bothering to look at his wrist, Koop answered, 'Damn near three hours now.'

'Maybe I oughtta go down and see if they're okay.'

'Naw,' said Koop. 'If the captain wants us he'll holler for us.'

The crewman nodded half-heartedly. Then he asked, 'Is he still in charge?'

'Who? The captain?'

'Yeah. I mean, Vishinsky seems to be giving the orders now.'

'He's still the captain.'

'You think so?'

'I'll tell you when I don't.'

'What's she like in bed?'

Koop drew in a breath. He'd known it would come to this, sooner or later.

'None of your damn business,' he growled.

The crewman grinned at him.

Yuan's voice came through the speaker set into Koop's bubble helmet. 'We're coming up.'

'Okay,' said Koop, adding silently, Good.

Koop peered at them carefully as they climbed up through the hatch set into the dome's floor. The four of them seemed unchanged by their experience with the artifact.

The cyborg was still as stolid and menacing as ever. The old woman was the same. Tamara was smiling, but there wasn't any joy in it. Her smile was like a cobra's. The captain – well, maybe he did look a little different. More serious. Quieter. Like he had a lot on his mind, a lot to think about.

'Isokuru,' said Yuan to the crewman, 'go power up the shuttle.'

'Hai!' The crewman made a perfunctory bow and started through the airlock.

Koop edged over to the captain's side. 'Did you see it?' he asked in a near-whisper.

Yuan pressed his lips into a thin line and nodded. 'I saw it.'

'What was it like?'

He shook his head slowly. 'I don't think I can describe it, Koop. I don't have the words for it.'

Koop glanced at Tamara, then asked, 'Do you think I—'

'It's shut down now,' Yuan said. 'We don't know how long it'll stay shut. It kept Tamara in there for more than an hour.'

Before Koop could say anything more, Tamara tapped Yuan on the shoulder.

When he turned toward her she gestured to Elverda and Dorn. 'We're not bringing these two back with us.'

Yuan felt his brows hike. 'We're not?'

'No. Kill them now. Let this be their final resting place.'

Perspiration trickled down Yuan's ribs. 'Why don't we just leave them here? They wouldn't last long.'

'Kill them. I want to bring absolute proof back to Martin that they're both dead.'

'Oh, so he's not Mr. Humphries anymore.'

Tamara gave him a pitying, almost disgusted look. 'Kill them both. Now.'

Yuan's hand slid to the sidearm at his hip. His hand was trembling, he realized. Elverda lifted her chin and stood before him at her full height like an Incan queen facing her doom regally. Dorn stood beside her, impassive as a machine.

'I told you to kill them,' Tamara insisted.

This isn't a computer game, Yuan was saying to himself. These are real people, real living human beings. Even if the cyborg is half machine, he's still a man. In his mind's eye he saw the blood splashed across the old commander's chest, the startled look in his sightless eyes. It must have hurt when the blade went in, Yuan thought. It must have hurt like hell.

'Kao Yuan, you're not fit to be captain of your ship,' Tamara snarled. 'I'm taking over. You're nothing but a gutless coward.'

Coward? Yuan's inner voice echoed. Coward? Yuan saw again what the artifact had showed him. He saw himself at the end of his life, respected by everyone, surrounded by his devoted children and grandchildren and great-grandchildren. He saw warmth and safety and admiration. He saw love.

'Koop!' Tamara's voice cut through the vision like a diamond-bladed saw. 'Kill them both and leave this pathetic coward with their bodies.'

'Me?' Koop squeaked.

Yuan's mind was racing. I'm not a coward, he said to himself. I'm on the wrong path and if I murder these two I'll never be able to get off that track, never be able to reach the path that the artifact showed me.

'Stand down, Koop,' he said to the Hawaiian. 'That's an order.'

Koop looked relieved, Tamara furious.

'When Humphries hears about this—'

'Hears about what?' Yuan replied softly. 'That I refused to murder two unarmed prisoners?'

'That you've disobeyed his orders,' she snapped. 'He'll kill you. He'll have you roasted on a spit.'

Yuan laughed at her. 'No, he won't. I understand what my path has to be, Tamara. I've seen the end of my life. Humphries isn't going to kill me. I'm going to live a long, long time – and raise a big family.'

'You're crazy! The artifact's unhinged your mind.'

'No. The artifact's shown me how to live.'

Tamara uttered a guttural growl and flicked her right hand. The stiletto-slim blade snapped into her hand.

'No!' Yuan shouted, reaching toward her. She slashed his arm. Blood spurted. Koop remained rooted where he stood, eyes popping, mouth open but no sound coming from it. Yuan clapped his other hand over the slicing wound that pumped blood through his grasping fingers.

Tamara whirled and sank the bloody blade into Dorn's human side. She felt it scrape along a rib, then sink deep into his chest. The cyborg grunted and tottered backward a step.

Yanking the blade free, Tamara turned to face Elverda. The old woman put out her arms defensively, but she was frail, her arms bone thin, no barrier at all to the knife.

Then Dorn's mechanical arm flashed out. His metal hand closed on Tamara's fingers. Bones snapped and she screamed in sudden agony. The blade dropped clattering to the floor as Tamara sank to her knees, her face white with pain and shock.

Dorn released her, then collapsed himself, his tunic darkening with blood. Yuan and Koop both rushed to him, leaving Tamara gasping and staring wild-eyed at her mangled right hand.

Elverda knelt beside her just before she fainted from the pain.

Salvage Ship *Vogeltod*:
Two Months Later

'Let me get this straight,' Valker said to Kao Yuan. 'You want me to hand *Hunter* over to you?'

'To its rightful owner,' said Kao Yuan, nodding toward Elverda Apacheta, sitting on the front few centimeters of the big recliner in the middle of Valker's compartment.

It had taken two months for Yuan to track own *Hunter*, which he had released after taking Dorn and Elverda aboard his own *Viking*. After seeing the artifact, Yuan realized that he had to return the sculptress and her cyborg companion to their own ship and let them find their own destinies among the asteroids.

Yuan still bore a scar from Tamara's knifing; he refused to allow nanotherapy to remove the scar. Something to show my grandchildren, he thought. A reminder of the wrong path I was on.

Dorn recovered, albeit slowly, from his chest wound, thanks to stem cell therapy. Tamara's crushed fingers had healed completely. Yuan made it clear to the crew that she was a prisoner; she had free rein of the ship, except for the bridge. She was not permitted to communicate with headquarters.

'When Humphries finds out what you've done,' she warned, time and again.

Yuan would simply shake his head, grinning. It doesn't matter what Humphries threatens, he told himself. I've seen where my life leads. I'll get through this, one way or another.

At last Yuan found Elverda's ship under tow by *Vogeltod*, heading for Ceres. *Vogeltod*'s skipper, Valker, had graciously welcomed them aboard his vessel and brought them to his own quarters to discuss the situation.

Valker sat behind his oversized desk, smiling handsomely at his two visitors. Elverda smiled back, a little uncertainly, from her perch on the recliner. Yuan, wearing a crisply clean uniform with captain's stripes on its cuffs, was sitting on the edge of Valker's bunk, the only other available seat in the jam-packed compartment.

'You're Elverda Apacheta,' Valker said, more of a statement than a question.

'Yes. I am the owner of the *Hunter*.'

'You're a very famous woman,' Valker said, his smile going even brighter. 'I looked you up. I've never met a sculptress before. I'm honored to have you aboard my ship.'

She smiled back at him. 'You are very gracious.'

'No, not at all.' Valker's smile turned almost shy. Then he suggested, 'Why don't we have some refreshments while we're talking? It's almost dinner time.'

'I'd like to get this settled as quickly as we can,' Yuan said.

'We have an injured man aboard Captain Yuan's ship,' Elverda said. 'I don't want to leave him for very long.'

'I see,' said Valker. 'Okay. Let's talk business. When we found *Hunter* she was drifting and abandoned. That makes her a derelict, according to IAA regulations. We took claim of her and we're bringing her back to Ceres.'

Elverda objected, 'But she's not salvage—'

'No, she's not,' Valker agreed, stopping her with an upraised hand. 'But she *was* a derelict and we have a legal right to sell her for the best price we can get.'

'I am her owner,' Elverda said.

'You were her owner, dear lady. Now she's my property. Mine, and my crew's.'

Yuan said, 'I'm not sure the courts at Ceres would agree with you.'

With a laugh, Valker replied, 'That's what makes horse races. And why we have lawyers.'

'But I don't want to travel all the way back to Ceres,' Elverda objected.

Valker said, 'Then make me an offer.'

'An offer?'

'Right here and now. How much are you willing to pay for the ship?'

Elverda glanced at Yuan, then said, 'But I have no money.'

'She's worth at least half a bill,' said Valker.

'I have no money,' Elverda repeated.

Valker sighed. 'Then I guess we'll have to go to Ceres.'

Yuan gripped the edge of the bunk's mattress,

thinking hard. I could accept his decision and go back to *Viking* with Elverda. Or I could return to my ship and then blast this scavenger into a cloud of hot plasma and retake *Hunter* for her. I could. It would be easy. But what would the consequences be? You already have to deal with Tamara and probably Humphries. You're already in deep trouble. How can you reach your proper path in life if you continue to live by violence?

The artifact had changed Yuan, profoundly altered his outlook on life by showing him a goal, a path, a tao that he yearned deeply to achieve. He thought about consequences now. He looked farther ahead in time than he had ever done before, and realized that until he had seen the artifact he had been merely zigzagging through life, bouncing from one event to the next, jittering like a dust mote being pushed and jostled by the forces around it, with neither control nor care about what happened next. Now he looked ahead, as far into the future as he could. He knew his life would end happily. But how to get to that destiny? That was his problem.

Valker saw the look on Yuan's face. He had seen it before and knew what it meant: trouble, big time. The man was determined to help this old lady, and he had a fully armed attack ship at his command.

'Isn't there some way . . .' Elverda began, but her plaintive question died in her throat before she could finish it.

'What were you using the ship for?' Valker asked. He had seen from the IAA registry that there was no crew listed, only one other person aboard the vessel, some-body named Dorn. A priest, according to the records. But there was no dossier on the man. His history was a complete blank.

'It's a personal mission,' said Elverda, suddenly looking uncomfortable.

'Personal?' Valker's smile turned doubtful. 'You mean you don't want to talk about it?'

Elverda seemed to struggle within herself for a few heartbeats. Then she said, 'I am assisting Dorn.'

'The priest.'

'Yes. His objective is to find the bodies of those who were killed in the wars and left to drift through the Belt.'

Valker blinked at her. 'Salvage dead bodies?'

'To give them proper funeral rites,' said Elverda. 'I know it seems outlandish, but—'

Leaning back in his big desk chair, Valker said, 'Not at all outlandish. I understand salvage. Families must be willing to pay handsomely to have the bodies of their dead returned to them.'

'It's not for money,' Elverda said. 'We never even thought of that. We simply give them final rites, as they deserve.'

With a low whistle, Valker steepled his fingers in front of his face, thinking hard. They're two nutcases, this old woman and her priest. Wandering around the Belt picking up bodies. To give them funeral rites? That's weird. She could be lying, of course. There could be something else in this.

'I see,' he said at last. Leaning forward, he placed

both his big hands on the desktop. 'Okay. You're involved in something that's . . . it's religious, isn't it?'

Elverda nodded slowly.

'Okay. I won't stand in your way. You can have your ship.'

Elverda gasped. 'I can?'

Yuan asked, 'For how much?'

'Nothing. For free. A gift from Captain Valker and his crew.'

'Do you mean it?' Elverda seemed on the verge of tears.

'Of course I mean it,' Valker said, getting to his feet and coming around the massive desk. '*Hunter* is all yours. And maybe you can get your priest to say a prayer for me and my crew. Might do us some good.'

'Certainly! Of course!' Elverda rose, clasping her hands together in gratitude. 'Bless you, Captain Valker.'

Yuan stood up too, his face showing more suspicion than appreciation.

Valker walked them from his compartment to the airlock, where *Viking* and *Vogeltod* were mated together. Elverda kept thanking him and he acted as if almost embarrassed by her gratitude. As he saw them through the airlock, Valker thought that it would be simple to hand over *Hunter* to them and then have all three ships go their separate ways. Once he was sure that Yuan's *Viking* was safely out of the picture he could always track down *Hunter* and retake it. Without falling under the guns of *Viking*. The old woman and the priest were the only crew aboard *Hunter*. Kill them,

Valker said to himself, and then their ship is yours again, free and clear.

He laughed as Elverda kissed him on both cheeks before leaving *Vogeltod*.

Tamara was lying on the bunk in her compartment, watching the wall screen. It showed *Hunter* disengaging from the little salvage vessel. Small puffs of cold gas jets pushed *Hunter* away from the smaller ship for a quarter of an hour. She listened to the radio chatter between the cyborg, who was apparently piloting *Hunter*, and Yuan, on *Viking*'s bridge.

'We're ready to light the main engine,' came Dorn's deep, methodical voice.

A moment's pause, then Yuan said, 'You're clear for ignition.'

Tamara saw a flash of blue-hot ionized gas and *Hunter* seemed to leap out of her vision, hurtling deeper into the Belt.

She counted the seconds. It took Yuan only thirty-four of them to get to her compartment's accordion door and rap on its frame.

'Come in,' she called.

He slid the door open and ducked one single step into her quarters. 'I thought you'd want to know that we're heading in now.'

'To Ceres,' she replied.

He grinned at her. 'No. To Selene. Headquarters. Humphries wants to see us. Both of us.'

BOOK III

Six Months Later

Nor blame I Death, because he bare
The use of virtue out of earth:
I know transplanted human worth
Will bloom to profit, otherwhere.

Ore Ship *Syracuse*:
Backup Command Pod

The pod was more of a home to Theo than his own quarters. He spent most of his free time in it, watching over *Syracuse*'s slowly failing systems, nursing the old bucket along day by excruciating day.

He was well past eighteen now, taller than his mother. His body had filled out some; he was growing into manhood. Less than six months remaining, he said to himself as he checked the navigation display. We're on our way back to Ceres. Will we make it?

He remembered seeing an old novel about a man who tries to go around the world – Earth, of course – in ninety days. Or was it eighty? The story was set a couple of centuries ago, and at one point the character is sailing across the Atlantic Ocean in a steam-powered ship. But they run out of coal for the steam boiler. So he has the crew cannibalize the ship's wooden structure, tearing the planks apart until there's nothing left above water but the ship's steel skeleton, its boiler, engine and paddle wheel.

That's what we're doing, Theo told himself. Cannibalizing old *Syracuse* as we limp back to port. It's a race to see if we can get to Ceres before the old bucket falls apart.

One hundred and sixty-seven days, he read off the ship's navigation computer screen. If my calculations are right. If I haven't messed up somewhere. One hundred and sixty-seven days to go.

Theo had taught himself a fair amount of astronomy over the past three-plus years. With all the ship's antennas out, he could not receive guidance signals from Ceres or anywhere else. Nor could he probe ahead with radar. It was impossible to determine where the ship was, or even its heading, through the ordinary electronic systems. So Theo learned the stars from the ship's library and learned to navigate by them. Using the stars, he kept *Syracuse* on its course back to Ceres.

He hoped.

At the moment, his attention was focused on their dwindling water supply. He had strictly rationed the water he, his sister and mother used. Angela had accused him of being a tyrant more than once. But Mother had merely smiled and accepted his estimates of how much water they could afford to use for drinking, for cooking, for bathing.

The recyclers aren't perfect, he told his sister time and again. We're losing water every day.

And without water for the fusion reactor their electrical power would fail. No electricity meant death: no power for the air recycler, no lights, no heat. They would freeze in the dark. Or suffocate.

So Theo shut down the sections of the ship they weren't using. Only this backup command pod and their living quarters received electrical power and breathable air. And the tube-tunnels connecting them. The rest of the ship was dark and airless.

The water recycler. It was Theo's daily burden. Every day he climbed down the tunnel to the equipment bay where the fusion reactor sat side by side with the recyclers and the now dormant main propulsion engine. Every day he nursed the cranky collection of pipes and filters, cleaning its grids tenderly, patching leaks in the connection seals, stealing sections of pipe from other parts of the ship and cannibalizing parts for the recycler's electrical motors.

He dreamed at night that he was trapped in the maze of piping, sloshing in water that was spurting from the recycler, going to waste, gushing across the deck and out into empty space. Once he dreamt that the water's inexorable current carried him outside the ship, too. He woke in a cold sweat, shivering. And berated himself for wasting the water of his perspiration.

Angela stepped through the hatch of the command pod.

'Reporting for duty,' she said, with a crisp salute and a challenging grin.

Theo glanced at the digital clock. 'You're three and a half minutes early, Angie.'

'Early bird gets the worm,' she said.

'But who wants worms?'

They both laughed. Theo got up from the command chair and Angela slid into it lightly. They had all lost weight on their enforced diet, but Angie had slimmed down best of all. She looked fine to Theo, a real beauty now.

'Any problems?' she asked, her eyes scanning the control board. Most of the telltale lights were dark now; only the systems they absolutely needed for survival were still functioning.

'Everything's percolating along,' Theo replied.

'Mom's got a problem with the microwave again,' Angie said. 'She thinks she can fix it, but you ought to give her a hand.'

'Gotcha,' said Theo. 'After I check the beast.'

Angie looked up at him. 'Trouble again?'

'No, but if I don't look in on that glorified clanker every spitting day it springs leaks just to devil me.'

'Maybe it misses you. Maybe the recycler loves your company.'

'Sure. And maybe water falls out of the sky. But not here.'

Aboard *Vogeltod* Valker was facing a grumbling crew.

'You never shoulda let them go in the first place,' said Nicco. He was a short, swarthy man with a thick mop of curly black hair and the faint trace of a scar running from the corner of his mouth across his cheek.

Valker's usual smile faded. If Nicco's pissed at me, he thought, the rest of 'em must be ready for mutiny.

Behind him, the others of the crew – all eight of them – nodded and muttered agreement. They had all jammed into the galley for this showdown, leaving *Vogeltod* cruising on automatic. The compartment felt steamy from the press of their bodies. Valker smelled sweat – and anger.

'It's been six goddamn months,' Kirk said, his voice almost breaking with pent-up resentment. 'Six months with nothing in our pocket. Nothing!'

Valker put on his brightest smile for them. 'Come on, guys, we've had dry spells before—'

'We had them and their ship in our hands,' Kirk insisted, pounding the palm of one hand with his other fist. 'The captain of the *Viking*, too.'

'And you let them go!'

Sitting at the head of the galley's narrow table, Valker leaned back, seemingly completely at ease.

'Now look,' he said. 'That *Viking* was an attack ship. Do we want to tangle with a ship that can blow us away like *that*?' He snapped his fingers.

Nicco and several of the others shook their heads.

'Besides,' Valker went on, 'it was a Humphries Space Systems ship. Even if we could've knocked it off we'd have HSS after us. You want that?'

'No . . .' Nicco said hesitantly.

'But what about the other one?' Kirk demanded. '*Hunter*? It wasn't armed. Nobody aboard her but that old woman and the cyborg.'

'A whole ship, intact.'

'And you let them go.'

'That's what we're after,' Valker said. 'That's the one we're looking for.'

'For six goddamn months.'

Spreading his arms, Valker said, 'It's been a lean six months, I know. If we'd run across something else we would've taken it. You know that. But this region's been pretty damned empty.'

'Then we oughtta move to an area where there's better pickin's.'

'You're right,' Valker said smoothly. 'That's just what I intend to do. I hate to give up on *Hunter*, though. She could have fetched a pretty penny for us at Ceres.'

'Six months is long enough.'

'Too long.'

'Okay. I hear you,' Valker said to them. 'Just give me another few days. If we don't find *Hunter* by then, we'll move to another sector.'

'Not in a few days,' Kirk said, baring his teeth. 'Now.'

Valker broadened his smile. 'You're not giving the orders on this ship, Kirk. I am.'

'Well maybe we oughtta change that.'

Slowly Valker got to his feet. He stood a good six centimeters taller than Kirk. 'If you want to—'

'CONTACT,' boomed the computer's synthesized voice over the intercom speakers in the galley's overhead. 'CONTACT WITH AN UNIDENTIFIED SHIP.'

Valker held up a clenched fist. 'There you are, guys! We've found her!'

Cargo Ship *Pleiades*: Solar Storm

Although Victor Zacharias cruised through the Asteroid Belt in silence, emitting no signals that another ship could detect except an occasional microsecond pulse of search radar, he still listened to whatever chatter *Pleiades*'s antennas could pick up. Sometimes he thought the only thing that kept him from outright madness as he sailed alone through the empty months was the inane entertainment broadcasts from Earth and the Moon.

He was leaner now, harder. His years of enforced labor on *Chrysalis II* had toughened not only his outlook but his body as well. His arms were hard ropes of muscle, his midsection flat and firm. The midnight black beard he had grown made him look satisfyingly menacing, he thought. I'll shave it off when I find Pauline and the kids, he told himself.

He sat alone in the galley, his softbooted feet propped up on one of the swivel chairs, and watched an educational vid from Selene. An earnest young scientist was walking the viewer through the new liquid mercury optical telescope at the Farside Observatory. With a pang of memory, Victor saw the original Farside facility that he had helped to design: the ten-kilometer-square spread of dipole antennas that made up the main radio telescope, the old twenty-meter reflector spun from lunar glass, the labs and workshops and dormitory facility for the Farside staff.

But the scientist-narrator was pretty much of a bore, Victor thought, droning on about details of the new telescope. He switched to an entertainment channel from Earth.

'And what did these Godless scientists bring us?' thundered a florid-faced man in a white suit. 'Floods! Drought! Storms that drowned whole cities! Those were the fruits of the secularists who brought on the greenhouse warming and the biowars and all the other horrors of our age! They brought down the wrath of God upon us!'

The preacher marched back and forth across his stage as he went on, 'It was only when the Faithful returned to their God, only when the people of this great nation accepted the Lord as their salvation, that some measure of peace and stability returned to the land.'

Victor flicked through a dozen more channels before stopping at an erotic film. Two women, three men, clad in nothing but glistening perspiration. I wonder where this is broadcast from? Victor asked himself. Certainly nowhere in the United States, not with the New Morality in control of the media.

The scene shifted to a dimly lit Asian temple. Four, no five naked women were making love together. Victor leaned back in his galley chair and thought about moving to the bunk in his compartment. But then I might miss something, he rationalized. Suddenly a squad of barbarian warriors burst into the temple. The women squealed daintily as the men cast off their furs and weapons and delved into them.

'WARNING,' the ship's intercom blared emotionlessly. 'THIS IS A WARNING FROM THE INTERNATIONAL ASTRO-NAUTICAL AUTHORITY'S SOLAR WATCH. A FORCE-FIVE SOLAR FLARE HAS ERUPTED IN THE LOWER LEFT QUAD-RANT OF THE CHROMOSPHERE. RADIATION FROM THIS EVENT WILL REACH LETHAL LEVELS FOR ALL UNPRO-TECTED PERSONS AND EQUIPMENT. FURTHER BULLETINS WILL BE BROADCAST AS THE SOLAR STORM DEVELOPS. TAKE ALL NECESSARY PRECAUTIONS AND STAY TUNED FOR NEW INFORMATION AS IT DEVELOPS.'

Switching to the IAA's dedicated information chan-nel, Victor saw that the deadly radiation cloud from the flare would miss Mercury, but envelop Venus and Earth within a few hours.

No word yet on how intense it'll be when it reaches the Belt, he saw. The cloud of hard radiation belched out by a solar flare was guided through the solar system by the twists and kinks of the interplanetary magnetic field. A cloud that wreaks havoc on Earth's telecommunications might not come within a hundred million klicks of Mars even when the two planets were at their closest.

Plenty of time to get into the storm cellar, Victor thought as he switched back to the pornography. I just hope the storm doesn't foul up the signal from Earth.

Without any working antennas *Syracuse* was cut off from the storm warning. But the ship's radiation sensors pinged while the family was eating its meager breakfast. They were down to two meals per day: a breakfast of juices and protein bars, and a dinner that Pauline tried to make attractive and nourishing.

'Radiation alarm,' Theo said, his mouth half filled with the last of his morning's protein bar.

'Solar storm?' Angela asked.

Theo nodded. 'Prob'ly. Might be the precursor wave of high-energy protons and heavier stuff.'

Pauline said, 'We'd better get to the storm cellar, then.'

'Right,' said Theo. 'I'll go up to the control pod, see what the instruments show, and check out everything. We might have to fly on remote for a few days.'

Looking at Angela, Pauline said, 'You help Theo into his suit.'

'I won't need a suit,' Theo protested.

'It's extra protection and you'd be foolish not to take advantage of it,' Pauline said firmly. 'I'll check the food stores in the storm cellar. If I recall from the last one we were almost out of juices there.'

'I restocked the juices,' Angela said, getting up from the galley table.

'Good.'

Theo got to his feet and followed Angela out to the airlock area, where the space suits were stored.

'I really don't need this,' he grumbled to his sister once they were out of Pauline's hearing. 'Mom's being a tight-ass.'

'Don't let *her* hear you say that.'

'Tight-butt. Okay?'

Angela grinned as Theo sat on the bench in front of the lockers and began tugging on his suit's leggings.

'The suit gives you an extra layer of protection against radiation,' Angela recited from memory. 'It could be the difference between life and death.'

'If we get so much radiation that the spittin' suit saves my life, half the equipment still running on this bucket will barf out,' Theo said sharply.

'You're always such an optimist, Thee.'

It'll be two days before the storm hits, Victor saw on the wall screen's display. He was exercising on the treadmill in *Pleiades*'s gym, a small, almost claustrophobic metal-walled chamber jammed with equipment that Victor thought of as implements of torture. Necessary torture, though. It would be all too easy to bloat into a boneless slug aboard ship. Exercise was necessary, vitally so.

Two days before the cloud of high-energy protons and electrons smothers this region of space. There's lots of heavier ions in the cloud, too, he saw as he studied the latest IAA bulletin. The ship's magnetic field will deflect most of the crud, but rad levels will still go up in here. I'll have to spend a couple of days in the storm cellar.

Communications from Earth had fizzled out once the storm cloud reached the Earth/Moon region. For entertainment, Theo had to fall back on the chips that Cheena Madagascar had stocked in the captain's compartment. The woman had interesting tastes, Victor discovered. He knew from his own experience that

Cheena was a vigorous heterosexual, but her assortment of entertainment vids was much, much broader.

I'd better bring some of the better ones to the storm cellar with me, he told himself. Not much else to do in there while I'm riding out the storm.

Then he remembered that Pauline and the kids would probably be hit by the same cloud of deadly radiation. *Syracuse* has a storm cellar, he thought. Pauline will make sure they're safe.

But how many storms has battered old *Syracuse* gone through? How many more can the ship take before its vital systems break down?

Like most deep-space ships, *Syracuse*'s storm cellar was a tight little compartment lined with thick metal walls that held a heavy liquid mixture that absorbed incoming subatomic particles. After a storm, once it was safe to leave the cellar, the liquid was flushed into the propellant tank for the fusion torch engine; eventually the absorbed particles were fired out the engine's thruster.

Theo stared worriedly at the wall screen as he sat on the padded bench that ran along the cellar's oval interior. The screen showed the level of absorbent remaining in the supply tank.

'How does it look?' his mother asked. She was sitting beside him. Angela sat across the minicompartment, where the food locker stood.

Theo thought for a moment before answering, 'Depends on how intense the storm is, Mom, and how long it lasts.' He didn't voice the rest of it: we might get through this storm, but we'll be out of luck if another one hits us.

Angela looked concerned, almost frightened. 'We'll be all right, won't we, Thee?'

He made himself smile at her. 'Sure, Angie. We'll be okay.' He wished he actually felt that way.

Valker worked hard to keep smiling. Cooped up with the rest of the crew in *Vogeltod*'s minuscule storm cellar was a strain, by any measure.

And just before the storm's radiation blanked out the ship's communications there had been that tantalizing blip on the radar screen. A ship, Valker was convinced. It had to be a ship, not a rock. No asteroid gives a profile like that.

It wasn't *Hunter*, the ship they'd been seeking all these past months. But it was a ship. Valker was certain of it. It was running silent for some reason. No tracking beacon, no telemetry coming out of her. All the better. A derelict, most likely. But she was intact, as far as the radar profile could show. All in one piece, not busted up. It's a ship that we can take and sell back at Ceres for a pretty dollar.

Valker couldn't wait for the storm to subside. The smell of the other men crowded into the cellar gave him even more incentive to get out and take that ship, no matter who it belonged to or who might be aboard her.

Selene: Humphries
Space Systems Headquarters

As the flunky in the conservatively dark suit led them through the warren of cubicles filled with quietly busy HSS employees, Yuan thought that Tamara seemed strangely cool, confident. She looked quite calm, almost serene, as if she were looking forward to this meeting with Martin Humphries. Yuan tried to picture how Humphries would react when he admitted that he had let Dorik Harbin and the old woman go free. Humphries doesn't like to be disobeyed. This isn't going to be easy, he told himself.

Yet Tamara seemed unconcerned, almost at ease. He wondered if she really was that relaxed or whether it was all an act, a front of bravura that she really didn't feel.

There's nothing for me to worry about, Yuan told himself. He thought back to the vision that the artifact had shown him. You're going to live a long and fruitful life, he repeated in his mind over and again. Yeah, he replied silently. Maybe. But the instant they had presented themselves at the corporate headquarters' reception desk, the bountiful young redheaded receptionist's smile had evaporated.

'Mr. Humphries wants to see you both,' she'd said ominously. 'Himself.'

Himself. Martin Humphries himself wants to see us, Yuan thought as the flunky in the dark tunic and slacks led them through the maze of cubicles. Report to him personally. Tell the most powerful man in the solar system that you not only failed to carry out his orders, you turned his intended victims loose, sent them on their way to wander through the Belt, free and unharmed. He's not going to like that.

Humphries Space Systems headquarters occupied one entire tower of the two that supported Selene's Main Plaza. Fifteen stories of offices and god knows what else. Yuan had heard that Martin Humphries once lived in a grandiose mansion built at the lowermost level of Selene, as deep as he could get, safe from the radiation and meteoroids that peppered the Moon's airless surface. But that mansion had been burned to ashes by Lars Fuchs, and Humphries nearly killed. Now the man lived over in Hell Crater, surrounded by the casinos and shopping arcades, the hotels and brothels of that resort facility.

But he's here in his office today, Yuan thought. To see us. And deal with us.

Yuan told himself there was nothing to fear. He tried to concentrate on the vision he'd seen at the artifact. I'm going to live to be an old, old man. I'm going to enjoy my grandchildren and great-grandchildren. A distant voice in his mind tried to warn him that he could experience much pain and sorrow during such a long life, but Yuan tried to dismiss that from his thoughts. Nothing Humphries can do will prevent the outcome the artifact showed me, he insisted to himself.

Down a long corridor flanked with closed doors on either side. Discreet little brass nameplates on each door. Yuan could see a trickle of perspiration sliding down the side of Tamara's face. She's not as cool as she's pretending to be, he realized. She was wearing a sleek pearl-gray jumpsuit that clung to her coltish figure like plastic wrap. Trying to look her best for Martin Humphries. I wonder if that will help her?

'In here, please,' said the flunky as he opened an unmarked door at the end of the corridor.

They stepped through and the flunky closed the door behind them. The room was the size of a spaceport departure gate, thickly carpeted, its walls covered with smart screens that displayed art treasures. Yuan recognized the *Mona Lisa*, a painting of royal children by Velazquez, some others. His eye was caught by a painting of a fallen banyan tree, its magnificently intertwined trunk ripped out of the ground by some overpowering force.

'Captain Yuan and Ms. Vishinsky,' said the young woman sitting behind the desk at the far end of the anteroom, her voice flat, toneless. 'Mr. Humphries will see you immediately.'

She pressed a key of her desk pad and another unmarked door swung open.

Yuan found himself smiling. He bowed slightly to Tamara and whispered, 'After you.'

She gave him a swift glance, fiddled nervously with the buttons on the bodice of her coveralls, and strode to the open doorway. Yuan followed closely behind her, thinking, She's scared now. Her confidence is melting away.

The office was smaller than the anteroom, but still big enough to land a shuttlecraft. A man got up from behind a broad, immaculately clear desk and stonily gestured toward the two low-slung sculptured chairs in front of his desk.

Tamara said, 'You're not Martin Humphries.'

'No,' the young man replied curtly. 'I'm his son, Alex.'

Alex Humphries resembled the holos of his father so closely that Yuan wondered if he was a clone. His hair was dark, his face firm, slightly round, but with a strong jaw. He was taller than Yuan had expected, and wearing a casual open-necked royal blue shirt over than denim jeans. His eyes were hard and gray as lunar rock.

'I thought we were to see Martin Humphries,' Yuan said as he lowered himself into the slingback chair.

'My father seldom leaves his home over in Hell Crater,' said Alex Humphries.

Tamara asked, 'Then you're running the corporation?'

Alex smiled coldly. 'That depends on who you ask. My father thinks he still runs it, but I have the day-to-day responsibility. I do his dirty work and he stays over at Hell Crater and amuses himself.'

'It never even occurred to me that Mr. Humphries had a son,' Yuan said.

'He has two of them. My baby brother Van lives on Earth.'

'I see.' Yuan nodded.

'I also thought we'd been summoned here by your father,' said Tamara.

Alex leaned back in his swivel chair. 'My father is very disappointed in you. Angry, you know. So furious that he almost came over here today to deal with you personally.'

'But you're going to deal with us, instead,' Tamara replied.

'He expected you to carry out his orders.'

'He expected us,' Yuan said, 'to murder an old woman and a cyborg who fancies himself a priest on some sort of a holy mission.'

'But you didn't do it.'

'No, we didn't,' Yuan said. Then, glancing at Tamara, he added, 'To be specific, *I* didn't do it. I was in command, it was my responsibility, my decision, not hers.'

'What happened?' Alex Humphries asked, his voice suddenly cold, his eyes hard, demanding.

Tamara was staring at Alex, Yuan saw. Trying to figure him out, he thought; trying to gauge what lay behind those steel gray eyes.

Yuan began to explain, 'The cyborg and the old woman are no threat to your father—'

'That's not your decision to make.'

'They'll never return to the Earth/Moon sector. They'll die out there in the Belt, searching for the bodies of the dead.'

Alex's brows rose. 'Is that really what they're doing?'

'Yes.'

'Searching for bodies?'

'Mercenaries killed in the wars and left to drift in space.'

'But why?'

'The cyborg was a mercenary. He's the one who wiped out the *Chrysalis* habitat.'

'Dorik Harbin.'

'He calls himself Dorn now,' Tamara interjected. 'He claims that the alien artifact changed him, turned him into a priest.'

'The artifact,' Alex said, edging forward in his chair. 'That's what I want to ask you about. My father had a bad experience with it.'

Tamara relaxed visibly. She even smiled at Alex Humphries.

Looking at Yuan, though, Alex asked, 'Harbin claims the artifact changed him?'

Yuan nodded.

'And the woman? Elverda Apacheta? It changed her, too?'

With a slight shrug, Yuan answered, 'It must have. She's willing to spend what's left of her life roaming through the Belt with Harbin to find the corpses from the war.'

Alex appeared to relax slightly. 'You've both seen the artifact?'

'Yes,' said Tamara.

'My father's forbidden me to go to it. He doesn't want anyone to see it.'

'But you want to see it, don't you?' Tamara asked.

'Of course! An alien artifact. Who wouldn't want to see it? Why do you think my father had that asteroid moved out of its original orbit? Why do you think he's placed guards around it?'

'It's a powerful experience,' Yuan said. 'Truly life-changing.'

'What did you see?' Alex asked eagerly. 'How did the artifact affect you?'

Yuan hesitated. How to talk about it without sounding foolish? he wondered.

Misunderstanding their silence, Alex explained, 'You see, I want to *understand* that artifact. It couldn't have been made by human beings; it's got to be an alien creation. Intelligent extraterrestrials left it there for us to find. Why? When? How does it work?'

'I don't know if human minds will ever be able to understand it,' Yuan admitted.

'I can't believe that,' Alex Humphries said, with some heat. 'I won't believe that.'

'You haven't seen it,' said Yuan.

'How did it affect you?' Humphries asked again. 'How did it change you?'

Haltingly, almost embarrassed by his experience, Yuan described his encounter with the artifact as accurately as he could remember it. Alex listened and nodded, his hands resting on the desktop, fingertips to fingertips.

When Yuan was finished, Alex turned to Tamara. 'And you?'

'Nothing so dramatic,' she lied. 'I sort of relived my childhood, that's all.'

'You don't feel different? Changed?'

'Not really.'

'Strange,' Alex muttered.

For long moments he was silent, while Yuan wondered what was going on in his head. Whatever it is, Yuan told himself, remember that you're dealing with one of the most powerful men in the solar system here. He could snuff you out like clicking off a light switch. He wants to run Humphries Space Systems and keep his father off the throne.

'Here's what I think,' Alex said at last. 'That artifact somehow influences the pattern of your thoughts. You know, we have brain scanning devices that can show the neurons in your brain flashing on and off. Our own neuroscientists can map out a person's patterns of thinking. Right?'

Yuan bobbed his head up and down. Out of the corner of his eye he could see Tamara leaning forward temptingly. She had undone several buttons of her bodice.

'Well, this artifact goes a step or two farther,' Humphries continued. 'It allows your deep unconscious thoughts to come up to the surface, where you can see them clearly. It allows you to see who you really are, who you really want to be.'

'Like a mirror,' Tamara breathed.

'Right! Like a mirror of your own soul.'

Yuan considered for a moment, then said, 'Then it's not showing you what *will* be. It's showing what *could* be.'

'Like the Ghost of Christmas Yet to Come,' said Alex.

Yuan felt disappointed. Nothing is certain, he realized. That beautiful vision . . . Then he realized the truth of it. That beautiful vision is something to aim for, a goal to guide my life, a star to steer by.

'It can be a tremendously powerful force, that artifact. I've got to find out how to control it, how to use it.' Humphries's hands clenched into fists.

He turned to Tamara. She seemed completely relaxed now, in charge of herself.

'It could be enormously powerful, couldn't it?' she suggested.

'Enormously,' said Alex Humphries. 'Whoever understands how to use it has a tremendous edge over everyone else.'

Yuan saw vast dreams glittering in those steel gray eyes.

'In the meantime, what do you intend to do with us?' Tamara asked, her voice low, smoky. Yuan had heard that tone from her before.

Alex blinked, the spell of his fascination with the artifact's power broken. Sitting up straight in the desk chair again he said, 'Well, my father wants you both skinned alive, you know.'

'Is that what you want?' Tamara purred.

His face went utterly serious. 'That depends.'

Yuan started to speak, but Tamara leaned even closer to the desk and said meltingly, 'I'd be glad to do whatever is necessary to help you understand the artifact.'

'What do you want us to do?' Yuan asked.

'You two go build new lives for yourselves. As far as HSS is concerned, you're both fired. I'll provide you with a healthy separation payment, then you're on your own.'

Tamara looked disappointed. 'On my own? With your father wanting me dead? He'll hunt us down—'

'You won't have to worry about that,' Alex said. 'I'll see to it that he doesn't bother you.'

'How can you do that?' Yuan asked.

Alex took in a breath before answering. 'Fair enough question.' He hesitated a moment. Then, 'Yes, my father wants to prevent anyone from learning that he collapsed when he saw the artifact. He was perfectly willing to order murders.'

Tamara shrank back from him a little.

'But I've had a university-full of medics and psychologists trying to put his ego back together. I've convinced him that the best thing to do is allow you two to go your own ways – providing you never mention you ever heard of the artifact.' Alex's voice grew iron hard. 'Not to anyone. Ever.'

Yuan agreed. 'That's fine with me.'

'It'll bring down the wrath of god on you if you speak a word about it,' Alex warned. 'It would be your death warrant.'

Tamara nodded reluctantly, then asked, 'What about Harbin and the old woman? They actually saw him at the artifact.'

'I'll protect them,' said Alex. 'I won't let my father harm them.'

'You can do that?' Yuan asked.

Alex smiled grimly. 'I can try.'

And Yuan realized what was going on. *He's playing a power game against his father. And we're pawns in his game. As long as his father knows there are people* alive who can tell about his collapse, Alex has the upper hand.

Yuan turned toward Tamara, but her eyes were still fastened on Alex Humphries.

If he noticed her focus on him, Alex gave no outward sign of it. He asked, 'All right, then. You'll come with me.'

'With you?' Tamara asked. 'To where?'

'The artifact, of course. We're going to study it. I want to find out how it works, who put it there, *why* they put it there.'

Somehow, Yuan wasn't surprised. But he heard himself ask, 'We're going back to it?'

'Of course. Right away.'

Ore Ship *Syracuse*:
Backup Control Pod

The jolt nearly knocked Theo out of his command chair. Angela, standing behind him, was thrown to the floor.

'COLLISION,' blared the ship's computer. 'PROPELLANT TANK SIX RUPTURED.'

Theo got out of his chair, helped Angela to her feet.

'Propellant tank six?' she muttered, slightly dazed.

'It's been empty for years,' Theo said. 'No loss.'

With both of them on their feet, Theo said, 'Check with Mom, see if she's okay.'

As his sister bent over the intercom panel, Theo scanned his working controls. Cripes! he thought. First a solar storm and now a collision. How much more can we take? Spin rate's increased, he saw. A whole section of the rim's been ripped open. Must've been a sizable rock that hit us, maybe a meter across or more.

He pecked at the control keyboard. Got to fire the spin jets, slow us back to normal. Otherwise the increased angular momentum will start to shake us apart.

But when he called up the spin jet display, half the lights were in the red.

'Damn!' he spat.

'What's the matter?' asked Angela, looking frightened.

Tracing the schematic display with a forefinger, Theo answered, 'The collision cut the circuitry to the spin jets on that side of the hull. The system won't fire with one set of the jets out.'

'Can you override?'

'No, dammit. I'll have to go outside and repair the circuit manually.'

Immediately Angela said, 'I'll back you up.'

'Okay,' said Theo. 'We'll both get into suits but you come back here and take the command chair while I'm outside. If I get into trouble, you'll be ready to come out and help.'

'Right,' Angela said. No argument.

As they clambered up the tube tunnel toward the living quarters and the main airlock, Theo felt the ship vibrating, a slight tremor that would only get worse, he knew, unless he could get the cold-gas jets to slow their spin back to normal.

'How's Mom?' he shouted to Angela, a few rungs of the ladder above him.

'She sounded okay. She said she was working on the air filters when the collision hit.'

'She wasn't hurt, was she?'

'You know Mom. She'd have to lose an arm or a leg before she'd admit she got hurt.'

Pauline was waiting for them at the hatch to the airlock. 'I've pulled out your suits and checked their air tanks. Both suits are ready for use.'

'Thanks, Mom,' Theo said.

Pauline helped them into their suits, checked the seals, then sent Angela back toward the control pod. Once she reported on the intercom that she was safely at her post, Pauline started to pull her own suit out of its locker.

'What're you doing, Mom?' Theo asked.

'I'll be your backup. Help me into my suit, please.'

'But Angie—'

'Angie's in the pod. If you get into trouble, I can be outside with you in three minutes, the time it takes to cycle the airlock. Angie's fifteen minutes away.'

Theo recognized the tone of his mother's voice. All that arguing would do was delay the repairs he needed to make. It would never change his mother's mind, or blunt her determination.

'Okay,' he said, with a defeated sigh. Yet inwardly he knew his mother was right, and he appreciated her wisdom.

Once outside, Theo used his suit's maneuvering jets to skim halfway around the ship's rim.

'How does it look?' Pauline's voice sounded calm enough, but he thought he detected just a trace of anxiety in it.

Shaking his head inside the suit's glassteel helmet, Theo replied, 'Like some giant robot ripped the whole section apart.'

'That bad?'

'Could've been a lot worse. The rock must've come in at a flat angle. It grazed the hull, just plowed along this one section and then went on its way.'

Angela's voice cut in. 'Can you fix the circuitry?'

'Yeah, sure. But it's going to take time.'

And air. Theo knew his mother had filled his suit's tanks, but every breath he took sucked up precious oxygen. Then there's the maneuvering jet propellant. Cold nitrogen, same as the ship's rim jets use. How much more do we have in store? We can take nitrogen out of the air we breathe, but that ups the oxy percentage, which can start its own cascade of problems.

He shook his head again, this time to clear away all the disturbing thoughts. No time for that, he told himself. Fix the problem at hand.

He didn't realize how long he'd been at his task until Angela called. 'You've got one hour of air left, Thee.'

Looking up from the welding job he'd been doing, he floated out to the limit of his safety tether with the welding laser in his gloved hand.

'Almost finished,' he said. He wished he could reach inside the helmet and scratch his nose. The headband he wore kept the sweat out of his eyes, but he could feel it trickling uncomfortably down his cheeks and soaking the collar of his shirt. No time for complaining, he told himself sternly. Get the job done.

At last he called to Angela, 'Check the circuit schematic, Angie. It should be all green now.'

'It's amb . . . no, it's gone to green!' Her voice sounded jubilant.

'Okay. Fire the jets. One-second burst. Just see if they actually work.'

'Firing.'

Theo saw a puff glitter from the nearest jet: cold

nitrogen gas immediately dissipating into the vacuum of space.

'Works fine!' Angela sang out.

'Okay,' said Theo. 'Check the spin program and slave the jet controls to it. I'm heading in.'

Two years ago, even one year ago, he wouldn't have trusted Angela to get it right. But she's grown a lot, Theo thought. Then he grinned to himself. So have I, I guess.

He got as far as the open outer hatch of the airlock. Then his earphones crackled:

'Unidentified vessel, this is *Vogeltod*. Do you need assistance?'

At first Valker was disappointed that the ship on his main screen wasn't his quarry, *Hunter*. But it was a ship, running silent, no signals coming out of it, either before the solar storm or now, after it.

'Is she a derelict?' Valker wondered aloud.

Nicco, sitting at the communications console, said, 'I can hail her.'

Valker thought it over for about a second, then replied, 'Do that. Politely. According to the rules.'

Nicco grinned as he pressed his transmission key. 'Unidentified vessel,' he called, his voice light and sweet. 'This is *Vogeltod*. Do you need assistance?'

No answer. Only the crackle of interference from the natural background emissions of the Sun and stars. Then:

'This is ore ship *Syracuse*!' a young voice shouted eagerly. 'Yes! We've been damaged and we urgently need help!'

'Put them on screen,' Valker commanded.

Nicco made an elaborate shrug. 'No visual. Only voice. And it's kinda weak, like it's a suit radio, not the ship's comm system.'

Valker leaned on the comm key built into his command chair's armrest. '*Syracuse*, we hear you. You're damaged, you say?'

'Yessir. We've been on a powerless trajectory for almost four years now, ever since we were attacked.'

'Attacked? By who?'

'We don't know. The attacker slagged our antennas so we couldn't call for help. I'm talking to you through a suit radio.'

Nicco half stood at his console and took a little bow. The other crewmen razzed him.

'We'll rendezvous with you,' said Valker, waving to the crew to be quiet. 'How many aboard your vessel?'

'Rendezvous will be tricky, sir. Our radar's out. We're blind as well as deaf and dumb.'

'That's all right. We'll match vectors and board you. How many in your crew?'

'There's just my mother, my sister and me.'

Valker's smile showed almost all his teeth.

'Hold tight. I'll come aboard myself.'

'That's great! That's wonderful!'

Valker cut the connection and his crew whooped with glee.

'Two women!'

'And only one man to protect them!'

'He sounds like a kid.'

'Keep your pants on, you apes,' Valker said, raising one hand to silence them. 'Nicco, check the IAA registration for *Syracuse*. Kirk, match our vector with theirs, get us close enough for me to jump across in a suit.'

'You? By yourself?'

'That's right. I don't want you baboons scaring the ladies.' Before they could complain he added, 'Or making the lad suspicious. Easy does it. They're not going anywhere without us.'

Theo was so excited it took him three tries to punch out the code on the wall pad that controlled the airlock. He stood fidgeting inside his space suit as the 'lock cycled from vacuum to normal air pressure, all fatigue forgotten, all the worries and fears that he had carried inside him like a gnawing tumor for more than three years, gone, disappeared.

We're saved, he kept telling himself. We're saved. We're saved.

In his helmet earphones he heard his mother and sister bubbling.

'It's a miracle!' Angie said, her voice brimming with joy.

'I never thought it could happen,' Pauline said, just as elated. 'In all this emptiness, to run into another ship . . .'

Theo heard his mother's voice catch, sensed her struggling to hold back tears.

When he finally clomped out of the airlock, Angela and Pauline were both half out of their space suits, down to nothing but their leggings. As soon as he pulled the helmet off his head they both wrapped their arms around his neck and broke into wet, blubbering sobs. Theo wanted to dance a jig, but they were pressing too close to him and he was afraid of tramping on their feet.

'We're saved, Theo, we're saved,' his mother said. 'You've brought us through it.'

'We did it together, Mom. You, Angie and me.'

Angie said, 'Let's get these leggings off and put on some clean clothes. I want to look presentable. You too, Mom.'

Pauline laughed through her tears. 'Yes, yes, of course. We want to look our best.'

Ore Ship *Syracuse*: Living Quarters

Valker beamed a brilliant smile as he sat in the cushioned armchair that Theo had avoided using since his father had left them. It had been his father's chair, but now Valker sat in it, perfectly at ease, a big-shouldered, handsome smiling stranger in a hodgepodge of a uniform that seemed to be made up of odd bits and pieces from half a dozen other outfits.

'Very comfortable quarters you have here,' said Valker smoothly.

Pauline had put on a clean set of pale blue coveralls that complemented her sandy hair nicely. Angela was wearing an actual dress, something she hadn't done since they'd left Ceres. Theo was shocked to see how really good-looking his sister was, and how Valker stared admiringly at her. Angie had pinned up her hair and put on lip gloss. She had also left the top three buttons of her dress open; Valker seemed especially impressed with her breathing.

Pauline sat on the sofa, her daughter beside her. 'I'm afraid we don't have much food left,' she said. 'We've been rationing it out all these months, to make it last long enough for us to get back to Ceres.'

'I understand,' Valker said, his eyes never leaving Angie.

Sitting nervously on the edge of the smaller armchair, on the other end of the coffee table from Valker, Theo said, 'It's a good thing we were in our suits when you hailed us. Otherwise we wouldn't have known you were nearby.'

'Oh, we would've boarded you anyway,' said Valker. 'We're in the salvage business. At first we thought your vessel had been abandoned, like so many others in the Belt.'

'Salvage business?' Pauline asked.

'It's not much, but it's a living for me and my poor excuse of a crew.'

'How many in your crew?' Theo asked.

'There's nine of us, plus me. I'm the skipper.'

'How many women?' asked Pauline.

Valker shook his head. 'None. Women cause trouble on long missions. They don't mean to, but men just naturally start to compete over them.'

Theo understood. 'I guess that's normal, unless you're family.'

'You bet it is.'

Angela spoke up. 'Are your men homosexuals?'

Pauline glared at her daughter.

Valker threw his head back and hooted laughter. 'My crew? No. Not at all. Quite the opposite.' Still chuckling, he added, 'Although, after they've been out on a mission long enough, they'll take whatever they can get.'

Angela flushed, but said, 'You wouldn't do that, would you?'

'I haven't had to . . . so far.'

Theo wanted to make Angie disappear. She's giving this stranger all the wrong impression, he thought.

Pauline changed the subject. 'If you could give us some propellant for our fusion drive we could get back to Ceres within a few weeks or less.'

'Certainly,' said Valker. 'No problem. We'll repair your antennas, too, so you can communicate again.'

'No need for that,' Theo said.

'You're wrong, lad. You can't go barreling into the Ceres sector deaf, dumb and blind. There's too much traffic in the region. It'd be dangerous for you and all the others.'

Theo glanced at his mother and saw that she didn't want Valker's men coming aboard *Syracuse* either.

'We appreciate your willingness to help,' Pauline began.

Theo interrupted. 'I can go back to your ship with you. If you'll give me a spare antenna from your stores I can bring it back here and set it up, no sweat.'

But Valker shook his head once more. 'It's not that easy, son. We don't have spare antennas. Our antennas are built into the ship's hull, just like yours. But we have the materials to lay down a new set of antennas for you. Materials and men to do the job.'

'I can do the job myself if you just give me the materials,' Theo said.

Valker looked at him, smiling toothily. 'I understand. You're scared to let my men aboard your vessel. Two beautiful women and nine hungry men. Right?'

'Ten men,' Theo corrected. 'Including you.'

'Including me, that's right,' Valker acknowledged, laughing. 'But you don't have anything to worry about, son. I guarantee that my men won't bother your mother or sister. That's a promise.'

And he held out his right hand. Theo glanced at his mother, thinking, I've got no choice. Reluctantly, he took Valker's hand in his own.

The three of them went with Valker to the airlock. Theo couldn't help but be envious as he watched the man pull on his nanofabric space suit.

'I'll be back with two men to help you install a new set of antennas,' Valker promised as he pulled the suit's cowling over his head and inflated it into a clear bubble. 'Once that's done we'll transfer enough hydrogen to get you back to Ceres.'

'That will be wonderful,' Pauline said.

Valker grinned at her. 'Always happy to help a lovely lady in distress.'

He waved and stepped into the airlock. Theo punched out the code that sealed the hatch and started the airlock cycling.

Once the hatch shut and the panel lights indicated the lock was pumping down to vacuum, Pauline swung around and slapped her daughter on the face, hard.

Angela was too stunned to cry. Theo saw the stinging marks of his mother's fingers on Angie's face, white against her reddened cheek.

'Talking about sex!' Pauline hissed. 'Are you crazy?

322

Ten sex-starved men and you make them think . . .'
Her voice faltered.

'I didn't mean . . .' Angela said, her voice quavering.

Theo tried to get his mother's attention. 'I couldn't refuse his help. They'd just come aboard anyway.'

Pauline said, 'Thee, get your sister out of sight. Find a place to hide her. I don't want those men to get a glimpse of her while they're on board our ship.'

'What about you, Mom?'

'I can take care of myself,' Pauline said. 'It's Angie I'm worried about.'

Theo started to object. Before he could, though, Pauline said in a softer tone, 'I'm an old lady, Thee. You saw the way that man was staring at Angie. He had no interest in me.'

'I'm not so sure, Mom. He—'

'Thee, we don't have time to debate the issue. Get Angie to a safe hideaway, quickly. Before they all come aboard.'

Back in *Vogeltod*, Valker's crew crowded around him as soon as he stepped through the airlock hatch.

'What's the word, skipper?'

'What's goin' on over there?'

'How big a crew?'

'What about the women?'

Valker silenced them with a gesture, then broke into his widest grin. 'Just like he said over the radio. One crewman, a teenaged kid. And two women, a mother and her daughter. Both good-looking. The daughter's hot to trot, too.'

323

They all laughed.

Nicco asked, 'What about the mother?'

'Good-looking, like I said. Elegant. Tries to be cool, but it'll be fun melting her down.'

Selene: Hotel Luna

Alex Humphries personally escorted Yuan and Tamara Vishinsky to the Hotel Luna. Although the hotel's formal entrance was up in the Main Plaza, a wide powered stairway led down to the lobby, past sheets of genuine liquid water that slid glistening down tilted slabs of granite quarried from the lunar highlands.

'The water's recycled, of course,' Alex said as they glided down the stairway. 'It looks pretty impressive, though, here on the Moon.'

Yuan nodded appreciatively and noticed that Tamara was standing as close to Humphries as she could without climbing into his clothes.

There were pools of limpidly clear water on either side at the bottom of the stairway, with fish swimming in them.

'Aquaculture,' Humphries commented. 'Selene gets more protein per unit of energy input from fish than from meat animals.'

'You mean people eat those fish?' Tamara asked, her eyes wide and fixed on Humphries.

He nodded. 'You can pick one out for your dinner.'

She laughed appreciatively.

The hotel lobby was bigger than any Yuan had ever seen, lavishly carpeted and decorated with oriental tables and comfortable leather-covered easy chairs. Ornate displays of artificial flowers sprouted from imitation Ming vases.

Humphries walked them to the reception desk, where a bowing assistant manager led them to adjoining rooms two levels below the lobby.

'This is our bottom floor,' the slightly pudgy man said in a self-effacing whisper. 'Our very best.'

He opened a door and motioned Yuan inside. Impressive, Yuan thought. Roomy without being too big. Nice decorations. One entire wall was a smart screen that showed, at the moment, a satellite view of the Grand Canyon on Mars.

'Thanks,' he said to Humphries.

'You're comped for everything,' Alex told him. 'For three days. Then we leave for the Belt.'

'May I add,' murmured the assistant manager, 'that our shops up on the lobby level offer the very latest designer fashions and a complete line of accessories.'

Yuan realized the man was telling him that he needed some new clothes. He nodded wordlessly and closed his door.

'And your room is here,' the assistant manager said, opening the next door.

Tamara looked inside. 'Very luxurious,' she said to Humphries.

The assistant manager handed her the key chip, glanced at Humphries, then bowed and scurried down the corridor.

'I think you'll be comfortable,' Humphries said.

Tamara realized he was several centimeters taller than his father, clone or no clone. Looking up at him, she asked, 'Would you like to come in?'

He smiled. 'I don't think that would be wise.'

'Really?' she breathed.

'Look,' he said, 'I've pulled you out of a cesspool full of trouble. My father isn't happy with you—'

'It wasn't me who let Harbin and the old woman go,' Tamara said. 'Yuan did that.'

'But you killed Commander Bolestos, didn't you? He didn't just conveniently drop dead. You stuck a knife in his ribs.'

Humphries could see sudden anger flare in her eyes. But she controlled it immediately.

'It was wrong, I know,' she said contritely. 'But he wouldn't have allowed us to see the artifact.'

'That's no reason to kill a man.'

'You're right,' she murmured, her head drooping. She looked up at him through lowered lashes and added, 'I realize that now . . . since the artifact.'

'There's been enough killing,' Alex Humphries said. 'Too much. Now we're going out to the artifact and try to understand it, learn from it.'

'If that's what you want.'

'That's what I want,' he said fervently. 'My father doesn't want the IAA or the universities near it, and I think he's right about that. But he can't stop me.'

'Of course he can't.'

'I'll need your help. Yours and Yuan's.'

'I'll do whatever you want me to,' Tamara said, her head still lowered.

Alex tucked a finger under her chin and lifted her face. 'You will?'

'Anything,' she whispered.

He stepped into the hotel room with her and pushed the door shut. She realized that this man was his father's clone, after all.

Cargo Ship *Pleiades*: Bridge

'You're talking to yourself,' Victor Zacharias muttered. 'That's not a good sign.'

So who else do I have to talk to? he asked silently. I'm a wanted thief in Ceres, I can't chat with anyone there.

He got up from the command chair and strode the four paces it took to go from one end of the bridge to the other. Then back again. Maybe I should go to the gym, work up a sweat. Instead he returned to the command chair and turned on the comm console.

He scanned the news channels constantly, desperately hoping for some word about *Syracuse*. For months he had plotted possible trajectories for his ship, paths through the Belt that were based on little more than guesswork. I don't have a firm fix on what her position was when I left the ship, and I have no idea of what Pauline might have done with the propulsion fuel we had left in the tanks. Or how much fuel was left. Or how she might try to swing into a trajectory that'll bring them back toward Ceres.

It was madness to attempt to calculate where *Syracuse* might be, but it was a madness that kept Victor sane. Otherwise he would be cruising blindly through the Belt, a single ship trying to find another speck of a ship in the enormous vast emptiness.

His dreams were racked with nightmares. He saw one disaster after another: The ship struck by an asteroid that ripped her apart, Pauline and the kids flung into the vacuum, their eyes bursting from their heads, their screams piercing his skull. Or drifting out to Jupiter, the ship's systems failing one by one, dying of hunger, of thirst, suffocating as the air recyclers failed and they all choked to death, emaciated and helpless.

The broadcasts from Ceres were strictly utilitarian, traffic reports for the most part. No word of a lost ship found, no word of his wife and children saved.

Still he listened. And watched the broadcasts from Earth and the Moon. And checked the frequency that *Syracuse* would use to beam out its beacon and telemetry data.

'Maybe Theo's fixed the antennas,' he hoped aloud. 'Maybe they're signaling for help.'

Nothing. Only the crackle of interference from the depths of space. No word from his lost family.

'I'm going to have to stay in the storm cellar?' Angela complained.

She had changed into strictly utilitarian coveralls, but still Theo noticed how well his sister's body filled the gray jumpsuit. As he pulled the heavy hatch open, Theo said, 'Seal this hatch once you're inside. Don't open it for anybody, understand?'

'Just because Mom's afraid—'

'Stuff it!' Theo snapped. 'Mom's got a right to be afraid and if you had any sense you'd be scared out of your skull.'

Angela fell silent.

'Ten men who haven't seen a woman in who knows how long,' Theo went on. 'You want to be gang-raped?'

'Theo!'

'That's what they'll do, Angie.'

'That nice Captain Valker wouldn't let them hurt me.' But she stepped inside the cramped radiation shelter.

'Valker would be first in line.'

'That's crazy, Thee.'

'Listen to me,' he said. 'There's food and water in here. You can stay here for a week if you have to. Seal the hatch and don't open it for anybody. Not until I knock on it like this.' And he rapped his knuckles on the hatch's metal face three times in rapid succession, then a second's pause, then three more quick raps.

'Got it? One-two-three, wait, one-two-three.'

'Like a waltz,' Angela said.

'A waltz? Yeah, I guess maybe it is.' Theo ducked down a bit to survey the interior of the metal-walled shelter. Cabinets stocked with supplies, food freezer and microwave, water tank half full.

'That's it, then,' he said at last. 'You'll be okay in here until we get rid of Valker and his crew.' Silently he added, I hope.

Pauline was in the command pod, fretting about the irony of the situation. We're found by a gang of scavengers, she said to herself. I suppose that's only to be expected. Who else would find a damaged ship drifting through the Belt?

But the way that man stared at Angela. And she enjoyed his attention! She's letting her hormones do her thinking for her. I've got to protect her. And Theo too. They'll murder Thee if they think he's getting in their way.

How can I pull us through this? How can I get them to repair the ship without hurting us? Without killing us? Valker said they're salvage operators; that means they want our ship. But to get it . . .

She squeezed her eyes shut, trying to blot out the vision that she foresaw. They'll kill us all. But only after they've had their fun with Angie and me. Maybe even with Thee. Then they'll take *Syracuse* back to Ceres and sell her for salvage. Or scrap, more likely.

One teenaged boy and two women against ten scavengers. Angie's out of their sight but they can find her easily enough if they want to. And poor Thee, they'll kill him right off if he tries to fight them.

What can I do? Pauline asked herself again and again. How can I stop them?

Valker, she thought. He's their captain, their leader. He can control them, maybe. If I can control him.

Salvage Ship *Vogeltod*: Airlock

'I don't get it,' said Kirk, almost in a snarl. 'Why don't we just go over there and take that ship? Push the kid out an airlock and screw the two women until our cocks fall off.'

Nicco, standing beside Kirk, laughed and agreed. 'Yeah, why not?'

Valker smiled benignly at his two crewmen. 'Because I say we're not going to do it that way, that's why.'

'If we put it to a vote the crew would go my way,' Kirk retorted.

'Now listen,' said Valker, planting his fists on his hips. 'I don't pull rank often, but I *am* the captain of this woebegone crew and you'll follow my orders.'

'Why should we?'

'Because I say so. That ore bucket will fetch us a decent price back at Ceres, but once we show up with her in tow what's the first thing the rock rats' inspectors will ask?'

Before either Kirk or Nicco could reply, Valker answered his own question. 'What happened to the owners?'

Kirk shrugged. 'How should we know? We found the vessel abandoned and adrift.' Turning to Nicco, 'Right?'

'Right!'

'It's not that simple,' Valker insisted. 'It never is.'

Scratching intently at the scar along his cheek, Nicco said, 'I don't know what's wrong with just taking their ship and the two women, bang! Like that.'

'We're going to do it my way, share and share alike.'

'That's what I've been saying,' Kirk argued, with a smirk.

'Just like in the army,' said Valker. 'The officers and the enlisted men share everything fifty-fifty.'

'Only there's a hundred enlisted men for every officer,' Nicco grumbled.

'That's right. And there's nine of you apes and only one of me. But we'll share everything fifty-fifty.'

'Yeah?' Kirk asked, suspicious.

'Two women. The nine of you mugs in the crew get one and the captain gets one. Fair enough, eh?'

'The hell it is!'

'All right,' Valker said, laughing. 'Suppose I appoint you two to be officers? My first and second mates.'

'Then the other seven—'

'They get one of the women and the three of us get the other one.'

'And the kid?'

'We push him out an airlock – *after* he rebuilds the ship's antennas. I'm not towing a vessel into the Ceres sector that's deaf, dumb and blind.'

Kirk looked at Nicco, who made an affirmative shrug.

'Fair enough?' Valker asked them.

'Fair enough,' said Kirk, grudgingly. Then he added, 'Uh, which of the women do we get? Or do we take turns with the two of 'em?'

With Valker directing them, Kirk and Nicco set up a flexible access tube that connected *Vogeltod*'s main airlock with the zero-g hub of the wheel-shaped *Syracuse*. Now they didn't need space suits to transfer from one ship to the other. Valker was the first to glide through the spongy tube and enter *Syracuse*, with his two crewmen close behind him.

Without much enthusiasm Theo greeted them as they floated through the inner hatch of *Syracuse*'s airlock. Speaking hardly a word he led them along the tube tunnel to the lockers that fronted the main airlock, where Pauline was waiting for them.

'Welcome aboard, gentlemen,' she said, forcing a minimal smile.

'Where's your lovely daughter?' Valker asked, his teeth showing.

'She's been taken ill,' said Pauline. 'Some sort of a fever. I've confined her to her quarters.'

Valker's grin didn't diminish by a millimeter. 'That's too bad. Awful sudden, wasn't it?'

Looking more serious than ever, Pauline said, 'I don't know what it could be. I'm hoping it's not contagious. Once you get an antenna working I can query the medical people at Ceres about her.'

Valker nodded understandingly. Turning to his two crewmen, he ordered, 'All right, you heard what the lady said. Let's get the materials aboard and start building a new set of antennas.'

Neither man moved.

Then he said to Theo, 'You'd better get into your suit, son. We have a lot of work ahead of us, outside.'

'Right,' said Theo. He turned to the row of lockers and began pulling out his own hard-shell space suit.

'Still using those?' Valker asked.

Pauline replied, 'We're not rich enough to afford the nanosuits, I'm afraid.'

'Too bad. If I had an extra one I'd loan it to the lad.'

Theo sat on the bench and began tugging on his leggings.

'Nicco, give the boy a hand. Kirk, you get back to our ship and start transferring the antenna materials.'

Kirk started to say something, but a glance at Valker made him shut up and head back to *Vogeltod*.

Theo obviously did not appreciate being called a 'boy' or a 'lad,' but he said nothing as he reached for his thick-soled boots.

'I useta work in a suit like this,' Nicco said, tapping his knuckles on the torso of Theo's suit, still hanging in the locker. 'The nanosuits are a lot better.'

'I suppose they are,' Theo said guardedly.

Valker said to Pauline, 'I can get a diagnostic hand-set from our infirmary, maybe find out what's ailing your daughter.'

'I think not,' said Pauline. 'If she has something contagious I don't want you and your crew coming down with it.'

'I understand,' Valker said, thinking, You don't want me to see the girl in bed, eh?

Nicco held the space suit torso high enough for Theo, crouching, to get his head and arms into it.

'You take care of him,' Valker told his crewman, 'then go back to *Vogeltod* and help Kirk bring up those supplies.'

With a sly grin, Nicco touched one finger to his brow and said crisply, 'Aye, skipper.'

To Pauline, Valker said, 'I'll have to see your communications setup if we're going to rebuild your antennas.'

'That's up in the command pod,' she replied.

'You'd better lead me there.'

Pauline shot a glance at Theo, who was pulling his glassteel bubble helmet over his head.

'I'll be all right, Mom,' Theo said.

'Nicco will take good care of him, don't worry,' Valker assured Pauline.

Without another word, Pauline went through the hatch that led into the family's living quarters and, beyond that, to the tube tunnel that connected with the command pod. Valker followed behind her, close enough for her to feel his breath on the back of her neck.

Smelter Ship *Hunter*: Galley

Elverda held both her gaunt, bony hands around the mug of hot tea, feeling the warmth seep into her palms. She stared at her hands: all bones and tendons, like a bird's claws, their skin mottled with age spots. *Once, these hands carved monumental sculptures*, she said to herself. *Now they can barely lift a cup of tea.*

Rejuvenation therapies have their limits, she thought. *So do old women who've outlived their usefulness.* Then she recalled the vision the artifact had revealed to her. *One last sculpture*, she told herself. *A final tribute to him. Can I hang on long enough to do it? How much longer can I go on? And once I'm dead, what will happen to Dorn?*

As if on cue, the cyborg stepped through the hatch and sat heavily in the chair at the head of the table. He stretched out his prosthetic leg and flexed it several times, slowly.

'Are you all right?' Elverda asked.

'The leg feels stiff. The bearings need lubrication.'

She started to get up from her chair. 'I'll find—'

'No need,' Dorn said, stopping her with one upraised hand. His hand of flesh. 'I can handle it later.'

Elverda settled back in the galley chair. 'You're certain?'

'Yes. Thank you anyway.'

'De nada,' she said. She picked up the mug of tea again, then asked, 'Did your radar sweep turn up anything?'

'Nothing.'

'No bodies?'

'Not even any debris.'

'Are you sure we're at the right location?'

He nodded ponderously. 'I checked with Ceres. The battle took place here. I wasn't in it, but I was given to understand that at least a dozen mercenaries were killed.'

'Which corporation did they serve? Astro or Humphries?'

The human half of Dorn's face frowned slightly. 'What difference does it make?'

'We could check their corporate headquarters. Perhaps they've already picked up the bodies.'

'No,' he said, flexing the leg again. 'The corporations never picked up their dead. They simply wrote them off their accounting ledgers.'

'Inhuman,' Elverda murmured.

'Humans often perform inhuman acts. I myself am the foremost example of that sorry fact.'

'That wasn't you,' Elverda said quickly. 'That was someone else. Another person. Not you, not who you are now.'

'Still . . .' He bowed his head briefly, as if uttering a swift prayer. Then, 'The fact remains that there are no bodies to be found at this location.'

'Which means?'

'Which means that they have drifted much farther than I anticipated.'

'Or they were destroyed in the battle.'

Dorn seemed to consider that for a moment. 'We'll do a spiral search pattern.'

'For how long?'

'A few days, at least. If we don't find anything we'll move on to the next battle site.'

'That would be the last one, wouldn't it?'

'The last one that I know of. I'm certain there are others.'

Elverda hesitated, then plunged ahead. 'What if there aren't any others? What if we've found all the bodies that there are to find? What then?'

He stared at her, one eye an unblinking red camera lens, the other all too human.

'Then my mission is finished,' he said.

'And what do you do then?'

He didn't answer. He can't, Elverda said to herself. He's built his life around this mission and once it's over his life will have no purpose, no meaning.

Then she realized, Nor will mine, once I finish his sculpture.

With Nicco beside him in his nanosuit, Theo hung at the end of his safety tether and surveyed the gashed length of hull where *Syracuse*'s antennas used to be. He could see the ship's innards through the long rip, the torn and empty fuel tanks that had once held hydrogen propellant for the fusion drive.

340

'Hafta patch that up,' Nicco said over the suit-to-suit radio link, 'before we transfer any fuel to ya.'

'We have other fuel tanks,' said Theo. 'Undamaged. On the other side of the wheel.'

'Oh. Okay, good. But the antennas come first,' Nicco said. 'Skipper wants them antennas workin' before we do anything else.'

Nodding inside his bubble helmet, Theo said, 'Fine with me. But we can't put them here, the skin's too torn up.'

'Where, then?'

Pointing with an extended arm, Theo said, 'Over on that section, by the command pod. That way gives us the shortest path for the circuitry.'

'Show me,' said Nicco.

Theo felt distinctly nervous about disconnecting his safety tether. The suit's propulsion pack can jet you around the ship for hours, he told himself. You can always jet back to an airlock, the tethers are just an extra safety precaution. He knew it, but he still felt edgy about being outside the ship with this scavenger.

And Mom's in the pod with their skipper, he realized.

'I'm coming out,' said Kirk's voice in Theo's helmet earphones.

'Wait,' he replied. 'We're moving to the next section of the hull. Bring the supplies there.'

'What the hell am I supposed to be, a donkey or something?' Kirk complained. 'How come I have to carry all this junk?'

'Too heavy for you?' Nicco jeered.

'Just 'cause it's weightless don't mean it's easy to handle, wiseass,' Kirk shot back. 'Come on down here and give me a hand.'

'Okay, okay,' said Nicco. Theo could see his teeth grinning.

'I'll be over at the next section, by the pod,' Theo said, pointing. 'I'll see you both there.'

'Yeah.' Nicco pulled himself hand over hand along his tether, heading for the open airlock hatch where Kirk waited with the materials to paint a new antenna set onto the undamaged section of the hull.

Theo unclipped his tether and squeezed the control stud at his waist. The jet pack surged against his back and he lunged across the slashed section of hull, heading toward the backup control pod.

Once there he clipped the tether to a cleat and looked inside the pod. His mother and Valker seemed to be in earnest conversation. Wish I could hear what they're saying, Theo thought. If he tries anything with Mom I'll . . .

You'll what? he asked himself. What can you do? Bitterly, he thought that it would have been better if they'd never seen Valker and his crew of scavengers. If I hadn't been in this suit when they hailed us . . .

Suddenly an idea popped into his head. The suit radios don't have much range, but we're closer to Ceres now. If these scavengers found us there might be other ships close enough to hear me!

But so would Valker's crew. So what? Theo asked himself. We can't be in more trouble than we are now.

Realizing that he had to act fast or not at all, Theo

raised his gloved hands before his face so he could see the keypad built into his suit's left wrist. He punched up a different frequency from the suit-to-suit freak he'd been using with Nicco and Kirk.

He licked his lips, then said, 'This is ore ship *Syracuse*. We are damaged and need assistance. Three people aboard. Propulsion system down. We are adrift and need assistance urgently.'

He saw Nicco and Kirk sailing toward him, towing a mesh net bulging with cans and tubes: the materials to spray new antennas onto the hull.

Kirk came up close enough almost to touch helmets with him. 'That wasn't smart, kid,' he snarled.

Back on *Hunter*'s bridge, Dorn sat heavily in the command chair. Elverda took the smaller seat beside him.

'I've been thinking about your question,' he said slowly. 'About what to do once we've recovered the last of the bodies.'

Elverda looked at him questioningly. 'What will you do?' she asked.

The human side of his face almost smiled. 'I suppose what I will do is try to find a way to die.'

'No!' she snapped. 'You mustn't!'

'What point—'

The comm computer's message light began blinking. Elverda touched the RECEIVE key.

'This is ore ship *Syracuse*,' came a weak voice, barely audible over the crackling hiss of interference. 'We are damaged and need assistance. Three people aboard.

Propulsion system down. We are adrift and need assistance urgently.'

'*Syracuse?*' Dorn gasped.

'You know the ship?' asked Elverda.

It was several moments before he replied, 'Dorik Harbin tried to destroy it.'

Ore Ship *Syracuse*:
Family Quarters

'He was using the alternate frequency on his suit radio to call for help,' Kirk said, his face set in an angry grimace.

Theo stood between Kirk and Nicco like a prisoner under guard. Valker lounged, completely at ease, in the big armchair that had been his father's. Pauline was on the sofa, sitting tensely, her fists on her knees, her eyes on her son.

'I do that whenever I'm in the suit,' Theo improvised. 'It's my normal routine.'

'Is it now?' Valker asked, one eyebrow cocked dubiously.

'We didn't hear any distress call from you when we found you,' Nicco said.

'I was just about to send out a call when I heard your message,' Theo said.

'Why call for help when we're already here?' Kirk demanded.

Valker answered before Theo could reply. 'Because he's scared of us, that's why. Isn't it, son? You see a gang of roughneck scavengers and you're worried about your mother and sister. Right?'

Theo hesitated, then admitted, 'That's part of it, I suppose.'

'Can't say I blame you,' said Valker. 'Mighty courageous of you, really, trying to protect your mother and sister.'

Nicco piped up, 'Whatsamatter, kid, don't you trust us?'

Getting to his feet, Valker said, 'I wouldn't trust us, Nicco. Not if I was a young lad facing a shipload of desperados like us.'

He placed a strong hand on Theo's shoulder. 'But you see, son, there's a matter of salvage rights here. We found you, and it would complicate the situation if somebody else showed up.'

'We're not salvage,' Theo snapped. 'We're not abandoned or adrift. This ship is occupied by its rightful owners and we're on a course that'll take us back to Ceres in a few months.'

'Are you now?'

'Yes,' said Pauline. 'We are.'

'We'd only be salvage,' Theo said, 'if the ship was abandoned.'

'That can be arranged,' Kirk said, with a smirk.

'None of that, now,' said Valker. 'The boy's right. This isn't a salvage operation. We're here to help these people.'

Kirk started to reply, but caught the look in Valker's eye and snapped his mouth shut.

To Theo, Valker said, 'You don't have to be afraid of us, son.'

'I'm not your son.'

'Now listen,' Valker said, a little more iron in his voice, 'I'm not your enemy. We can help you, but you've got to trust us, at least a little. We're fixing your antenna problem, aren't we? We're going to transfer some of our fuel to you. What more do you want?'

Theo had no answer for him. He simply glowered at Valker, sullenly.

Pauline got to her feet. 'Theo, you're tired. Why don't you go to the galley, make yourself some dinner, and then go to sleep.'

He looked into his mother's eyes and saw that her suggestion was really a command.

Nodding, Theo said, 'Okay, Mom.'

'And take these gentlemen with you,' Pauline said, gesturing to Kirk and Nicco. 'They must be hungry, too.'

Tight-lipped, Theo repeated, 'Okay, Mom.'

He left the family room, Nicco and Kirk marching behind him like a pair of guards.

Valker turned back to Pauline. 'Alone at last,' he said, grinning.

'I don't want them to hurt my son,' Pauline said.

'Now why would they do that?'

'You know perfectly well. If you kill the three of us you can bring this ship back to Ceres and sell it as salvage.'

Valker nodded. 'True enough. Or we could put you into the command pod and send you off. No blood spilled that way.'

'But you'd be murdering us just the same.'

'That's what *they* want to do.' Valker jerked a thumb toward the hatch that Kirk and Nicco had just gone through.

Pauline's chin rose a notch. 'And what do you want to do?'

'Me?' Valker's grin faded a little. 'I'm not a killer. I'm more of a lover.'

Pauline said to herself, So there it is. Out in the open. He's offering me our lives. But for how long?

'Can you keep your crew under control?' she asked. He nodded wordlessly.

'I don't want any of them touching my daughter.'

Valker puffed out a breath. 'That will be a pretty tough assignment.'

'Or hurting my son.'

'Hell, we can let him join our crew. The boy's got nerve; I like him.'

'But my daughter's got to be safe. From all of them, including you.'

Spreading his arms in a gesture of complete agreement, Valker replied, 'If you're willing to let me share your bed, why would I be interested in your daughter?'

She looked into his eyes: greenish blue, hazel eyes, the kind that changes color, the kind that can't be trusted. But what else can I do? Pauline asked herself. What else can I do to keep Angela and Theo safe?

Aboard *Hunter*, Dorn stared at the communications screen as if he could make it light up by sheer willpower.

'The message isn't being repeated,' Elverda said.

'No,' said Dorn. 'And it was very weak, almost as if it was made from a space suit radio rather than a ship's comm system.'

'No visual.'

'I have a fix on it, through,' Dorn said, tapping on the comm keyboard with his mechanical hand.

'You attacked their ship?'

'Dorik Harbin did.'

'When? How long ago?'

'Just after *Chrysalis*,' Dorn said, his voice barely audible. 'Nearly four years ago.'

'We must go to their assistance.'

He nodded slowly as he opened a comm channel and said, 'Attention *Syracuse*, this is *Hunter*. We've heard your message and are coming to your assistance.' Glancing at the navigation display, Dorn added, 'Estimated time of arrival at your position, thirty hours. Please confirm.'

No response. Nothing but the hiss from the Sun and stars.

Dorn looked at Elverda. 'They don't reply.'

'If their message came from a suit radio . . .'

'Perhaps they didn't get our message.'

'Perhaps they can't reply,' she suggested.

'You take over the comm console,' Dorn said. 'Tell the computer to repeat our message, with updated ETAs.' He turned to the navigation console. 'I've got to plot a course to their position.'

Strangely, Pauline felt neither apprehension nor excitement as she led Valker to her sleeping compartment. She felt numb. I'm doing what I have to do to protect the children, she told herself. I'm doing what I have to do.

As she started to slide the compartment door open, Valker's pocket communicator chimed.

'Damn!' he muttered, fumbling it out of his tunic pocket.

Pauline could hear Kirk's voice from the tiny speaker. 'Somebody's answering the kid's distress call. It's the *Hunter*! They'll be here in thirty hours.'

'*Hunter*? Check it out with Ceres and—'

'Already did. It's the same *Hunter*. Two people aboard, one of them a woman. No weapons registered.'

Valker broke into a wolfish grin. 'Good! Let 'em come! Like flies to honey.'

He clicked the communicator shut and jammed it back into his pocket. 'Your boy's bringing fresh meat to the table, Pauline.'

She knew what he meant, but she asked anyway, 'You're going to take that ship?'

'Why not? Only two people aboard her. They can disappear and we can bring her in for salvage. Get a good price for her, I'm betting.'

'But—'

'No buts,' Valker said, silencing her with a finger on her lips. 'This is business.'

He slid the compartment's door all the way open, saw her oversized bed neatly made against the far bulkhead of the compartment. 'But pleasure before business,' Valker said, ushering Pauline in to her own compartment. 'We have thirty hours. Plenty of time to get to know each other.'

Cargo Ship *Pleiades*: Bridge

The message electrified Victor.

'Attention *Syracuse*, this is *Hunter*. We've heard your message and are coming to your assistance. Estimated time of arrival at your position, thirty hours. Please confirm.'

'*Syracuse!*' he shouted. 'They're talking to *Syracuse*! My ship! Pauline and the children!'

He banged his comm key. '*Hunter*, this is *Pleiades*. Can you give me a navigational fix for *Syracuse*? My wife and children are aboard her.'

Several minutes dragged by. At last his comm screen lit up to show the bizarre image of a man whose face was half flesh, half finely etched metal. A gaunt, aged woman sat beside him.

The cyborg spoke in a deep, slow baritone, '*Pleiades*, you are listed as a stolen ship. Are you Victor Zacharias?'

'Yes, yes,' he answered impatiently. 'I took this ship to search for my family. Please give me a nav fix so I can go to them.'

Neither the cyborg nor the old woman responded. They merely sat there like mute sculptures, staring at him.

★　　★　　★

Dorn froze the image of Victor Zacharias's fiercely bearded face on the comm screen and turned to Elverda. 'What should we do?' he asked.

'He says he took the ship to search for his family. If they're aboard *Syracuse* . . .' She realized that she wasn't certain which course of action they should take.

'I could call Ceres to verify his story,' Dorn suggested.

Elverda shook her head. Pointing to the registration data for *Pleiades* that had automatically come up on their comm screen once the computer recognized the caller's name, she said, 'Ceres will give us the same information that the computer files have.'

The message light was blinking frantically.

'He's trying to talk to us,' Elverda said.

Dorn tapped the comm keyboard.

Victor Zacharias's bearded face suddenly became animated. '*Hunter!*' he said urgently. 'I'm trying to find my family! My wife and two children.'

Reluctantly, Dorn responded, 'I'm afraid you're listed as an outlaw. Ceres claims—'

'That I stole this ship,' Victor interrupted impatiently. 'It's true. I did steal it. To find my family!'

Elverda punched up the computer's file on *Syracuse* and touched Dorn's shoulder to get him to glance at the secondary screen: Missing since the *Chrysalis* slaughter. Four people aboard, all members of the Zacharias family.

'He's telling the truth,' Elverda said. Then, to Victor's image on the main screen, 'Mr. Zacharias, we don't want to be in the position of abetting a criminal.

Let us go to *Syracuse* while you go back to Ceres and turn yourself in.'

Turn myself in? Victor echoed silently.

'*No!*' he roared. 'I want to get to my wife, my children!'

It was impossible to read an expression on the half-metal face of the cyborg, but the woman looked troubled, concerned.

'Listen,' Victor said, toning down his fervor a little. 'I'll go back to Ceres and turn myself in after I see my family. I want to know that they're all right.'

'Their message said they need assistance,' the woman said.

'They've been drifting through the Belt for more than three years,' Victor pleaded. 'Of course they need assistance! We've got to help them!'

The cyborg started to say, 'The lawful thing to do—'

'Don't talk to me about legalities!' Victor insisted. 'My family needs help! They could be dying while we're here arguing!'

As unperturbed as a mountain of granite, the cyborg continued, 'The lawful thing to do is for you to return to the authorities at Ceres while we go to your family's rescue.'

'No!' Victor shouted. 'No! I've got to go to them! I've *got* to!'

'We'll take care of them,' the cyborg said, implacable. 'You'll see them when we bring them back to Ceres.'

'No!' Victor bellowed again. But his screen went blank.

'The bastard's cut me off,' Victor groaned. He wanted to batter the screen with his bare fists, smash it into a million shards. Instead, he buried his face in his hands and wept like a man who's lost his last chance for redemption.

Elverda stared at the suddenly blank screen. 'That . . . that was . . . cruel.'

Dorn nodded minimally. 'Perhaps it was.'

'He's trying to find his family.'

'If he's telling the truth. Perhaps he's really a thief and he wants to take our ship. Or *Syracuse*. Or both.'

'That's far-fetched.'

'Is it? Do you have any idea of how many people he has aboard his ship? Thieves. Pirates.'

'The data from Ceres said he was alone.'

Dorn almost smiled. 'I'm sure that if he's spent the past several months recruiting cutthroats to serve under him he wouldn't send updates to Ceres about it.'

Elverda had to admit that Dorn was right, but she said nothing to him. Then she realized that Dorn did not want to be confronted with the man whose ship Dorik Harbin had crippled.

'Remember that other ship? *Vogeltod*?' Dorn said. 'They claimed they were in the salvage business.'

'But . . .'

'It would be quite profitable to find a ship, get rid of its occupants, and sell it back at Ceres.'

'And you think that's what this man Zacharias is doing?'

'I'm not willing to take that chance,' Dorn replied. 'There are only the two of us here. I've got to protect you.'

'I don't think we need protection from a man who's trying to save his family.'

'If that's what he's truly doing,' Dorn said, looking up at the empty screen. Turning to the screen that showed the file on *Syracuse*, he noted, 'There are four people in the Zacharias family. He claims to be one of them. How did he get aboard *Pleiades*?'

Elverda nodded grudgingly. 'You think he's lying, then.'

Dorn ran his human hand across the etched metal of his chin. 'If he's telling the truth, if he really is who he says he is and is trying to rescue his family, he'll find a way to track us and let us lead him to *Syracuse*. A man desperate to save his wife and children will go to any lengths. A scavenging pirate will look for easier prey.'

Elverda hoped he was right.

Salvage Ship *Vogeltod*: Bridge

The bridge was crowded, hot and sweaty with *Vogeltod*'s entire crew jammed into the compartment. Valker had called them all in to plan how to handle the ship that was nearing them.

'The *Hunter*,' he said jovially. 'We haven't lost her after all.'

'Only two people aboard her?' one of the crewmen asked.

The man on duty at the communications console looked up from the data displayed on his screen. 'Two people,' he confirmed. 'One's listed as a priest and the other's a woman.'

'A woman?'

'She's over a hundred, for chrissakes. Some famous artist named Elverda Apacheta.'

Hunching forward slightly in his command chair, Valker remembered, 'I met her, back when that Humphries captain forced us to give the ship back to her.'

'That's the same ship that we've been looking for!'

'That's what I said: the *Hunter*.'

'The ship we let go,' Kirk said, throwing an accusing glare Valker's way.

With a widening smile, Valker said, 'And now she's coming back to us, nice and sweet.'

'So whattawe do?' Nicco asked, standing to one side of Valker.

'We take her, boys. They're coming to help *Syracuse* but they're walking right into our hands. A priest and an old lady.'

'On a nice, fat, shiny ship,' said one of the crewmen.

'She'll bring a good price at Ceres. Better than this creaking old tub *Syracuse*.' Valker laughed. It was all working out beautifully, he thought. Maybe we can leave *Syracuse*, let her drift. I can bring Pauline and her daughter here aboard *Vogeltod*. The crew'll be happy with the daughter and I can keep Pauline for myself – if I can keep Kirk and Nicco away from her.

'Yes, sir,' he said aloud. 'We ought to thank that kid for sending out his distress call. He's luring a good ship straight to us. What could be better?'

'You can have the old lady, skipper,' Kirk said, grinning. 'We'll take the two tarts from *Syracuse*.'

'Yeah,' one of the crewmen chimed in. 'I bet the daughter's still a virgin.'

'Not for long!'

They all laughed.

Holding up a hand, Valker said, 'First things first, boys. First things first. I hope none of you has religious qualms about slitting a priest's throat.'

After posting his men for seizing the approaching *Hunter*, Valker got up from his chair, ducked through the hatch, and started down the passageway that led to his quarters. He didn't have to look behind him to know that Kirk and Nicco were trailing him.

'Come on in, fellas,' he said amiably, sliding open the door to his compartment. 'Have a drink on me.'

They stepped in, Nicco carefully shutting the door behind him as Valker went to the cabinet where he kept his liquor. Not much left, he saw. Most of the bottles were perilously close to empty. He pulled out the fullest, brandy from one of the L-4 habitats between the Earth and Moon, and opened it with a satisfactory pop of its plastic cork.

'Good times coming,' Valker said, pouring three meager drinks.

As he accepted his glass from Valker's hand, Kirk said, 'You banged the mother, didn't you?'

Valker grinned at him. 'That I did, Kirk. That I did.'

'How was she?' asked Nicco.

'Not half bad. Kinda tense at first, but I soothed her well enough.'

Kirk swallowed more than half his drink with one gulp, then asked, 'When's our turn?'

'In due time. We've got to grab *Hunter* first.'

'That shouldn't be much of a problem,' said Nicco. 'An old woman and a priest.'

'What's a priest doing out here?' Kirk wondered.

'Isn't he the one who's supposed to be finding the dead bodies?' Nicco said.

'Yes, that's him,' said Valker. 'Some sort of religious fanatic.'

'Well, he'll be a dead body himself in a few more

hours,' Kirk said. Then he finished his drink with another swift gulp.

'Speaking of dead bodies,' Valker said, without offering to refill the drink, 'we've got that boy to take care of.'

'We shoulda done that already,' Nicco grumbled.

'Naw,' said Kirk. 'Let the kid finish swabbing the antennas. Let him do the work. Then we'll finish him.'

Valker took a genteel sip of his brandy, then mused aloud, 'Maybe we ought to take care of the kid before *Hunter* gets here. No sense having him around when we take the ship. Get rid of him now.'

Kirk glanced at Nicco, then shrugged. 'Wouldn't take much. We go out with him, finish the antenna job, then we yank out his air line and send him jetting into deep space.'

Nicco giggled. 'He might be the first guy to reach Alpha Centauri.'

Valker saw that Nicco's glass was empty, too. Taking both glasses and putting them down on the cabinet, Valker turned and laid a hand on each of their shoulders.

'Good thinking, lads.' Gently he nudged them toward the door. 'Now you go out there and take care of the boy. I want him out of our hair by the time *Hunter* gets here.'

Victor Zacharias unconsciously scratched at his thick beard as he scowled at his communications screen. The system displayed a graph showing the direction from which *Hunter*'s message had come, but not the ship's distance from him.

That damned half-robot, he growled inwardly. Telling me to turn myself in to the authorities. Victor refigured the keyboard beneath his fingers to call up the propulsion controls, then lit *Pleiades*'s fusion torch engine to full thrust, heading along the vector of *Hunter*'s message.

They'll be gone by the time I get there, he realized. But maybe I can pick up their ion trail. If it hasn't diffused too much. Maybe I can track them and let them lead me to Pauline and the kids.

Maybe.

Ore Ship *Syracuse*:
Pauline's Quarters

She stayed in the shower until the ship's life support computer shut off the hot water. As she toweled dry, Pauline said to herself for the ten thousandth time, You did it to protect Angela and Thee. It's all right. You did what you had to do. You didn't have any choice, really.

Still she felt grimy.

As she dressed she thought that it could have been worse. Much worse. Pauline had wondered, as she watched him strip and climb into bed with her, grinning like a wolf, if she could actually allow another man to make love to her. She closed her eyes, picturing Victor in her mind. I'll fake it, she told herself. I'll please him as much as I can. It doesn't matter what he does to me. I've got to protect Angela.

To her surprise, Valker was a gentle lover, even thoughtful. All his swaggering, smirking attitude dissolved as he genuinely sought to bring pleasure to her. With some surprise, Pauline remembered what she had learned all those years ago, before she'd met Victor: you never know what a man is truly like until you're in bed with him.

Once dressed she walked absently into the family room. Everything was still the same. All the chairs in their places; the sofa, the lamps and wall screens. But I'm not the same, she told herself. I've been unfaithful to my husband. I allowed that grinning hyena to use me. Then the truth slapped her in the face: I enjoyed it! I enjoyed having sex after all these years. My body overpowered my mind.

She sank into the nearest chair, guilt flooding through her like a tidal wave, and burst into racking sobs.

A noise from the galley startled her.

Stanching her tears, she went to the hatch and saw Theo sitting at the table, his back to her, scraping the remains of a meal from his plate.

Pauline hurriedly wiped her face, rubbed her eyes. She had to swallow hard before she could get any words out. 'Thee?'

He turned and smiled at her. 'Hi, Mom. Where've you been?'

Ignoring his question, 'How long have you been here? In the galley?'

His youthful face wrinkled slightly with thought. 'Oh, ten, maybe fifteen minutes. I thought I heard the shower running.'

'Yes,' she said, sitting beside him, hoping he wouldn't notice her reddened eyes.

'I've got to go out again, finish the work on the new antennas.'

'Have you checked on Angela?'

'No, didn't get a chance to do that. Those two apes were with me all the time I was out. I just got rid of them no more than a half-hour ago.'

'I don't think anyone's aboard right now.'

'Yeah, but they'll be here in a few minutes to finish the antenna work. Maybe you can call Angie on the intercom while I start to suit up.'

Pauline nodded. 'I'll do that.' Silently she added. If the intercom is working today.

Angela was startled by the intercom's sudden chime. She'd been pacing around the circular interior of the storm cellar, counting her steps: two hundred and fifty-three, two hundred and fifty-four . . . Nothing better to do, locked in the pod alone. Then the intercom chimed.

She touched the keypad and her mother's face appeared on the tiny wall screen.

'Are you all right?' they asked simultaneously.

Pauline broke into a tight smile. 'I'm fine, Angela. What about you?'

'I'm bored out of my skull. There's nothing to *do* in here!'

'Good. Just stay there. It's the safest place in the ship for you.'

'But—'

'No buts, Angela. Stay in there. Stay where it's safe.'

The screen went blank.

Angela stared at it for long moments, thinking, If it's safe in here, that means it's not safe outside, where Mom and Theo are.

Despite his headband, sweat trickled into Theo's eyes, stinging, forcing him to blink. But through the glassteel of his helmet he looked with some pride at the finished antenna set that he and the two men from *Vogeltod* had painted along *Syracuse*'s curving hull.

He hung at the end of his safety tether, Nicco and Kirk on either side of him. Battered old *Syracuse* swung slowly through the dark emptiness, *Vogeltod* still attached like some mechanical parasite. The steadfast stars looked down on Theo, unblinking, solemn, terribly far away.

'Try transmitting now, Mom,' he said into his helmet microphone.

In his earphones he heard his mother's calm, steady voice, 'This is *Syracuse*, testing its communications system. Testing, testing, one, two, three.'

Turning to Kirk, hovering in his nanosuit alongside him, Theo switched to the suit-to-suit frequency and asked, 'Did it work?'

Kirk grinned and made a circle with his thumb and forefinger. 'They heard her on *Vogeltod* loud and clear.'

Switching back to the ship's frequency, Theo said, 'Sweep through the comm channels, Mom. See what you can pick up.'

For several moments he heard no reply. Then, 'Thee! I'm getting Ceres! And video from Selene! And Earth! It works, Thee! It works!'

Theo thought he should feel wonderful. Ecstatic. Triumphant. Instead he merely felt tired.

'Turn on the tracking beacon,' he said. 'And the telemetry transmitter.'

'Yes,' Pauline replied. 'Green lights! They're working. At last, they're working.'

'Good,' he said, feeling flat and somehow disappointed. 'We'll come in now.'

'You did it, Thee,' said his mother, her voice trembling slightly. 'You did it.'

'I had help,' he replied, eying Kirk and Nicco, who were drifting closer to him.

He clicked back to the suit-to-suit frequency. 'Okay, we can go back inside now.'

Nicco was close enough to see his toothy grin and crooked scar. Kirk had slid around behind him.

'We're goin' in, kid,' Kirk said. 'You're not.'

Aboard *Pleiades*, Victor cursed long and loud as he desperately tried to pick up the ion trail from the exhaust of *Hunter*'s fusion drive. I must have misjudged their distance, he said to himself between bouts of swearing.

'Maybe you got the motherhumping vector wrong,' he muttered to himself.

He set up the communications keyboard and checked the transmission he'd heard. No, the vector's correct, he saw. They must have been farther away than I estimated.

The comm screen's yellow message light was blinking. Automatically, Victor tapped the keypad to play it back.

'This is *Syracuse*, testing its communications system. Testing, testing, one, two, three.'

Pauline's voice!

Suddenly Victor's hands were shaking so badly he could hardly manage to work the keyboard. They've fixed the antennas! He thought. Theo did it. Or Pauline. They're alive! She's alive!

Sure enough, the strong steady signal of a tracking beacon came through on its normal channel. With tears in his eyes Victor read off the name and registration that appeared on his comm screen: *Syracuse*.

Ore Ship *Syracuse*: Outside

Even though he half expected it, it happened so fast that Theo didn't know what to do. At first.

Nicco suddenly wrapped him in a bear hug, pinning Theo's arms to his sides. Behind him, he felt Kirk click open his tether and then start banging and yanking on his life support backpack.

He didn't have to ask what they were doing. They're going to kill me, he thought. And then they'll go back into the ship and rape Mom. And Angie.

Theo struggled but Nicco was surprisingly strong and held his arms pinned. The scavenger was grimacing with the effort, though, his inflated helmet pressing against Theo's glassteel bubble. Theo was bigger than he and flooded with adrenaline. The two of them grunted and strained. Theo could see sweat breaking out on Nicco's face, see his lips pulling back over his mottled teeth in an angry snarl.

'C'mon,' Nicco grunted to Kirk. 'Whatcha doin' back there?'

'Got his radio. But the goddamn air hoses are inside the pack,' Kirk growled. 'I gotta pull off the whole fuckin' tank.'

'Punch a hole in it!' Nicco shouted.

'Yeah . . . yeah . . .'

Theo felt Kirk hammering on his air tank. They'll kill me! roared a voice in his head. They'll kill me!

The three of them were floating weightlessly away from the ship, twisting and spinning as they struggled. Theo rammed a knee into Nicco's groin and heard a satisfying screech of pain. He pulled his arms free and punched Nicco in the face as hard as he could. His gloved fist bounced off the inflated helmet but Nicco sailed backward, away from him, as Theo recoiled in the other direction with Kirk still hanging on his back.

My suit's like armor, Theo thought gratefully. Kirk was swearing at the top of his lungs, still banging away at the air tank behind him. Theo tried to twist around and get Kirk off his back, but the scavenger had locked his legs around Theo's middle. Fumbling for the kit buckled to his waist, Theo pulled out the first tool his fingers clutched, a smallish wrench. With all his might he pounded it against Kirk's knee.

'Sonofabitch!' Kirk yowled. Theo realized that the nanosuits were too soft to offer much protection against such blows.

Kirk unwrapped his legs from Theo. 'You shitfaced little bastard! I've got you now, asshole!'

Theo felt something click in his backpack and suddenly he was whooshing away from the two other men, jetting madly away from *Syracuse*, spinning wildly out into dead empty space. He saw the ship whirling insanely with the figures of the two nanosuited scavengers hovering near it.

'I'm gonna fuck your mother!' Kirk's voice taunted in his helmet earphones. 'And then your sister!'

'Me too!' Nicco added gleefully.

Theo knew he was going to die. The oxygen was spurting out of his life support tank and Kirk had disabled his radio. But all he could think was, I've failed. I've failed to protect Mom and Angie. I've failed them. I've failed them.

Valker was at *Syracuse*'s airlock, waiting for them with his fists on his hips and a disgusted sneer on his face.

'You two sure blew that one,' he grumbled as Kirk and Nicco began to peel off their nanosuits.

'We got rid of the kid, didn't we?' Kirk snapped.

'One kid, and he damn near beat you. And you shot off your stupid mouths good and loud. Now the mother's locked herself into the command pod and the daughter's hiding somewhere.'

Nicco shrugged elaborately. 'We'll find 'em. The ship ain't that big.'

'What you're going to do,' Valker said, with steel in his voice, 'is get back to *Vogeltod* and help the crew when the *Hunter* gets here.'

'And what're you gonna do?' Kirk asked, his voice heavy with suspicion.

'I'm going to try to sweet-talk the mother into coming out of the pod.'

'You could blast her out.'

Valker shook his head. 'Two numbskulls. We want this ship as intact as possible when we sell her at Ceres. Don't you think the rock rats' inspectors might wonder why the control pod hatch has been blasted open? And where the ship's original owners might be?'

'Yeah, well . . .'

'I keep telling you dim bulbs: you catch more flies with sugar than with vinegar.'

Nicco made an obscene gesture.

'She knows you killed her son. You made that clear enough for anybody this side of Ceres to figure it out. Now I've got to sugar that woman until she unlocks the pod hatch.'

'Come on,' Kirk growled to Nicco. 'Let's go find the daughter.'

'Get back to our ship,' Valker insisted, 'and get ready to take *Hunter*. The girl will still be here after we've taken it.'

Nicco nodded reluctantly. 'Okay. You're the skipper.'

Kirk grinned nastily and said to Valker, 'Well, after you've sweet-talked the mother out of the pod,' he snickered, 'save some for us.'

BOOK IV

Atonement and Redemption

For this alone on Death I wreak
The wrath that garners in my heart;
He put our lives so far apart
We cannot hear each other speak.

In Memoriam A.H.H.,
Alfred, Lord Tennyson

Smelter Ship *Hunter*: Bridge

'There's something strange here,' Elverda called as she sat in *Hunter*'s command chair, eyes riveted on the main screen.

Dorn replied over the intercom, 'Strange? In what way?'

'I'm getting a radar image of *Syracuse*,' she replied. 'It's rather fuzzy at this range, but it doesn't look right.'

'I'll come to the bridge.'

He was in the workshop again, she knew. Elverda worried about him; his mechanical systems needed maintenance, a thorough overhaul, much more detailed than the two of them could provide aboard the ship.

Dorn stepped through the hatch and stood behind her.

'It looks like a double image,' Elverda said. 'Could there be something wrong with the radar's resolution?'

He glanced at the console settings, then said, 'Perhaps there's another ship mated to *Syracuse*.'

'Another ship? But they didn't say—'

The radio speaker came to life. 'This is *Syracuse*, testing its communications system. Testing, testing, one, two, three.'

'Nothing about another ship,' Elverda said.

'Why would they be testing their comm system?' Dorn mused. Pointing to the radar image on the screen, 'Look. They're emitting a tracking beacon and telemetry now.'

'Maybe their comm system was down?'

'That is a second ship mated to them, but it's not emitting any signals.'

'Curious.'

Dorn turned Elverda's chair so he could see her face. 'It might be dangerous,' he said.

'Dangerous? How?'

'Remember that scavenger ship, *Vogeltod*, and its captain?'

'Valker,' Elverda murmured.

'Suppose someone like them is using *Syracuse* as bait for a trap, to lure us to them. Then they could seize this ship and . . .'

'And kill us,' Elverda finished for him.

Dorn nodded solemnly, but then his eye caught a small blip on the radar screen hurtling away from the image of the doubled ship.

'That's a body!' Dorn said, with absolute certainty.

Valker was at *Syracuse*'s backup command pod, frowning unhappily as he talked to Pauline through the locked hatch.

'It wasn't my doing,' he said earnestly. 'They did it on their own.'

'You murdered my son,' Pauline said. Her voice was muffled by the hatch, but he could hear the anger and hatred in her voice.

'*They* murdered your son. Not me.'

'They're part of your crew.'

Valker bit back a nasty reply, took a deep breath. 'All right,' he said. 'All right. They boy's gone and there's nothing that either one of us can do about that.'

'Go away. Leave us alone.'

'I can't do that, Pauline. And you've got your daughter to think about now.'

No response from beyond the blank hatch.

'They know she's aboard the ship. They'll turn your ship upside down searching for her. And when they find her . . .' He let the thought dangle.

After a few heartbeats, Pauline said, 'You can't let them hurt her.'

'I might not be able to stop them,' Valker said.

'We've got to protect Angela.'

'I can try,' he said, 'if you'll cooperate with me.'

'Cooperate.' Pauline pronounced the word as if it were a death sentence.

A smile easing across his attractive features, Valker coaxed, 'Look, my crew of lowlifes are all back in *Vogeltod*, getting ready for *Hunter*'s arrival. You and me and Angela are the only ones here aboard *Syracuse*. If we're quick enough we can get Angela out of wherever she's hiding and bring her to you, here at the command pod.'

'Then what?' Pauline asked.

'Then while my crew's taking over *Hunter*, you can disengage from my ship and take off for Ceres. You and Angela. You'll be safe there.'

Another silence, longer. Valker counted off the seconds. She's no fool, he told himself, but she might be desperate enough to go for it. After all, what other choice does she have?

'You'll let us go to Ceres?'

'Sure! It's not that far, you'll be able to make it there in a few weeks. My guys'll be busy taking over *Hunter*. It's a fine ship, intact. It'll bring a good price when we take her in to Ceres. They'll forget about you and your daughter. Once we get to Ceres with *Hunter* to auction off, they'll have their pick of the women there.'

Valker nodded, pleased with his logic. It almost made sense to him. *As long as she doesn't remember that she's got no propulsion fuel.*

'But we don't have any time to waste,' he added sternly. 'We've got to get your daughter out of hiding and set up your command console so you'll be able to disengage from my ship at the touch of a keypad.'

Pauline was shaking like a palsied woman as she sat in the command chair, listening to Valker's honeyed words, frantically trying to decide what she should do. She heard Valker's voice, muffled by the locked hatch, heard the earnestness in his tone, the urgency in his last few words.

Why would he let us go? she asked herself. *His men killed Theo. He knows I'll report that once we get to Ceres. Why is he so willing to help Angie and me?*

The memory of his naked body pressing against hers sprang into her mind. *Don't be an idiot!* she warned herself. *He's not in love with you. He's not even infatuated with you. He's nothing but a smooth-*

talking murderer who'll end up killing you and Angie both. After he and his crew have had their fun with us.

She tried to think of some other option, some alternative that she could turn to. There was nothing. Except . . .

With an effort of iron will she suppressed her trembling. She rose to her feet and went to the hatch. She touched the keypad on the bulkhead and the hatch slid open.

Valker stood there, an expectant smile on his face. Handsome face, she thought. Dangerous face.

'I'll reconfigure the control console,' she said, without preamble. 'You return to *Vogeltod* and deal with this approaching ship. I'll bring Angela to me once you're off this vessel.'

His brows rose slightly. 'You don't trust me?'

'Not entirely.'

Valker shrugged good-naturedly. 'Can't say I blame you.'

He stepped into the pod and went straight to the command chair.

'What are you doing?' Pauline demanded.

'Punching in the command code to disconnect the access tunnel. That's what you want, isn't it?'

'Yes,' she said.

'There's a price, you know,' he said, without looking up at her.

'I expected there would be.'

Valker straightened up and turned toward Pauline. 'When we all get back to Ceres I'm going to quit this crazy scavenging business. It's coming to an end anyway; the rock rats are seeing to that.'

'And what will you do?' Pauline asked mechanically.

'With my share of what we make from selling off *Hunter* I can set myself up in business. Nothing grand. Maybe selling jewelry or other luxury items imported from Earth.'

'And a little smuggling on the side?'

Valker laughed. 'No, I'd be strictly legitimate. But I'd want you with me, at my side. We'd make a good team, together.'

This is his price for Angie's safety, she realized. Aloud, she replied, 'I'll . . . I'll have to think about it.'

'I want your promise, Pauline. Now.'

'I still have a husband,' she insisted.

'He's dead and we both know it.' He looked at her intently, his face totally serious. 'I want you, Pauline. For keeps.'

'I can't—'

'I'll protect your daughter. I'll protect you both. But I want your promise, right here and now.'

Pauline closed her eyes and heard herself murmur, 'Very well, I promise. As long as you protect my daughter.'

Victor paced restlessly about *Pleiades*'s bridge, debating inwardly about whether he should send out a call to Pauline or not.

She's out there, he told himself. I've got a good fix on her tracking beacon and I'm homing in on it. I'll be with her in two days, max.

I should call her, tell her I'm coming.

Yet something made him hesitate. He remembered his brief encounter with that scavenger ship, *Vogeltod*. What if he's out there with Pauline and the kids? Theo couldn't repair the antennas without help, we didn't have the stores on board to do the job. If he had, he wouldn't done it years ago, right after we were first attacked, right after I left them.

No, Victor said to himself. Theo had to have help from somebody, and whoever that somebody is he's not emitting a tracking beacon. He's running silent. Why?

His train of logic frightened him. Because he's holding Pauline and the kids prisoners, using them to lure other ships to him so he can capture them and sell them as salvage.

But what's he doing with Pauline and the children? Victor's blood ran cold as he imagined the possible scenarios. He replayed Pauline's short test broadcast. She sounded all right, he told himself: calm, under control.

But what if . . . what if . . .

When he finally stretched out on his bunk and closed his eyes to sleep, the 'what ifs' filled his mind.

Alone

Theo knew he had less than an hour left to live. Pinwheeling through space, he tried to ignore the stars swirling dizzyingly around him and concentrate on the condition of his suit. The diagnostics displays splashed on the inner surface of his helmet confirmed his worst fears. Kirk had punctured his main oxy tank; the oxygen jetting from the puncture had acted as a miniature rocket, thrusting him away from *Syracuse*, away from Mom and Angie, away from any possibility of help.

His radio was gone; there was no way he could call for help. Big spitting deal, he thought: the nearest help is out at Jupiter.

The suit's auxiliary oxygen tank held a half-hour supply. In half an hour I'll die, Theo knew. No, he corrected himself, less time than that. A lot less.

He tried to look back toward *Syracuse* but the ship was already too far away from him to see. Besides, his spinning motion made it almost impossible to focus on anything for more than a few seconds. It made his stomach queasy to watch the universe whirling around him.

They've got Mom and Angie, he realized. Valker and his bastard crew have Mom and Angie and there's no way I can do a thing about it.

Squeezing his eyes shut, he muttered to himself, 'You might as well die. You're not good for anything else.'

Dorn sat in *Hunter*'s command chair as tensely as a bird dog that's spotted a partridge.

'That's a body,' he repeated.

Elverda strained her eyes, but saw only a featureless blip on the radar screen. 'How can you be certain . . . ?'

But Dorn was already tapping on the navigation keyboard, maneuvering *Hunter* toward the radar contact. Elverda felt the soft nudge of the maneuvering jets. Minutes passed and the radar blip grew larger, sharper, better defined. Sure enough, Elverda could make out arms and legs.

'Matching velocity vectors,' Dorn muttered, bent over the keyboard as he called up the propulsion program. 'Setting up a rendezvous trajectory.'

Hunter glided after the figure. Elverda could see that it was tumbling, spinning slowly as it coasted through space. She thought she saw the arms moving but knew it must be her imagination.

'Was there a battle here?' she asked Dorn.

'None that I know of.'

'Then what's a body doing out here?'

He shook his head slowly. 'Maybe we'll find some evidence on the corpse to tell us what happened to it.'

'Can we get close enough?' she asked.

Dorn got up from the command chair. 'I'll get into a suit and go outside for him. You take the con.'

She nodded as she slid into the chair, warm from his

body. 'Couldn't we use the grapples? Then you wouldn't have to go outside.'

'That would be tricky,' Dorn replied. 'I can try, but I'd still better be suited up, so I can go out if I have to.'

Elverda understood that standard safety procedures called for her to suit up, too, so she could serve as a backup, if necessary. But she knew she'd be no good at it: too old, too slow, too tired to be of any use. Dorn didn't mention the subject and neither did she.

Pauline went with Valker down the tube tunnel to the ship's zero-g hub, where the scavengers had set up the flexible connector to link *Syracuse* with *Vogeltod*.

'I mean it about Ceres,' Valker said, his face utterly serious. 'I want to start a new life with you.'

She nodded. 'As long as you protect my daughter.'

'Of course,' he said. Then he grasped her by the shoulders and kissed her, hard.

Taken by surprise, Pauline closed her eyes as he pressed against her lips. Then he let her go, grinned, and headed lightly along the spongy tube. At the hatch on the *Vogeltod* end he turned and waved, beaming a bright smile. Pauline made herself smile back at him.

As soon as the hatch at the far end of the tube closed behind Valker, Pauline slammed shut the hatch on *Syracuse* and punched the intercom console on the bulkhead alongside it.

'Angela!' she said sharply. 'Angela!'

'Mom?'

Pauline felt a grateful sigh gust out of her. For once the intercom was working.

'Get out of there and meet me at the hub. Right away. It's urgent.'

'But Theo said—'

'Never mind what Theo said! Get here at once, do you hear me?'

'Yes. I'm coming.'

'Quickly!'

Elverda wished she were a better pilot. Dorn had set up a rendezvous plot on the navigation program, but a really sharp pilot would be able to edge *Hunter* much closer to the body that was spinning out there.

They were close enough to use the cameras now, in addition to the radar. The image on her main screen was clear and sharp: a human body encased in one of the old-fashioned hard-shell space suits.

Best not to touch anything, she told herself as she scanned the control board. We won't get close enough to use the grapples; he'll have to go out and retrieve the corpse. He's done it before, hundreds of times. He knows what he's doing.

Still, she wished she could help, wished he didn't have to leave the ship.

Then she sat up straight in the command chair. 'It moved!' Elverda said aloud. It moved both its arms!

'Dorn!' she called into the intercom. 'I think it's alive.'

For a moment he didn't answer. Then, 'Alive? How can that be?'

'It moved its arms.'

'I don't believe—'

'There! The arms moved again!' She pointed to the image on the main screen.

'That's impossible,' said Dorn.

'It's not a dead body,' Elverda insisted. 'At least, it's not dead yet.'

At first Theo thought he was hallucinating. Oxygen deprivation, he told himself. The brain's starting to break down. He seemed to see a ship spiraling out there, a big wheel-shaped vessel. And it was drawing closer to him. He squeezed his eyes shut for a moment, took a deep breath of what precious little was left of his oxygen. When he opened his eyes again the ship was still there, swinging around against the background of stars as he pinwheeled.

Could it be real?

'Hey!' he yelled. 'I'm here! Come and get me!'

Then he realized how foolish it was. Kirk had ripped the radio out of his backpack. Theo began to wave at the oncoming ship, swinging both his arms frantically.

Pauline hovered in the zero-g hub of *Syracuse*, alongside the closed hatch of the connector tube. Valker could come back through that hatch at any second, she knew. Where is Angie? Why is she taking so long to—

'Mom! Here I come!'

Angie's voice! Pauline pushed herself to the opening of the tube tunnel that led from the storm cellar and saw Angie diving toward her headfirst, arms flat by her sides, hurtling like a sleek dark-haired torpedo.

'Look out, Mom!' Angie yelled, reaching out to the ladder rungs set into the tube's sides.

Pauline watched aghast as Angela neatly slowed her rush, tucked into a compact ball, and landed lightly on her softbooted feet at her side.

'You told me to be quick,' she said before Pauline could open her mouth to speak.

'You . . . you could have broken every bone in your body,' Pauline said, once she found her voice.

Angie laughed lightly. 'Tunnel diving. Theo showed me how to do it. It's easy when you're going upwards, weightless. Gets trickier when you're going downhill, down to the rim.'

Pauline nudged her daughter toward the tube that led to the backup command pod. 'Come along, we don't have any time to lose.'

Grabbing one of the tunnel's projecting rungs, Angie pulled herself lightly along. 'Where's that Captain Valker? And the other men? Where's Theo?'

Following behind her daughter, Pauline said, 'Theo's dead. Valker's men killed him.'

'Dead?' Angie's wail echoed off the tube walls. 'Theo's dead?'

Pauline swatted her daughter's behind lightly. 'Keep moving. We'll be dead too if we don't get to the pod before those murderers get back here.'

'But what happened?' Angie asked as she resumed clambering along the rungs. 'What's going on?'

'We're going to do just what your father did,' Pauline said grimly. 'We're going into the pod and blast ourselves out of here before Valker and his crew can get their hands on us.'

Capture

'She's veered off,' said Nicco, scowling at the main screen on *Vogeltod*'s bridge.

'I can see that,' Valker snapped from the command chair.

'Something's spooked her,' said the scavenger sitting at the navigation console.

'Maybe,' Valker conceded. 'Or maybe they're just being careful.'

'Should we hail them?' Nicco asked.

Valker thought it over for a moment. 'No. I don't want them to know we're here. Let them think *Syracuse* is alone and needs their help.'

'But they'll see us when they get closer.'

'*If* they get closer,' Kirk growled. 'They're moving away from us now.'

'But they're slowing down,' Valker pointed out. 'Strange behavior.'

'What the hell are they up to?'

'Wait and see,' said Valker. 'Wait and—'

The communications screen lit up to show an image of Elverda Apacheta's arid, withered face. Nicco immediately put it on the main screen.

'Attention *Syracuse*,' the old woman said. 'This is *Hunter*. We have been diverted temporarily. We estimate rendezvous with you in approximately five hours.'

'Diverted?'

'By what?'

Valker fought down an impulse to reply and ask the woman why they changed course. Instead, he made a soothing motion with both hands and said, 'Calm down, boys, calm down. She'll be here in five hours.'

'Yeah, but—'

'Kirk, go to the boys at the airlock and tell them they can stand easy for another four hours and more. We won't be boarding *Hunter* until then.'

He got out of the big padded chair, stretched his arms up to brush the overhead, then started for the hatch.

'And where're you going?' Kirk demanded.

Valker grinned. 'Back to *Syracuse*, to keep the ladies happy.'

'How about taking us with you?' Nicco said.

'Not yet. You maniacs would scare that woman out of her skull. I need her to produce the daughter first. Then we'll have them both.'

'We can find the daughter without the mother's help.'

'You stay right here and keep an eye on *Hunter*. That's our prize. The two women are just icing on our cake.'

'Yeah,' Kirk sneered. 'Looks like you're going over there to lick the icing.'

'You'll get yours soon enough,' Valker said, grinning. Then he ducked through the hatch while the other crewmen snickered behind his back.

Theo was coughing so hard his eyes watered. Not much oxy left to breathe, he knew. But the ship was edging closer, close enough for him to make out the glassteel windowed bulge of what must be her bridge, and ports and other pods along her curving flanks. Airlock hatches, too. Through his tear-filled eyes Theo saw several of them as the ship rotated ponderously, drawing ever closer.

'Come on,' he muttered, but the effort started a new fit of coughing. I'm breathing my own fumes, he realized. It's only a matter of minutes until I choke to death.

His vision was blurring badly, but he thought he saw one of the airlock hatches slide open. He could see the figure of a man standing at the lip of the hatch, outlined against the dim red lights of the hatch's interior.

He knew he couldn't call to them; his suit's radio was gone. But he waved both his arms frantically. He felt hot, beads of sweat trickling down his face, along his ribs. Coughing again. Can't catch my breath!

It all went gray, foggy. Don't pass out! Theo commanded himself. Stay awake!

But you need oxygen to stay awake, he said to himself. 'Sfunny, he's so close, he can almost reach out his arm and grab me, but I'm gonna be dead by the time he gets his hands on me.

Everything slid into blackness.

*　　*　　*

Sheathed in a nanofabric suit, Dorn stood at the lip of the open air-lock hatch, his eyes riveted on the space-suited body spiraling out there in the emptiness. Its arms had been pumping until a few heartbeats ago, proving that the person inside the suit was still alive. But now the arms had stopped, slumped, extended motionless from the figure's shoulders in a weightless crouch, like a drowned man floating facedown in the water.

Dorn checked the control pad of the propulsion pack on his back. 'I'm going out after him,' he told Elverda.

'Are you tethered?' she asked.

'He's too far for a tether to reach,' Dorn said, stepping off the hatch's rim and into nothingness. 'This is a free-flight mission.'

She said nothing, but Dorn could sense her apprehension. Squeezing the control rod, he felt a sudden thrust push at the small of his back. He jetted the few hundred meters to the inert body, wrapped his prosthetic arm around it, and looked into the transparent bubble helmet.

'It's a man,' he called to Elverda. 'Very young. He seems unconscious.'

'Or dead?'

'We'll see.' With his human arm Dorn fumbled with the oxygen hose from his own life support pack. He found the emergency port on the unconscious man's suit and pumped fresh oxygen into it.

The youngster coughed, shuddered spasmodically, banged his nose against the glassteel bubble of his helmet.

But his eyes opened. 'Wha . . . who are you?' The lad's voice was rasping, painfully dry.

'You're all right now,' Dorn said. 'I'll bring you aboard our ship.'

'My mother! My sis—' Coughing overtook him.

Dorn said, 'I'm taking you to our ship. Don't try to talk.'

Jetting back to the airlock, Dorn stood the youngster on his booted feet and turned to close the hatch. But his prosthetic arm would not move. It was frozen.

Valker floated into the zero-g hub of *Syracuse* and started 'downhill' along the tube tunnel that led to the backup control pod, where he'd left Pauline. The going was easy at first: he merely had to flick his fingers against the rungs built into the tube's curving side. But as the feeling of weight grew he grabbed onto a rung, turned himself around, and started clambering down the rungs with the lithe agility of a circus acrobat.

Voices! Valker stopped for a moment, listening. Yes, there were voices echoing up the tube. Two women. Pauline and her pretty young daughter. Valker licked his lips and began descending the rungs even faster than before. But silently.

'I was afraid of this,' Dorn said sorrowfully as he eased himself into one of the galley chairs. His prosthetic arm was still jutting out from the shoulder, bent at the elbow, as if a cast had been wrapped around it.

Theo couldn't help staring at the cyborg. The old woman had introduced herself as Elverda Apacheta;

the name meant nothing to Theo. But this half-man with one side of his face formed by etched metal, one eye an unblinking camera, one arm and one leg built of alloys and plastics and filled with bioelectronic circuitry – Theo couldn't take his eyes off Dorn.

'You need major maintenance,' Elverda said as she sank wearily into the chair on the opposite side of the galley table.

Dorn puffed out a grunt. 'That is an understatement.'

Theo took the chair at the end of the narrow table. 'I need to get back to *Syracuse*,' he said. 'My mother and sister are in danger there.'

'Danger?' Elverda turned toward him.

'A gang of scavengers has attached themselves to my ship,' Theo explained. 'I hate to think of what they'll do to my mother and sister if we don't get there fast.'

Dorn's human eye closed briefly. Then he said, 'Their ship is named *Vogeltod*?'

'You know them?'

'We know them. They're undoubtedly waiting for us to rendezvous with your ship so that they can board us and take over this vessel.'

'We should get away,' Elverda said, 'as quickly as possible.'

'But my mother!' Theo protested. 'My sister!'

'What good could we do?' Elverda asked.

'We can't just leave them in the hands of those bastards!'

Dorn said, 'He's right. We must do what we can.'

'With one hand?' Elverda scoffed.

'I can help you repair the arm,' Theo offered. 'While we're on our way to *Syracuse*.'

Dorn contemplated him for a silent moment. Then, 'What do you know about bioelectronic circuitry? Micromechanical systems?'

'Some,' Theo replied. 'Not much, I admit. But if you've got manuals, instruction vids, I can learn while we're on our way back to my ship. At least . . .' He stopped himself from going on.

Dorn almost smiled. 'At least you have two working hands. I understand.'

Pacing the narrow confines of *Pleiades*'s bridge Victor saw that *Hunter* was heading for *Syracuse*. Good, he said to himself. Then he recalled that the half-machine creature on *Hunter* had wanted him to head back to Ceres and turn himself in. Screw that, he thought.

They heard Pauline's signal, Victor knew. They'll get to her before I do. He nodded to himself. Good. Fine. The sooner Pauline gets help the better.

Then his comm screen showed the seamed, aged face of the old woman. 'Attention *Syracuse*,' she said. 'This is *Hunter*. We have been diverted temporarily. We estimate rendezvous with you in approximately five hours.'

Five hours, Victor thought. He returned to the command chair and pecked out his navigation program. At the rate I'm moving I'll be there in a little more than six hours.

For the first time in months, Victor smiled.

Ore Ship *Syracuse*:
Backup Command Pod

Valker stopped his descent and, clinging to the rungs in the shadows of the dimly lit tube tunnel, he listened to Pauline and her daughter. He could clearly hear their voices echoing up the tube, even though the two women were speaking in hushed whispers.

'Fire off the pod?' the daughter asked. 'But—'

'We've got to get away from those men,' Pauline said urgently. 'We can escape in the pod and let the people in *Hunter* pick us up.'

'But what good would that do?' the daughter demanded. 'They'll just come after us, whether we're in *Hunter* or here.'

Impatiently, Pauline answered, 'We're alone here. Alone against ten of them. At least aboard *Hunter* we'll have a better chance.'

Valker could make them out, down at the end of the tube. Pauline was working the bulkhead-mounted pad that controlled the hatch into the command pod.

'That Captain Valker isn't so bad,' the daughter was saying. 'He wouldn't let them hurt us.'

'Angela, for god's sake!' Pauline snapped. 'Don't be a fool.'

'But—'

'We can't trust him.'

Valker sighed philosophically. The woman's right. Even if I want to protect her and her daughter, the roughnecks behind me won't leave them alone. Too bad. I might have changed my whole life with a woman like Pauline at my side. Too bad.

As soon as the hatch slid open Valker called to them. 'Hello ladies! Good to see you've recovered, Angela.'

Staring up at him, they looked up like a pair of guilty waifs suddenly caught in a police spotlight.

Pauline pushed her daughter through the hatch and started into the command pod herself. Valker clambered down the rungs as swiftly as a monkey, then dropped the final few meters and slammed his palm against the hatch's control panel, stopping Pauline from shutting it.

'You weren't thinking of leaving, were you?' he asked, stepping into the cramped little pod.

Pauline backed away from him until her hip bumped against the control board. Angela stood off to one side, half smiling at him.

'Please don't go,' Valker said, with exaggerated courtliness. 'The fun is just beginning.'

'This is weird,' Theo muttered as he lifted Dorn's prosthetic arm out of its shoulder socket.

The cyborg was sitting stolidly on a stool by the workbench. An interactive maintenance vid was running on the wall screen of the workshop. The arm felt heavy in Theo's hands; he put it down carefully on the workbench's top, littered with tools.

'Can you feel any of this?' Theo asked.

Dorn nodded slightly. 'It isn't pain, but the sensation isn't pleasant, either.'

Jabbing a thumb toward the wall screen, Theo said, 'According to the vid, this shoulder joint should be self-lubricating.'

'Pressurized air lubrication, I know,' said Dorn. 'But the shoulder seizes up. The lubrication fails.'

Theo asked the voice-activated program for a list of possible failure modes.

'Air leakage,' he said, studying the list. 'That must be it.'

'Or erosion of the bearings.'

'I can test the bearings,' Theo said. Pointing, he asked, 'That's an electron microscope, isn't it?'

'The maintenance program should have a sub-routine for testing the bearings.'

'Right.'

Half an hour later, as he was replacing the bearings in the shoulder ring of Dorn's arm, Theo said, 'The bearings are all well within specification.'

'Then it must be a pinpoint leak in the air lubrica-tion,' said Dorn. 'We don't have the equipment to find a microscopic hole in the seal.'

Theo thought a moment. 'Maybe we can—'

Elverda's voice on the intercom interrupted him. 'The navigation program estimates rendezvous with *Syracuse* within one hour. I can see another ship mated with her.'

'That's the scavengers,' Theo said.

'They'll want this ship,' said Dorn.

'They'll want to kill us all, including my mother and sister.'

Dorn gestured with his human arm. 'We'd better get me back together, then, and hope the arm doesn't freeze up again.'

Lifting the arm in both hands and working its end into Dorn's prosthetic shoulder, Theo said, 'Maybe we can use a quick and dirty fix.'

'Quick and dirty?'

'Yeah.' The arm clicked into the shoulder socket. As Theo reached for the air hose attached to the work-bench's side, he explained, 'We replenish the air in the bearings, get it up to the right pressure, then we spray a plastic sealant around the joint, so the plastic covers whatever pinhole might be in there.'

Dorn thought a moment. 'Like spraying sealant on a leaking tire.'

'Right. It ought to hold, at least for a while.'

Dorn nodded. 'It's better than nothing.'

Valker disabled the circuit that fired the explosive bolts that would separate the backup command pod from the main body of *Syracuse*, talking to Pauline and Angela nonstop as he bent over the console.

'My crew's drooling with anticipation over you two,' he said, his usual smile replaced by a tight-lipped, unhappy frown. 'It's not going to be easy to keep you out of their hands.'

'Then let us get away from here,' Pauline urged.

Valker shook his head. 'No. That won't work. They'll go chasing after you. And when they catch up with you, nothing will stop them. Not even me.'

'Then what are you going to do?' Angela asked, her voice trembling.

'They'll be busy taking *Hunter* once it gets here. But after they've got her, they'll want to celebrate.'

'Leave my daughter alone,' Pauline said. 'Give me to them.'

'Mother!'

'That might work,' Valker said, 'for a while. But only for a while.'

Pauline swept the cramped pod with her eyes, looking for a tool, a weapon, something, anything.

Valker straightened up, the disconnected firing keys to the separation bolts in his hands. 'Ladies, I'm afraid you're in for a rough time.'

Cargo Ship *Pleiades*: Bridge

Victor called up the nav program for the eighth time in the past half-hour. 'Estimate rendezvous with *Syracuse* in ninety-three minutes,' he read aloud from the screen. 'Ninety-three minutes. I'll see Pauline and the kids again in a little more than an hour and a half.'

Punching up the radar image, he saw the wheel shape of *Syracuse* clearly enough, although there seemed to be a strange sort of bulge on one side of the vessel's hub. And there was the blip of *Hunter*, also heading toward Pauline. His fingers worked the keyboard and the screen showed that *Hunter* would arrive at *Syracuse*'s position in less than an hour.

They're thirty-some minutes ahead of me, Victor thought. I'll get there half an hour after they do.

He checked the comm program. No messages from *Syracuse* since Pauline's call. Why not? Victor asked himself. You'd think they'd be beaming out a steady call for help. Why aren't they?

He sagged back in the command chair, unwilling to believe what logic was telling him. That one message was their last gasp. They're dead now. All of them. Pauline. Theo. My little Angel.

He pounded both his fists on the chair's armrests. To come this close! And still be too late. Victor bowed his head. He wanted to weep.

But instead he raised his chin and glared at the radar image on the main screen. No. I won't give up. Not until there's not a shred of a chance that they're still living. Not until I see their dead bodies with my own eyes. Not until then. Not until then.

Valker's communicator buzzed in his tunic pocket. His eyes still on Pauline and Angela, he fished it out of his pocket and held it up to his ear.

'What?'

Nicco's voice answered, 'Radar shows another ship heading this way. Running silent.'

Valker's brows knit. 'Running silent?'

'And heading this way like a bullet, about half an hour behind *Hunter*.'

Breaking into a broad grin, Valker said into his comm unit, 'What did I tell you, boys? This *Syracuse* is our good luck charm. She's like a magnet, drawing ships to us. Now we've got two vessels we can salvage.'

'I don't like it,' said Nicco. 'Why's she running silent? Who is she?'

'Maybe another band of salvage operators, just like us,' Valker mused.

'That could be trouble.'

'Not if we're ready for 'em and they're not ready for us.'

Nicco said nothing.

'I'm coming over to *Vogeltod*,' Valker said. 'We've got to take *Hunter* fast and be ready for this other ship when it gets here.'

'An old woman and a priest,' Nicco replied. 'Shouldn't be much trouble.'

'Right. Let's nail them quick and clean.' He clicked the communicator shut and said to Pauline, 'I've got to attend to business back on my ship. Don't do anything foolish while I'm gone.'

Pauline glared at him.

As Valker started up the tube ladder toward the ship's hub, Angela asked her mother, 'What can we do?'

'Wait,' Pauline said, in a hushed voice.

'Wait for them to come and get us?'

'Wait until that smiling ape gets back aboard his own ship. Then we go over to the main airlock as fast as we can and get into our suits.'

'The space suits? Why?'

'We're getting off this ship.'

'But you heard him,' Angela objected. 'They're going to take the ship that's approaching us. It wouldn't do us any good to—'

'We're not staying on this ship with that gang of rapists waiting to get their hands on us,' Pauline said. 'I don't care if we die of asphyxiation in the suits, we're getting away from here!'

On *Hunter*'s bridge, Theo slid into the communications chair. 'We're close enough for a tight laser beam transmission,' he said. It was a statement, not a question.

'You want to speak to your mother and sister?' asked Elverda.

Theo nodded. 'I want to let them know I'm alive, without that Valker or his crew hearing me.' Silently he added, But I don't know how long I'm going to stay alive. The two of us – Dorn and me – against ten of them.

Dorn was standing behind Elverda, in the command chair, moving his prosthetic arm in a circle, testing its bearings.

'Do you know how to activate the laser?' Elyerda asked Theo.

'Yes ma'am,' he replied, his fingers playing across the console's keyboard. Looking up at the comm screen he saw the battered hulk of *Syracuse* looming close enough almost to touch. A tiny red dot showed where the laser was aimed. Theo played the controls, marching that red dot across the vessel's curving hull until it locked onto the optical receiver built into the backup control pod. The dot suddenly changed to green and Theo pressed the key that opened the communications link to the receiver.

Okay, he said to himself. Nobody hears this except Mom, on the receiving end of the laser beam.

'Mom, Angie,' he called. 'It's me, Theo. I'm on *Hunter*. They picked me up after Valker's thugs tried to kill me. I'm okay. I'm coming back to help you.'

No response. Theo pressed the REPEAT key, but still there was no answer from *Syracuse*.

'They're not in the control pod, I guess,' Theo said,

as much to himself as to Elverda and Dorn. 'But the intercom should relay the message.'

Victor was weighing the possibilities. That's definitely another ship attached to *Syracuse*, he told himself. On his main display screen he could see the smaller vessel linked to *Syracuse* like a lamprey eel that's attached itself to a hapless fish.

And there's *Hunter*, heading in.

He couldn't be patient any longer. He got up from the bridge's command chair and went to the communications console.

'Attention *Syracuse*,' he said, his voice brittle with tension. 'This is *Pleiades*. I heard your call and I'll rendezvous with you in . . .' He glanced at the digital clock readout on the screen. '. . . in seventy-eight minutes.'

Pauline was in the locker area just outside *Syracuse*'s main airlock, checking the seals and connections of Angela's suit, when the intercom speaker in the overhead announced, 'INCOMING MESSAGE.' She ignored the statement. Getting Angie suited up and ready to escape the ship was more important.

'Another message,' Angela said. 'That makes two.'

Satisfied at last that her daughter's suit was spaceworthy, Pauline reached for the leggings of her own suit and sat on the bench that ran in front of the lockers.

'Never mind the messages,' she said. 'The important thing is to get off this ship before Valker comes back.'

Angela stood stiffly in the cermet suit, the visor of her bubble helmet raised.

'But aren't you going to check the messages?' she asked.

'They're probably for Valker, from his crew.'

'But—'

'There's nobody out there to send messages to us, Angie,' Pauline said, grunting with the effort of tugging on her heavy boots.

'Maybe it's from that other ship heading toward us,' Angie insisted.

Pauline almost smiled. She's still young enough to hope for a miracle.

'That's the *Hunter*. The only people aboard her are an old woman and a priest. I'm hoping that we can get to them before Valker seizes their ship. Maybe we can get away on their ship, if we're lucky.'

Angela gave her mother her stubborn scowl and clomped to the comm panel mounted on the bulkhead. 'It wouldn't hurt to hear what they're saying,' she said, holding her gloved hand up to the panel.

She's right, Pauline realized. Shrugging, she said, 'Go ahead, then.'

Angela pressed the comm unit's ON button and said, 'Play first message, please.'

They heard, 'Mom, Angie. It's me, Theo. I'm on *Hunter*. They picked me up after Valker's thugs tried to kill me. I'm okay. I'm coming back to help you.'

'Theo!' both women cried in unison.

'He's alive!'

'He's coming back!'

Pauline redoubled her efforts to get into her suit. 'We've got to get to him before Valker's crew takes over that ship,' she said.

'We should send him a message,' said Angela. 'Warn him.'

'No, we can't do that,' Pauline countered. 'Valker and his people would hear any message we sent, unless we used the laser unit and that's back in the pod.'

'Besides, we need *Hunter* close enough for us to get to,' Angela agreed.

'That's right,' Pauline added silently, But not so close that Valker and his scavengers get to her first. She slipped into the hardshell torso and Angela came away from the comm panel to help her seal it to the leggings.

Back on *Vogeltod*'s bridge, Valker listened to Victor Zacharias's message.

'*Pleiades*!' he exulted. 'That's a fine ship. And there's only one man aboard her, a thief, at that.'

'Unless he's picked up a crew,' Kirk muttered.

'Good point,' said Valker. 'Let's break out the weapons.'

Like everything else aboard *Vogeltod*, the weapons supply was a hodgepodge of pieces stolen, scavenged, or bartered from other ships. There were four genuine laser pistols, complete with compact power packs attached to their belts. There were two cumbersome laser welders that could cut metal and easily slice flesh, although it took two men to carry each one of them and their bulky power packs. There were a variety of tools such as cordless drills and wrenches that could be used

404

as knives or bludgeons. There was even an old-fashioned air pistol that fired tranquilizing darts, although Valker wondered if the tranquilizer was still potent after all the years the darts had lain unused. Finally, there was a belt of minigrenades, powerful enough to blow down an airlock hatch.

Valker looked over his grinning crew, each of them now carrying sidearms or tools-turned-weapons strapped to their hips. Two of the men hefted one of the bulky laser welders and its power pack between them. Valker himself had taken a laser pistol and flung the belt of minigrenades across his broad shoulder.

'You look like a band of real fierce pirates,' he said, laughing.

'We're ready for anything,' said Kirk, brandishing a power drill whose bit was almost as long as his forearm.

'Yeah!' Nicco agreed. 'And after we've taken these two ships, we get the two babes. Right?'

Valker had to force his smile, but he said, 'Right.'

Smelter Ship *Hunter*: Airlock

Standing at the lip of the open airlock hatch, Theo saw clearly the curving flank of *Syracuse*, the long ugly gash in one of the fuel tank sections, the stumps that had once held the missing command pod, the new antennas he had painted on the adjoining portion of the hull, the backup command pod.

They were approaching the ship from its top, the side opposite the place where *Vogeltod* hung mated to *Syracuse* by the flexible connector tube.

Theo was in his hard-shell space suit with a new backpack that Dorn had provided; the cyborg stood beside him in a nanofabric suit.

'The living quarters are on the other side of the pod,' Theo told the cyborg, pointing with an outstretched arm. 'The main airlock is—'

He saw that the airlock hatch was open, subdued red light glowing from it.

'Is Valker using our airlock?' he wondered aloud.

'I doubt it,' said Dorn.

'Then who . . . ?' Theo saw two space suited figures outlined against the airlock's dim red lighting.

'Mom?' he called over the suit-to-suit frequency. 'Angie?'

'Theo! We're coming over to you.'

'Okay! Great! Make it quick!'

Theo turned to Dorn. 'Tell Ms. Apacheta to goose the fusion drive as soon as we get them aboard. Maybe we can take them in and get away from here before Valker's crew can board us.'

Dorn shook his head inside the inflated bubble hood of the nanosuit.

'Too late,' he said, pointing.

Half a dozen nanosuited men were jetting up from between the spokes of *Syracuse* and heading straight for them.

Standing at *Vogeltod*'s main airlock in his nanofabric space suit, Valker heard Theo's call to his mother and sister.

'The kid's still alive,' he growled.

'And the women are trying to jump over to *Hunter*,' Kirk said.

'Let 'em,' Valker snapped. 'We'll get there first. Come on.'

He squeezed the knob that controlled his suit's propulsion unit and jetted out of the airlock. Five of his men followed him. He had left Nicco and three others behind to take over *Syracuse*.

As they maneuvered through the spokes of the big wheel-shaped *Syracuse*, Kirk laughed maliciously. 'Nicco's gonna crap himself when he finds the sugar-pots ain't on the ship.'

'So what?' said Valker. 'Once we take over *Hunter* we've got the women, too.'

He could see *Hunter* hanging in the emptiness, rotating slowly. There's the airlock, Valker said to himself. And two people standing in it.

'Hey, there's the women,' one of his crew called out.

Turning slightly, Valker made out a pair of figures in hard suits jetting toward *Hunter*'s open airlock hatch.

'Good,' he said. 'Let 'em get to the airlock first. We'll hit 'em while they're all crammed in there together.'

'What about hitting one of the auxiliary locks, too?' Kirk asked.

'They'll be sealed tight. Why blow a locked hatch when we've got one wide open and waiting for us?'

Then Valker thought a moment. Turning to the two men handling the big welding laser, he said, 'Slice a chunk out of the main thruster cone. I don't want them lighting off their fusion engine and getting away from us.'

'Elverda,' Dorn was saying into his suit microphone, 'as soon as I give the command you must push the main engine to full thrust.'

'I understand.' Her voice sounded tense in his earphones.

The two women were a scant hundred meters from the airlock hatch and coming on fast. But the half-dozen scavengers were not far behind them.

'Crank the command chair to the full reclining position,' Dorn told her. 'You'll be able to take the acceleration better that way.'

'Don't worry about me,' she replied immediately.

But Dorn did worry. She can't take a full g's acceleration, he thought. Even with the stem cell therapy she received, her heart can't take the strain. But if we don't get out of here before those men come aboard . . .

'I'm programming the propulsion system for a one-g acceleration,' Elverda was saying, her voice tight but calm. 'Tell me when.'

'Crank the chair down,' he repeated.

'Yes. Certainly.'

Theo nudged him with an elbow. 'Here they come!'

In their space suits, it was impossible for Dorn to tell who was the mother and who the daughter.

Close behind them six other figures were speeding toward them: the scavengers from *Vogeltod.*

'Hurry!' Theo urged.

Dorn saw two of the scavengers peel off, away from the others. They were carrying some kind of bulky equipment. A weapon? he wondered.

'I'm ready to light off the fusion drive,' Elverda's voice reported.

Theo was attaching a tether to one of the cleats on the hull just outside the airlock hatch. Before Dorn could ask him why the youngster jumped out into the vacuum and reached for the nearer of the two women. He pushed her toward the airlock, then stretched his arms out toward the other one.

Dorn grabbed at the woman as she coasted into the airlock and helped stop her headlong rush. 'You're safe now,' he said.

He could see the frightened expression on her face

through her glassteel helmet. 'For how long?' Pauline asked.

Theo clutched at his sister's outstretched hand and tugged her toward the airlock.

'Thee! Look out!' Angela screamed.

One of the scavengers was speeding toward them. Theo pushed Angela toward the airlock hatch and turned to face the approaching man. He could see Kirk's face through the bubble of his nanofabric suit, lips pulled back in a savage grin. He was brandishing a long, deadly looking power drill.

'I'm gonna finish you once and for all, kid.'

Theo jetted up and away from the scavenger, but the tether reached its limit and stopped him with an abrupt jerk that pulled Theo upside down. Kirk swung around, fiddled with his propulsion unit's controls, and came swooping after him.

Theo dived toward Kirk, holding his end of the buckyball tether in both hands, and flicked it like a whip. Kirk flew into it, and Theo spun around him, wrapping the tether around Kirk's middle, trapping one of his arms against his torso. Screaming curses, Kirk flailed at the tether with the drill, but the buckyball material was too tough even to scratch.

Theo raced back to the airlock hatch, where Dorn, his mother and sister were standing. A burst of light splashed off the airlock hatch. They're firing lasers at us! Theo realized.

Theo planted his boots on the airlock deck just as a blast of energy slammed into his back. He staggered into his mother and sister.

'Thee?'

'I'm all right. They hit my backpack.'

'They've also hit the hatch control,' said Dorn. 'We can't close the outer hatch.'

'They're almost here!' Angela said, and Theo saw the scavengers racing toward them, with Valker in the lead, a laser pistol in his hand.

'Fire the engine,' Dorn shouted.

'Firing,' said Elverda.

Hunter shuddered as if it had been hit by a bomb. But it did not move away from the men approaching the airlock.

Cargo Ship *Pleiades*: Bridge

Victor was close enough to hear the suit-to-suit chatter from the other ships. He recognized Theo's voice, and his wife's. Then there were others, men's voices, cursing, yelling. It sounded as if some sort of struggle was going on. A fight.

He stared at his main screen as if he could get himself there by sheer willpower. Still fifteen minutes away, he saw from the numbers on the nav program.

What's happening? he asked himself. What's going on there?

He could see *Syracuse* gleaming sharply in sunlight against the starry background of infinity. There was another ship linked to it. And *Hunter* had arrived and matched their velocity vector.

A burst of flame from *Hunter*'s main thruster! Victor saw the ship shudder. A half-dozen figures were flitting around the vessel, most of them clustered at the main airlock.

Fourteen minutes and thirty seconds. Victor knew he had to do something. But what?

Standing in the crowded airlock, pistol in his hand, Valker smiled at his prisoners.

'No sense fighting,' he said amiably. 'Your ship is crippled and you're not going anywhere.'

Theo could see the other scavengers crowding around the air-lock hatch. Kirk glowered at him murderously.

'Let's go inside,' Valker said, motioning with his pistol. 'It's not polite to leave your visitors hanging outside your door.'

Besides, Theo said to himself, the air in your suits must be running low. He saw red lights splashed across the inside of his own bubble helmet. That laser shot's smashed up my life support pack, he realized.

Dorn said slowly, 'You've destroyed the control for the outer hatch. If I open the inner hatch the air in this entire section of the ship will blow away into vacuum.'

'Tell whoever's at your bridge to seal the airtight emergency hatches,' Valker said. 'That way only one small section will go to vacuum and you can pump air into it again once the inner airlock hatch is closed again.'

'Yes, that is the answer,' Dorn said. He called Elverda. 'Are you all right?'

'Yes,' her voice answered. 'But the engine . . . it failed.'

'Our guests,' Dorn's voice dripped irony, 'disabled the thruster.'

'Tell her to close the emergency hatches,' Valker reminded.

'*Now*,' Kirk stressed.

'Close all the emergency hatches,' Dorn said. 'We're going to use the section next to the main airlock as an extension of the 'lock.'

413

'Why . . . ?'

'Please do it,' Dorn urged. 'We have visitors among us.'

Within minutes all ten of them were crowded into the locker area, with the inner airlock hatch safely sealed and the section of the ship refilled with air.

'Take off your helmet, lad,' Valker said to Theo. 'Let's see if the air pressure's okay.'

Burning with anger, Theo lifted his helmet off his head.

'The air's fine,' he said.

'You two, please,' Valker said to Pauline and Angela, gesturing with his pistol. Turning to Dorn, he added, 'And you.'

The two women lifted off their helmets. Dorn deflated the hood of his nanosuit and pulled it back off his head.

Valker peered at him. 'You're the priest?'

'Yes.'

'You're a cyborg,' Kirk said, as he pulled his own hood off his face. 'A fuckin' freak.'

'Very observant of you,' Dorn replied.

As they all wormed out of their space suits, Elverda's voice came from the overhead speaker: 'We have a message from the approaching vessel.'

'Play it,' Valker commanded.

They heard, 'This is *Pleiades*. Estimate arrival at your position in nine minutes. Will match your velocity vector.'

Standing before the bench in front of the lockers, his bubble helmet in his gloved hands, Theo felt a jolt of electricity surge through him. That's Dad's voice! he said to himself. He glanced at his mother; she recognized the voice, too. So did Angie.

Valker grinned his widest. 'Here comes our profit, boys,' he said. 'Walking right into our laps.'

'If he's alone on that ship,' Kirk cautioned.

'Even if he isn't,' said Valker. 'I'm going up to the bridge and guide our pigeon to us. You boys stay here by the airlock. When he comes in, you grab him.'

He turned to Dorn. 'Come on, cyborg. Lead us to the bridge.'

Elverda got up from the padded command chair and went to the communications console. She activated the laser comm system, hoping that it would lock onto the optical receiver of the oncoming ship.

As soon as the screen's ready light flashed green, Elverda said urgently, '*Pleiades*, this is *Hunter*. We have been boarded by scavengers who intend to take our ship and yours. We have three people from *Syracuse* with us. We need help. They're going to kill us all unless we can find a way to stop them.'

Victor heard the fear in Elverda's trembling voice, saw the anxiety in her worn face.

'How many men do the scavengers have?'

'I don't know. Four or five, I think, maybe more.'

'Where are they?'

'Down at the main airlock, but I think their leader is coming to the bridge.'

Victor thought swiftly. 'Do you have an airlock near the bridge?' he asked.

'Yes, immediately adjacent.'

'Please open it. I'll board your vessel through it.'

'Very well. Please hurry.'

'I will.' He scanned the control board, saw that the nav and propulsion programs were set to match the velocity vectors of the other ships. Then he got up from the command chair and headed for the equipment bay where tools were stored. I'm going to need some kind of a weapon, he told himself. Something to make the fight more even.

As they walked along the slightly sloping passageway that ran along *Hunter*'s inner rim, Valker kept his pistol in his right hand, although he allowed his arm to relax naturally by his side. The kid and the two women were a few steps ahead of them, trudging reluctantly, grudgingly toward the ship's bridge; the cyborg paced along beside him, matching him stride for stride.

'What's it like,' Valker asked, 'being half machine?'

Dorn's half-metal face turned slowly toward him. 'What's it like, being entirely animal?'

Valker laughed. 'I mean, does your machine half feel pain? Is it stronger than normal human flesh?'

Lifting his prosthetic arm slightly, Dorn said, 'This hand could crush that pistol you're carrying.'

Instinctively, Valker twitched the gun away from the cyborg.

'Not to worry,' said Dorn, quite solemnly, 'I'm a priest, not a warrior.'

416

'You're not a fighter, then?'

'Not normally.' Dorn raised his left arm higher, then let it fall to his side. 'Besides, this arm is prone to a mechanical version of arthritis, now and then.'

Valker asked, 'You've always been a priest?'

'No, not always. Once I was a soldier. A mercenary. I've seen battle. I've . . . killed people.'

'But not anymore.'

'Not unless I'm provoked,' said Dorn, with a slight nod to the two women and the young man walking ahead of them.

Smelter Ship *Hunter*: Bridge

Her fingers moving swiftly on the electronic keyboard, Elverda opened the emergency airlock next to the bridge as she watched in the main screen the lone figure of a man jetting across the gap between *Pleiades* and *Hunter*. Glancing at the control board's telltale lights, she saw that he entered the airlock and cycled it.

Through the open hatch of the bridge she heard voices approaching; Dorn's deep, slow tones and the lighter, faster patter of another man: Valker. As she got up from the command chair two women stepped through the hatch, followed by the same young man Dorn had brought aboard earlier, then Dorn himself and the tall, broad-shouldered, smiling Valker, who was still chattering blithely away. And holding a pistol in his right hand.

He had to duck slightly to get through the hatch. Then his eye caught Elverda's and he beamed a bright smile at her.

'Hello again, Ms. Apacheta,' he said.

Elverda smiled back tentatively.

'It's good to see you again,' he said, putting more wattage into the smile.

Drawing herself up to her full height, Elverda said, 'We meet under unusual circumstances, Captain Valker.'

Valker raised the pistol and glanced at it as if he hadn't realized it had been in his hand. 'This? Well, this is business, dear lady. I'm afraid we're going to have to take your ship, and the one that's just made rendezvous with us.'

'Like hell you will!'

A scruffy, stubby, dark-bearded man in a rumpled short-sleeved tunic and shorts stepped through the hatch, a laser spot welder in one hand. His bare arms and legs were knotted with muscle, his onyx eyes blazed fury.

Valker whirled around at the sound of his voice, leveling the pistol in his hand. Dorn wrapped both his arms around Valker's body, and young Theo punched the scavenger solidly in the jaw. Valker's legs buckled, his head lolled back on his shoulders.

'Victor!' The older woman rushed into the arms of the fiercely bearded man. The younger followed her by a half-step. They both broke into sobs.

Dorn let Valker's unconscious body slip to the deck. Theo bent down and took the pistol from his hand. Dorn slipped the belt of minigrenades off his shoulder, stared at them for a long wordless moment, then with a growl flung them across the bridge.

It took a few minutes, but Elverda got it sorted out despite the blubbering. Even young Theo Zacharias – who turned out to be the bearded man's son – had tears in his eyes.

'This is a helluva family reunion,' said Victor Zacharias, his arms around his wife and daughter, a happy grin on his face.

Dorn brought them all back to reality. 'There are nine other scavengers: six aboard this vessel and three on *Syracuse*.'

'Hunting for Mom and Angie,' Theo said grimly.

Victor's dark eyes flashed. 'They didn't—'

'Angie's fine,' Pauline said immediately. 'They didn't touch her.'

Elverda stared at the woman, then turned to the main screen, above the control panel, and pointed. 'Look. Four men are crossing over to your ship, *Pleiades*.'

'It'll take them a little while to realize I'm not aboard her,' said Victor.

'Then what?' Theo asked.

'How many are still on this ship?' Victor asked.

Elverda worked the electronic keyboard. The main screen broke into a dozen smaller views, each showing a section of *Hunter*'s interior. Only two scavengers were visible, both by the main airlock.

'We've got to get them before the others come back,' Theo said.

Victor stepped closer to the multi-eyed screen. 'They're both armed.'

Valker groaned and pushed himself up to a sitting position. He looked up at Theo, rubbing his jaw. 'Nice punch, kid. Try it again sometime when my arms are free.'

Theo started toward him, but Dorn blocked him with his prosthetic arm. 'Perhaps we won't have to fight the others.' Pointing to Valker, 'We have a hostage here.'

Valker laughed bitterly. 'Some hostage. You think those cockroaches would give up taking two whole ships, just for me?'

'We'd better get those two before the others come back,' Victor said.

'Defeat them in detail,' Dorn muttered.

Victor looked at him. 'You talk like a soldier.'

'I was a soldier, once.'

Hefting the pistol he'd taken from Valker, Theo said to his father, 'Let's go for them, then.'

Victor looked into his son's eyes, then nodded. Turning to Dorn, 'Can you lock him up someplace?'

'One of the storage bays,' Dorn replied. 'It's on the way to the main airlock.'

'All right,' Victor said. 'Pauline, you and Angie stay here on the bridge with Ms. Apacheta. Keep all the airlock hatches sealed.'

'We can't close the main airlock's outer hatch,' Elverda said.

'That's all right. Just don't open any others.' Victor waved the squat gray cylinder of his spot welder in Valker's direction. 'Get moving.'

Valker climbed to his feet and went without protest, his usual smile gone, replaced by a glum resignation. But just as he was about to step over the hatch's sill, he looked back at Pauline for just the flash of an instant. Elverda saw her cheeks redden.

Dorn locked Valker in the nearly empty storage bay, then hurried to catch up with Victor and his son.

'They tried to kill me,' Theo was telling his father. 'Punctured my suit's main air tank and pushed me off into space.'

Dorn could see Victor's fists tightening. 'But your mother, Angela, they haven't hurt them, have they?'

Theo shook his head. 'Not that they didn't want to. We hid Angie in the storm shelter.'

'And your mother?'

Theo hesitated a heartbeat before answering, 'Nobody attacked her.'

They strode down *Hunter*'s curving main passageway in silence for several moments. Then Victor turned to Dorn, 'We'll have to find a weapon for you.'

'No,' said Dorn. 'I'm a priest, not a warrior.'

Theo began to object, 'But we're going to need—'

'I will fight to protect my companion,' Dorn said to Victor, 'or you and your family. But I will not willingly kill anyone.'

Victor stared at him for several paces along the passageway. At last he said, 'Don't get in our way, then.'

As they approached the main airlock, Victor said to Theo, 'This spot welder puts out a stream of high-energy pulses. Doesn't carry very far, though. That pistol you're holding is more powerful.'

Theo glanced at the pistol. It bore the imprint of Astro Corporation. Valker must've taken this from a ship he captured, he thought.

'Both those men are in space suits,' Victor went on. 'Puncture the suits. Rip them open so they can't get off the ship.'

'Right,' Theo agreed.

Dorn said, 'Wouldn't it be better to let them get off this ship? Let them have *Pleiades* and leave us in peace.'

'So they can steal other ships and kill their crews?' Victor snapped, almost snarling. 'No. There's no law out here. It's up to us.'

'Vengeance is not justice,' Dorn murmured.

Victor glared at him, then answered, 'This isn't vengeance. This is extermination. You heard what Valker called them: cockroaches. You don't let cockroaches go free. You kill them.'

Dorn stopped walking. 'I can't help you do that.'

'Then go back to the bridge,' Victor said.

'I could take those two men for you. Without killing them.'

Victor stared at the cyborg.

'If I succeed, you will have them without risk to yourself or your son. If I fail, then you can attack them your way.'

Theo tapped Dorn's prosthetic shoulder. 'Is your arm working okay?'

Dorn lifted the arm, turned it in a full circle. 'Your maintenance work is holding fine.'

'Let him try it, Dad,' Theo urged. 'What do we have to lose?'

Victor looked from his son to the cyborg and back again. At last he reluctantly murmured, 'All right.'

Cargo Ship *Pleiades*: Bridge

Suspicion smoldering in his mind, Kirk flicked through *Pleiades*'s internal camera views. Every section of the ship seemed empty, abandoned.

'There's nobody here,' said the scavenger at his elbow. 'This's a ghost ship.'

'Your great-grandmother's a ghost ship,' Kirk growled. 'He's aboard somewhere. He's hiding.'

One of the other crewmen piped up. 'He sure don't have a crew with him. He musta been alone.'

'He's in here someplace,' Kirk insisted, watching each camera view intently for a few moments, then skipping to the next. 'We've gotta find him.'

'It's a big ship, Kirk. There's only the four of us. It'll take a day or two to search every compartment.'

'So it takes a day or two!'

'Yeah, but while we're playin' hide-and-seek with the bastard, Valker and the other guys got the women.'

Kirk glared at the crewman. Gritting his teeth in indecision, he finally admitted, 'Maybe you're right.'

'Least we can call Valker and tell him the bum's hiding out someplace.'

'Yeah. Let's call Valker.' The others all agreed.

Kirk tried his suit radio. No answer. Grimacing with anger, he turned to *Pleiades*'s comm console.

'Valker, this is Kirk.'

No reply.

'Valker, this is Kirk. We can't find anybody on *Pleiades*. We're coming back.'

Still nothing but the hiss of the comm signal's carrier wave.

Kirk snatched up the power drill he'd lain on the control board. 'Something's wrong. Let's get back to *Hunter*.'

Nicco, meanwhile, was feeling equally frustrated aboard *Syracuse*. He and the two scavengers with him had searched the living quarters, the command pod, and even the storm cellar. No sign of the two women.

'They ain't here,' Nicco said as he stepped out of the radiation shelter's cramped womblike interior.

'They've gone?'

'Looks like it.'

The other crewman said, 'This is a pretty big ship. We've only searched a quarter of it.'

'The rest is in vacuum,' Nicco told him. 'No air. All shut down. They can't be in there.'

'Not unless they're in suits.'

'Suits only hold a few hours' air; they can't stay in 'em for long.'

'Maybe they can hold their breaths for a couple hours,' said the first crewman. 'I bet they both got big lungs.'

Nicco did not laugh. Frowning with frustration, he said, 'C'mon, we better get back to Valker. Maybe he can figure this out.'

Dorn stopped a good fifty meters before the airlock area.

'You two wait here,' he whispered. 'Give me three minutes, then come ahead.'

Victor nodded. Theo licked his lips, thinking, If this cyborg can't handle those two scavengers I'll kill them both. I'll cut them up with this laser. I'll chop them into pieces.

Then he saw the look on the human half of Dorn's face and remembered the priest's words: *Vengeance is not justice.*

Dorn walked slowly, deliberately, toward the main airlock. The two scavengers that Valker had left were lounging at the inner airlock hatch, which was sealed shut. They stiffened at the sight of the approaching cyborg, gripped their weapons in their hands. One had a cordless power drill, the other an elaborately wicked-looking knife with a serrated blade.

'What're you doin' here?' asked the taller of the two, the one with the drill.

'Captain Valker sent me,' Dorn replied, shifting his steps slightly so that the one with the knife was on his prosthetic side.

'Valker? What for?'

'Why di'n't he come himself?'

'Or call us on the intercom?'

Dorn was within arm's reach of the pair of them. They seemed wary, distrustful. They both edged half a step backward as Dorn approached them.

The one with the knife lifted its blade so that its point was level with Dorn's prosthetic eye.

'Why don't I just carve you up here and now, 'stead of waitin'?'

Praying that his arm would work properly, Dorn grabbed the blade in his metal hand and twisted. The blade bent and the man holding it yowled in sudden pain. His partner, jaw dropped wide, fumbled for the power button on his drill as he backed away from Dorn.

Yanking the knife out of the first one's hand, Dorn growled to the other, 'Drop that toy before I shove it up your colon.'

For an instant both men stood frozen in shocked silence. Then Dorn heard Zacharias and his son running up the passageway. Seeing the weapons in their hands, the scavenger dropped his power drill to the deck with a dull clunk. The would-be knife wielder raised his hands over his head.

'Good work,' Victor said to Dorn. 'That's two of them.'

'There are seven more,' said Dorn.

Sitting in the bridge's command chair, Elverda heard Kirk's call from *Pleiades*, saw the angry irritation in his chiseled features.

'Should we reply to him?' Pauline asked.

'No,' said Elverda. 'Not until the men return.'

Angela stared at the frozen image of Kirk on the screen, but said nothing.

Elverda cut off the message and pulled up a view of the passageway where Dorn, Victor and Theo were leading the two scavengers back from the main airlock.

With Pauline standing on one side of her and Angela on the other, Elverda asked softly, 'The men did not harm you?'

'No,' Angela said.

Turning to Pauline, Elverda dropped her voice to a near-whisper and asked, 'Will you tell your husband?'

Pauline glanced at her daughter, then replied, 'I suppose I will, sooner or later.'

'He'll want to kill Valker.'

'Mother!' Angela blurted. 'He raped you?'

Pauline pressed her lips together, then replied, 'No, he didn't rape me.'

'But . . .' Angela's eyes went wide as she realized what her mother implied. 'You mean . . . willingly?'

'Not willingly. I had no choice,' Pauline said, her voice flat and cold.

Angela's mouth hung open but no words came out.

'Your husband will kill Valker,' Elverda repeated, 'once he knows.'

Pauline said nothing.

'Look!' cried one of the scavengers. 'That's Nicco and the others comin' over from *Syracuse*.'

Kirk and the three crewmen with him were jetting back to *Hunter*. He twisted in the emptiness and saw the three sunlit figures heading toward him.

'What's goin' on with you?' Kirk asked over his suit radio.

'Damn ship's empty,' Nicco's voice answered. 'The women are gone.'

'They must be hiding.'

'They're gone. And Valker ain't answering us.'

Kirk nodded grimly inside his inflated helmet. 'We can't raise Valker either. Something's gone wrong.'

The two groups of scavengers came together like gliding vultures, shifting clumsily in their flight.

'You think they got Valker?' Nicco asked.

'Don't see how,' Kirk replied. 'He had a pistol. The priest and the kid were unarmed.'

'The women musta gone aboard *Hunter*.'

'Or drifted into space.'

'What about the guy from *Pleiades*?' one of the crewmen asked. 'Where'd he go?'

They coasted toward *Hunter*'s main airlock. Kirk saw that the hatch was open; the dimly lit airlock chamber looked empty.

'All right, hold it,' Kirk said as they glided to *Hunter*'s curving hull. 'We gotta take stock before we go in.'

'Take stock of what?'

'The situation.'

'There's seven of us against a priest, a kid, and an old lady.'

'And maybe the two other women.'

'And maybe the guy from *Pleiades*, too.'

'We got weapons and they don't.'

Kirk sneered at them. 'Weapons? You got a coupla power tools and some wrenches.'

'I've got a pistol,' Nicco pointed out.

'Yeah, and they prob'ly got Valker's pistol. And the grenades he was carrying.'

That quieted them.

'Where'd you leave the heavy welder?' Kirk asked the two men who had disabled *Hunter*'s main thruster.

'We put it on a tether after we were done with it.'

'Go get it,' Kirk said. 'We might need it to burn through some hatches.'

Smelter Ship *Hunter*: Bridge

'So that's how they disabled our fusion engine,' Dorn said, looking at Elverda.

She was still sitting in the command chair as they listened to the suit-to-suit talk between Kirk and the other scavengers.

'Maybe we can retrieve that heavy laser before they do,' Theo suggested.

'No.' Victor shook his head. 'They're already outside, suited up. They'll get to it long before we can.'

'I'm still in my suit,' Theo pointed out. 'So're Mom and Angie. Angie and I could—'

'No,' Victor repeated firmly.

'Then what do we do?' Pauline asked.

More to Dorn than the others, Victor said, 'Once they get that heavy laser they'll be able to burn through any of the hatches we try to keep locked against them.'

'Yes,' said Dorn.

'They'll punch their way from the main airlock right up here to the bridge,' Victor muttered.

'And free Valker on their way,' Theo added.

'All we have is this one laser pistol.'

'And those grenades,' Theo said, pointing to the belt that lay on the far side of the deck.

'Stay in your suits,' Kirk told his men as they came through the inner hatch of the main airlock. 'They might try somethin' cute, like cutting off the air in this section of the ship.'

Nicco glanced over his shoulder at the two men lugging the heavy welder and its power pack. 'You guys oughtta be up front,' he said.

'Why do we hafta lug this clunker?' one of the men complained. 'How 'bout you takin' it for a turn?'

'Whatsamatter, girls?' Nicco asked, laughing. ''Fraid you're gonna break a fingernail or somethin'?'

The men glared at him but shuffled up to the front of the line, where Kirk stood peering down the passageway, left and right. He stepped to the wall screen and tapped its directory.

'Okay,' he said, tracing a path on the main display. 'The bridge is this direction.'

They started along the passageway, Kirk in the lead, the two men with the welder grumbling right behind him, then the rest, with Nicco bringing up the rear.

Kirk tried to raise Valker on his suit radio, again to no avail.

'They musta killed him,' he mused aloud.

'Then we're gonna hafta elect a new captain,' said one of the men toting the laser welder.

Kirk grinned toothily. 'I nominate me.'

From up the passageway they heard Valker's sneering voice, 'Over my dead body!'

'It's the skipper!'

The passageway ran along the rim of the ship's wheel, so that although it felt flat as long as the wheel was turning, it curved up and out of sight in both directions. Valker came striding toward them, smiling grimly. The two men Dorn had disarmed came into sight behind him.

'Where've you been?' Kirk demanded.

'They ganged up on me, that half-robot priest, the kid, and some other guy – he must be from *Pleiades*.'

Grinning at the bruise on Valker's jaw, Kirk said, 'Only three of 'em?'

'They caught me by surprise. Then they locked me in a storage bay. Then they brought in Gig and Kelso, here.'

Nicco came pushing through the group. 'How'd you get out, skipper?'

Valker gave him a sour look. 'Accordion-fold door. They thought locking it would keep me inside. One kick is all it took.'

'So the guy from *Pleiades* is aboard?' Kirk asked.

Nodding, Valker added, 'And the two women from *Syracuse*. They're all up in the bridge, one tidy little package.'

Raising the power drill he was carrying, Kirk shouted, 'So let's go get 'em!'

Victor and the others watched the scavengers' impromptu reunion in the main passageway. Turning from the bridge's screen, Victor muttered, 'We've got to stop them.'

433

'Yes,' agreed Dorn. 'But how? There are ten of them.'

'Close all the emergency hatches.'

'They'll burn through them with that big laser.'

'I know. But that will take them time.'

'So what good will that do?'

'Theo,' Victor said, pointing to the belt lying on the deck, 'get those grenades and come with me. You,' he said to Elverda, 'seal all the hatches. Now.'

As Elverda called up the life support program, Victor and Theo headed for the hatch.

Pauline reached for his shoulder. 'Victor, what are you going to do?'

'Stop them,' he said.

Dorn watched the two of them go, then, after a moment of indecision, followed after them.

The hatch up the passageway swung shut with a sharp clang. Turning, Valker saw the hatch behind them bang shut. They could hear more thumps in the distance.

'The bastards're sealing all the hatches,' Kirk growled.

Valker grinned at him. 'What else can they do? They're just postponing the inevitable.'

'They might try to pump out the air.'

'So we stay in our suits,' Valker said, pulling up his hood and inflating it.

He motioned to the two men carrying the heavy laser welder. 'Now ain'tcha glad we brought this beauty along with us?'

Nicco laughed. 'We'll burn right through the hatches.'

'No need to,' Valker said, pointing to the control keypad on the bulkhead beside the sealed hatch. 'Just burn out the pad and get to the manual override. Won't take more'n a minute.'

'For each hatch,' Kirk said.

'So what?' Valker snapped. 'They're not going anywhere. And we're not going away.'

Following his father's example, Theo peeled back the plastic sheeting that covered the passageway's structural tubing and wedged the pebble-sized grenades into the exposed metal framework in a complete circle, from the deck to the overhead and then back down to the deck on the other side.

Dorn stood in the middle of the passageway, arms folded against his chest. 'I see what you intend to do. But blowing away this section of the wheel won't stop them. They're already in space suits. They'll merely jet through the open area to the next hatch.'

'Not if they're in the section that we blow away,' Victor said.

'No, they'll still be able to jet back to us,' Dorn countered. 'Unless they're killed or injured by the blast.'

'That's the general idea,' said Victor.

'I can't be a party to that.'

'You don't have to be. Just stay out of my way.'

Theo spoke up. 'You can show us how to fuze the grenades so we can set them off from the bridge.'

Dorn did not reply.

Victor strode down the passageway to where Dorn was standing. 'Now listen. These scavengers would kill you and your friend without blinking an eye. They'd kill my son and me. They'd rape my wife and daughter and then kill them, too. You expect me to let them do that?'

For several heartbeats Dorn did not reply. At last he said, 'I spent a lifetime killing. My soul is drenched in blood. I can't help you to commit murder.'

And he walked away, past Theo, back toward the bridge.

Victor glowered at his back. 'Finish the job, Thee,' he said to his son. 'I'm going to the bridge.'

Smelter Ship *Hunter*:
Main Passageway

'Ow!' Nicco yelped, wringing his hand. 'That's hot!'

Valker laughed. 'What do you expect? The circuit's been melted by a laser beam. Put your gloves back on.'

Nicco scowled at the blackened hole in the bulkhead where the hatch's control pad had been. Kirk pushed past him, wiggled his nanogloved fingers in the air, then reached in and found the manual switch.

The hatch popped open a crack. Kirk kicked it all the way open, then made an exaggerated bow. 'This way, gentlemen.'

'That's three,' Nicco said, still wringing his burned hand as the scavengers trooped through the open hatch. 'How many more?'

Valker turned to the wall screen display of the ship's layout. 'Four . . . five . . . and then the galley and finally the hatch to the bridge itself. Six more to go, men.'

'And then we've got 'em!' one of the crewmen exulted, waving the laser pistol he carried in the air.

'And then we get the women!' shouted Kirk.

Back on the bridge, Theo saw his father's jaw clench as he watched the main screen's camera view of the scavengers advancing along the passageway. And then we get the women, Theo repeated silently. He's one of the dog turds that tried to murder me. Dad's perfectly right: Kill them or they'll kill us.

Dorn still stood with his arms locked across his chest, immobile as a statue, except that his head swiveled back and forth from watching the main screen to staring at Victor. What's going through his mind? Theo wondered. He said he'd killed a lot of people and now he doesn't want us to kill these scum. But what else can we do?

Suddenly the cyborg let his arms drop to his sides and started toward the closed hatch.

'Where are you going?' Victor demanded.

'To them.'

'What? What do you think—'

'You're going to kill them. Kill me, too.'

Before he realized what he was saying, Theo blurted, 'That's crazy! You're not one of them!'

'I was, once. Just like them. Worse. I'll die with them.' Dorn reached the hatch and started to tap out the command code with his prosthetic hand.

Victor said, 'You're going to warn them?'

'No,' Dorn replied. 'I'll simply join in their fate.'

Elverda protested, 'They'll kill you as soon as they see you!'

'What difference does that make?'

Pushing herself up from the command chair, Elverda crossed the bridge to Dorn's side. 'I can't let you kill yourself.'

'I'm going to die anyway,' he said softly. 'We all will, sooner or later. Why prolong the misery?'

'Because I need you,' Elverda answered. 'If you die, I'll die too. I'll have no reason to go on living.'

Theo stared at them. The cyborg with his death wish. The old woman trying to save him from himself. His mother and sister, frozen speechless. And his father in that fierce beard he'd grown, looking as implacable as death itself.

Turning to the main screen, Theo said loudly, 'They're through the third hatch. They'll be entering the section we mined next.'

Everyone turned to the screen.

Theo went to the command chair. 'Might be a good idea to pump the air out of the passageway before we blow the grenades,' he said, leaning over the control panel.

Valker himself was now taking a turn at lugging the laser welder. Trotting up the passageway behind him, Nicco toted the power pack.

'How're we doing on juice?' Valker asked over his shoulder.

Nicco peered at the colored bar of the indicator. ''Bout halfway down. We can recharge off the ship's current if we hafta.'

Valker said, 'That'd take some time. I don't want to keep those ladies waiting.'

Nicco laughed. Behind him, Kirk was leading the other seven men. They stopped at the closed hatch. Nicco lowered the power pack to the deck; Valker propped the bulky welder on one hip and aimed it at the control pad.

'Warning,' said a deep voice. The men all looked up at the intercom speaker set into the overhead. 'Warning. This passageway will be evacuated to vacuum in thirty seconds. Air pressure will be reduced to zero.'

'Bastards!' Kirk snapped.

Valker was grinning inside the inflated hood of his nanosuit. 'Seal up or breathe vacuum, boys,' he said, almost cheerfully.

'They think they can stop us?'

'They're gettin' scared.'

'Desperate.'

'They can't think of anything else to do, I guess.'

Should be enough air in the suit tanks for an hour, at least, Valker thought. Plenty enough to get through the last of these hatches and into the bridge. I'll let Kirk lead the charge: that guy with the beard took my pistol. Let Kirk go in first. He's a hothead, he'll charge right into the gun. Then we can cut the bearded one down and the kid and the cyborg, too.

'Everybody okay?' Valker asked. They heard him through their suit radios and nodded.

'Then let's get through these frigging hatches!'

'The entire passageway is in vacuum,' Dorn announced, his eyes on the control board, his back to Victor.

'Why'd you warn them?' Angela asked.

Dorn glanced toward Elverda, but did not answer.

'They're going into the section where we planted the grenades,' Theo said, feeling perspiration trickle down his ribs.

Dorn started toward the hatch again.

'Where do you think you're going?' Victor demanded.

'Dorn!' Elverda said sharply. 'No!'

'I have to,' the cyborg replied.

Victor stepped between Dorn and the hatch. 'Stay here. You can't stop this.'

For a long silent moment Dorn stood eye to eye with Victor, unmoving. Then he said, 'I belong with them. Kill me too.'

'I don't want to kill you,' Victor said.

'Yes you do. You simply don't know it yet.'

'They're entering the section we mined,' Theo said, turning from the main screen to the two men confronting one another. 'If we're going to blow those grenades we've got to do it now.'

Before Victor could reply, Dorn said, 'I'm the man who attacked your ship. I am Dorik Harbin.'

'What?'

Theo felt his guts clench with shock. He saw his father reach for the pistol he'd tucked into his waistband.

'He was Dorik Harbin,' Elverda said, rushing to Dorn's side. 'But he's changed, he's—'

'I wiped out the *Chrysalis* habitat,' Dorn said, his voice flat, emotionless. 'Then I attacked a ship named *Syracuse*.'

Victor stared at the cyborg. He couldn't get a word out of his throat. But his right hand pulled the pistol from his waist.

'He's not the same person!' Elverda pleaded. 'He tried to kill himself. He's spent his life atoning for his sins.'

Victor raised the pistol to the level of Dorn's eyes.

'You attacked my ship? You nearly killed my whole family!'

'So kill me,' Dorn said softly. 'Release me from life.'

Theo stood frozen at the control panel and stared at his father. His father held the gun at arm's length, unwavering, pointed at the cyborg's face. His mother and sister were clutching each other, still in their space suits, their faces torn with fear and uncertainty.

'Please!' Elverda begged, pushing herself between Dorn and Theo's father.

Dorn grasped the old woman by her shoulders and lifted her off her feet. Placing her down gently to one side, he turned back to Victor.

'So kill me,' he said.

Smelter Ship *Hunter*: Bridge

'You attacked our ship,' Victor said, the words barely struggling past his gritted teeth. 'You tried to kill us.'

Dorn said nothing.

'But you survived,' Elverda reminded. 'You lived through it.'

Victor grimaced. 'No thanks to this . . . this . . . monster.'

'So kill me and get your revenge,' Dorn said.

Victor stared at the cyborg. Kill him! urged a savage voice within his mind. Kill him. He deserves to die. He *wants* to die.

Victor's finger froze on the pistol's trigger. He closed his eyes briefly, but when he opened them again Dorn still stood before him.

'No one will blame you,' Dorn said.

'Don't do it!' Elverda pleaded.

'I can't,' Victor groaned, dropping the pistol to his side. 'By all the fiends of hell, I can't do it.'

'Then don't kill those other men, either,' Dorn said softly.

Theo looked up at the screen again and saw that Valker and his crew were marching along the passageway to the next hatch.

'Dad!' he called.

Victor seemed in a daze. His father stared at the main screen but didn't seem to understand what he was seeing.

'Dad, now!' Theo called.

Dorn turned toward Theo. 'Don't murder them.'

Sudden rage boiled through Theo. They tried to murder me. They want to rape Mom and Angie.

Dorn repeated, 'Don't—'

'The hell I won't!' Theo yelled, and he slammed his fist onto the control key that ignited the grenades.

In the airlessness of the passageway the detonations made no sound, but the scavengers were jolted off their feet as the bulkhead around the closed hatch in front of them was torn apart by sudden flashes of explosion.

Through his suit radio Valker heard his men shouting and swearing as he struggled to his knees. Weight seemed to be dwindling, as if he were suddenly floating. Kirk and others were sprawled in a heap, drifting up off the deck, arms and legs thrashing. The entire section of the passageway had been blasted loose, tearing itself out of the ship's wheel-shaped structure and lumbering off into empty space.

Nicco was tangled beneath the laser welder, but in the sudden near-weightlessness he pushed it off with a grunt and a string of curses.

'They've torn this whole section out of the ship!' Kirk yelled, pushing himself to a standing position. The effort made him float off the deck altogether; his hooded head bounced off the overhead.

Hovering in a weightless crouch, Valker realized there was enough light to see by. The passageway sections must have individual battery-powered emergency lights, he reasoned.

'Anybody hurt?' he asked.

'Fuck that! We're drifting away from the ship.'

'We're headin' for friggin' Pluto or someplace!'

'Calm down,' Valker said, making a soothing motion with both hands. 'Calm down. We ain't dead yet.'

'Won't be long, though.'

'Bullshit!' Valker snapped. 'We've got more than an hour's worth of air in our tanks and enough fuel in our jet packs to get back to the ship.'

'This time we blow a hole in their bridge first off,' Kirk snarled. 'No more pussyfootin' around.'

Victor dashed to the control board and clapped his son on the back.

'You did it, Thee! Good work!'

Theo stared at the main screen. The outside cameras showed the torn section of *Hunter*'s hull spinning slowly away from the ship.

'Now let's get ourselves out of here,' Victor said.

'We have no propulsion,' Elverda reminded him. 'They disabled our fusion thruster.'

Theo jabbed a finger on the key that opened the suit-to-suit radio frequency.

'. . . got more than an hour's worth of air in our tanks and enough fuel in our jet packs to get back to the ship.'

Valker's voice, Theo recognized.

Then Kirk's snarling, 'This time we blow a hole in their bridge first off. No more pussyfootin' around.'

Theo turned to his father. 'They're coming back!'

'But now they're vulnerable,' Victor said. 'They're floating in vacuum, in space suits.' He brandished the laser pistol.

'You think the gun has enough charge to get them all?' Theo wondered.

'All we need to do is puncture their suits. A pinhole will do.'

'No,' Dorn said. 'Please!'

Victor glared at him. 'Listen. Just because I couldn't shoot you in cold blood doesn't mean that I'll allow those cutthroats to get back to this ship.'

'Don't murder them,' Dorn begged. 'Choose life over death.'

'Tell that to them!' Victor snapped.

'There must be another way.'

Theo looked into the cyborg's half-human face. 'Maybe there is another way,' he said.

Pauline hardly recognized the fiercely bearded man who had come aboard *Hunter* as her gentle, thoughtful husband—until the moment he failed to kill Dorn. Victor, she thought. Despite everything, despite the years of anguish, he couldn't kill the man who's caused all our troubles. Not in cold blood. Not Victor. He couldn't.

But she saw that Victor was perfectly ready to do whatever he had to in order to protect her and Angela. What would he do if he knew that I've slept with Valker? How will he feel about me?

446

She looked at Angela, standing beside her, and at the elderly woman who tried to save Dorn from his own guilt-ridden death wish. *Angie knows about Valker now*, Pauline told herself. *But she won't tell her father; she won't breathe a word about it, not to Victor or even to Theo. It's our secret. I'll have to talk to her about it, explain what happened. Make her understand. If I can. If I can.*

She realized Theo was asking something of Dorn. With an effort, she forced her thoughts aside and focused on the others on the bridge.

'Do you have suits for yourselves?' Theo was asking Dorn.

Elverda replied, 'Nanosuits, yes. There are several in the locker by the main airlock.'

'Why should they need suits?' Victor demanded.

Theo jabbed a thumb at the main screen. The scavengers were floating out of the twisted wreckage of the severed hull section.

'They're going to be coming here. We'd better get off this vessel and into *Pleiades*.'

Victor grinned with understanding. '*Pleiades* has propulsion. Her fusion engine works and she's got enough fuel to get back to Ceres.'

'Right,' said Theo. 'Let those dog turds have this ship. It can't move. It's a derelict, thanks to them.'

'And we'll get away on *Pleiades*,' said Victor.

'But we've got to be quick,' Theo urged.

'Wait,' Pauline said.

The men turned toward her.

'They've got their own ship: *Vogeltod*. Its main engine works and they've got fuel for it in her tanks.'

'I know,' Theo said. 'I'll have to take care of that.'

Victor bent over the control panel. 'We've got to put some distance between us and those scavengers.'

Dorn came up beside him. 'With only the maneuvering jets, we can't go far.'

Theo told him, 'Move us toward *Syracuse*.'

'*Syracuse?*' his father demanded. 'You mean *Pleiades*.'

'*Syracuse*,' Theo replied. 'And their ship, *Vogeltod*.'

Space Race

'Anybody hurt?' Valker asked again.

He was clinging by one hand to a cleat on the outer skin of the broken hull section, spinning slowly in the middle of nowhere, with nothing but the emptiness of the universe all around him. Along the curve of the section he could see his men pulling themselves out of the wreckage, slowly, still in shock from the explosion.

'Well?' he demanded. 'All you huskies in one piece?'

'My hand still hurts,' Nicco complained.

'I twisted my leg.'

'My insides don't feel so good.'

'That's the zero-g,' Kirk's scornful voice countered. 'Don't up-chuck in your hood.'

A scattering of snickering laughs.

The broken hull section turned enough for Valker to see the rest of *Hunter* gleaming in the sunlight, one section of its wheel-shaped hull gone, the shattered ends blackened by the explosions.

'All right, all right. Pull yourselves together. We've got to get back to that ship and give those pissants what they deserve.'

★   ★   ★

Once they got to the auxiliary airlock, Theo saw how simple it was for Dorn and Ms. Apacheta to get into nanosuits. Just like pulling on a set of coveralls. He hefted the new backpack that Dorn had given him, feeling its weight settled on his shoulders, then went to his sister.

'I'll check out your backpack,' Theo said to Angela.

'Let your mother do that,' Victor said. He was still in his nanofabric suit, its hood pushed back against his shoulders.

'You sure you know what you're doing?' Victor asked as he checked Theo's backpack.

'Yes, sir.'

'I ought to be doing this myself,' Victor muttered. 'If anything goes wrong . . .'

'Nothing's going to go wrong, Dad. It's my idea; I'll do it. You take care of Mom and Angie.'

Despite his father's beard Theo could see the uncertainty, the anxiety in his face.

'I can do it, Dad,' he insisted. 'You can trust me.'

Victor looked up into his son's eyes, then clasped him on the shoulder of his bulky hard suit. 'I know you can do it, son. It's just that . . . if anything should go wrong—'

'Then you'll be with Mom and Angie, protecting them.'

Theo lowered his bubble helmet over his head, sealed it to the suit's collar, but left the visor open. Dorn had volunteered to stay aboard *Hunter* in Theo's place, but neither Theo nor his father completely trusted the cyborg. He's too fond of death, Theo said to himself. This job needs somebody who wants to live through it.

'It shouldn't take long to wreck the controls,' Victor said.

'I know,' said Theo.

'They'll come straight to the bridge as soon as they see you're ramming *Hunter* into their ship.'

'If they're smart they'll jet back to their own ship and get out of here before *Hunter* smashes into them.'

'No, they'll come after you. They'll want to prevent the collision so they can keep *Hunter* for salvage.'

'I'll zip out before they can get to me.'

Victor nodded minimally.

Theo could feel the eyes of his mother and sister on him. And the cyborg and the old woman, too. He remembered a word from his history lessons: *kamikaze*.

'Is it just my eyes, or is *Hunter* moving away from us?' Kirk asked.

The ten scavengers had floated free of the torn-out section of *Hunter*. Gripping their makeshift weapons, they were jetting back toward the vessel. Valker had appropriated the laser pistol that one of the men had carried.

'Hard to judge distance out here,' he muttered.

Then he saw three glittering puffs of gas from the man-euvering thrusters on one side of *Hunter*'s broken hull.

'They're moving her!'

'Towards *Syracuse*!' Nicco bellowed, pointing at the distant wheel shape of the battered cargo ship.

'And *Vogeltod*!' Kirk snarled. 'The bastards're going to ram us!'

'Power up, boys,' Valker commanded. 'We've got to stop *Hunter* before it hits our ship!'

'Look! They're leavin' *Hunter*!'

'Headin' for *Pleiades*!'

'Let's get them!'

'First things first, boys,' Valker said, his voice high with excitement. 'We've gotta stop *Hunter* from plowing into our ship.'

'But they'll get away on *Pleiades*!'

'Let 'em,' Valker insisted. 'We've got to save our own ship first. Nicco, take Ross and Turk and get back to *Vogeltod*. Disconnect her from *Syracuse* and get her the hell out of the way. The rest of you come with me.'

We'll take *Hunter* before she rams our ship, but we'll lose our best prize, Valker admitted silently: *Pleiades*, an intact, first-rate ship. And the two women. He saw Pauline in his mind's eye: beautiful and strong. With her I could become anything I want to be. But I'd have to get rid of these apes first. And even before that I'd have to take care of the people with her.

That includes her daughter, Valker realized. Or maybe I could take them both. He grinned, inside the bubble of his nanosuit hood. Both of them. Mother and daughter. Maybe I could . . .

He shook his head. Forget that. If you don't move fast you're going to lose your own ship and die like a chump out here.

Jetting between Angela and Victor, Pauline saw *Pleiades* looming larger as they approached.

'It's working.' She heard Dorn's heavy voice in her helmet earphones. 'Some of them are racing back to their own ship.'

Victor said, 'But the rest of them are reboarding *Hunter*.'

'Theo's still on *Hunter*!' Pauline cried out. 'Alone!'

Smelter Ship *Hunter*: Bridge

Sitting awkwardly in his hard suit on the bridge's command chair, Theo heard the scavengers' suit-to-suit radio chatter as he worked frantically to dismantle the navigation program and controls.

I've got maybe five minutes, he told himself as he feverishly pecked at the navigation keyboard.

'Navigation program cannot be erased,' said the computer's maddeningly calm voice, 'without authorization from the ship's captain.'

'Erase it!' Theo shouted. 'Emergency override!'

Coolly, the computer replied, 'Voiceprint identification does not match the captain's. Emergency command not valid.'

Theo was already out of the command chair before the computer's stubborn refusal was finished. He rummaged through the tool bin built into the end of the control console. The best he could come up with was a hand-sized laser welder, similar to the one his father had brandished earlier, good for spot welds on electronics equipment and not much else.

'It'll have to do,' Theo muttered to himself.

On the main screen, above the control console, he saw *Syracuse* slowly, slowly growing larger as *Hunter* inched toward it. The scavenger's ship was still attached to it. Good! Theo said to himself. Maybe I'll get them both, after all. But he wished he could push *Hunter* faster.

Then, on one of the auxiliary screens that displayed views of the ship's interior, he saw Valker and a half-dozen of his men pushing through the open airlock and sprinting up the passageway toward the bridge.

Knowing he had only moments, Theo used the butt end of the hand laser to smash the transparent covers on the navigation controls and then fired pulses of infrared energy to slag the circuitry.

'It's not much,' he said, 'but it's the best I can do.'

He snapped his visor shut and clumped off the bridge toward the emergency airlock: He could hear the pounding footsteps of Valker and his crew approaching. Theo ducked into the airlock, fidgeted impatiently while it cycled down to vacuum, then stepped off the outer hatch's rim into the nothingness of empty space.

Valker was the first of the scavengers to bolt into the bridge. He immediately saw that the key controls on the main console had been smashed, their circuits melted.

'Sonofabitch!' he snapped. 'The little bastard's screwed us, but good.'

Kirk came up beside him. 'I can fix this. Rewire—'

'How long?' Valker asked.

'Huh?'

'How long would it take you?'

'Half an hour,' said Kirk. 'Maybe a little longer.'

Valker sneered at him. 'And just how long do you think it's gonna take this clunker to smash into *Syracuse?*'

Kirk scowled back at him.

'I'd say it'd be a lot less than half an hour,' Valker answered his own question.

'Yeah. Guess so.'

Valker bent over the communications console and tapped on its keys. 'Nicco! You uncouple the ship yet?'

A moment's hesitation, then, 'Got the access tunnel disconnected. Powering up the maneuvering jets right now.'

'Good. Get our ship the hell out of the way. This bucket's going to ram right into *Syracuse* in another ten–fifteen minutes.'

'We'll be outta the way, Skip.'

Nodding with satisfaction, Valker turned back to Kirk and the rest of his men.

'So whattawe do now?' Kirk asked.

'Get to *Pleiades* as fast as we can,' Valker replied. 'She's our prize. Her, and those women aboard her.'

Standing in *Pleiades*'s open main airlock in their nanofabric space suits, Victor and Dorn could see the lone figure of Theo in his hard-shell suit floating across the gulf that separated the ship from *Hunter.*

And behind him, seven nanosuited scavengers erupted from *Hunter*'s airlock.

'They're not returning to their own ship,' Dorn said calmly.

'No,' Victor agreed. 'They're heading here.'

'Your son has a good lead on them.'

But Victor was thinking, Seven of them. And we've only got this one pistol. The hand welder's useless in this kind of fight: its range is too short.

'Once Theo comes aboard,' he said to Dorn, 'we've got to power up and get away from them.'

'You'd better go to the bridge, then,' Dorn replied.

'Not until Theo gets here.'

'That may be too late.'

'Wow,' said Angela, glancing around at the spacious, well-appointed bridge of *Pleiades*. 'Talk about luxury.'

Pauline said, 'Your father lived here alone for all those months.'

'How could he control such a large ship by himself?' Angela wondered aloud.

Elverda said, 'Dorn reconfigured *Hunter*'s controls so that one person could handle it. Your father must have done the same here.'

With a small smile of appreciation, Pauline started to say, 'I didn't think Victor knew how—'

'Pauline!' her husband's voice blared over the intercom. 'We've got to power up the main drive and get away from here.'

She looked at Elverda. 'Do you know how?'

The sculptress shook her head. 'I could do it on *Hunter*, but these controls are strange to me.'

'Pauline, did you hear me?' Victor's voice sounded strained with tension.

'Victor, I don't know how to do it!' Pauline said.

Angela plunked herself down on the command chair. 'Talk me through it, Dad,' she called out. 'I'll do it.'

'Talk you through it?' Victor shouted.

'I'm in the command chair,' Angela's voice replied, bright and eager. 'There's an electronic keyboard in front of me.'

Theo was almost within arm's reach; the scavengers close behind him and coming up fast. Victor closed his eyes momentarily, trying to visualize the command keyboard.

'Extreme right end,' he said. 'The key's labeled "propulsion."'

'I see it,' Angela said. 'Oh, good! The whole keyboard's changed to the propulsion program.'

Dorn reached out with his prosthetic arm and helped Theo to remain standing as he glided into the airlock.

'Made it!' Theo said, exultant.

'But not soon enough,' said Dorn, pointing to the scavengers, barely a hundred meters away.

Cargo Ship *Pleiades*: Main Airlock

Standing at the open airlock hatch, Victor watched the seven space-suited figures approaching *Pleiades*. They're going to get here before we can get the fusion drive going, he realized, then added, If Angie can figure out how to do it.

Turning to Theo, he commanded, 'Get up to the bridge and power up the fusion drive! *Now!*'

Without even lifting the visor of his helmet Theo banged the wall control that opened the airlock's inner hatch. Alarms hooted and emergency hatches farther up the passageway slammed shut as Theo dashed out, heading for the bridge.

Victor looked down at the pistol in his hand. The indicator along its barrel showed it was fully charged.

'Don't fire until you see the whites of their eyes,' said Dorn.

'Don't try to stop me,' Victor warned.

'You can prevent them from boarding this ship without killing them.'

'Can I now?' Victor's voice echoed the scorn he felt.

'Warn them. Remind them of how vulnerable they are.'

'Men don't always behave logically, especially when their lives are at risk.'

'Warn them,' Dorn insisted.

Victor stared at the cyborg for a long, silent moment. At last he said, 'Words won't stop them.'

Dorn reached out his prosthetic hand. 'Let me have the pistol, then.'

'No!'

Patiently, Dorn explained, 'I'm a good enough shot to hit that big laser welder they're carrying. Perhaps a warning from you and a disabling shot from me will discourage them. In any event, you don't want them to use the laser to ruin the fusion drive's thruster, as they did to *Hunter*.'

Victor thought it over for half a second. *Maybe all he wants is to get the gun away from me. He could probably crush it in his metal hand. Then we'd be totally defenseless.*

'I don't want them here any more than you do,' Dorn said, his metal hand still extended. 'But we at least should warn them that we'll defend ourselves if they don't leave us.'

He could take the gun from me, Victor was thinking. *And probably break every bone in my hand while he's doing it.*

'Killing should be our last resort,' Dorn said.

Reluctantly, Victor handed him the pistol. Then he clicked on the radio frequency that the scavengers were using.

'Don't come any closer,' he said sternly. 'We're armed and we'll defend ourselves.'

The seven approaching figures did not waver. They were close enough now to see the weapons they were brandishing.

Valker answered, 'We're armed too. And we outnumber you.'

Dorn raised his prosthetic arm and, holding the pistol in his human hand, cradled it in the metal one.

'You're hanging out there like targets in a shooting gallery,' Victor said. 'One puncture of your suit and you're a dead man.'

The scavengers kept coming.

Using both hands, Dorn raised the pistol to eye level. He pressed its infrared finder with his thumb, walked the red spot in the IR scope center to the flank of the welder that Valker carried cradled in his arms. He squeezed the trigger.

The welder flared as the laser pulse punched a hole of molten metal into its side. Valker twitched and yelped and let go of the bulky tool. It floated weightlessly for a moment, then jerked as the cord connecting it to its power pack pulled it short. The smaller man carrying the power pack let go of it, and the two pieces floated away from him.

Victor heard the scavengers cursing and muttering.

'Go back to your ship,' Victor told them. 'Leave us alone.'

Valker hung in emptiness, watching the laser welder and its power pack tumble slowly away. Kirk was beside him, an arm's length away, the five other members of his crew hovering around them.

'Go back to your own ship while you can,' he heard Victor's voice in his suit's radio speaker. 'You can have *Hunter* and *Syracuse*. Leave us alone.'

'You're willing to give us two ships that are gonna mangle each other while you take the one that's in perfect condition?' Valker shot back. 'A sweet deal – for you.'

'Go back to your own ship,' Dorn said. 'My next shot will kill you.'

Valker heard the cyborg's threat, as calmly unemotional as an ocean wave surging onto the shore.

'I thought you were a priest,' he shot back.

'Don't push me,' Dorn said. 'The killer inside me can break through and cause havoc.'

The airlock of *Pleiades* was close enough for Valker to clearly make out the two men standing inside its open hatch. One of them – the cyborg, he guessed – was holding a pistol rock steady in both hands.

He's pointing it straight at me, Valker realized. One puncture of this suit and I'm a dead man. The freak's right: we're exposed out here. He could kill four or five of us before we got to the hatch.

'All right,' he said, fingering his jetpack controls. 'All right. You win. For now.'

Kirk growled, 'You're gonna let them go?'

Valker made a toothy grin for Kirk. 'You want to go in and be a hero? Go right ahead. Be my guest.'

But Kirk had slowed down, too. All seven of the scavengers hovered in the emptiness, close enough to *Pleiades* almost to touch it, while Dorn stood inside the airlock with that one pistol locked in his unwavering hands.

'A whole fucking ship!' Kirk whined.

'You gotta know when to fold your tent, boys,' said Valker, 'and silently steal away.'

With enormous reluctance, the scavengers started back toward *Vogeltod*, which now was separated from *Syracuse* and slowly edging farther away from it.

'We'll get them,' Valker assured his men. 'Once we're back in *Vogeltod*, we'll power up and—'

'And chase us all the way back to Ceres,' Victor's voice cut in. 'Good. Do that. I'm sure the rock rats will be glad to see you, after what we'll tell them about you.'

Valker scowled and started to reply, 'Oh yeah, well you just might—'

'Hey!' Kirk yelled. 'They're gonna hit!'

As Theo ducked through the hatch of *Pleiades*'s bridge, still awkward in the clumsy hard suit, he saw Angie – also in her hard shell – sitting at the command chair, his mother and the elderly sculptress on either side of her.

Lifting off his bubble helmet as he went to the command console, Theo said, 'Dad wants me to—'

'I think I've got it all set up, Thee,' Angela said happily. 'All I've got to do now is press this key, the one that says "ignition."'

Theo swiftly scanned the electronic keyboard. 'I think you're right, Angie. I think you've done it.'

'So let's light the fusion torch and get out of here,' Angela said.

Theo glanced up at the main screen. 'Oh, for the love of god – they're going to crash!'

462

They all stared at the screen as *Hunter* slowly, inexorably, plowed into *Syracuse*. In the vacuum of space there was no noise, but Theo saw the two ships smash together in a rending, pulverizing collision that tore both ships into mangled shards of metal.

That was our home, Theo realized. He saw *Syracuse* tear apart, whole sections of its wheel-shaped structure ripping loose, the tube-tunnels where he went diving as a kid breaking apart, pipes and pumps from the cranky old water recycler flung into space, a shape that looked like the old sofa from their living quarters spinning end over end.

'It's gone,' Pauline whispered. 'Our home . . . it's gone.'

'*Hunter*, too,' said Elverda Apacheta, her voice almost reverent. 'Dorn will never finish his quest now.'

'But we're here,' Theo said. 'We're alive and we're safe.'

'And we're heading for Ceres,' Angela added, pressing her fore-finger on the ignition key.

Pleiades surged into acceleration as its fusion torch drive lit up.

Habitat *Chrysalis II*:
Council Chairman's Office

Big George Ambrose sat behind his desk like a smoldering red-haired volcano. The unpretentious office seemed crowded to Theo, with his parents and sister, Dorn and the sculptress taking up every available chair.

'There's nothing illegal with salvaging,' George said guardedly, after listening to their story.

Victor had shaved his beard and looked more normal, Theo thought. Grayer, his face thinner, but now he looked like the father Theo remembered.

'Nothing illegal with salvage,' Victor agreed. 'But when you seize ships that are occupied by their rightful owners, that's not salvage. It's piracy. And murder.'

George frowned.

'They would have murdered my wife and daughter,' Victor continued. 'After raping them.'

'They did try to kill me,' said Theo. 'Dorn and Ms. Apacheta saved my life.'

'I guess we'll have to go after 'em, then,' Big George muttered, clearly unhappy.

'They can't have gone far,' Victor said. 'They'll have to stop for fuel sooner or later.'

'We don't have a military force, y'know,' George grumbled. 'Never needed a fookin' army until that bastard wiped out the old habitat.'

Dorn slowly rose to his feet. 'That bastard was me.'

George's eyes went wide. 'What?'

'I was Dorik Harbin. I attacked *Chrysalis*. I also attacked these people's ship, *Syracuse*.'

'That was another person,' Elverda said quickly. 'He's not the same man.'

But George got up from his desk chair, seething. 'You're Dorik Harbin?'

'I was.'

'You wiped out *Chrysalis*? Killed more'n a thousand helpless people?'

'I did.'

Moving swiftly around the desk, George reached for Dorn. 'I'll break your fookin' back!'

Everyone seemed frozen by Big George's sudden rage. Except Theo, who pushed between George and Dorn and laid both his hands on George's chest.

'Leave him alone!' Theo snapped. 'He saved my life.'

George snorted like a dragon. Fire blazed from his eyes. He grabbed Theo by the front of his coveralls, lifted him off his feet with one hand and tossed him onto the desk top with a painful thud.

'Stop!' Victor shouted, going to his son. 'You'll be just as bad as he was.'

Dorn remained as unmoved as a rock. George wrapped his big hands around the cyborg's neck. 'You bastard!' he shouted. 'You bloody bastard!'

Elverda pushed herself up from her chair and slapped at George's beefy arm. 'Don't you dare!' she snapped. 'You leave him alone!'

Big George blinked at her, his expression suddenly changing into a naughty little boy's, confronted with an angry schoolteacher. His arms dropped to his sides.

Elverda waved a finger in George's face. 'He's tried to atone for what he did. He's a changed man. Don't you dare hurt him.'

'Give him a fair trial, at least,' Theo said, getting off the desk, rubbing his bruised hip.

Dorn was still standing perfectly motionless, unmoved, like a statue, like a man awaiting execution.

George took a step back, sagged onto the edge of his desk. 'Dorik Harbin,' he muttered, his chest heaving.

'Go ahead and kill me,' Dorn said. 'I deserve it.'

'That'd be just as bad as he was,' Theo repeated.

'We'll have a fookin' trial, all right,' George said darkly. Going back to his chair and thumping heavily into it, he called to his desktop communicator, 'Security. Send a squad to my office to take a prisoner into custody.'

Only then did anyone notice that Elverda had sunk back into her chair, her face gray, gasping for breath.

Elverda opened her eyes. She saw that she was in a hospital cubicle. The lights were turned down low; the compartment smelled clean, brand new, as if it had just been opened for her. A faint beeping sound made her turn her head toward the bank of monitoring sensors lining the wall to her left.

I must have fainted, she realized. The pain was less now. Almost gone. But she could still feel it throbbing deep inside her like a lurking demon.

She tried to sit up and the bed automatically lifted behind her. She saw a shadowy figure in the compartment's only chair.

'Dorn?' she whispered.

The cyborg stirred out of sleep. His human eye opened; the other one glowed red in the dimly lit chamber.

'How do you feel?' he asked.

Elverda considered the question for a moment. 'Not bad,' she said, then added with a sardonic smile, 'considering the condition I'm in.'

'You haven't lost your sense of humor.' Dorn reached for a remote control wand on the bedside table and the lights came up a little.

The sullen pain in her chest notched up a bit, and the sensors' beeping quickened.

'The doctors say you need to go to Selene for a full rebuilding of your heart,' Dorn told her.

I'd never survive the trip, Elverda said to herself. Aloud, though, she asked Dorn, 'I thought you were under arrest.'

He nodded. 'There are two armed guards outside your door. I go on trial tomorrow.'

'Tomorrow?' Elverda felt a pang of alarm. The monitors beside her bed changed their tone slightly. 'How long have I been unconscious?'

'Not quite thirty-six hours. The rock rats move swiftly. George Ambrose wants the trial held right away.'

'I'll speak for your defense.'

'No need. I don't want a defense. They have every right to execute me.'

'No!' she snapped. And the monitors' beeping pitched still higher. 'They may have a right to execute Dorik Harbin, but he's already dead.'

Dorn almost smiled. 'Not dead enough,' he muttered.

The Trial

It took less than forty-eight hours for Big George to arrange for the trial of Dorik Harbin.

Dorn stood alone in a darkened video studio, bathed in a pool of light. In the shadows armed security guards ringed the cyborg while communications technicians operated a trio of video cameras, all focused on Dorn. The technicians' monitors showed that every citizen of *Chrysalis II* could watch the trial by television from their quarters.

The etched metal of the prosthetic half of his face glinted in the pitiless glare of the overhead lights. From his office, Big George read the charge against Dorik Harbin: one thousand, one hundred seventeen counts of murder.

'Do you admit that you deliberately killed the inhabitants of the original *Chrysalis*?' George's disembodied voice rumbled in the TV studio like an approaching thunderstorm, seething with barely repressed fury.

'I do,' said Dorn.

'What d'you have to say in your defense?'

'Nothing.'

'Nothing? Nothing at all?'

'Nothing,' Dorn repeated.

Suddenly there was a hubbub in the darkness beyond the pool of light in which Dorn stood. A door swung open and Elverda Apacheta rolled herself to his side, sitting in a powered wheelchair.

'I have something to say in the defense of this man,' she announced. Dorn saw that her pallor was still sickly gray; an oxygen tube was hooked to her nostrils; her eyes were rimmed with red.

Before Dorn could stop her, Elverda struggled to her feet and said, 'This is not the same man who attacked your habitat. Dorik Harbin has been dead for many years now. This man, Dorn, has spent those years atoning for the sins of Dorik Harbin.'

'That doesn't matter,' Big George's voice spat. 'The only question here is whether or not he murdered the people of *Chrysalis*. He admits that he did it. It's time to vote on the verdict.'

Dorn and Elverda saw a screen light up on the wall before them. Numbers flickered, too fast to follow.

Finally the numbers stopped. Big George's voice announced, 'It's almost unanimous. The verdict is guilty.'

'No!' Elverda gasped. Dorn rested his human hand on her frail shoulder.

'Now for the penalty,' George went on, sounding as implacable as an avalanche. 'We've never executed anybody before, but if ever a man deserved the death sentence, this is the one. How do you vote—'

'Wait!' Elverda shouted. Dorn could feel her trembling beneath his hand. 'You don't need to kill him.

470

You can exile him. You've done that before: permanent exile for criminals. Exile this man if you want to, but don't kill him!'

'What he's done deserves more than exile,' Big George's voice boomed. 'He should never have the chance to hurt anybody again. Death!'

'He'll never return here,' Elverda promised, shuddering, almost breathless. 'Exile him. Don't stain your hands with his blood.'

For long moments there was no reply; only profound silence. At last, his voice a low growl, George responded, 'All right then, we'll vote on it. Execution or exile.'

Dorn slid his arm around Elverda's bone-thin shoulders to support her as the electronic vote was swiftly tabulated on the wall screen. She slumped against him, her strength almost gone.

Once the numbers stopped scrolling across the screen, they read sixty-seven percent in favor of exile, thirty-one percent for execution, two percent abstaining.

At last the voice of Big George Ambrose came through the speakers, like a pronouncement from the heavens:

'The vote's been verified. Dorik Harbin is hereby exiled from *Chrysalis II* for life.'

George sounded very disappointed.

The studio lights winked out. Elverda sagged against Dorn, her head lolling back on her shoulders. He grasped her in both his arms.

'Medic!' Dorn shouted, suddenly frantic. 'She's collapsed!'

A Higher Law

The funeral service was brief and attended only by Dorn and the Zacharias family. And the security guards that followed Dorn everywhere. Big George would not willingly place himself in the same section of the habitat as Dorn; the people of *Chrysalis II* may have voted leniency for Dorik Harbin, but George would not be party to their decision.

The International Consortium of Universities had offered to send a representative to the solemnities, but Dorn decided not to wait. He went ahead with the funeral the day after Elverda died, her heart too frail to support her any longer, despite the stem cell therapy that had saved her life after her first heart attack. Her final words were to Dorn:

'It's time for me to leave you. I'm too tired to go on.'

He was kneeling at her bed in the habitat's small hospital, like a grieving son at his mother's bedside.

She stroked the etched metal of his skullcap with her skeletal, bloodless hand. 'You must go on without me, Dorn. Can you find the strength to do that?' Her voice was a feather-light whisper.

He didn't answer.

'There's something that a very brave and wise man said, nearly two centuries ago,' Elverda rasped. 'He said, "Life persists in the middle of destruction. Therefore there must be a higher law than that of destruction."'

Dorn muttered, 'A higher law.'

'Gandhi said that. Can you believe it? Can you follow its path?'

'Is that what you wish?'

'Yes,' she said, with all of the little strength left in her. 'Follow the law of life. You have much to give. You have much to live for.'

'I wish I thought so.'

'Do it for me, then. My dying wish. Live! Turn your back on death. Make your life mean something.'

For long moments he was silent. At last Dorn said, 'I'll try. I promise you – I'll try.'

But by then Elverda Apacheta was dead.

Dorn commandeered an equipment pod for her sarcophagus and, with all four of the Zacharias family helping him, placed it in one of the habitat's airlocks and fired it out into space.

'She will become an asteroid, circling the Sun just as her *Rememberer* does.'

Theo thought he saw tears glimmering in Dorn's human eye. He heard his mother and sister sobbing softly behind him.

Hours later, feeling utterly wretched, Theo returned to the quarters that the rock rats' administrative council had granted them: a string of three adjoining living units, with connecting doors between them.

Bone tired, weary and discouraged, he looked around the spare little compartment. The message from Selene University still flickered on his desktop screen. Where do I go from here? he asked himself. Not to Selene: they've made that clear enough. The university doesn't want me. They turned down my application.

He heard a snuffling sound from the compartment next door. Putting his ear to the connecting door he listened for a moment. Angie's crying, he realized.

Theo tapped on the door and called, 'Angie?'

The sobbing stopped. 'Thee?'

'Are you all right?'

He slid the door back and saw that her eyes were puffy and red, her cheeks runneled with tears.

'What's the matter?' Theo asked, stepping into her compartment.

'It's Leif,' she said, and broke into sobs again.

'Leif? The guy you were seeing . . .?'

'Leif Haldeman,' Angela choked out, wiping at her eyes.

'He was on *Chrysalis*,' Theo realized. 'He was one of the people Dorik Harbin killed.'

Angela's red-rimmed eyes widened. 'No! He was on a mining ship when the attack happened.'

'Then he's alive?'

'He's married,' Angela said, struggling to hold back another burst of tears.

Theo tried not to laugh, not even smile. 'Oh,' he said.

'He's a father.'

He put his arm around his sister's shoulders and held her close. 'Don't worry Angie. There are lots of other guys in the world.'

'But I loved him!'

He lifted her chin and smiled down at her. 'Come on. Fix your face and come with me.'

'Where?'

'To the nearest bar. We can drown our sorrows together.'

'Our . . . you've got sorrows too?'

He sighed. 'Yep. Selene University doesn't want me. No scholarship. It's been too long since I first applied.'

'But that's not fair!'

'No, I guess not. But we've lost more than four years, Angie. And there's nothing we can do about that.'

There was only one restaurant in the habitat, the *Shoo-Shoo*, owned and operated by an Italian cook and his Japanese wife. Neither Angela nor Theo was in the mood for eating, but the hostess-owner took one look at the two downcast young siblings and presented them with a delicate sushi selection before she brought the wine they ordered.

Wisely, she sat them at the sushi bar instead of a table. It was mid-afternoon: most of the tables were empty but there were half a dozen customers along the curving bar, chatting amiably with the sushi chefs (both sons of the owners) and one another.

Angela took an experimental sip of the red wine that Theo had picked at random from the list displayed on the bartop screen.

'Ugh!' She put the stemmed glass down. 'People actually drink this?'

Theo felt his mouth tingling. 'I guess it must be an acquired taste.'

'Try the sake,' said the young man sitting on Angela's other side.

'Or a beer,' suggested the guy sitting on the next stool over. 'Straight from the brewery on Vesta.'

Before long Angela was deep in conversation with the two of them: mining engineers who began explaining how nanomachines took atoms of selected metals out of asteroids and bypassed the old smelting process. Theo watched as he sipped at his wine and realized that Angie would not be lovelorn for long. Men are attracted to her. She's sort of beautiful, I guess. Not like me.

On his other side, a few chairs down, a pair of older men were discussing Dorn's trial.

'I never saw Big George so worked up,' said one of them. 'He wanted that cyborg executed. I thought maybe he'd do it himself.'

The other shook his head. 'Just about everybody in the habitat is a newcomer. They didn't see the massacre, like George did. It didn't affect them personally.'

'I don't know. I had a brother-in-law on the old *Chrysalis*. I voted to execute the bastard.'

Theo was about to tell them what he thought when a lithe, dark-haired young woman slid into the chair beside him.

'This seat isn't taken, is it?' she asked, in a near-whisper.

Theo shook his head, immediately forgetting the other men's conversation. She was really good-looking, he thought, with intriguing flecks of gold in her deep brown eyes. She wore a form-fitting dark zipsuit with insignias of rank on the cuffs and a stylized logo on her left breast. She must be a member of some ship's crew, Theo guessed.

'Are you working on a ship?' he asked, knowing it sounded terribly awkward.

She nodded. '*Hyades*. Medical officer.'

'Oh.' Theo had run out of things to say.

One of the sushi chefs slid a small porcelain bottle of sake to the young woman, and a tiny cup.

'We make the run out to Jupiter station,' she said as she carefully poured some of the hot sake into the little cup.

'Jupiter station,' Theo muttered. 'I wish I could go there.'

The young woman sipped at the sake, then said, 'They're looking for people.'

'Scientists. People with degrees.'

'Technicians, too. You don't have to be a scientist.'

'You still need a degree.'

She focused those gold-flecked eyes on Theo, as if thinking over a problem. Then, 'Their chief recruiter is here on the habitat. He'll make the trip back with us on *Hyades*.'

Theo nodded glumly.

As if she'd made up her mind about the problem, she said, 'I could introduce you to him. He's looking for technicians.'

Theo didn't know what to say.

'It couldn't hurt,' coaxed the young woman, with a shy smile.

'I guess not,' Theo agreed.

She dug into a hip pocket and pulled out a communicator. 'I . . . don't know your name.'

'Oh! I'm Theo Zacharias.' He held out his hand.

'Zacharias?'

Theo nodded, wondering if he should spell it out for her.

She hesitated a moment, then took his hand in her own as she said softly, 'Altai. Altai Madagascar.'

New Lives

By the time Theo returned to the *Shoo-Shoo* restaurant from his meeting with the Jupiter station's recruiter he was beaming with happiness. Until he saw his parents sitting at one of the restaurant's tables, with Angela and Dorn.

Dad's not going to like my news, he said to himself. Drawing in a deep breath, he headed for his family.

The restaurant was filling up. The customers at the other tables were casting uneasy glances toward the cyborg, but Theo ignored them as he hurried to join the group. He grabbed the empty chair between his father and sister, and started to say, 'I've got news for—'

Victor Zacharias cut off his son's words with a dark scowl. 'Since when do you encourage your sister to drink wine? In the company of strangers, no less.'

Angela, across the table from Theo, tried to suppress a giggle. And failed.

Theo blinked at his father. 'Dad, Angie's an adult.'

'That doesn't mean—'

Pauline laid a hand on her husband's arm. 'It's all right, Victor. It's nothing to get upset about.'

'I wasn't drunk,' Angela said. Then she hiccupped.

Victor tried to frown at his daughter, but slowly a smile spread across his face. 'Maybe I'm overly protective,' he admitted.

Angela nodded vigorously.

Turning to Theo, Pauline asked, 'What's your good news, Thee?'

He glanced at his father, then replied, 'I've landed a position on the Jupiter station. It's only—'

'Jupiter?' His father seemed startled.

'You're going to leave us?' Pauline asked.

'I'm going to Jupiter, too,' said Dorn.

Ignoring the cyborg, Victor asked, 'How in the world could you do this? Why didn't you talk it over with your mother and me first?'

Because you'd say no, Theo replied silently. Their surprise and displeasure was about what he'd expected. 'I met with their recruiter less than an hour ago. A girl I met here at the sushi bar introduced me. It's only a menial position, really. I'll be a junior-level technician. But I can take university courses electronically and work toward a science degree!'

'Jupiter,' Pauline murmured.

'The girl who introduced me is the medical officer on the ship that'll take me to Jupiter,' Theo went on. 'She's really elegant.'

'They took you on?' Victor demanded, suspicious. 'Just like that?'

'They need people, Dad. They're having trouble getting qualified people.'

'I'm not surprised,' Victor grumbled. 'That outpost is a long way from civilization.'

'They'll train me on the job,' Theo went on enthusiastically. 'It's a great opportunity.'

'Jupiter,' Pauline repeated. 'It's such a long way off.'

Angela asked, 'How long will you be there, Thee?'

'I'm contracted for two years.'

'You've signed a contract with them?' Victor asked darkly. 'Without asking me? Without *telling* me?'

'I'm telling you now, Dad. The pay's good, if that means anything to you.'

'Two years,' Pauline murmured.

'At least,' said Theo.

They fell silent, each thinking their own thoughts. Pauline looked at her husband. Victor knew what she was trying to tell him. Theo's grown up. It's time he went his own way. This was inevitable. But he saw the pain in his wife's eyes. Leaving for Jupiter. Just like that. Spur of the moment. The boy has no common sense.

'I'm going to Jupiter, too,' Dorn said again.

'On the *Hyades?*' Theo asked.

'Yes.'

'We'll be on the ship together, then.'

With the bare minimum of a nod, Dorn said, 'Big George wants me off the habitat in two days.'

'But *Hyades* doesn't shove off for a week,' said Theo.

'I've made arrangements to live on the ship, starting tomorrow. That will keep George's blood pressure down to normal, almost.'

'What will you be doing at the Jupiter station?' Angela asked the cyborg.

Dorn made a one-shouldered shrug. 'I think they want to study me. They're making deep dives into the Jovian ocean, and a man who's already half machine may be very useful to them.'

Pauline started to say, 'You'll be leaving in a—'

'So there you are!' called a voice from halfway across the quiet restaurant.

Heads turned. Cheena Madagascar threaded her way between tables, her eyes aimed at Victor. She was wearing a shiny black suit that fitted her like a second skin, polished knee-length boots, a flaming red scarf knotted around her throat.

Victor stumbled to his feet, his face flushed. Theo and Dorn rose, too.

Without being asked, Cheena took the unoccupied chair at the foot of the table.

Flustered, Victor introduced, 'Cheena Madagascar, the owner and skipper of *Pleiades*.'

Cheena made a brittle smile. 'Not anymore, Vic. You screwed me out of my ship.'

Victor sputtered as he resumed his seat. Theo almost laughed. He'd never seen his father looking so flummoxed. Then he realized: Madagascar; that's Altai's last name, too. And they look so much alike. . . .

'I'm Pauline Zacharias,' said his mother, smiling steel-hard at Cheena.

Cheena nodded. 'And you must be Angela. And Theo. And you're the one we voted to exile.'

Before anyone else could speak, Victor said, 'I've brought *Pleiades* back to you. I'm sorry I—'

'Can it, Vic. I don't own *Pleiades* anymore. The insurance consortium owns it. They paid off on the bird when you stole it and I bought a new ship, *Hyades*.'

'*Hyades?*' Theo blurted. 'Then Altai is your daughter?'

'Smart fella,' said Cheena. 'Like your father.'

'So what do I do with *Pleiades?*' Victor asked.

'You don't have to do a thing. Insurance agents are taking it over right at this instant. They'll probably want your hide, but that's not any of my business. Not anymore.'

With that, she got to her feet, blew Victor a kiss, and sauntered away from their table.

Victor ordered another bottle of wine.

It wasn't until they were in bed that night that Pauline asked, 'Just who was that woman?'

Glad that it was too dark for her to see his cheeks reddening, Victor cleared his throat before replying, 'I told you, she owned *Pleiades*. I stole it from her.'

'And now her insurance carrier has repossessed the ship?'

He stared up at the shadowy ceiling of their bedroom. 'Yes, and they want me to pay for damages – the difference between what they paid Cheena and what *Pleiades* is worth on the open market.'

Pauline fell silent and Victor was glad of it. He closed his eyes and tried to change the subject.

'Big George says he'll hire me for the new construction program. There's a lot of building going on here, and new projects in the planning stage.'

'Then we can stay at Ceres?' Pauline asked, sounding pleased at the prospect.

'For as long as they keep building. We won't have to be rock rats anymore and I'll be able to pay off the insurance debt, in time.'

'Angela wants to go to Selene, to the university.'

'The Moon? But how—'

'She says she'll work her way through. She'll take classes part-time and find a job.'

'Doing what?'

He sensed his wife's amusement. 'She learned a lot while we were on *Syracuse* without you. She's got a good head for math.'

'Do you think she'll be all right, on her own? She's never—'

'Victor, dear, it's time for Angie to go out on her own. We can't keep her with us forever.'

He nodded reluctantly. 'I suppose not. But with Angie going to Selene and Theo going to Jupiter—'

'It will be just you and me, Victor. The two of us, alone together.'

'The way it was in the beginning,' he said, reaching toward her.

Pauline melted into his arms, but asked softly, 'Just how well did you know this Cheena woman?'

He froze. *There it is*, Victor said to himself. For the flash of an instant he thought about lying his way through, but he heard himself say, 'When I was forced to work on her ship, we slept together.'

'That's what I thought,' Pauline said, her voice

484

gentle, far from accusative. 'She had that possessive air about her.'

'I didn't have much choice,' he tried to explain. 'She was captain of the ship and—'

'And we'd been separated for years,' Pauline finished for him. 'You didn't even know if we were still alive.'

'I didn't have much choice,' he repeated.

'Neither did I,' Pauline whispered.

It took a moment for Victor to understand what she'd said.

'You and Valker?'

He couldn't see her face in the darkness, but he heard the remorse in her voice. 'Once.'

'He forced you?'

'Not really. I was trying to protect Angie. He would've gone after her.'

'I should have killed the bastard when I had the chance.'

'It's over and done with,' Pauline said. 'Let Big George and his people take care of Valker.'

It took Victor several moments before he could reply, 'Over and done with.'

'It's time to start our life together again.'

'Time to start new,' he muttered, wondering if he could. 'Fresh.'

She leaned into him and they kissed, neither of them knowing what the future would bring, each of them hoping for the best.

Epilogue

There was a Door to which I found no Key:
There was a Veil past which I could not see . . .
        — *The Rubaiyat of Omar Khayyam,*
            Edward Fitzgerald

Asteroid 67-046: The Artifact

Tamara Vishinsky absolutely refused to see the artifact again. All the way out to the asteroid Tamara had been Alex Humphries's willing bed partner. She knew that what the artifact had showed her the first time was the absolute truth: her way to wealth and power lay in her ability to manipulate wealthy and powerful men. It was her path to comfort, to safety. Her way to escape poverty and danger.

During the days of their full-g flight to the Belt she had noticed Yuan regarding her with amused tolerance. Fool! she thought. All he wants from Humphries is to open his stupid restaurant in Shanghai. I want more. Much more. And I'll get it.

But once their ship established orbit around the asteroid Tamara knew she could not face the artifact again. She remembered the pain of its revelation, the aching remorse of reliving her miserable childhood. Not again, she told herself. Never again.

Alex Humphries seemed keenly eager as they rode the shuttlecraft down to the asteroid's surface, his cold gray eyes glittering with anticipation.

'This could be the most powerful force the human race has ever encountered,' he said, as much to himself as to her. 'I'm going to link to capabilities no one's ever even dreamed of.'

Sitting beside him in the padded shuttlecraft seat, Tamara suddenly realized that if he was right, if the artifact empowered Humphries the way he anticipated, she would lose him forever. Her safety, her future, would vanish.

'Do you think it's really a good idea to expose yourself to the artifact?' she asked, in a whisper. 'I mean, look what it did to your father.'

Alex Humphries was silent for a moment. Then, 'All right. You go look at it first.'

'Not me!' she blurted. 'It was too painful the first time.'

'And you're afraid it will be painful for me?'

'Disabling. It crippled your father, didn't it?'

'Temporarily.'

'Don't risk it. Let Yuan go in. He *wants* to see it again.'

Humphries fell silent again for several long moments. At last he asked, 'That first time you came here: why did you kill Commander Bolestos?'

She blinked with surprise. 'He . . . I didn't think. . . .'

'He was in your way,' Humphries said softly. 'Is that it?'

Scrambling in her mind to find an excuse, she finally admitted, 'Yes, that was the reason. I had to get past him to see the artifact.'

'And once you saw it, the experience didn't change you at all, did it?'

'Not really, but it might hurt you, Alex.'

He smiled at her and patted her knee. 'We'll see. We'll see.'

A full security team was waiting for them at the glassteel dome that protected the opening of the tunnel that led deep into the asteroid's interior. Humphries ordered them to stay at the dome.

'Captain Yuan knows the way down,' he told the chief security officer. The man stepped aside as Humphries strode to the tunnel entrance.

Turning, Humphries said to Tamara, 'You can stay up here. You don't want to see the artifact again, do you?'

Looking uncertain, Tamara stammered, 'No . . . I . . . but, but don't you want me to go with you?'

'No,' Humphries said, cold as honed steel. 'You stay here.' He pointed to the chief of the security detail. 'Captain Bolestos will take care of you.'

'Bolestos?'

The young security officer pulled his laser pistol from its holster.

'The son of the former commander here,' Humphries said.

Wide-eyed, Yuan looked from Humphries to Tamara to the grim-faced security captain with his drawn pistol.

'Alex!' Tamara called to Humphries. 'Don't leave me! Please!'

'Come on,' Humphries said to Yuan, turning his back on her. 'You come with me.'

Slowly, fearfully, Yuan followed Humphries into the down-sloping tunnel. For several minutes neither man said a word. Then a scream echoed off the tunnel's rock walls.

'What was that?' Yuan shouted, knowing the answer, dreading it.

Humphries didn't even turn his head. 'Justice,' he said. And he continued down the tunnel.

They ducked their heads where the tunnel was low, then found themselves in the grotto just outside the artifact's chamber. The rocks glowed with cool light. The ceiling vaulted above them. The partition that closed off the artifact's chamber was wide open.

Humphries licked his lips. 'Me first.'

'Fine,' Yuan said.

Humphries looked surprised for an instant, then his eyes went hard. 'You're afraid of it?'

'No. I want to see it again.'

'Then . . .?'

'I can wait,' Yuan replied.

Humphries nodded. 'All right. Wait here.'

He stepped across the faint groove in the dusty floor that marked where the partition rested when it was closed. The walls of the tunnel glowed coolly, bathing him in a golden glow. He felt his pulse thumping in his ears. A whiff of an odd scent tickled his nostrils; something that he vaguely remembered. . . .

Hesitating, Humphries turned and saw Yuan standing back there, watching him. Tamara was afraid of the artifact, he said to himself. What did it do to her to make her so fearful? Could it harm me? The thought sent a shudder of alarm through him. It drove my father insane – temporarily. What will it do to me?

His pulse thundering now, Humphries stepped farther into the chamber. The light was bright but warm, like sunlight on a tropical beach. He did not notice the partition sliding smoothly, silently down the chamber's entrance, closing him inside.

Turning the corner in the stone tunnel he stood face-to-face with the artifact.

Nothing. The chamber seemed empty. Humphries felt his brows knit with puzzlement, then anger. To come all this way . . . Were they lying to me? Is this all some elaborate fraud?

The odor he had noticed seemed slightly stronger here. It brought back a memory from his childhood: Christmas morning with the huge tree and all the decorations and the brightly colored packages beneath it.

Then he noticed a tiny glow on the far wall of the rocky grotto, nothing more than a candle's flickering. But as he watched the glow brightened, grew until it was like a lamp shining in his eyes, a spotlight, a miniature sun blazing its intensity. Humphries threw an arm over his eyes; the light was painful, searing, yet he could not take his eyes from it.

And within the light, shadows. Something formless shifting, moving, slowly taking shape. It was his father. Three-year-old Alex saw his father looming above him, reaching for him, cradling him in his arms. Young Alex felt the warmth and happiness of his father's love. For a moment.

Other people crowded around Martin Humphries, separating Alex from his father. Alex was a teenager now and his father was distant, aloof. He watched as his father drifted farther and farther away from him. And changed.

Martin Humphries grew larger. The figures around him shrank until they were dwarves, midgets, vermin scurrying beneath his father's feet. Martin Humphries pointed at one and the figure exploded in a flash of flame. Alex felt pain, like a red-hot iron pushing through his guts.

His father was becoming grotesque, hideous, larger and larger as he turned into a ravening monster, terrifying everyone his fiendish eyes fell upon. Martin Humphries laughed like Satan enjoying the torment of damned souls, and suddenly Alex realized that this wasn't his father, it was him, Alex, who had become the monster.

He sank to his knees, unable to tear his eyes away from the vision of torture and pain. Is this what my father saw? he asked himself. Is this what my life will become?

He saw the cyborg, Dorn, and the aged Elverda Apacheta: hostages in his power maneuvers against his father. Marionettes, their strings in his own hands. And he saw Tamara: beautiful, cunning, ruthless Tamara staring at him with the eyes of a needful child. She reached toward him with both hands but Humphries saw her cut down by the hand of death. His own hand. Dripping with her blood.

On his hands and knees, Alex Humphries tried to crawl away from the damning, accusing visions. But he couldn't move. He could not will his body to obey the commands of his fevered mind. He cried out in anguish, then collapsed onto the stone floor, sobbing.

The vision faded slowly, leaving Alex on the grotto floor, soaked with perspiration, trembling with fear. And understanding.

The artifact didn't drive my father insane, he realized. Dad *was* insane. The artifact merely brought his madness out into the open, showed it to himself. It's taken years for him to recover from that revelation.

Slowly, painfully, Alex scrabbled to the rock wall and pulled himself to his feet.

And I'm heading into the same abyss as he did. I'm becoming my father! Alex squeezed his eyes shut. No! That's not me, he said to himself. That's not me. But a voice in his head told him, That will be you. Eventually. Inevitably.

His sweat-soaked shirt sticking to his skin, Alex pulled himself to his feet and staggered out of the grotto. The metal partition slid upward, releasing him.

'That's not me,' he whispered to himself. 'And it never will be.'

Yuan rushed to him.

'Are you all right?' he asked. 'The partition closed. You were sealed in there for more than an hour.'

'An hour?'

'More. Are you okay?'

'I'm okay,' Alex said shakily, fighting off the urge to collapse into Yuan's arms. He forced himself to stand steadily on his own feet. 'It was . . .' He tried to smile. 'It was pretty intense.'

He leaned his back against the rough rock wall and slid down to a sitting position. I should have waited, he said to himself. I shouldn't have turned her over to Bolestos so soon.

Then he noticed Yuan looking at the beckoning glow beyond the open partition.

'Can I go in now?' Yuan asked.

Alex waved a weak hand at him. 'Sure. Go ahead.'

Yuan bounded through the open partition and disappeared into the artifact's inner chamber.

He wants to see it again, Alex thought. He's not afraid of it because he has nothing to be afraid of. I do. I'm heading along a path that will make me exactly like my father.

'I've got to change,' Alex murmured. 'Let my father run the corporation if he wants to. There are better things for me to do.'

Yuan came back out of the artifact's grotto in what seemed like a few minutes, grinning hugely, happy with what he saw.

'When we get back to Selene,' Alex said, his voice weak, strained as if he'd just run ten kilometers, 'you go build your restaurant. I'm quitting Humphries Space Systems.'

'Quitting?' He seemed shocked.

With a faint smile, Humphries said. 'I've got better things to do.'

'What better things?'

'There's still a lot of rebuilding that needs to be done on Earth. There's millions of people who need help, need a chance to pull themselves out of poverty and misery.'

Yuan looked puzzled. 'You want to help them?'

Alex's smile grew stronger. 'If I can,' he said. 'It's better to build than to destroy.'

Chrysalis II

Theo said his goodbyes to his family at their quarters in *Chrysalis II*. His mother and sister teared up as they embraced him. He promised to stay in touch and they both said they would message him every week, once he arrived at Jupiter station. His father shook his hand solemnly, his face frozen into immobility.

Before he himself started sniffling, Theo slung his slim travel bag over his shoulder and left them there, striding down the passageway to the docking port where *Hyades* was set to depart for Jupiter.

There were forms to fill out before they would allow him to board the fusion torch ship. Theo tapped out his information blindly, automatically, wanting to get aboard the ship as quickly as he could, wanting to stay with his family at the same time.

Can't have both, he told himself as he pecked away at the keyboard. At last the security program was satisfied and granted him clearance to board *Hyades*.

As Theo stepped through the spongy access tunnel connecting the ship to the habitat he saw that there was a ship's officer at the open hatch, checking credentials with a handheld scanner. And another man, just in front of the hatch.

His father.

'How'd you get here ahead of me?' Theo asked, astonished.

Victor grinned at his son. 'The old man can still outrun you,' he said. Then he added, 'I didn't have to go through all the busy-work you had to fill out. I saw you at the console, tapping away.'

Theo nodded. 'I . . . I guess I ought to get aboard, Dad.'

'I know,' Victor said. 'I just wanted to . . . well, I just want you to know that I respect you, Theo. You saved your mother and sister. You've grown into a real man.'

Blinking at the tears that sprang up in his eyes, Theo stood there dumbfounded, not knowing what to say.

Victor wrapped his strong arms around Theo, who dropped his travel bag and embraced his father.

'I love you, son.'

'I love you too, Dad.'

'Good luck. Good voyage.'

'Thanks, Dad.'

He picked up the bag and hurried past the waiting officer and through the hatch. Turning, Theo waved once to his father, then stepped through the inner hatch into the ship's main passageway.

Dorn was standing there, arms folded across his chest.

'Welcome aboard,' he said gravely.

'Thanks,' said Theo, brushing at his eyes.

'Today we begin our new lives,' said Dorn.

'Yeah. Guess we do.'

With a hint of a smile, Dorn said, 'I have a message for you from the ship's medical officer.'

'Altai?'

'Altai Madagascar. She wants to see you in the infirmary as soon as you've stowed your bag in your quarters.'

Theo broke into a happy smile. A new life, he said to himself, looking forward to it.

BEN BOVA

Titan

Winner of the John W. Campbell Award

Titan Alpha has landed: the most complex man-made object to reach Saturn's largest moon. The ten thousand men and women of Habitat *Goddard* are once more at the frontier of science.

From their huge, artificial paradise hanging in orbit above Saturn, some of them dream of landing on Titan's surface. Others will do anything to prevent such a landing. And yet others have darker, secret plans.

But almost immediately, *Titan Alpha* goes silent. And minor, inexplicable faults start to affect *Goddard*. Is there a basic design flaw that could threaten the lives of everyone on board? Or has one of the many malcontents exiled to space decided to sabotage the probe or even the whole expedition?

HODDER

BEN BOVA

The Silent War

The Asteroid Wars III

The story of the men and women who risk everything to mine the riches of the asteroids began in *The Precipice* and continues in *The Rock Rats* – coming to a thrilling climax in *The Silent War*.

Martin Humphries, wealthy, ruthless and obsessed, has exiled his rival Lars Fuchs to the depths of space and taken Fuchs' wife, Amanda Cunningham, for his own. Now he rules space exploration almost unchallenged.

But for Humphries, nothing short of total domination will ever be enough. He wants a son – Amanda's son. He wants Fuchs to die. He wants to control the Moon. And if the free space prospectors of the asteroid Ceres stand in his way, he promises to destroy them.

But another power is building its strength in secret, waiting for a chance to seize the Humphries empire.

HODDER

BEN BOVA

Mercury

The closest planet to the Sun, Mercury is an airless, heat-scorched world where temperatures rise to four times higher than the boiling point of water.

But this vision of hell is also a planet with unlimited solar power – worth a fortune to the space tycoon Salto Yamagata if he can find a way to harness it. He has hired the enigmatic Dante Alexios to establish a research station on the surface of the planet and find a way to turn that solar energy into portable power satellites.

But Yamagata is secretly also preparing the way to a very different dream: he wants to travel to the stars themselves. And Alexios has his own obsession, a plot to lure an old enemy to this hellhole of a world and take his revenge for one of the worst disasters in human history.

HODDER

BEN BOVA

Saturn

Ten thousand men and women, exiled from Earth, are riding a man-made habitat to the planet Saturn. They form a volatile community – one that needs only a spark to set off an explosion that could end in disaster.

Some are innocents like Holly Lane, revived after dying many years ago from cancer, or Manuel Gaeta, a stunt man who intends to land on the surface of Saturn's biggest moon, Titan.

Others are idealists, like Edouard Urbain, the habitat's chief scientist, opposed to allowing any human to set foot on Titan.

And some have much more dangerous plans. Malcolm Eberly, a swindler who was freed from prison by agents of the Holy Disciples, has been placed aboard the Saturn-bound habitat to take over its government.

As the mammoth spacecraft nears its destination Eberly manoeuvres to take control of the habitat. His manipulations lead to murder. Meanwhile, frustrated by Dr Urbain's intransigence, Gaeta prepares to fly solo through the rings. What he finds there changes everything.

HODDER